Sin & Magic

Also by K.F. Breene

DEMIGODS OF SAN FRANCISCO
Sin & Chocolate
Sin & Magic
Sin & Salvation

DEMON DAYS VAMPIRE NIGHTS WORLD
Born in Fire
Raised in Fire
Fused in Fire
Natural Witch
Natural Mage
Natural Dual-Mage

FINDING PARADISE SERIES
Fate of Perfection
Fate of Devotion

DARKNESS SERIES
Into the Darkness, Novella 1
Braving the Elements, Novella 2
On a Razor's Edge, Novella 3
Demons, Novella 4
The Council, Novella 5
Shadow Watcher, Novella 6
Jonas, Novella 7
Charles, Novella 8
Jameson, Novella 9
Darkness Series Boxed Set, Books 1-4

WARRIOR CHRONICLES
Chosen, Book 1
Hunted, Book 2
Shadow Lands, Book 3
Invasion, Book 4
Siege, Book 5
Overtaken, Book 6

Sin & Magic

By K.F. Breene

Contact info:
www.kfbreene.com
books@kfbreene.com

Chapter 1

ALEXIS

"HELLO, YES, MAY I speak to Detective McLaughlin, please?" I asked the woman on the phone.

My ward, Mordecai, was on the mend, healing at incredible rates now that his human body was no longer rejecting his shifter magic, so I had a little time to look after my obligations. When I told a spirit I'd do a certain thing, I followed through. Which was why I was currently speaking to someone at a police station in New York City. I was making good on the final request of the uptight ghost I'd encountered at the magical showcase in the non-magical zone. A detective in life, the poor sod had hoped to use me to resolve his final case.

"Whom may I ask is calling?" the woman asked.

"Jane. Fon...tain." I grimaced. I should've practiced giving the fake name. I hated lying—I was no good at it. "Jane Fontain. I have some information Detective McLaughlin is looking for. Probably. Should be looking for, at any rate."

"Please hold."

I drummed my fingers on my beat-up, round table straddling the line between my tiny kitchen and small living room. It was as close as we had to a dining room.

Daisy, my other ward, a fourteen-year-old going on fifty, sauntered into the kitchen with threadbare sweats and brown hair snarled at the back of her head.

"'Mornin','" she mumbled, her sleepy eyes barely open. Bright light streamed through the kitchen window, cutting across her face as she passed it. She reeled back like she'd been slapped before putting up her palm to shield her eyes. "What's up with the weather?"

Near the ocean in San Francisco, late August was usually a hovering fog bank. The air was so thick with moisture that the street glistened. Curly-haired people walked around like they'd just stuck a fork in an electric socket. But every so often, Mother Nature gave us a treat, and cleared away the dull gray muck for a day or two of lovely blue skies and warm sun. This was weather we could expect in October. It was a little early.

The music coming through the phone switched from one cool jazz song to the next.

Daisy yanked open the freezer door. "What time are you starting again?" she asked, staring into the icy depths. I really needed to defrost it one of these days.

I sighed and scrubbed my hand across my face. I needed to do a lot of things. But they'd have to wait, because I'd gone and said I'd work for Demigod Kieran, Valens's possessive and dangerous son, who wanted to help his deceased mother cross over from the land of the living. All signs pointed to Valens holding her spirit hostage somehow. I needed to find out how, and fix the problem.

All without ending up dead myself.

This was what I got for my stick-to-itiveness when it came to helping spirits: I got myself in trouble. Because if there was one certainty in life, it was that you didn't want to mess with Valens. He was one of the most ruthless and cunning Demigods in the world, and he ran magical San Francisco like a despot. Not even the best spies could get away with visiting the city undetected. People who had been contract killing for decades were brought up short after one trip into Valens's territory. Everyone knew it. Everyone (rightfully) feared him.

And somehow I thought I could get one over on him? Me. The twenty-five-year-old nincompoop whose magic mostly worked on dead people?

I was about to join them.

I rubbed my eyes. "Twelve. Someone is supposed to meet me here and escort me to Kieran's office."

Daisy pulled out a beat-up ice cream carton before slamming the freezer door shut. "I thought it was in the government building." She sidled over to the utensil drawer. "Why would they need to escort you?"

"Why do they hide in my bushes? Why do they follow me around? They've been misguided into thinking I'm important."

I grimaced with the lie, and then grimaced with outing myself by grimacing. Thankfully Daisy's back was still turned.

I wasn't sure if I was important, but I knew exactly why Kieran's guys were hiding in my bushes, watching me. Protecting me.

I wasn't the Ghost Whisperer I'd always thought I was—the lowly peon who couldn't find a decent job with the mostly useless skill of seeing and hearing ghosts.

It took Kieran muscling me into a proper magical assessment for me to learn that almost no one could see and hear ghosts like I could. And that I wasn't actually a Ghost Whisperer at all. Instead, I was something much more dangerous: the heretofore unknown daughter of an unbalanced Demigod of Hades, who'd saddled me with one of the most feared types of magic in history. I was a Spirit Walker, the rarest form of Necromancer.

Ghost Whispering no longer seemed that bad. Which was why I planned on letting the kids think it was still my jam.

Daisy extracted a spoon before setting the ice cream carton on the counter. She didn't open the cabinet for a bowl.

"Daisy, that ice cream carton isn't your personal trough. You need to use a bowl." I pinched the bridge of my nose. "Which is beside the point, because you can't have ice cream for breakfast."

She huffed in annoyance before reaching up to the cupboard and extracting a chipped blue bowl.

"*Can't* have ice cream for breakfast," I repeated. "As in, cannot."

"It's okay. I'm going running with Mordie later. I'll burn the calories right off."

"No, that's not why—"

The cool jazz cut off, replaced by a gruff voice. "Hello, Mr. Hamshaw?"

"No, this is…" My mind went blank trying to remember my fake name. "I'm waiting for Detective Miller," I rushed to say, then clenched my jaw. Dang Daisy and her poor breakfast choices—I'd just said the spirit's name! "Detective McLaughlin, I meant. I'm on hold for Detective McLaughlin."

Silence filled the line.

"Hello?" I asked, watching Daisy peel off the top of the ice cream carton.

"Who is this?" the man asked, his voice guarded. Not a surprise since I'd just asked to speak with a murdered detective.

"Jane…" I wracked my memory. "Fonda. Fontain!

Sorry, my ward is trying to eat ice cream for breakfast and—"

"Damn it, Mordecai!" Daisy yelled, startling me into silence. She stared down into the carton for a beat before her face screwed up in anger. She spun around and trudged out of the kitchen, carton in hand.

"What is it you need…Jane?" the man said slowly.

"I have a message for Detective McLaughlin. It's from an old co-worker of his."

"I'm Detective McLaughlin."

"Oh right. Ah, look, this is going to sound crazy, but I said I would pass it along, so…Jim Miller said to tell you eight-seven-seven in terminal three. I don't have anything other than that. Eight-seven-seven, terminal three. He thought that would mean something to you."

Silence filled the line again and Daisy's voice drifted down the hall.

"If you finish something off, *put it in the garbage can.* Don't just close it back up and put it away. What is wrong with you? I only wanted ice cream because I saw the carton—don't you turn over and go back to sleep. This is serious." I heard a sound like skin slapping skin.

"Ow. I heard you," Mordecai hollered. "Stop punching me!"

I put my hand over the bottom of the phone. "Daisy, stop hitting your brother," I yelled. "We didn't get him patched up so you could beat on him."

"He deserves it," Daisy yelled back. "Leaving empty cartons of ice cream in the freezer is bullshit."

"We only have ice cream because of me," Mordecai said. "Ow, would you stop?"

"We only went without ice cream for years because of you, too," Daisy said. "Stop squirreling away. What, all those practice sessions and you can't take a chick's punch?"

"You're in the practice sessions, too!" Mordecai yelled.

I leaned back in my chair so I could see around the wall and down the short hallway. "Stop fighting, you two. Take it out in practice."

"He's not in a vulnerable position in practice," Daisy said, and another punch landed.

She had a point.

I pulled the phone from my head, checking to make sure there was still someone on the line.

"Hello?" I said.

"How is it you knew Detective Miller?" the man asked.

I squinted an eye when someone down the hall screeched. It was impossible to tell who it was.

"Well, that's the crazy part I was talking about," I said, leaning forward again. The kids would survive. "You remember that movie a long time ago where that kid reveals that he can see dead people? Well, I'm magical, and I can, in fact, see dead people. Kind of like the people you have on staff, but a lot more effective. Jim was haunting a criminal—Romaro or Romano or something, I try not to get names—and his last request was that I get this message to you. So there you go. Take it or leave it, it's up to you, but that's all I know."

"This was...when?"

Daisy stomped back in the kitchen, empty-handed.

I put my hand over the bottom of the phone again. "Where's the carton?" I asked her.

"Let that idiot throw it away. He should've done it in the first place."

"Daisy—" I shook my head and returned to the call. I did not have the patience. "This was...about four weeks ago now," I told the detective. "I was paid to send the ghosts across the Line—honestly, it doesn't matter. You'll just think I'm weird. Bottom line, Jim really wanted someone to get that message to you. Eight-seven-seven in terminal three. He didn't elaborate and I didn't ask. I'm just passing it on. My conscience is clear." I leaned back with a farewell on my lips.

"How is it you know Romano?" the man asked before I could get away.

Daisy opened the refrigerator, leaned against the door, and stared into its depths.

"Daisy, you're wasting electricity," I admonished her. "Get in and get out." I returned to the call. "Sorry, we've gotten some charity in the last few weeks and it has resulted in more than enough food to go around. It's causing all sorts of unforeseen problems. Anyway, I don't know Romano. He showed up at my booth at what they call a magical showcase, asking that I banish a few ghosts. Before I banish an entity, I let them speak for five minutes. Jim gave me that message to pass on. Eight-seven-seven—"

"How did Jim die?"

"I don't know. I ignored him for most of his five minutes."

Silence stretched across the line.

"I know how that sounds," I rushed to say. "But I'm not in the habit of listening to descriptions of grisly violence. I try to tune that sort of thing out. But as I said, he got my attention at the end of his five minutes and made sure I heard that message and who to give it to. After that, Jim-the-spirit was okay to leave."

"Jeez, whoever you're talking to sounds dense," Daisy muttered.

"To leave?" the detective asked.

"To go across the Line. To rest in peace."

"I see." The man's tone suggested he thought I was hiding something. "You're magical, did you say?"

"Yes. So anyway, good luck. Hope you get your man. Bye." I pulled the phone away from my head, ignoring the detective's "Wait—", and tapped the button to end the call. He seemed like the type who would call me in for questioning. That was not something I wanted any part of.

"Did he believe you?" Daisy asked as she pulled out a carton of milk.

"He was too busy being suspicious to believe me. He probably thinks it's a trap, or maybe that I'm a criminal snitch, or…who knows." I stood from the table and swiped my hands together. "No longer my problem. I did what I promised. End of story."

She shook her head slowly. "You should've used that letterhead I stole from Denny's dad. It couldn't come back to bite you, that way."

Denny was a guy Daisy had kept on the hook for a while—even after she stole shifter medicine from his dad's vet shop and blackmailed him to stay silent about it. Mordecai and I had nagged her until she stopped seeing him.

"I didn't leave my name," I said. "How could they possibly find me?"

She rolled her eyes at me as she pulled a box of cereal out of the pantry. "You used your cell phone, dummy. They could trace it."

"They don't trace every call, give me a break. And besides, Kieran prepaid the phone service for a year. Given what I know about his obsessive need to control every situation, it's probably in his name. If there's a problem, they'll go straight to him. Still not my problem."

"Unless you two fall out. Then he could just turn you over to the cops."

"He's a Demigod, Daisy. A Demigod of Poseidon's line—one of the Power Three." She looked at me with a blank face. It occurred to me that she had some gaping holes in her education. "The Power Three gods are the original brothers. Zeus, Hades, and Poseidon. Many believe they are the most powerful of the gods. Demigods of their line often have more power, though how much more, I couldn't say." She continued to stare at me with a blank expression, and I realized that it wasn't a lack of knowledge, it was a lack of interest. "Right. Anyway, he might not be in charge of a specific territory yet, but he's one of the most powerful people on the entire planet. If he wants me dead, he'll kill me himself. He won't even need to hide the body. The man could literally just say 'oops' and walk away. I'm a nobody living in the cracks between the magical and non-magical societies. No one would be bothered."

"And you took a job working for him?" She clucked her tongue. "Suicide."

I let my mouth drop open as I stared at her incredulously. "Have hormones clouded your brain, or something? You *helped* me set up that job. You got him to buy me a Burberry, and you negotiated a higher salary. You're just as much at fault as I am."

"I'm a good business manager. I don't advocate which jobs my client should and should not take. That would be unethical." The cereal pinged off the sides of the bowl.

I threw up my hands. "You're talking gibberish. Look. He's not going to kill me. We both know that. Not unless I piss him off or something—"

"He's a ticking time bomb."

"Besides, the cops aren't going to come after me over this. It was a hazy message delivered by a magical lunatic. Chances are they'll probably ignore it like people have ignored most of my other warnings. But if they do manage to decipher it, and then actually find something... Well, I doubt they'll want to seek me out and share the glory. It's over. My job as a Ghost Whisperer is behind me. Onward to bigger and better things."

"Now who's talking gibberish? You're just about to start working for a possessive Demigod with daddy issues."

I hated losing arguments to hormonal teenagers who thought they knew everything. But she did have a point.

"Touché," I ground out. "Now go get Mordecai up. Your training starts in an hour. If you guys eat too late, you'll throw up your breakfast again."

"I'm not his mother," she replied, adding milk to

her bowl.

"I'm his mother...ish. And yours...kinda. And I'm telling you to go get him up."

"Ugh!" She gestured at her bowl. "Why didn't you tell me to do that before I filled my bowl? Now it's going to be soggy."

"Then give him that bowl as a punishment for getting up late, and make yourself a new one."

She cocked her head at my bad parenting. Then nodded with a determined expression. "He deserves it." She stalked off down the hall.

"And someone throw away that empty ice cream carton," I hollered.

I eyed the clock. I had a few hours before my first real business meeting. More time than I'd ever taken to get ready for anything. But it felt important to create an impression today—something to set the tone for my business relationship with Kieran. I needed to look business savvy and experienced, as well as competent and confident. Most of all, I needed to look independent and aloof.

I didn't need him for anything. I could survive on my own. I'd been doing it since my mother had died six years ago. And I certainly wasn't hung up on his core tightening appearance, his incredible charm, and his awe-inspiring strength and power. I would show him that none of those things fazed me, and I was in it for the job. End of story.

Chapter 2

ALEXIS

A FIRM RAP sounded at the door and butterflies exploded in my stomach.

"It's that tough guy who won't fight," yelled Frank, my miserable excuse for security. He was great at watching and reporting what went on outside my door—even though he either didn't know, or refused to use, names—but given that he was a ghost, and couldn't do anything, physically, about trespassers, he wasn't ideal for protection.

"He means Zorn," I mumbled to myself. Zorn was one of Kieran's Six, a group of guys who had given some sort of blood oath to protect Kieran.

I gave myself a once over in the mirror, straightening my second-hand suit top before sliding my palms down the badly ironed fabric over my thighs. With the pad of my middle finger, I corralled a loose strand of blonde hair back into the bun at the back of my head. I'd debated wearing my hair long, but for a professional and, dare I say, uptight look, a bun felt more appropriate.

I took a deep breath, checking my nearly nonexistent eye makeup and extremely light coat of pink lip gloss, when the front door burst open. I startled and stuck my head out of the bathroom.

Daisy trudged through the front door with a red face dripping with sweat. Mordecai followed, his dark skin shining and his expression pulled down with fatigue.

I grinned and strode down the hall. "Hard workout today?"

"Wuh—water," Daisy managed.

Mordecai nodded grimly, tripping on nothing and staggering into the kitchen.

"Why is Zorn here already?" I heard Daisy ask Mordecai. Then: "Get off," followed by a grunt. She'd likely elbowed him.

Zorn filled the doorway. Over six feet tall and with a solid frame, his grim face and muscular body would give pause even to the battle-hardened. Neither the perfectly tailored, pristine suit he wore nor the expensive watch wrapped around his wrist did anything to detract from the murder and violence that raged in his stare. One look made a person's spine turn to jelly.

I hid it easily. I was used to being the least powerful person in the room, whether in the magical world or among non-magical Chesters, people who thought magical people should all be burned at the stake like in old days.

"Hey," I said, stalling at the kitchen entrance. "Almost ready."

Frank, the front yard poltergeist who stood behind Zorn with a puffed-out chest, nodded. Clearly he thought I was talking to him.

"They've got the girl fighting, did you know that?" Frank asked, stepping closer to Zorn as though they were buddies. A look of unease crossed Zorn's face. He couldn't see Frank, but he could feel his presence. It was a disconcerting feeling if you weren't used to it. "Girls fighting! Imagine that."

"I know," I said, stepping into the kitchen to grab my water bottle out of the fridge. "She's been training all week."

"What?" Mordecai asked, sagged against the counter with both hands wrapped around a glass of water. He was one year older than Daisy, and used to be just as skinny. After a single week of training, the muscles in his arms were more defined and a spark of confidence burned brightly in his light hazel eyes. The training, given for free by members of the Six, was really improving him, both physically and mentally.

Just another way Kieran had wormed into my life, improving it for the better. He had a good game, I'd give him that.

The cunning bastard.

"Frank," I said by way of explanation, rolling my eyes and heading back toward the door.

"You've got to put a stop to that nonsense," Frank said, now edging around Zorn to get closer to the door.

I crossed the entryway to grab my chief prize, a Burberry medium buckle tote, in pink! It was the only piece of fashion I owned, given as payment for speaking to Kieran's deceased mother, something the other Ghost Whisperers he'd hired hadn't been able to do. I prized it above all other inanimate objects. It spoke of lavish lifestyles, classy people, and expensive vacations. And it was mine!

"Women shouldn't be fighting like men! It's unseemly," Frank went on, shoving himself in front of Zorn.

"Women can do whatever they damn well please," I told Frank, slipping the fantastic bag onto my shoulder, admiring its weight. A smile crept up my face, my annoyance at Frank drifting away.

I was wearing a Burberry. A *Burberry!* First-tier fashion rested on my arm. My mother was probably turning over in her grave with envy.

"A woman's place is in the home, looking after the children," Frank returned. Zorn glanced around him, and though he was a hardened man who seemed immune to danger…he took a giant step back.

"She doesn't have any children," I told Frank, filing Zorn's weakness away.

"Then she should be seeing to her studies and helping you around the house."

"Frank, may I remind you that your views of the world are out of date. You know, given that you're dead." His expression soured at my words. He thought pointing out his lack of an earthly body was a low blow. Luckily, I didn't much care. "If Daisy wants to learn to fight, she can."

"Is that ghost telling Lexi that I shouldn't be allowed to train with you?" I heard Daisy say incredulously. She must've gotten a nod because she went on. "For the first time in my life, I wish I could see that miserable sonuvabitch." She raised her voice. "Tell him that I just beat Mordecai in two out of three fights. Girls can not only fight, but when trained correctly, they can fight damn well. Actually, just banish that miserable bastard."

"I said you could fight, not swear, Daisy," I berated.

"You only win because you fight dirty," Mordecai said.

"You're bigger, getting stronger every day, and a guy. Of *course* I fight dirty, you donkey. If I didn't, you'd wipe the floor with me. Do you think enemies are all a lovely bunch of fluffy unicorns who care about rules? The real world is a shitty place, Mordecai. A real shitty place. There is no place for morals when you're fighting for your life, there is only staying alive."

Daisy had been in and out of the non-magical orphanage and foster care system since she was little, exposed to horrors I couldn't even imagine. Her self-proclaimed miracle was me finding her on the streets and taking her in. She claimed she was living her dream—a fact that made my heart squish with both happiness and sadness. She was a bright, loyal kid with *so much* to offer. She deserved more than the half-life I was able to provide.

I took a deep breath and sucked it up. This new job would hopefully remedy that a little. With more money, I could buy them things most people took for granted. Like heating.

"It's just practice," Mordecai mumbled.

"It's never just practice," Daisy returned.

"Don't mind her," I told Zorn. I glared at Frank, who wisely backed away to give me room. He didn't like when I forced him. "The practices have amped her up a little."

Zorn turned sideways so I could pass, his expression thoughtful. "She's correct. She's what, fourteen?"

"Fourteen going on fifty, yeah." I shut the door behind me and motioned for Zorn to lead the way.

He swept his hand toward the sidewalk. "Ladies first."

I tried to hide a pleased smile. I'd been called an awful lot of things in my life, but lady was seldom one of them. The suit was a winner. Or maybe it was the Burberry...

Jack, the member of the Six who cooked for us the most, waited off to the side with his enormous arms glistening in the sunlight. His hands were braced on his hips and his sculpted chest rose and fell with deep breaths.

"How is the girl doing?" Zorn asked him as we passed.

I frowned. Zorn didn't usually take an interest in the kids. He was the only one of the Six who never helped them train.

Jack's eyebrows lifted and a grin lit his face. "She's a feisty little cheat. You teach her something, and she somehow finds a way to twist it into a new move that you"—he held up his thumb—"didn't see coming, and"—he held up his first finger—"didn't realize would hurt so much. She's a firecracker."

Zorn looked back at the closed front door, the small crease between his brows the only indication he was thinking and not powering down like a robot.

"What?" I asked.

As if coming out of a trance, he shifted his gaze to me. His expression wiped clear before hardening. "Let's go. We'll be late."

Without another word, he held out a set of car keys

before stalking toward a black BMW parked behind my rusty old Honda.

"Just look at her, all sweaty and—she looks like a drowned rat," Frank said as Daisy led Mordecai out of the front door.

"Frank, can it, will ya?"

"Is he still talking about me?" Daisy planted her fists on her hips. "I wish I had the power to banish him. He'd be gone so fast…"

Zorn looked at her while standing next to the Beemer with the keys held out. He didn't say a word.

"No wonder Daisy calls you a zombie," I said to Zorn. I snapped my fingers at him. When that didn't yield a response, I pushed the keys back toward his body. "You can drive. Let's go."

Impatience crossed his features. He jingled the keys. "This is your car. It's a signing bonus for a high-level contract. Demigod Kieran must uphold his reputation."

"Oh my God, what did he just say?" Daisy stalked forward, fatigue draining away.

Mordecai followed. "But you haven't signed anything yet. And he knows you like designer labels. This might be another attempt at a leash, Alexis. He's good at manipulation."

"Yours isn't even a high-level contract," Daisy said, crossing her arms over her chest. "For him, it's medio-cre, at best. What's his game, here? Is he trying to bamboozle you with this freaking awesome car he has to know we'd all love?"

"All good insights and questions." I pushed Zorn's hand again. "Let's hold off until I sign the contract, mmkay? We can easily write in something that denotes a company car. One that actually fits in around here. Because I'm not sure if you're aware, but this isn't a nice neighborhood. A car like this will stick out."

"Guys popping in and out of bushes sticks out," Frank mumbled, looking over the car.

He did have a point. People probably thought I was a drug dealer. The car wouldn't help.

"Come on, we can go in my car." I ticked my head at the Honda.

Disgust crossed Zorn's face. "I'm not riding in that."

"Oh well…" Daisy dropped her hands. "Look at you, Mr. Fancy Pants, in your high-dollar suit and your 'I'll cut a bitch' eyes. Too good for your origins, huh?"

Zorn zeroed in on her again, and while many would've flinched under that flat stare filled with malice, she didn't so much as blink. Apparently, she had pieced together more about him than I'd ever tried to.

He snapped the keys into a newly closed fist and turned toward the BMW. "I'll drive."

"You could've saved us the argument and driven in the first place." I winked at the kids and reached for the door handle.

"Wait—" Daisy held out her hands before looking down at herself, then back at the house. "If he's changed something, I need to see it. You cave too easily, Lexi, you know you do. He'll add in some bonus that'll help Mordie or me, and you'll go along with whatever horrible thing he's trying to trap you into doing."

I held up a hand to stop what I knew was coming. "There is no way you're getting into this car looking like that. If it becomes mine, I don't want sweat stains."

"Simply unsavory," Frank muttered.

"It's leather. It'll just wipe off," Mordecai said reasonably.

"No." I wiggled my finger at Daisy as Zorn sat into the driver's seat.

"Get in," Zorn barked. "We're three minutes behind schedule."

"See?" I tapped my bare wrist. "The robot is worried about his schedule. I'll just have to go alone. How will I manage?"

I got into the passenger's side.

"This isn't wise," Mordecai said. "You're not good at this type of stuff, Lexi. Which is why you're in this situation in the first place."

"When I was young, children were seen and not heard," Frank said.

"Just go." I slammed the door with a pleasing *cush* and breathed in the delicious new car smell. "Go. The longer we stick around, the more likely they are to force their way into the car."

"You let those kids rule you." Zorn slid the car in gear and moved away from the curb.

"Not rule me so much as...keep me from doing anything harebrained."

"You're not a great authority figure."

"Gee thanks, Zorn. Wow. What a great insight. It really warms my heart."

"It's a good thing. Kids in their situation need to be hard. You've forced them to be independent, while shrouding them in a loving environment. You've created a strong pack mentality—your success is their success, and vice versa—and your bumbling and incompetence have forced them to be leaders and caregivers themselves. Their sense of responsibility will help them get ahead. They'll be the top of their trade."

Heat pricked my eyes at what he said about the kids. The sting of the insult lowered my brow. For someone who was usually silent, he sure knew how to pick his words for maximum impact. "That was a good back-handed compliment, Zorn. On a related note, you don't have many friends, do you?"

His jaw clenched.

At the end of the street, I expected him to take a right, heading toward the magical zone. Instead, he took a left, which would take us farther into the dual-society zone.

San Francisco was divided into three zones—magical, where magical people lived under the rule of Demigod Valens and the magical governing body, non-magical, where only those without magic resided, and what I called the crack between the societies, the dual-society zone.

Neither government really cared what went on in the no-man's land between the magical and non-magical zones. It was a crusty place without a lot of money or curb appeal. Generally, criminals, poor people, and outcasts lived in the crack.

"Are you taking me somewhere to kill me, you sly dog?" I said with mock humor.

"If only," he answered.

Shivers washed over my body. When it came to Demigod Kieran, surprises were dangerous. They put me off-balance, which meant he was more likely to get what he wanted.

I hated when Daisy was right.

Chapter 3

ALEXIS

W E STOPPED IN front of a ramshackle building with five ground-level doors and three "available for lease" signs. On the other side of the street, sand from the beach spilled out onto the sidewalk and into the gutter. Blue sky stretched over the crisp blue of the ocean. This was the edge of nowhere—a dirty beach, deep into the dual-society zone, where few people would willingly hang out.

"What's this?" I asked, not reaching for the door handle.

He paused in getting out. "Your new headquarters. Demigod Kieran wants to keep you under the radar for your own protection. Setting up an office in this part of town should help with that goal."

"Well then, yes. It is very clear he bought me this expensive car with his reputation in mind. I can see the correlation."

"Your sarcasm is draining."

"So is your face, Oh Expressionless Wonder. I'd say

we're even."

He grunted and stood from the car. I sighed and did the same.

Part of me was intensely relieved. I'd avoided the magical zone my whole life. My motivations had changed, but my aversion was no less intense. I was about to tamper in Valens's business, so I was all too happy to stay out of his territory.

The other part of me was really annoyed, because if I didn't have a high dollar office to report to, why the hell would I need a high dollar car? It felt like confirmation Kieran was trying to sweeten me up for something, and I'd probably have to refuse out of principle.

I gazed at the car wistfully. The kids were right, I really did love designer labels.

"You coming?" Zorn barked, standing at the leftmost door in the decrepit building. A piece of yellow police tape fluttered not far away, trapped in a straggly bush.

"Jesus. Give a girl a moment to collect her thoughts." I positioned my handbag *just so*, lifted my chin to show my confidence, and strutted forward like I was in complete control of all things.

Kieran needed me more than I needed him. Now that Mordecai's illness had been cured, the kids and I could scrape by. But without me, Kieran's mother would continue to be trapped in the world of the living.

I needed to remember who had the upper hand, and use that to my advantage—or at least as a means of bolstering my confidence.

But as soon as I walked through the door and into the office, all of that washed away.

Kieran stood at the back of a small but lavish room, wearing a white T-shirt and faded blue jeans that hugged his muscular body. Raven hair, cut short on the sides and longer on top, matched the color of his regal, high-arching eyebrows. A narrow nose ended above luscious and shapely lips that softened his strong jaw and sharp cheekbones, turning severe into ruggedly handsome. Incredibly ruggedly handsome.

Large shoulders stretched the white cotton, pulling at the seams. Cut pecs stood out over his flat stomach, which I knew from (brief) experience was a glorious six-pack bordering on an eight-pack. Powerful thighs gave those jeans something to show off.

The man was a legend, but none of that could compete with those entrancing, stormy blue eyes—wild and vicious and passionate. His delving stare hit me like a Mack truck before reaching down into me, all the way to my soul. The world dropped away, and all I knew was him, this moment, and the incredible desire surging through my body.

His large hand swung up and touched the center of his chest, like he was reaching for his heart. My own heart quickened at the movement.

"She has refused the car, sir," Zorn said, and just like that, the moment shattered.

My exhale was audible. I may have staggered, just a little, but I passed it off like the rug had grabbed my heel. No biggie.

A grin wrangled Kieran's kissable lips. "As I told you she would. Were the kids the deciding factor?"

Zorn grunted and moved off to the corner of the small office.

With the spell of Kieran's hotness broken, for now, I could finally take a look around.

The outside of the building hadn't been touched, but the interior had been completely re-done. The walls were painted a soft gray that somehow didn't close the room down. A beautiful rug stretched across the refinished hardwood floor. A desk took up the center of the room with two leather chairs in front, an executive chair behind it, and a plant to the side. File cabinets lined the back wall, beside a door that led into what looked like a smaller office. Oil paintings decorated the space, one above a bookshelf stuffed with various titles.

"Alexis," Kieran said, and his deep, raspy voice vibrated down low. "It's nice to see you again. I hear Mordecai is defying all expectations. Only a week after his procedure and he's training like he's worked out all his life."

I swallowed, not an easy task given that all the spit had dried up in my mouth. "Yes. Thank you again for doing that. He's...better than new."

"Yes, so I hear. With a good appetite." Kieran sauntered forward, almost lazily, and thick, heady magic washed over me. The man had power in spades. It felt unlike anything I'd ever experienced. "And how about you? Are you ready to get to work?"

"I need to look over the final contract to make sure it's everything we agreed upon."

His cocky grin turned into a full-fledged smile, and my insides did worrying flips. I hadn't forgotten how attractive and charismatic he was, but in just a week, my memories had *grossly* downplayed his effect on me. I was not prepared for this. My confidence was wavering like an inflatable dancer at a used car lot.

"That we agreed upon?" he asked, stopping in front of me and looking down into my eyes. At six-two, he was only five inches taller than me—less when I wore heels, like now—but with his robust body, confidence bordering on arrogance, and intense power and strength, I felt tiny. Insignificant. "Or that Daisy and I agreed upon?"

I shrugged, the movement stiff. "When it comes to things like this, it's one and the same."

His gaze roamed my face before stopping on my lips. His smell drifted around me, salty sea foam, and rich, decadent chocolate. "Everything is as we agreed," he said softly. "Except for the car. You will take it."

"I don't respond well to commands."

His eyes sparkled. "Yes, you do. You just haven't realized it yet." He stepped over to one of the visitor chairs facing the desk, then lowered a large hand to its back as though preparing to pull it out. "Please, have a seat."

I stalked forward, passing the chairs and walking around the desk, and took the large leather chair facing him.

"Thank you," I said, clasping my hands on the desk and waiting for him to sit in the visitor seat.

Gaze rooted to mine, he slowly moved around the chair he'd been touching before sinking onto its cushion. "If you'll just reach into the first drawer—"

Before he could finish, I opened the drawer on my right, expecting a folder. Instead, I saw office supplies.

"On the left," he finished, laughter in his eyes. "I'm left-handed. I keep the important things on that side."

"Obviously." I sniffed. "I was just looking to see if my bag would fit." It was a terrible cover, but I went with it anyway. "Too small." I took my bag off my arm and set it on the bare desk. There wasn't even a calendar on it.

Kieran leaned back and crossed an ankle over his knee. "High fashion suits you. It brings out your arrogance, which can be quite helpful in certain situations."

"You would certainly know," I mumbled, pulling open the top left drawer and breathing a small sigh of relief when I saw the file folder. It lay atop more office supplies. How much writing and paper-clipping did he expect me to do from this desk? "I was born for big things," I said distractedly, placing the file folder on the desk and flipping it open.

"Yes, you were."

Kieran's suggestive tone drew my eyes to his. The depth of his stare, and its openness, made my heart flutter and sent tingles across my skin. I ripped my eyes away, not understanding the look or the tone, but knowing I'd better be careful because both threatened to suck me under and lose me to the tide.

"Right," I said with a business savvy, can-do attitude. "Let's see." I scanned the various stipulations that Daisy had demanded I put in. Some of them I wouldn't pay much attention to: working hours, overtime, and other logistical details. I hated schedules. But she'd want to see it all in writing, and since she'd taken such an interest in being Miss Business Manager, I would go with it. Other aspects of the deal were more to my interest. The bonus for quick completion was on point, as was the salary, ten percent higher than what he'd originally offered. Medical, retirement, donuts on

Wednesday—all the things I'd been denied while working retail jobs for non-magical blowhards.

I tried to hide my smile. I really did. And failed miserably.

Then I saw something that made the smile slip. "What's this…" I tapped a line. "Training is mandatory?" We'd talked about it, sure, but I hadn't expected he'd enforce it.

"Yes." Kieran steepled his fingers. "I have brought your true nature out into the open. My efforts to hide that information might fail. I am also using your services in a way my father will not be pleased with. In other words, I'm putting you in danger. It is my responsibility to protect you in every way I can. Obviously I have my guys guarding you and your home, but you need to learn how to protect yourself in the field—to get in touch with your surroundings and, most importantly, to use your magic."

I bit my lip, fear biting into me like jagged teeth. I wasn't sure I wanted to learn how to use my real magic. Everyone had heard the same horror stories about Spirit Walkers. Some vicious guy would walk through a war zone and rip souls from living people's bodies. He'd then assume control of the spirit, and stuff them back in, using the person like a puppet. The act sounded harsh and brutal, and I didn't know if I had it in me. I didn't know if I wanted it in me.

"There is more to your magic than the horror stories you've heard, Alexis," Kieran said, as though reading my mind. "Much more. Your magic isn't evil. *You* aren't evil. I'll make sure you don't fall into the hands of someone that would use you in that way. But the magic is a part of you, and you need to learn how to use it. If the worst should happen, heavens forbid, you will need everything in your arsenal to survive. Your magic will help you do that."

I blew out a breath. "Do you even know anyone else who has magic like mine?"

"No. No one on earth, *at present*, has magic like yours." He tilted his head. "That we know of. Most of our knowledge about it comes from written record, rumor, or myth."

Right. Until recently, he hadn't known about me, either.

"But the Demigods of Hades…" I started.

"Have different powers. They can manipulate spirits, and they can travel beyond the Line into the spirit realm, but they cannot rip a spirit from its living body, like a Spirit Walker can." He paused for a second before continuing. "That I have heard of. The last person with magic like yours was killed by Demigod Zander fifty years ago in England. The man was a puppet of the pope—a dark secret kept in the strictest confidence."

"If it was so secret, how did they find out? And why

did the Demigod kill him?"

"Zander killed the man because he was a high-profile assassin. It took a Demigod to finally bring him down. Zander learned of the man's master because Demigods are ruthless, Alexis..." Goosebumps spread across my skin. Kieran was not excluding himself from that group. "Zander extracted the information by using his magic to torture the man. Or maybe to twist his brain. There are many ways."

I barely stopped myself from pushing back from the desk, standing, and running—not striding, but fucking running—for the door.

"The man was an assassin, Alexis," Kieran said, leaning forward in his chair. "You won't be. In fact, you're signing on to a rescue mission. You are already using your magic for good."

"But...with training..."

"You choose how to use your magic. I'll simply employ someone to show you how."

"But if no one like me exists, how will I learn?"

Kieran leaned back again. "You'll start with the basics, both in fighting and magic. You're a type of Necromancer in your basic skill set, so you'll learn rudimentary skills you would've been taught years ago had your initial assessment been legit. Once you're set on the basics, we'll decide on additional training."

I nodded slowly. I did need the help. Even when it

came to non-magical combat. Sure, I had a couple of years of martial arts training and a couple months of boxing, picked up when someone offered a poor girl some classes out of pity, but I hadn't kept up the practice. If danger came my way right now, I was totally vulnerable. The kids wouldn't tell me to push back on this one since it was in my best interest.

I blew out a breath. "Fine. But I'm not taking that car."

"Your vehicle is a rust box waiting to die. If you need to get out of a situation fast, peddling the ground like Fred Flintstone won't be conducive to staying alive."

I arched one of my eyebrows indignantly. "I'll have you know that that Honda is way more reliable than a BMW. It runs just fine, thank you very much, and it's near impossible to kill."

"How about speed? How many minutes does it take to get up to sixty? How much coughing and shaking does it do at a hundred?"

I gritted my teeth. Plenty of minutes and lots of shaking.

"And how does a BMW stand up to something like a Ferrari?" I asked. "Or are you telling me Valens's car isn't faster than the Beemer?"

Kieran shifted and his eyes glimmered. "My father has many cars, and some of them are faster, yes. But my father won't be the one following you." His expression turned somber and a vicious gleam replaced the amusement in his eyes. "He'll leave that to his minions. Whom I will need to make disappear before they can tell him of your efforts. I would like to avoid that. Listen, Alexis..." He braced his hands on his knees. "You must know this is a fragile and precarious situation. It's dangerous, to say the least. If you run into trouble, I'll need to know about it immediately. *Immediately*. Do you understand?"

I nodded, the weight of the situation pressing on my shoulders.

"I will protect you, but we won't be together at all times," he went on. "I have cultivated a presence in certain areas of my father's government that I need to maintain until the last possible moment. This is just the first step in a dangerous journey. I can't let it interrupt my overall goal. If at all possible, I'd like you to get my mother across the Line without him knowing how it was done."

I widened my eyes with the realization that Kieran wanted to free his mother, but he wouldn't stop there. He intended to tear down his father. The Demigod in front of me sought vengeance against another Demigod, and if I fulfilled my task, I'd likely be the spark to ignite the war. A war that would be fought on home soil.

My breathing increased as anxiety pooled in my gut. What had I gotten myself into?

Chapter 4

ALEXIS

"**I**'D BETTER LET *all* the spirits go, then," I said, my mind suddenly churning. As they said: in for a penny, in for a pound. "Your father has at least one other spirit trapped—the teen in the government building—but I'd bet there are more. If I let them all go, he won't be able to pin down an actual motive. Well, other than someone wanting to release the spirits. That, or he'll suspect his spirit-trapping person decided to take the job and shove it."

Kieran watched me silently, his face blank. Zorn's head turned slowly, now watching me, too. They didn't seem amused.

"You already thought of that, huh?" I nodded and pretended like I was back to looking over the contract. "Give me a break. I'm just getting up to speed."

But once my mind started churning, I couldn't stop it. My gaze drifted to the side as I thought on the situation.

"The girl in the government building didn't do anything truly heinous, just lashed out in teen rage. Magical people do things like that all the time. Why did he single her out, I wonder? Oh! Maybe something about that girl struck a personal chord with Valens. That might be the tie-in. And if he did go after her for personal reasons, there must be others. Many others. Valens isn't exactly an easygoing guy, as your mother found out the hard way."

I cleared my throat. I should probably rein it in a little.

"I only saw a few ghosts in the government building," I went on, "and, of those, only the girl seemed put out, so he can't be storing them all there. I'll need to find his little strongholds. If the spirit trapper has to continually strengthen them—which he probably does since the girl in the government building said he stops in periodically—there can't be *that* many. He'd run out of energy." I ripped my gaze to Kieran before pointing at him. "We could take down the prison walls when you're in a meeting with Valens. That would give you a strong alibi. You'd be in the clear." I chewed on my lip. "Of course, Valens's people are excellent at solving unsolvable crimes. My last assessment, the scene at the magical showcase, and the ghosts I talked to in the government building lobby—it won't take him long to find me, even if you run interference. I have an awful lot of breadcrumbs littered around. I'll need witness protection…if there is such a thing from Valens."

"No one will implicate you. I'll ensure it," Kieran said, and that vicious gleam in his eyes flashed at me. I shivered, knowing he wasn't lying when he said Demi-gods were ruthless.

I shrugged. "That's if any of this has merit. It's all assumption so far."

Zorn huffed and glanced downward.

Before I could defend myself with the obvious—I'd *told* them I didn't have any real experience—Kieran spoke.

"Getting back to what you said earlier, no, we hadn't thought of letting all the spirits go at once, because…" He shook his head and a smile blossomed. "Because all of this is utterly foreign. You talk about ghosts as if they're as normal as roses in spring. I still haven't totally acclimated to the idea of my mother being trapped in the world of the living. I only found out because a high priestess arranged for a Ghost Whisperer's entertainment as thanks for my keeping silent on…certain matters." I felt my eyebrows lower. Man-whore. "I'd had no idea my mother wasn't resting in peace. That she was somehow trapped. Since then, I've received very little information I could actually use. Certainly nothing to the extent of what you've just so easily laid out with barely a thought." He was silent for a beat, looking at me with an unreadable expression.

My face heated. "It's all guesswork at this point…" I mumbled.

"You continually blow my mind, Alexis. I've never met anyone like you. It's…refreshing."

I looked down at the contract, not seeing it. "Right. Well." I opened the right drawer and extracted a pen. "First, I need to spend more time assessing the situation. The government building is a good place to start. I want to talk to that teen again. If I keep my head down and pretend I have a function there, I doubt anyone will notice me. I stay pretty invisible in the dual-society zones. I'm good at it."

"There isn't a day in your life where you are invisible, Alexis. You draw attention wherever you go."

Something in his tone set my body to humming. More heat infused my cheeks, and at this point, I probably looked sunburnt.

I pushed it away, desperately trying to keep focus. I was working, and he was bad news. Best to avoid any strange and exhilarating feelings he created that he shouldn't.

"Bria," he said, his fingers steepled again and his gaze rooted to me.

"Who's Br—"

A short woman with shoulder-length, platinum blonde hair stalked into the room from the little office. The sleeves of her Green Day shirt were torn off, revealing two tattoos—a snake curled around her right bicep, its eyes ruby red, and a panther crawled down her other forearm. Each ear had a mess of earrings and a stud adorned her button nose.

"Hi," she said by way of introduction, nodding at me. "You're a queer one, aren't you?"

"Wh-what?" I put my hand to my chest like I was about to clutch pearls. For some reason, the loudness of her appearance contrasted strangely with the radio silence she'd maintained throughout my meeting with Kieran. It unsettled me. I hadn't even felt a twinge of a presence.

Yes, I needed training. Clearly.

"You're a queer one, I said." A finger showcasing a short pink nail waggled at me. "Your soul is like a strobe light. Sometimes it burns brightly and sometimes it just simmers on idle. It's a first."

"Alexis, this is Bria, a level-five Necromancer." Kieran gestured at her. "She has thorough knowledge of her craft and excellent fighting skills. She's also savvy in a bind. She'll be training you."

"So…" I pointed at her before pulling the finger into a fist and lowering my hand. However small her stature, the woman was intimidating. Something about her suggested she'd be happy to dole out fat lips. "You can see spirits, too?"

Kieran stood, the movement stretching his T-shirt

in all the right places. "Bria, take care of her. You know the requirements."

She nodded and her gaze drifted down my body. "Why would you wear a suit to a place like this?"

I ran my hand down my front. "I thought we were going to the magical government building."

"Ah." Her hand rested on her hip and her fingers tapped her jeans. "So you wanted to stand out in a bad way, then? Make a mockery of his reputation, that sort of thing?" She nodded. "I dig that. Good idea."

"She's off-kilter right now, Bria," Kieran said as he stepped around the desk into my space. His smell wrapped around me, comforting and sexy and delicious. I hated it. "You'll want to watch yourself when she recovers. You'll get a shock you aren't expecting."

"Quite a shock," Zorn mumbled.

"My gracious. She's affected the mighty Zorn?" Bria made an O with her lips. It melted into a smile. "I can't wait."

Zorn scowled at her and then looked away.

"I thought you could start here…" Kieran's side bumped mine as he bent, reaching for the bottom right drawer. His arm skimmed my leg, revving up the low hum in my body. "You smell good, Alexis," he murmured.

"I showered," I blurted, flustered by his proximity.

The new girl would think I was a huge doofus.

Kieran extracted another file folder. He laid it in front of me, but didn't move away. Instead, he leaned over me to open it, his side now resting snugly against mine. Fire sparked in my middle.

"This is unprofessional," I murmured with a wispy voice. Bria snickered.

A *huge* doofus.

The first page in the file was a photograph of a shabby house hunkering within a mess of brambles. A blurry image, human-like, stared out of a cracked window. Boards covered the front door and the steps leading to the porch lay at odd angles, many of them badly broken.

"Lovely. Summer home?" I said, leaning closer to look at the man in the window. "It's a spirit, right? It's kinda...'not there' looking."

"That's the general consensus, yes," Kieran said, turning the page. "The home has been abandoned for decades, and it's reputed to be one of the most haunted places in the country. Tours go by every Halloween, and mediums often go there to practice."

"How do they get in?" I tapped the boarded-up door in the picture.

"The boards have been removed, and the steps and porch marginally fixed up. A key is required to enter." He turned the page, revealing another picture of the house. This time, an orb floated in one of the windows.

"I get it, I get it, it's haunted." I scooted my chair away from his warm body.

"I suggested we go there," Bria said, crossing her arms over her chest and sagging in apparent boredom. "I want to see what I'm working with." She nodded at me, clearly indicating that she wanted to assess my magic for herself. "We're going to meet a Medium. She's supposed to be the best Ghost Whisperer in the city. You guys will have something to talk about." She winked at me.

I groaned. I hated mediums, with all their bells and whistles. Literally. They created an awful racket.

"Which zone is this place in?" I asked, standing.

Kieran straightened as I did. "The magical zone, on the outskirts by the east wall. There is very little traffic there, except for the ghost seekers. Occasionally, my father's office will allow non-magicals in via a chartered bus, but that's usually only around Halloween."

"Wait…" I held up my hand. "Your father owns it?"

"No. It's a condemned building, owned by the magical government." A crease formed between Kieran's brows. "But my father does retain control over it. His office schedules the visits." I shot him a look, and he shook his head. "This is what I'm talking about. That didn't dawn on me."

"What?" Bria asked, unfolding her arms. "I had the medium request admittance. We're in the clear as far as the books go…"

"It's a house stuffed with spirits controlled by a guy who traps spirits." I widened my eyes and held up my hands. "So yeah, obviously we need to go there. We don't need to meet a medium, though. Those buggers just get in the way."

A slow grin curved Bria's lips and a dimple dotted her chin. "We're going to get along just fine."

Not if she kept making me feel like a dweeb, we weren't.

"Who do you want to send, sir?" Zorn asked.

Kieran studied me for a moment. Frustration crossed his expression. "Send Jack. Tell him to stay out of sight. I'll want a full report." He leaned in to me. "I can't risk being spotted with you. If you have any problems, you have my number."

I glanced at my handbag. "Yup. It's in there with all the numbers I had to re-input after they were somehow deleted from my iCloud. So weird, that. Especially since they were all guys. Good thing I was late to the technology game and had a little black book, huh?"

Bria coughed into her fist before muttering, "Serves you right for getting involved with a Demigod."

"I'm not involved." I stalked around the desk to get away from his suffocating proximity before reaching over and grabbing my handbag. "I just always seem to be in the wrong place at the wrong time. I'm unlucky."

"Very, yes. Very unlucky." Bria ducked into the back room and returned with a camo backpack. "You should've played it smart and just banged the right-hand man with commitment issues. Way less stressful."

"Bria." Kieran had only uttered her name, but a savage intensity trickled through the room, his power filling up the space. My small hairs stood on end and my flight reflex made my legs and arms tremble.

To my utter astonishment, Bria grinned, completely unaffected. "I'm just kidding. Except about bumping uglies with a certain hard-hearted grump with a wicked tongue." She waggled her eyebrows at me. "And I do mean wicked." Jerking her head toward the exit, she said, "Come on. Time's a wastin'. Let's take that horrible suit out for a spin. By the by, have you ever purchased clothes that actually fit your body, or do you just really enjoy airing out your ankles?"

I sent a pleading look to Kieran before following her. He was sending me out into the unknown with a very cool nutcase, I was certain. Although, I had to admit, there was something about her that screamed *competent.* She didn't look much older than me—twenty-eight or nine, maybe—but the self-assurance in her bearing spoke of a woman that knew what she was capable of.

"Be safe," Kieran said as I neared Zorn. "Don't take chances."

"We're visiting a bunch of dead people and you wouldn't even let me bring a cadaver for show and tell purposes," Bria said, pausing in the door. "What sort of chances do you think are possible?"

Zorn held out the car keys without looking at Bria. She snatched them out of his hand. "Thanks, silver-tongued devil."

Her grin said it all. He was the hard-hearted grump she'd been talking about.

My mouth fell open. I had not seen that coming. She seemed too edgy to be bumping uglies with a straight-laced, prim-suit-wearing guy like Zorn.

"You comin', flood waters?" she said.

I started moving, belatedly realizing she held the keys for the Beemer.

"Crap, I was going to reject that part of the contract," I grumbled. So much for digging in my heels.

"Regardless, you need something to drive," Zorn said. "Bria got a ride here in anticipation of you driving. This is the only mode of transportation."

I sent a narrow-eyed look at a smug Kieran. He'd made it impossible for me to easily reject the car. He had many super powers as a Demigod, but manipulation was where he truly shined.

Bria chuckled, clearly reading the situation. "You don't stand a chance against that Demigod." She disappeared through the door.

Chapter 5

KIERAN

KIERAN WATCHED ALEXIS go, recognizing the unsettled look on her face.

"Did I make a mistake, pairing them together?" he asked Zorn, suddenly unsure. "Alexis is incredibly powerful, but she has no experience in the magical world. Maybe I should've started her out with someone not as…"

"Impulsive?" Zorn shook his head and looked out the doorway. A car engine revved before tires squealed. Bria was clearly driving.

"Not impulsive…reckless," Kieran said, hooking his thumbs into his pockets and forcing down the unease.

"She's not reckless. She's a fast thinker with a life-time of experience."

"She stands out."

"In a good way. An *expected* way. Alexis stands out…in a bad way." Zorn quirked an eyebrow.

Kieran had to give him that. Alexis was a woman who marched to the beat of her own drum. She was breathtakingly beautiful, but dressed in unfashionable, ill-fitting attire, as though she didn't have a clue how to clothe a lithe, graceful body like hers. She shoved her hair up in messy ponytails, rarely bothered with makeup, and made constant use of frustrated, impatient scowls—and yet she had the poise and grace of a model. The unexpected dichotomy suited her to a T, and it was what had first drawn his notice.

Yes, she did stand out. In a sea of similar people, she was absurdly different. And he fucking loved it.

He'd have to hope Bria could tone Alexis down when it was needed. He didn't have any other options. Not so late in the game.

Kieran checked his watch. He had a meeting with the mayor of non-magical San Francisco in an hour. On paper, they were meeting to discuss the new magical showcase. After following Alexis to the old one, Kieran had shut it down. It had been a magical freak show of sorts, whereby people with powers showed off for a bunch of small-minded, non-magical, and cash-carrying morons. The conditions had been appalling, especially for the magical animals on display. He planned on opening a new, improved showcase in the neutral zone, allowing both magical and non-magical folk easy access.

The move would also give him a great reason to spend more time in the dual-society zone. Under the guise of overseeing the fair's progress, he'd be able to check in with Alexis more frequently without fear his father would grow suspicious. That was the plan, anyway. Valens was anything but easy to navigate.

Off paper, and unbeknownst to the mayor, Kieran also hoped to use this meeting to discuss his hidden agenda.

It was no secret that Valens deemed non-magical people beneath him. That fact created dissension in the already divided city, especially between the two governing bodies. Given apt assurances that someone else would assume the brunt of the risk, Kieran anticipated the mayor would jump at the chance to end the reign of the magical tyrant next door. All Kieran would then need to do was secure some of the mayor's weaponized forces. Just a fraction of what the mayor had at his disposal, when added to the units Kieran had been working to accrue, would be enough to equal Valens's standby battalion. It would give Kieran a fighting chance to take down one of the most fearsome Demigods in the world, a tyrannical leader who thought he was above the law.

"Keep in contact with Bria and Jack," he told Zorn, heading into the back office to get changed. He'd dressed down to be more on Alexis's level, not anticipating the strange suit she'd worn. It was on a level all its own.

He grinned. He fucking loved it.

"Sir," Zorn said after a moment. "I would like to train the girl."

Kieran paused in unzipping the garment bag hanging on the inside of the door. "Daisy?"

"Yes, sir. She's…got something. She's a diamond in the rough. Hard. Insightful. Durable. She's training with the wolf and holding her own."

"I heard. She has impressed the guys. What do you suspect she'd be good at?" Kieran finished unzipping, exposing his navy blue, tailored suit.

"I can't tell for certain, but a spy comes to mind. An assassin. A mercenary, maybe."

Kieran widened his eyes. It wasn't normal for Zorn to take an interest in someone, even when they had some natural ability. That this non-magical girl had drawn his notice meant she had something special.

"Get to it. I'm sure I don't have to remind you that your tolerance and endurance is far above that of most people. Don't push her hard enough to break her. Nor do I need to remind you that Alexis might be as dangerous as a kitten now, but someday soon she'll surpass anything you could imagine. She'll rip you apart if you harm one of her wards."

"Didn't need to be said, sir."

Kieran nodded and extracted his suit. "Oh, and tell the guys that I'll take cooking duty tonight. I want to get a first-hand account of Alexis's first day."

And a larger glimpse into her life. He wanted to find out all her secrets, and then he'd make her scream his name.

Chapter 6

ALEXIS

"THERE'S THE MEDIUM," Bria said quietly. She sat in the driver's seat of my new car, leaning her elbow against the window ledge and covering half her face with her hand. The rest was concealed by the visor pulled down in front of her.

She turned off the engine but didn't move to get out. Quiet settled between us as we stared out at the driveway of the plain, nondescript, though apparently incredibly haunted house. A woman with bright red hair waited beside a newer Mercedes parked in front of us.

"Kieran knew of her," Bria whispered. "She's the best in the area. Damned expensive."

"How much is expensive?" I whispered, too, not sure why we were being quiet but going with it.

"Five hundred bucks an hour."

"*Five hundred bucks an hour?*" There went being quiet. "What the hell? Who would pay that?"

"Your new boss, apparently. Highway fucking robbery, if you ask me, but he didn't, so there you go. Then again, he isn't going to spare any expense when it comes to his new pet. Demigods are all the same. If I were you, I'd ask for a bunch of expensive shit, starting with pants in a size *long*. Go ahead, you deserve it."

"A bunch of expensive shit...and a lovely little leash and collar, yeah." I shook my head and put my hand on the door handle. "Why are we waiting in here?"

"Sure, yeah, get a leash and collar, if that's what you're into. Diamond stud that shit. Kink can be fun. Just remember your safe word."

I could tell she had misunderstood me, since it was clear she wasn't kidding.

"No, I mean, leash and collar...as in...he'd try to control me. Like...he's possessive."

"Ah, right. Yeah, that's a given. Demigods are a huge buzz kill with all the controlling shit. Don't worry, they do it to everyone. That's what you get for banging him. Hindsight, though, right? He's hot, I get ya. Okay, first order of business—"

I put up a finger in indignation. "I did not bang him." No need to mention how close I'd come. I'd been freezing cold and in need of body warmth, and he'd been mostly naked—the saintliest of souls would have been tempted. "This is strictly a professional situation."

Her lips pulled down at the corners. "Fooled me. Okay, check this out. I'm using all of my senses to get a feel for what's around me. Feel for that weird little tingle between your shoulder blades that means some-one's watching you. Do you know what I'm talking about?"

I did, so I nodded.

She nodded with me. "Good. You're shit at it, be-cause you didn't know I was in that back room, so you'll need to practice a lot. Don't focus on any one thing with your eyes. You do that, and your brain ignores every-thing you're not focusing on. Let movement come and go around you. Anything out of the ordinary will trigger you. I assume so, at any rate. Your experiences in the magical showcase and the dual-society zone should've honed that ability." Without looking, she reached over and put her hand on my forearm. "I read a bunch of your file. Sorry to snoop. I have to get a little creepy when I gather information before taking an assignment, but you had so much crazy shit in there, I couldn't stop reading. Your whole situation is truly whack. I'm jealous." She pulled her hand back. "At that fucked up fair, you were probably always looking out of the corner of your eye, so you should be good at that."

I frowned, because she made it sound like the dual-society zone was dangerous, when actually, people mostly just minded their own business. I hadn't grown accustomed to looking out of the corner of my eye at all. Not even at the freak show, the magical showcase she was talking about.

Clearly, I should have been…

"We're in a car, so this is a moot point at the moment, but you'll want to key in to sounds around you," she went on. "Now, in addition to those things, I also tune in to my environment magically. It sounds like our abilities are similar, but I won't know how similar until we get in some field tests. For the time being, suffice it to say that I'm a kick-ass Necromancer, and can sense souls. I can feel…" She made a claw with her hand and touched the center of her chest. "What I'm doing right now is assessing what we're about to walk into."

I nodded even though I had no idea how to duplicate her efforts.

"I don't sense anyone other than the Medium," she said. "Not anyone living, I mean. She didn't bring an army or even a bodyguard. Not that I can feel at the moment, at any rate."

"You're always suspicious of foul play, then?"

"Yes. Always. You never know when some dipshit will turn on you and try to stick a knife in your skull. I know this for a fact. My old roommate was a real piece of work." She got out before grabbing her backpack from the rear passenger seat. "Come on."

I glanced at my purse, resting at my feet. Then at the dirty house with people crowded at the windows, staring out like they were starving and there was a pizza logo painted on the car.

Shivers raced across my skin. Those people would try and latch on to me with desperate abandon, I could already tell. They'd yell at me, anxious to be heard. They'd clutch at my arms, wanting to be felt. They'd cry, trying to find peace.

That house was filled with torment.

Suddenly, I wished I hadn't signed that contract. That I hadn't agreed to take this job.

"Hey." Bria wrapped on the window with her knuckles, her skull ring with the two rubies for eyes clattering against the glass. "We're good. There aren't any surprises. We've got a boring afternoon ahead of us. Let's go."

She had no idea what she was in for. Nothing but surprises awaited us in that house.

"Hello. Bria?" I heard through the glass as I pulled on the door handle.

A woman in her fifties, wearing a burgundy pants suit with the jacket flaring away from the white blouse beneath it, stalked forward with a smile. The combination of her tight, shoulder-length curls and her large red cheeks made her look like a doll. Her smile showed a chipped front tooth.

"I'm Clare Lawson. I'll be working with you today." The woman reached Bria and stuck out her hand.

Bria shook it without ceremony. "Hey, Clare. Did

you get briefed?"

"Yes, yes." Clare glanced at me. "And this is Alexis?"

"Exactly. Alexis has a unique way of working with spirits, so she'll do her thing while you do yours, and I'll see what's what."

"Well, great." Clare puffed out a breath with her smile, a little winded from striding over.

Dreading this with everything I had, I crawled out of the car, taking my phone but leaving my bag behind.

"Oh, there'll be a clean place to set down personal affects," Clare said, noticing.

I shut the door firmly. "It's okay. I don't need anyone's grubby paws on it." I pointed at the surly face staring at me through the window.

"Oh…" Clare's smile melted away in confusion as she turned to see what I was pointing at. Her confusion intensified.

"Let's do this." Bria stalked forward, her camo backpack slung across her shoulder.

"Yes, of course." With a last worried look at me, Clare followed Bria.

This in no way looked like a magical neighborhood. The desolate street boasted not a single car besides the Beemer, the sidewalks were cracked and the curbs were crumbling, and the abandoned houses sagged helplessly. On many of them, the siding and boards swung loose, blackened with dirt and covered in chipped paint.

Weeds choked front yards and bare tree branches twisted into the blue sky.

We were in a ghost town.

Without consciously intending to, I started down the disheveled sidewalk, moving away from the house we'd come to see. A strange buzzing permeated my senses. It seemed to emanate from the houses, vibrating along the rotted wood siding, draping over the doors and windows.

Three houses down from the first house, I held my hand up to one of the doorways. The buzzing beckoned me, asking that I enter.

No. Not me. The squishy part in my center. It was tugging at my spirit. My soul.

"Is this the spirit trapper?" I asked quietly, thinking about the magical electricity I'd encountered in the government building. It hadn't beckoned to me, but when I'd focused on it, it had buzzed.

A strange scratch between my shoulder blades invaded my thoughts, the feeling of being watched Bria had mentioned. I usually equated that feeling to dangerous things. But Kieran had vowed to protect me.

"Jack, is that you?" I called, stalling. If it wasn't, I'd be running.

"Yes," a deep male voice whispered. "I've got your back."

"Do you know if there is anyone in these houses?"

A soft rustling preceded Jack popping up like a jack in the box right next to the porch.

I jerked back, surprised. My foot hit a soft spot in the wood. A loud crack barely prepared me for my foot breaking through the porch.

"Shi—" I windmilled my arms, trying to shift my weight.

"I got ya." Jack was beside me a moment later—his huge arms wrapped around my middle, his legs braced wide.

I dangled for a moment, catching my breath, before tapping his Popeye forearm. "Thanks. I'm good."

"Sure, yeah." Jack lifted me while swiveling. My feet bumped down in front of the door. "Watch where you're stepping. If anything happens to you, the boss'll kill me."

"What's going on?" Bria called from near the first house, heading my way. "Are we going on a walkabout?"

"He paired you with the crazy Necromancer," Jack said, stepping to the side. "I heard that. Tough luck."

"Tough luck, yeah." I couldn't help but get sidetracked. "Is she really...with Zorn?"

"Yeah. Don't try to make sense of it, there is none. And don't engage if it's ever brought up. That shit is crazy. Best not to look it in the eyes."

My chuckle at his flabbergasted tone dried up

quickly, the strange buzz recaptured my focus. I gestured with my palm to the gaping doorway. "Is there anyone in these houses?"

"Squatters, maybe," Jack said, staring in. "Want me to check it out?"

"Yes, please."

He extracted a long knife from a holster in his leg before drifting into the house's murky low-lit interior.

"Wait, did you feel anything when you walked in?" I asked.

"Nah," Jack said. "Felt like any old doorway."

"What have we got brewing up here?" Bria stopped on the sidewalk in front of the house, her hands loose at her sides. If she was annoyed that I'd taken a detour, she didn't show it.

Clare, on the other hand, had thunderclouds rolling across her face. She stomped up the sidewalk toward us, her bag tinkling against her side.

"Okay. Go check it out." I waved Jack off.

"I don't sense any souls," Bria said, stepping onto the brittle front yard. "What's got your attention?"

"Isn't it odd that all these houses are deserted?" I asked her, closing my eyes to concentrate on that hum. After a moment, I felt something else, throbbing beneath the buzzing spirit welcome mat. Almost like a warning. It told me I did not belong, that the living had no business in a place of death. A place of rot.

I furrowed my brow. I'd never felt anything quite like it. But then again, had I ever concentrated this hard on a place?

"Not really," Bria answered. "This area housed a weird magical cult a while back. A self-proclaimed high priest sacrificed humans for power, and his disciples put their hands out for the scraps. It went under the radar for a while until they were caught kidnapping an influential Chester. That's when Valens finally put a stop to it. He was getting heat from the Chester government."

"How'd he put a stop to it? Let me guess, he killed them all?"

"Obviously, yeah." Bria made a funny face. "If you can kill Chesters and get away with it, fine. But when you get caught, he makes an example out of you." She narrowed her eyes at me before lowering her voice. I wondered if she was trying to keep Clare from hearing. "You know he's a ruthless kind of crazy, right? That he's unhinged and kills at the drop of a hat? I'd hate for this to be a surprise, being that you might be stepping on his toes."

A reminder I didn't need.

Jack drifted back into view, a graceful sort of lethal. Shadows slid across his large frame. All the training he'd done that morning with the kids, and still he looked ready for battle. The man was in great shape.

"Clear," he said, hovering near the inside of the door. He correctly assumed I was coming in.

"And no one else wants these fixer-uppers?" I asked, affecting a light tone as I crossed the threshold. An electric zing sizzled through me, tugging at my squishy center. The cage of my body held my spirit—my soul—in place, not allowing the force field, or whatever it was, to pull it away.

"Weird." I put my hand to my sternum, my mind churning.

"What?" Bria stepped up onto the porch. She eyed the doorway. "What am I missing? And what magic are you using, or do you know?"

I made a circle in the air with my finger. "If you come through, you don't leave."

"Like hell you don't," Jack murmured.

"No, I mean—" I screwed up my face and shook my head. I wasn't used to talking about this stuff. Up until recently, I'd had little to do with magical folk. As far as my power went, things just randomly happened and I largely ignored them. I'd never had to piece together a bigger picture before. "Spirits are invited in, and once they've crossed the threshold, they can't leave. It's a trap, like at the government building, but this trap actually invites them in."

Bria stepped up to the doorway and put out her hands, but her expression didn't change. She stepped through, her gaze finding me, and then stepped back out. She shook her head. Just like Jack, she didn't feel what I was talking about.

The crisp sound of a bell interrupted my thoughts. The medium was hard at work creating racket for no reason.

I blew out an annoyed breath and hurried farther into the house. The smell of mildew and stuffy air permeated my senses despite the still-open door and one cracked window. No signs of life disrupted the dust layering the ground or the furniture. Upstairs, the two small bedrooms lay bare, the hardwood floors scuffed and closet doors lopsided. The house was empty of people and souls.

"Why would he try to lure spirits in and then trap them?" I scratched my temple and made my way out of the house, scooting past the medium who'd moved into the living room. "Why would he expend the energy? It's not like the spell's targeted—this would work on any spirit."

"He, who?" Bria asked, before stopping at the front door and turning back. "No, no, Clare, I'll shadow her to the other houses. You see if there are any spirits lingering in this one. She seems to think there are."

"No, I don't—"

Bria elbowed me before I could finish. Then she pushed me along toward the next house with Jack following silently, blessedly leaving Clare behind.

"First order of business, get faster on the uptake," Bria said. "Now, what the hell are you talking about? I feel like a mime at a public speaking event."

"Sorry," I mumbled, because she was exactly right. I usually wasn't so slow, but this situation was throwing me for a loop.

I took a deep breath.

"I'm talking about the guy—or lady—who's trapping spirits here. Give me a second, though. I need to check something." I quickly moved through two more houses. Both were set up in the same way as the first, and both came up empty. "He's not even really trapping them. He didn't put up a wall blocking off the Line."

"Stop. Stop, stop, *stop.*" Bria yanked the strap of her backpack in frustration, moving it higher on her shoulder. "Start at the beginning. I still have no fucking idea what you're talking about."

I looked down the street at all the empty houses, each abuzz with magical activity. Each empty of spirits.

I smoothed back my hair. "The spirits in the magical government building have been barred from leaving."

Bria nodded with a furrowed brow. "That I did hear, yes."

"Right. Well, the same thing is happening here. In each of these houses."

Bria nodded again, her gaze darting to the empty dwellings around us.

"In addition," I went on, "these houses have a strange sort of lure. Each one, independently, is beckoning to spirits. There wasn't anything like that in the government building. It didn't want new spirits, it just wanted to keep the spirits already there…in place."

She nodded again, on board the information train.

"But here, unlike the government building, there is no wall between the world of the living"—I pointed at the ground, as if that would help—"and the Line…"

She held up a hand. "That's the part I'm missing. What is this wall you're talking about?"

I crossed my arms over my chest and stared out at nothing, thinking back. "It's a magical concoction of some sort. It looked like a sheet of various colors, draped in the air in front of the Line to block it off. No going around, no—"

She held up another hand. "Wait. You're telling me that you can actually *see* the Line? The place where spirits cross over into the afterlife—you can see it?" She put two fingers in front of her eyes. "With your eyes?"

"Yeah." I frowned at her in confusion. "I can see the Line, the crossing point, but not beyond it."

"Yes. The crossing point. The freaking Line." She leaned back, her eyes widening. "Holy shit, Alexis. You're a fucking fountain of power. No wonder Kieran is basically pissing himself in glee."

"Other Necromancers can't see it?"

She blinked comically at me. "Do you smoke a lot of ganga, or what? That info is pretty basic." Sensing that I didn't, and it wasn't, at least not for me, she ran a hand across her face. "Necromancers, especially strong ones"—she tapped her chest—"can feel the Line, and the plane around it. It's like bat sonar. We can create an image in our mind's eye from feeling it, but no, we can't actually see it. I wouldn't be able to draw it if my life depended on it."

That took me aback a little. I'd always thought my magic was less than interesting. I'd certainly never thought, in my wildest dreams, that I could do something above and beyond what highly paid magical workers could do. Then again, I'd never thought I could rip souls from people's bodies, either.

It was crazy that my mother had never reacted to any of my magic growing up. If she'd known how rare it was, or how surprising some of my skills were, she'd never given me any sign. No wonder the neighbors wouldn't let her play poker in their weekly games. She'd probably been banned for always cleaning them out.

I shrugged it off and struggled to get back on track. "Right, well, at the government building, the magical wall keeps any spirits inside from crossing over. It effectively keeps them in a magical box. They couldn't leave the building, not even to the beyond."

"And here...they can't leave the building, but they can crossover."

"Correct." I started walking again. "Here, he's bringing them in, but allowing them to cross over. He's not keeping them."

"What's the point?"

"And now we've come full circle. That was my question. Why expend the energy?"

She rubbed her nose, thinking. "Maybe this is someone's way of playing god. We can't all be Demigods, but some want the power of one. Maybe this is his or her way of feeling powerful."

"Or maybe Valens doesn't want any loose spirits messing with what he has going in that house at the end of the street." I forced myself to walk back to the house in question, with its waiting spirits.

"There were no entities," Clare said, catching up to us, still holding a bell.

"Great work, Clare," Bria said, her tone so seemingly genuine that I doubted Clare knew it was sarcasm.

"Do you think this was done by the same person who closed off the government building?" asked Jack, who'd been with me when I first felt the weird wall closing off the Line.

I stalled in front of the spirit-stuffed house and scratched my head, staring at the mess of faces in the window, all vying for space to look out. "I honestly don't know. But if it isn't the same person, they are obviously talking to each other. The principles of what they are doing is the same. And equally as fucked up."

"Oh good, you swear." Bria nodded in relief. "The suit threw me, I have to admit. I was worried you'd be a Mary Sue." She turned and looked down the street. "I can do magic summoning a spirit, and I can keep a spirit in a body, but I cannot cover a house with magic. I can't keep a spell stationary for an extended period of time. And I wouldn't have the first clue about blocking off the Line."

We all stared at the house for a silent beat until Clare finally said, "Shall we finally go in?"

This was why people hated Mediums.

Chapter 7

ALEXIS

"Now." CLARE PUSHED in close, right at my back. She had a large and small bell squished in her meaty hands. "If you'll just head on in and go to the right..."

Bria opened the door, walking into the depths. I stepped forward to follow, but as soon as she got out of the way, bodies dressed in ragged clothes crowded into the doorway. The side of a man's head was singed black, a woman's ear was half torn, and another man was missing a hand, the stump also singed black. Hands clawed desperately at a waiting Bria, standing in their midst.

"What?" she asked, confusion crossing her expression.

"I'll just squeeze in past you." Clare bumped me to the side as she passed, allowing me to backpedal.

"What's the problem?" Bria asked, leaning against the doorframe.

I sucked air into my lungs while shaking my head.

Hollowed eyes and twisted expressions stared out at me from beside her. Behind her, a man babbled about nothing.

"Those people look deranged." I pointed beyond her. "They are busted up and freaking out. One woman is screaming and beating her hand against her head. Their clothes and whatnot tell me they're from different walks of life, but they have similar issues, which means something in this house is probably messing them up."

"Yes, but…" She put out her hands. "It isn't messing me up. So we're good."

I shook my head and swallowed hard, eyeing the surly-faced man staring at me through the window. Streaks of black ate away at the skin on his right temple. A look of vicious ruthlessness barely hid the desperation in his eyes.

Jack leaned against the porch railing and crossed his arms over his chest, his gaze rooted to mine. Without knowing how, I knew he was asking me if I wanted to go. If I gave him a sign, he'd leave with me, right now, without question.

I blew out a breath, his support lending me strength.

"Don't touch me when we're in there," I told Bria quietly, starting forward.

"Got it." She stepped back and turned, totally at ease with the situation and my curt demand.

I wished I could say the same.

At the door, I dropped my head, slipping into a trance so I could pull my magic around me, creating a barrier between myself and the spirits. Usually I would infuse this same magic into inanimate objects so I wouldn't have to constantly expend the effort. If only I'd been allowed to bring my Honda, I would've had some supplies.

Another connection filtered into my anxiety-soaked mind.

I used my magic to push spirits away. I could infuse objects with it. What would be the difference in drawing them in instead of pushing them away? Surely that's all this spirit trap maker was doing.

But then he was trapping them. I still didn't understand the logistics of that. Not yet.

Tightening the magical barrier I'd set around myself, I lifted my head and faced down a barrel-chested man with a grim face marked with jagged white scars. Black scored the side of his body, blistering the skin on his arm and blackening what was left of his shirt. He blocked the door with grim determination.

"We don't need your kind here," he said in a raspy voice bubbling with liquid. Red appeared at the creases of his lips before overflowing and dripping down his chin. Blood, even in death.

My stomach swam. "And what kind is that?" I

asked.

His eyes squinted a little, nothing more than a flicker of movement. He shifted his weight before stepping to the side and turning, arms still crossed. Eyes tracking me.

"Well that was a sudden change of heart. You're not very good at sticking to your guns, I must say." I barely stopped myself from holding my breath as I crossed the threshold.

Unlike the other houses, this one didn't have a lure. It had a warning—do not cross. Except I had, and the magic dragged across my skin like little hooks, looking to catch in my squishy middle.

I frowned and stalled, taking in that feeling. Trying to categorize it.

A woman rushed at me, her arms held wide like she was coming in for a bear hug.

"No." The man shoved a grisly hand through the air. The tips of his fingers were gone, and the nails had melted away, too.

The woman staggered to a stop, her body stooped and eyes wide. Her mouth hung open, and if she'd been alive, a line of drool would be slipping down her chin.

Bodies edged toward me, some with hands hooked like claws, the faces curious, angry, or out to lunch. A man reached in before stalling, no doubt feeling my magic. Anger flitted through his eyes as he pulled his hand back slowly.

"You're the boss around here?" I asked the large man. I was gearing up to push further in. I'd never been around this many spirits at one time, and *never* had I encountered spirits this…tumultuous.

"We ain't got no bosses," the man said, his scars dancing across his cheek.

I nodded, edging along the shiny wooden floor toward the opening that led to a living room. Victorian-era chairs, all kept in great condition, were arranged in formations conducive to conversation. A light purple rug stretched across the floor, and through another shallow archway, I could see a dining room chair pushed up to a table.

The house thrummed around me, vibrating with power. The aching desire to cross over the Line echoed from one spirit to the next, each boosting the effect on my body.

I deepened the trance until the colors in the house shifted from the normal color spectrum humans could see to the dizzying ultra violets of the spirit world. The Line materialized, above and a little left of me, a burst of blues and purples spreading out from a solid black line that pulsed like the doorway to a black hole.

The Line didn't always appear in one specific place. It randomly moved around for reasons I couldn't decipher, but the colors and feelings were always the same: dark and scary, yet welcoming. The contrast denoted the fight between my logical human mind, taking in the majesty of the sight, and my emotional intuition, feeling the actual intent behind it. My brain versus my spirit.

A wall draped down in front of the Line, full of shifting shades of reds, pinks, and yellows. No entry.

"What are you thinking?"

Bria's voice startled me out of my focus. The Line and magical wall in front of it throbbed before disappearing, leaving me once again standing in a dilapidated house, surrounded by a bunch of manic spirits.

I took a couple deep breaths, allowing my heart to return to normal speed.

"The other houses invited spirits in, and kept them there—"

"Giving them the choice to stay or leave," Bria said with an impatient nod. "And if there were any, they've left."

"Right. But this house doesn't want wayward spirits. Those are being rebuffed. The spirits here can't leave. There's a wall in front of the Line, just like the one in the government building..."

"Valens isn't trapping all souls, he's trapping specific souls," Bria surmised. "You must've been right—the other houses are there to keep this house free of riffraff spirits."

"That's certainly what it looks like. And his guy is expending an awful lot of effort to do it, what with all the different spells…or whatever you call that magic." I dragged my lip through my teeth and checked the location of the Medium. She was out of hearing distance, waiting in the dining room. "But Kieran's mom isn't trapped in one location. She's free to wander. He's trapped the spirit of her skin. Somehow."

"I didn't even know that was a thing," Bria murmured, looking at the baseboards as though hunting for a pile of seal skin.

If only it would be that easy.

I shook my head, my gaze flitting from one jerkily moving spirit to another. Someone screamed. Another banged their head against the hall in repetitive thunks.

"He wouldn't put the seal skin here," I whispered, disgust for this place permeating every fiber of my being. "She bore his Demigod son. In life, he exiled her to a castle on a beautiful island, with servants and medical care. He'd never lock up part of her in a place like this, even in death. If nothing else, think of his reputation. What would people say if they found out? No, she'll be in a special place. She'll have her own digs."

I came out of my reverie to find Bria staring at me.

Heat infused my cheeks. "Obviously I'm guessing, but—"

"No, no." She held up her hands and cocked her head, as though backing down. "I wasn't judging. You're exactly right. Everything you said is spot on. I can't see what you do, but your assessment of Valens is correct. You're not so far under your rock after all, eh?" She smiled playfully.

I looked around again, feeling the correctness of that assessment.

"Speaking of rocks." Bria jerked her head toward the dining room, where she'd clearly told the Medium to wait. She seemed to agree with my assessment of them. That, or she was trying to keep the spillover of knowledge at a minimum.

We exchanged a look and headed into the dining room.

"Great, let's get started," Clare said when I pulled out a chair and sat.

The barrel-chested guy from the doorway drifted in behind me, hovering just above the ground. That neat trick meant he'd fully accepted his spirit status. Someone like him would usually succumb to the Line's welcome and leave the land of the living behind. He hadn't been given that chance. Instead, he was forced to stay here in torment.

Anger unfurled within me. This wasn't right. Valens was disrupting the natural balance between life and death. I felt that down to my bones. He needed to face judgment for what he'd done.

Clare's reaching hand caught my notice. The Line pulsed not far away, blocked off. A strange breeze ruffled my hair, and I couldn't tell where it was coming from.

"Alexis," Bria said, pulling my focus to her.

The breeze dissipated and the Line drifted away. The house and all its spirits remained.

"If you'll just take my hand, we can get started," Clare said, impatience lining her features.

"Oh." I reached out without thinking, then stopped myself as my brain caught up. "Nah." I took my hand back before noticing Jack's face in the window, watching what was going on. "I'm good."

"We need to create a circle of power," Clare said, her hand hovering in the air.

"You guys go ahead without me." I gestured between the two of them. "I have magic going and I'd rather not...you know." I pointed at her hand.

"We really must—"

"It's fine," Bria cut in, her gaze steady and confident. She had taken a page out of Kieran's book. "Leave her out of it."

"We won't know if the person we seek—"

"I'll know," I said. "Just tell me who you're looking for, and I'll tell you if they're here."

Clare's eyes narrowed and her lips thinned in annoyance. Finally, she dropped her hand.

"I can't guarantee results if we're not all participating," she said tersely, "but okay, have it your way. It'll be you Demigod Kieran goes after, not me."

"Understood." I nodded slowly, and noticed none of the other ghosts had followed us into the room with the large guy. "Did you use some sort of spell or whatever to keep the spirits at bay?" I asked Clare.

"They are giving you room to work," the big man told me, as though I'd asked him.

"No, we wouldn't want to—"

I held up my hand to Clare. "Never mind. The boss who doesn't think he's the boss just answered."

Bria's brow furrowed. Clare's lowered.

"Now, what I'm going to do is open up the veil, and see if any spirits would like to grace us with their presence," Clare said, lighting two red candles and one white one. She rang a bell that sounded strangely out of tune, then another bell that affronted me for reasons I couldn't identify. She nodded her head forward and raised her hands before moaning.

I leaned toward the big guy. "Why are a bunch of you burned?" I whispered.

"We must focus, Alexis, if we hope to reach the other side," Clare scolded. Bria started to chuckle.

"Do you feel it?" The big guy pointed in the direction of the Line. "You are living, but…can you feel it?"

"The Line, or the wall blocking off the Line?" I mouthed.

"What?" he asked.

Apparently, ghosts couldn't read lips.

"Join us," Clare boomed, filling the space with her voice.

Two men and a woman looked around in confusion before stepping forward. The big guy held up his hand, keeping them at bay.

"Join us!" Clare lifted her arms higher.

Bodies shifted and feet shuffled, more than a few of the spirits fidgeting. A guy standing in the throng took a step backward.

"When we meet the shield, it burns," the man said, his distasteful gaze on Clare. He wasn't impressed with her antics. "Many of us are strong. We siphon power from those who enter this space and the batteries in their toys. We use it to join together and attack the shield."

Wall, shield. Tomato, to-mah-to.

"And it burns you?" I whispered.

He held up his damaged hand in answer.

"Can you not change your appearance back to normal?" I asked, ignoring Clare's pointed glare.

"It doesn't heal, even when we shift form." His image flickered to that of a confident younger man, stacked with muscle. His skin was still just as blistered, his nails equally melted.

"Weird." I'd never heard of that. Then again, I'd never heard of any of this. "Bria—"

"Is anyone with us?" Clare called loudly. Her breath flickered the candles.

A little round instrument I hadn't noticed, laying in the center of the table amid the bells and candles and various accouterments, flashed green.

Clare, eyes closed, lifted her chin. "I'm sensing...a man."

I pointed at the large guy. He was certainly the closest. Then again, she could've been guessing. She would always have a fifty-fifty chance of being right.

Clare swayed. "John. John, is that you?"

"Do we have any Johns?" a middle-aged man behind me called out. "Any Johns?"

"I'm John," the big guy said. I felt like the rest of the pack should've known that, since John obviously gave the commands around here. But the situation they were in wasn't exactly ideal for casual conversation.

"There..." Clare's voice became reedy. "John, why are you here?"

"Why are you trapped, she means," I said. "Did you do something to Valens?"

I sure hoped Clare was in the know, and trusted, or I had no doubt this trip would grant her a visit from Kieran.

"I was one of his grunts," John said, drifting closer to Clare. He reached out a hand, his eyes defiant.

"No, you shouldn't—"

He put his hand on the top of her head.

"Oh!" Clare jolted and clutched at the table. "I'm making contact. He's here! He's touching me!"

He was siphoning energy from her.

"That's not cool, John," I said.

"She gets off on this," John said without remorse, "and I get energy. Even trade."

The man did have a point.

"Valens sent me to get rid of a certain non-magical politician," John said as Clare's face closed down in concentration. "But he didn't give me enough details. The politician had a full crew and the layout of his office wasn't anything like what I'd been told. Valens basically sent me in to die. So when they caught me, I sang like a canary. Gladly. I knew—"

"I sang," Clare said in a low, rough voice. She was mimicking John.

I grimaced. "That is…off-putting."

"They offered me protection from Valens—" John said right before Clare started speaking again, her voice blasting through the room.

"His fault…prepared. Got…what…" Clare straightened up a little and creases formed around her eyes. "John is saying that it was his fault he wasn't prepared, and he got what he deserved."

John bristled and his fingers tightened on the top of Clare's head.

She groaned, dropping her head forward. "His presence is strong," she said with a wispy voice.

"Valens deserved to get caught for what he was trying to do," John amended, his angry gaze directed down on his new energy source. "He did that shit all the time—sent someone into the non-magical zone badly prepared, then shrugged when they didn't make it back out. We were expendable. Not worth the effort of doing the job right. I wanted them to go after him, so I answered their questions."

"And they returned you to him?"

"Yeah." John rolled his shoulders. "I knew they would. Chesters ain't no better than Valens and his drones. I didn't care. I wanted to make sure everyone was on the same page."

"They… pressure on me… I sang. Ratted…out." Clare swayed from side to side.

"Clare, can you stop?" I said, pained. "Good work, though. John is, in fact, here. He's touching you right now. I'd advise leaving the house. He can't follow."

"No, I can't," John said. "That gives us a shock. It don't hurt as much as touching the shield, but it won't let up, neither."

Someone started to wail in the other room.

"So you ratted Valens out, and he trapped you in here?" I asked.

"Yeah. He brought me here and slit my throat. When I woke up, I was me…but not me. I was this." He spread his arms wide and looked down at his chest. "We'll stay here until we're torn apart, piece by piece. We watch everyone else get sliced to shit around us. Why do you think we're trying to break through that shield?"

Clare chimed another bell. The sound rang through my body, putting me on edge.

I pushed back from the table and walked into the living room, clasping my hands and monitoring my magical buffer. "How do spirits get torn apart?"

"Can't you feel that?" John followed behind me, his grisly hands still held out to the sides.

"The…vibration?" I asked, slipping into my trance. Trying to discern what he was talking about.

A pleasant smell drifted into my awareness, dense and gratifying.

"It's within that vibration," John said, and his voice changed. Became grimy.

I slipped a little deeper into the trance, floating on the currents of the house. Feeling the different spirits drifting around me. Feeling that warning at the door. The throb of that wall, or shield as they called it, pulsing power to block off the Line.

And then I did feel it. Grimy, like his voice had just been. Putrid. Oil slicked across fresh water. Sewage floating in a well.

"Do you feel it?" he asked, his voice a skeleton, a collection of bones clattering in the back of a moving vehicle.

"Yes," I said, opening my eyes, then startling.

Light smoke drifted around the room. Bria knelt at my feet, lighting more incense. Shimmering currents moved within the framework of the wall blocking off the Line, like the sheen of a bubble before you blew it into a sphere. The walls of the magically buttressed house buzzed, the haze of the fragrant smoke making them look like glass run through with millions of multicolored wires.

"What is that?" I asked, running my hand through the smoke.

"Necromancer's aids," Bria answered, wafting the smoke toward me. "Only a Necromancer can see the magic they reveal, and their power determines how much they see. In other words, you'll see more with this stuff than I will, since you have some serious *skillz*. Kieran stumbled on something incredibly cool, I don't mind saying. My creepy snooping didn't do you justice. Anyway, this stuff stinks, but it's helpful to see the layers of reality you can't see with your naked eye."

Every so often, a sludgy dark line slashed through

the magic, the darkness John had warned me about. Valens has essentially trapped these people in a burning building that was slowly, ever so slowly, roasting them alive.

Was this what Kieran's mom could expect? A slow, violent dismemberment of her spirit until there was nothing left? Would she go mad, reduced to muttering without coherent thought? Or would she waste away in time, pulling energy from her son just to stay afloat?

My heart sank as rage welled up inside of me.

The answer was no. None of that would happen to her. Because I was going to figure this out, and I was going to set this right. If I had to own my mantle as a soul stealer, or take on Valens directly, or both, I would. I would not allow this slow torture in purgatory. Not while I was breathing.

Chapter 8

ALEXIS

I SIGHED AS I rolled up in front of my house in the BMW. The failing light of the evening cast a murky glow through the fog. I'd been working all day, but nothing useful had happened after we left the house of doom. Bria had taken me to two other allegedly haunted houses. One was definitely haunted, with an old woman who was really ticked off that the current residents wouldn't just bugger off, and the other was just badly built. Wind could really mess with a person's mind. Neither had furthered my knowledge of what Valens was doing.

While we were "out in the field," as Bria called it, she'd walked me through a few training exercises, mostly consisting of feeling for souls. I'd learned how to (vaguely) feel the placement of a soul within a body.

I heaved a tired sigh and slipped the sleek little driving machine into park. I shut off the engine and pushed myself to standing. The day's events had taken a lot out of me, not helped by my constant worry over Kieran's mom.

It would kill Kieran to know that Valens might actually be eroding his mother's spirit. And I wouldn't feel comfortable until all of the spirits had been freed.

"You accepted the car. It's a nice little ride," Frank said, standing in the center of my lawn. "But your suit is still…unfortunate."

"Who asked you, Frank?"

"I'm just calling it like I see it, that's all. A guy likes a girl who can dress herself. Someone who knows when the hips in her pants are too roomy and her sleeves are the right length."

"Keep it up, bud. See what happens." I shrugged my Burberry a little higher on my shoulder as I reached the front door. Hand held out to grab the knob, I paused when the uncharacteristic roar of a large engine infiltrated the quiet thrust of the distant ocean.

The lovely morning weather had given way to a lazy, rolling fog, nearly obscuring the opposite side of the street. The red Ferrari seemed to burst out of it. My heart sped up and the breath caught in my throat as the car drifted toward my house.

"Why today, of all days?" I muttered, thinking about turning around, going inside, and locking the door behind me. I doubted Kieran would break it down. Then again, he probably had a key. It wouldn't surprise me.

The sweet ride put my new beauty to shame, and the two cars probably made me the most interesting person on the block. A title which I'd tried my whole life to avoid.

I stalked toward him with all the angry energy I could muster. Frank whistled a low, tuneless sound.

"That is a beaut," he said, stalking forward with me.

"Get back, you." I waved him away.

The raven head I was expecting gracefully rose from the driver's side door. His navy blue suit perfectly molded to his wide shoulders before artfully cinching down to his waist. He stared out at the street for a moment, then shut the door and started around the back of the seriously stylish car.

Billows of fog rolled in like tumbleweeds from the end of the street. They brushed past Kieran, fully obscuring the sidewalk opposite us in a thick, wet sheet. He was taking care of people noticing the car issue.

He reached the passenger side door, still not having looked in my direction, giving me a view of the rest of his body.

The pants matched the suit jacket, of course, tailored to fit those powerful legs before ending at shiny black shoes. Sparkling gold cufflinks set off his sleeves, and a pink-purple tie said he was secure in his masculinity.

I couldn't decide what I liked more, the white T-shirt and faded jeans, or the tailored power suit. He looked equally delicious in both.

"Now *he* knows how to fit clothes to his body," Frank said, at stage one of bromance.

"He has a bunch of money and a team of people making sure he gets it right," I grumbled.

Kieran pulled two bags from the seat of his car before shutting the door and finally turning toward me. Fatigue lined his face and heavy lids draped his eyes.

My annoyance eased. He'd clearly had a day, too, but he was still showing up to cook. That was pretty cool of him.

"Hey," I said, reaching for the bags.

He shook his head at my offer to lend a hand. "Well, how's things?"

His accent sounded as though he'd walked straight out of Ireland.

"Do you just affect an American accent most of the time?" I reached the door and pushed it open.

"Demigods can speak all languages in all dialects. It's one of our powers. We're made fer ruling, and can do it anywhere. But when I'm tired, things tend to slip. That's one of them." His American accent came and went. He sagged where he stood before jerking his head toward the inside of the house. "Go on. Shit before the shovel."

Surprised laughter bubbled up through me. It

wasn't the sort of expression I would have expected from him. I stepped into the house, glancing around at the mess. Shoes lay in a pile right in front of the door. Sweatshirts dotted the hall, and a couple random hair things littered the run-down carpet. Both kids lay in a heap on the couch, watching something on the laptop.

"Turn that off and clean this place up," I barked. "You've had all day." I trudged into the kitchen and dropped my handbag onto the counter. "I swear, when Mordecai was sick and we were all busting our asses just to get by, this place looked ten times better. Suddenly, we're a little more secure and everything has gone to hell."

"We've been working out all day," Daisy whined. "Would you get off my legs?"

A thud shook the floor as Kieran followed me into the kitchen.

"Ow!" Mordecai hollered. "What was that for?"

"I asked nicely," Daisy said. "You ignored me. Now look."

"I was moving! You didn't have to kick me off the couch."

"And you didn't fight half as much," I yelled.

"Hey, Demigod Kieran," Mordecai mumbled, stalling next to the kitchen opening. "Thanks again for the procedure."

A smile spread across Kieran's handsome face. "You

look stiffer than when you were sick."

"I hurt the same, just in a different way." Mordecai trudged off down the hall.

Daisy stopped near the table, her eyes narrowing at Kieran. "What are you doing here?"

"Daisy, give him a break," I said, moving to the paper bags. "He's my new boss, and he brought us groceries."

"Since when does the boss do manual labor?" Daisy asked, piling on the attitude. She wasn't the passive-aggressive type—when she was annoyed, she wanted everyone to know it.

"What can I tell ye? I couldn't pass up such a glowing welcome." Kieran smiled as he reached into one of the bags and pulled out a white paper bundle.

She sniffed. "Since when do you have an accent?"

"Daisy, seriously, give it a rest." I took out ingredients and set them on the counter. "He's here, this is happening, so let's be civil."

Daisy flung out a hand. "I'm just a little concerned, is all. He has stalked you most of the time he's known you, he's manipulated you into working for him, and now he's here, in your home, probably trying to get in your pants. He's getting too close, Lexi. You need protection from yourself."

"I'm in earshot," Kieran murmured tiredly, though not in anger. "In case you hadn't noticed…"

"She has a point," Mordecai said as he carried in two glasses and set them next to the sink. A waft of funk slapped me in the face. "Every time he comes around, he seems to want something."

"A big guy in a small kitchen," Kieran mumbled. "Hard to miss."

"Right now he probably wants you to take a shower." I waved my hand in front of my nose. "Mordie, you need deodorant."

"He's trying to cut corners and save some money." Daisy rolled her eyes. "I told him to spend the few dollars, but apparently his stink doesn't offend him like it offends everyone else."

"It's natural," Mordecai replied.

"So are farts, but you don't see people rejoicing when those waft around," Daisy said. "His feet, too, Lexi. My whole room *reeks.*"

"Our room." Mordecai left the kitchen, bending to grab a sweatshirt before disappearing from sight.

"It won't be yours if you keep up this stink," Daisy called after him. "We'll get a dog house and put you outside."

"Low blow," I heard from the back bedroom.

"I didn't mean because you're a wolf—" The door slammed, cutting Daisy off. "You're more sensitive than a chick," she yelled.

The door opened. "Anyone is more sensitive than

you. Rocks are more sensitive than you. You're a hard-hearted old cow!" The door slammed again.

I pointed at Kieran, who was shrugging out of his suit jacket with a mouth-watering grin.

"Did you say you wanted to go out to eat?" I asked. "Because if so, I'm in. Or how about Guinness for dinner? It's super filling. Any takers on leaving them here and heading down to the pub?"

"Mordecai is super moody lately," Daisy said, her gaze snagging on Kieran's upper body as he crossed the small space and dropped his suit jacket on the back of one of the dining room chairs. His white button-up stretched across his broad, muscular back and hugged his large biceps. "I don't know what his deal is." She shook her head before turning and kicking the shoes toward the door.

"Place them next to the door, don't kick them into a pile," I said. "And he's not the only one who's moody."

She stepped back into view and put a finger to her chest. "I've always been moody. That's my jam. Things are off-kilter when he is as moody as me."

I sagged against the counter. "Sleep in my room. I'll sleep on the couch. If that ends the fighting, I'm all for it."

"Or let me buy you someplace bigger," Kieran said, his brogue getting heavier by the word.

"Fat chance, Mr. Suave. We don't need your charity." Daisy went back to kicking the shoes. "But if you do buy a place, I'd be cool with breaking in and squatting there. Anything to get my own room." She stepped back into view. "But I'll take you up on staying in your room tonight, Lexi. I'll take the floor. Tomorrow, I am going to Febreze bomb my room, and throw all his stinky shit outside. That'll teach him." She rolled her eyes and moved off down the hall. "Hopefully."

"You can sleep at my house," Kieran said quietly, his tone teasing. "We'd have to sneak you past my father, though."

I bit my lip to try and hide a smile. "You live with your dad at your age?" I huffed. "What a loser."

"So." Kieran pulled out a bottle of wine before glancing around. "What was your day like?"

He opened the nearest drawer and looked inside before shutting it again and moving on to the next one.

"What are you looking for?"

"Two guesses, but I'm hoping you'll only need one."

I laughed, because yes, I should've known he was after the wine opener.

I stepped forward and reached for the correct drawer, not realizing he was doing the same thing. My fingers wrapped around metal. His warm hand wrapped around mine.

A jolt of electricity fired up my arm before settling into a delicious hum in my middle. His gaze slowly slid toward me. Without lifting his hand, he shifted, and his warm body grazed against my side.

My heart rate increased and my stomach flipped over before dropping down to my feet. The heat from his body, so close, soaked in deep, flash-boiling my blood. His thumb trailed across my knuckles and my core ached for his touch to slip down lower. It craved hard, fervent contact.

A horrifying realization struck—I wanted him desperately, and not just for his hot body. His confidence, his poise, his intense air of command—he was at the very top of the power pyramid, and had proven to be my own personal safety blanket. Despite his possessiveness and repeated attempts at manipulation, I trusted Kieran. I trusted him as a boss *and* as a man. Though he unapologetically strived to get what he wanted, he'd never once screwed me over. The opposite: he'd lured me in by helping my family. By making our lives better. Even now, he was here to cook a meal.

Without thinking, just reacting to this dawning realization, I angled my body toward him. The heat between us had grown blistering hot, eating through me. I longed to reach up and feel his hard chest before hooking my hand around his neck to pull those shapely lips closer.

I floated on the ardent tide of desire, letting my eyes drift closed. Electricity buzzed through me from his proximity. Magic danced and swirled between us, singeing my skin and forcing a moan from my lips.

He'd inherited his mother's seductive selkie magic, which pierced me in all the right ways, promising unimaginable pleasure. His father had passed down the raw power of the ocean, taking that sexy magic to the next level. It stole my breath away it felt so good.

"I love your sexy magic," I whispered with a thick, sultry voice I barely recognized. My core ached for him. My body burned.

"I'm keeping that magic in check, Alexis. It's taking all my willpower, but it's under control. This is your response to me. And me to you."

I blinked my eyes open, and his face was inches from mine. His gaze settled on my lips.

"I told you I would wait for you," he said softly. Confidently. "I knew all it would take was time."

I lightly shook my head, denying his effect on me.

His free hand touched down on the counter, blocking me in, and his other hand held mine hostage. His body pressed against mine.

"Do you not believe me?" His voice was dangerous. Thick and deep. Sexy as hell.

Without warning, a heady blast of desire shocked into me. It cocooned us in agonizing pleasure. Intense bliss sucked me under to a place from which I never wanted to emerge.

This time, he *had* unleashed his sexy magic, and it was better than anything I'd ever felt in my life.

Chapter 9

ALEXIS

I MOANED, UTTERLY lost to the feeling. Yearning sucked at my focus. I wanted him inside of me, thrusting hard.

Eyes closing again, I ran my hand up his chest, over the bumps of his pectorals and then along the width of his strong shoulders. His hardness pressed into me before he shifted forward, grinding deliciously against me.

I moaned in ecstasy.

"Does the selkie magic affect you like it's affecting me?" I asked, feeling his lips graze along my chin, leaving a trail of fire in their wake.

"It heightens my senses. It heightens the feel of you." He nibbled my bottom lip. "The first time I used it, it turned a woman into a mindless sex zombie. I swore I'd never influence anyone else with it. But then, no one else can withstand it like you can."

"I'm not withstanding it, I'm rolling with it. And you're not influencing me, I was already there."

"I know." His fevered lips skimmed the hollow of my throat, a viciously vulnerable area. "I want to fuck you so badly it hurts, Alexis."

He rocked forward, rubbing against my apex. The pleasure mounted, tight and sizzling. Pounding and white hot.

"*Hmm* Kieran…"

One hand fisting in my hair, he released the other from the drawer and felt firmly down my back, holding me against him. As soon as my hand was freed, I reached around him and grabbed his perfect, tight butt.

He groaned into my mouth and his magic switched over, from the sexy sultriness of the selkie, to the raw, brute force of Poseidon, slamming into me.

I gasped and arched, completely swept away.

"Yes," I exalted, wrapping my arms around his shoulders and throwing both legs up high on his hips.

He caught me without effort and leaned in harder, trapping my body against the counter and thrusting.

Thoughts drifted away. Pleasure increased. I climbed higher, wound tighter. I clutched onto him, digging in my fingers. Nearly there.

A door handle jingled somewhere in the background, barely permeating my fevered mind. A door swung open.

My ass hit the counter, hard. Cold air rushed against my front, replacing the hot press of his chest, and my hands fell, ripped away from the strong body they'd been clutching. I blinked into the sudden chill and confusion, only saved from pitching forward by his hand against my sternum.

"Wha…?" I couldn't even form a solid word.

Kieran moved so fast he blurred. His hands were on me, around me, lifting. My butt bumped down again. The faucet turned on. My brain couldn't process anything.

"Wha…" That was the only sound I could make as Mordecai entered my peripheral vision, trudging into the living room.

"Would ye mind peeling those?" Kieran asked, his accent heavy and his voice strained.

He'd deposited me on one of the dining room chairs in front of a spread of a few potatoes, a cutting board, and a peeler. He stood at the sink, rinsing something within the steady stream of water. On the outside, the scene looked domestic and tranquil. Normal.

But my insides were still burning for his touch, aching and tender. Electricity surged through my blood and passion throbbed in my middle.

"Mum…" At least that was a different sound.

"Hey." Mordecai ducked into the kitchen. "Do you need any help?"

"Rum…" I rubbed my eyes.

"You okay?" I heard.

"No." I opened my fists and rubbed my whole face this time. My body pounded, yearning for Kieran's touch. His magic still coursed through me. It felt so right, like a key sliding into a lock and turning. "I'm tired, and I had a hard day."

"Oh." Mordecai stepped a little farther into the kitchen, his head bowed in fatigue, and his eyes drooping. "Do you want to talk about it?"

"You've had a hard day, too. Go rest. We'll all catch up at dinner."

"Are you sure—"

"Ask her if she needs a chaperone, Pippin," Daisy hollered down the hall.

Daisy had watched *Lord of the Rings* one time, equated the sounds of Mordor with Mord-ecai, and had been peppering in references ever since. I now hated the movie purely from social annoyance.

Mordecai just stared at me. He knew I'd heard her. As they all kept reminding me, the house was small.

"Yes" was on my lips. The word was formed. I had so little control around Kieran that clearly I needed someone to run interference, but I didn't want to admit it. Not to the kids, not to Kieran, and especially not to myself.

"I'm good," I said, picking up a potato and staring at it. My hands shook.

"Cool. I'm going to take a cat nap on the couch. Jack

made me do sprints and…" He shook his head.

"Lots of water." Kieran only turned his upper body. He left his groin facing the cabinets. "I'll have one of the guys bring you something for sore muscles, but you need constant water. It'll help."

Mordecai nodded and hooked a thumb behind him. "I have my water bottle out here. I'll drain it. Thanks again. For everything. You don't have to let your guys train me, but I wouldn't work nearly as hard without them." He shook his head. "Not nearly."

"They've had a lot of training themselves. They know what the human body can withstand."

"I'm not human," Mordecai said with a strange tone. It was like a cocktail of pride, fear, and uncertainty.

"Which is why they are pushing you harder."

Mordecai nodded and drifted away.

"He needs to make his first change soon." Kieran sounded like he was talking to himself. "He's old for never having done it. It'll affect his psyche."

"How do you know?" I worked at sliding the peeler across a potato, being careful not to jerk my shaky hand to the side and take off some of my skin.

It took me a second to realize he hadn't answered me. I glanced up and my breath caught.

Kieran was facing me, his pants tented by his massive erection. His black hair stood up at odd angles, like he'd just run his fingers through it in frustration.

"Sorry about…" He didn't gesture, but I knew he was talking about putting distance between us right before I got where I was going. He lowered his voice to a whisper. "I didn't think you'd want your wards walking in on that." He paused, and a smile ghosted his lips. "I also didn't want to get kicked out by a couple of teenagers."

I forced out a breath, sagging against the table. He had a point. I would've been mortified if the kids had seen me like that, for so many reasons. His presence of mind was impressive. I'd barely registered Mordecai coming out of his room.

"They'll each need their own bedrooms, though," he went on, before reaching down and adjusting himself.

My gaze snagged on the motion, and fantasies of replacing his touch with mine brought my blood back to boiling. I wiped my forehead of moisture.

"He's a healthy teenage boy now. He'll need some privacy," Kieran said, leaning back.

"They're well used to changing in the bathroom," I said, returning to the potatoes. "They think of each other as siblings—there's no cause for alarm."

"You're not hearing what I'm saying." He stepped closer to the table. "I'm not sure how it is for girls, but for boys, he's at the age where his dick will be his favorite pastime. He'll be dreaming about girls while—"

"Ew, okay." I held up my hands to stop the words. "Got it. I know what you mean now. All clear."

"He needs his own room."

"I've already had *the talk* with him. He knows to deal with that stuff in the bathroom. Or shower. Or he can clean out the back shed and have his own personal wank shack. Whatever. He knows I won't pass judgment as long as he keeps it away from their shared room."

He shook his head before turning back to the counter. "That's an incredibly awkward conversation. How'd he take it?"

"It's only awkward if you're being awkward about it. It's a natural human situation. It's not a big deal."

"It will be when he doesn't think anyone is home, wants the comfort of his bed, and Daisy walks in on him. That won't be a good scene. Or if he thinks she's asleep and—"

"Okay, okay. Jesus, how often did you play whack-a-mole with yourself?"

"All the time. That's what I'm saying."

I pushed off of the chair and looked out into the connected family room, something I should've done before proceeding with this conversation. Thankfully, Mordecai was lightly snoring on the couch and Daisy was probably doing the same in my room.

"Well...I can move Daisy into my room permanently, I guess. But then I'll have to use the bathroom…"

Kieran stilled, his whole body going stiff. "What do you use? Your fingers, or a vibrator?"

I slid my forearm across my forehead, my body pounding again.

"None of your business," I forced out, my throat tight.

"Can I watch?" He glanced back, his tone teasing but his eyes on fire. "You can use both methods, and then compare them with my cock. See which one gets you off the best."

"Vibrator, easy." I cleared my throat. "It's got all the bells and whistles. Men just aren't equipped to compete."

"I'm not a man." His voice was deep and rich. "I'm a god."

Chapter 10

KIERAN

A N HOUR INTO a pleasant, though very frustrating, evening, Kieran plated the last of the steaks before turning and handing the plate off to a waiting Daisy. She took it without a word, then sauntered over to the table and placed it in front of Alexis's spot.

Alexis opened the second bottle of wine and set it down in the middle of the table. She glanced his way, quickly saw that he didn't need anything, and slid into her seat.

Kieran paused at the counter for a moment, basking in the easy family dynamic of these three completely different people. The kids were moody, and they gave plenty of attitude, but under it all was a deep love and respect for their provider. They'd be happy with absolutely nothing, so long as they were all together. They were content in a way Kieran had never experienced. No drama, no turmoil. Just family.

A pang of envy hit him. He'd give up everything for this easy, loving lifestyle. His mother probably would've, too. Maybe she'd even tried to establish this sort of life for them, but Valens had always called the shots, end of story.

Rage flashed through Kieran, hot and unexpected. Memories surfaced. Of his mother trying to hide her worry that his father would show up and force him into some painful exercise or another, or take him away entirely. Of her fierce and painful longing for the ocean, so close they could hear it crashing against the cliffs not far from their castle.

Next, images of the hospital accosted him. There, he'd watched helplessly as her frail body withered away day by day. He'd written dozens of pleading emails to his dad to give her back her skin and let her go. Kieran didn't need her as badly as she needed the ocean. He would've given anything to free her.

Instead, he'd been forced to watch her die slowly. Unable to help.

"Hey..."

A soft touch pressed against his bicep. It felt...comforting.

Alexis stood close, her feminine scent mixing with the thrilling feel of her magic. The kids studied him, concern in their expressions.

"You okay?" Alexis asked softly. She put out her other hand, as though trying to hold someone back. "No, no. Remember what I said? You have to learn when to let him come out of it. Touching him now will only keep him under."

Sorrow welled up inside him, the sharp bite of loss taking his breath away.

His mother was here. She wouldn't like to see him hurting. She never had.

"I'm fine." He tried to straighten up, but the heaviness of his plans pressed on his shoulders.

How the hell could he take someone like Valens down? He couldn't even get the non-magical mayor on his side. The meeting had been a bust. The man clearly hated how Valens ran things, but he'd hinted at some mutually beneficial dealings with the reigning Demigod. He wouldn't stand in Kieran's way, or so he said, but neither would he help him.

"Your mother says to sit down and eat. Your food is getting cold." Alexis's tone sounded just like his mother's.

He slipped an arm around her and hugged her close, sinking into the soft support of her compassion.

"Sorry," he muttered, knowing his mother would hear.

"No, we're not," Alexis said, slipping out of his grasp. "He's just grabby." She paused, staring at empty space. "That's all well and good, but I'm not the right one for him. I live in this place, and he lives...somewhere nicer. He needs a girl more his speed."

Kieran stilled, suddenly desperate to know what his mother had said.

"It's weird, isn't it?" Daisy asked as Kieran took a seat at the table. Daisy sat next to him, and Mordecai on the other side. The teens had separated the adults.

"What?" he asked as Alexis braced her hands on her hips, still staring at that spot where his mother clearly stood, there...but not there. In the same room, but a world away.

"When she talks to emptiness." Daisy shivered. "You know someone dead is in the room. It's gross." Her gaze darted to Kieran. "No offense," she muttered. "Sorry for your loss."

"It's not like it's a corpse. And it's not empty space to her," Mordecai said.

"Yes, Sharon the White, but—"

Mordecai bent over in laughter.

"What?" Daisy asked indignantly.

"Saruman. Not Sharon." Mordecai cut a large piece of steak before popping it into his mouth. He spoke around it. "It's Saruman the White. The wizard."

She waved the comment away as Alexis said, "Do you have any idea where your skin might be? Any idea at all?"

"She's still a dead person." Daisy cut off a bite of her steak and speared it with her fork. "Which is weird."

She popped the bite into her mouth, then moaned and rolled her eyes. "This is good. Kieran, you're a better cook than Jack, and he's great."

"I agree," Mordecai said, working at cutting off another piece. "I figured it would be bland and overdone because of where he's from. I've always heard meat is overcooked in Ireland and England."

Daisy nodded while digging in. "They err on the side of burnt."

Kieran laughed unexpectedly, the pain of his mother's loss momentarily eased by the banter of these two. "You're stereotyping me."

"Yeah." Daisy lifted her eyebrows at him, as if to say *obviously.*

"Well, don't tell Jack. You'd crush him," Kieran said, watching Alexis continue to stare at that spot where his mother apparently stood.

Her teeth snagged her plump bottom lip, thinking. She turned toward the edge of the counter near the fridge. "Wait, let me get a pen and paper… No, don't worry about dinner. I'm fine eating it cold. This is more important, trust me."

"Something is up with her magic, isn't it?" Daisy asked Kieran, her intelligent blue eyes piercing his focus. "It's changing."

He paused, not sure what Alexis had told them.

"That means yes," Mordecai said softly, nearly done

with his steak. The rest of his plate lay untouched.

"You're damn right that means yes." Daisy rested an elbow on the table and conversationally pointed the business end of her steak knife at Kieran. "She doesn't like the change, right?"

He held his tongue.

Daisy nodded like he'd answered. Mordecai leaned back with a sigh. They looked at each other for a moment, something passing between them.

"No, I did not know that," Alexis said into the silence. "Is there a code or something?"

"What is it?" Mordecai asked, dividing Kieran's attention between the kids and Alexis's one-way conversation. "What's the magic?"

After another non-answer, Daisy pointed with the knife again, only this time, there was a threat behind it. "We can't help her unless we know what's going on. Spill it, Demigod."

"She's a Spirit Walker," he said distractedly as Alexis scribbled something down. "Alexis, what is she telling you?"

"Your father has a trophy room," she said.

He shook his head, leaning forward to rest his elbows on the table. "It's not there. I've been through it."

"You forget"—she straightened up and tore a sheet of paper from the notepad—"the skin is a spirit now. You wouldn't be able to see it."

"Still, that trophy room isn't for those kinds of trophies." He held out his hand for the paper.

"He does think he has all the answers, doesn't he?" Alexis said, clearly speaking to his mother.

Something within him eased, just a little. The sorrow that suffocated him most nights pulled back. His mother was trapped in the world of the living, and while she'd clearly rather move on, from what he'd heard through Alexis, she didn't sound like she was suffering. Constant sickness no longer weighed on her every thought. A pile of meds no longer stole her attention. She'd been transported back to the days when she still cared about hot meals and whether Kieran's attitude needed adjusting.

Her salvation was close. Alexis would free her, he was sure of it.

"Give me the paper," he said in a thick voice filled with gratitude and hope.

Daisy paused, her mouth open, before lowering her knife and looking down at her plate. Mordecai, too, the good cop of their duo, found somewhere else to focus.

They'd recognized his lack of composure, and were giving him a moment.

Alexis had raised good kids. Kind kids, despite their attitude flare-ups. He understood now why his Six nearly fought over cooking dinner for them. Like him, they craved a sense of community, a taste of a family dynamic.

"Yikes, these might be tough," Alexis said, finding her seat.

He held out his hand again. "Let me see the list."

Alexis put it in his palm as she sat down. "Your fatigue and disorientation is because you're not used to this place. Kieran drew you here. You didn't elect to come. Wait—" She held up her hand and her brow creased.

Daisy leaned across the table, looking at Mordecai. "She's still talking to a ghost, isn't she?"

Mordecai nodded.

Daisy's lips thinned and she leaned back without a word, returning to her dinner.

Kieran scanned the list, recognizing a few rooms in his father's house and a warehouse he'd visited. The other places weren't familiar, and a few of the warehouses didn't have exact locations listed. His mother clearly knew of their importance, but not why they were important.

He dropped the notepaper to the table, wondering if those places were still operational—and, if so, what they were being used for. Uncertainty pinched his gut. Every time Kieran thought he'd turned up all his father's secrets and lies, something new popped up onto the radar. His confidence in taking on his father was dwindling. His preparations looked more and more like the hopeless dream of an upstart, exactly what the non-magical mayor had called them.

He blew out a breath. He might be able to free his mother, but taking down his father was starting to look like a suicide mission, and if he wasn't careful, he'd pull Alexis in with him.

Chapter 11

ALEXIS

A HARD RAP permeated the house.

I peeled an eye open, noticing the soft light lining the shades in the window. It was early morning, before the sun had completely risen.

Another series of knocks, knuckles flush to the door.

"What is it?" Daisy asked, stirring on the floor.

I glanced at the clock on my nightstand. Five-oh-two in the morning, much too early to be awake let alone knocking on someone's door.

The faint tinkle of metal on metal chased the sleep away. A key plunged into the lock.

I froze, listening. Mentally rolled through the list of everyone who had a key.

"Mordecai slept in his room, right?" I whispered.

Daisy bolted up to sitting, her eyes wide and staring at me in the dim light. My unease had triggered her warning mode.

"Yes. Remember? I berated him for forcing me to

leave?" she said. "He wasn't put out about it, so then I throttled him. He was already under the covers. He wouldn't have left after that. He hates moving when he's comfortable."

I nodded, the foggy memories from last night coming back to me. I'd had the equivalent of a bottle of wine, and Kieran's proximity had made me doubly drunk. Anything not related to desire and a near eight pack of muscles hadn't sunk in too deeply.

The lock tumbler clicked over.

"Then who the fuck just opened our door?" I rolled out of bed and ducked for the bat, resting against the wall in the corner.

It wouldn't be Kieran, not when he knew Daisy was sleeping on my floor. He'd lingered at the front door last night, his gaze resting on my lips, his body close. The kids had already gone to bed, disapproval in their sleepy eyes as they drifted down the hall. They'd clearly thought I'd buckle and give in to him.

I totally would've. I wouldn't have been able to help it. Not after seeing the haunting sorrow that crossed his beautiful features whenever he spoke of his mother. Not after eating the fabulous dinner he'd labored over after a hard day. Not after an evening spent talking to him about everything and nothing as if we'd known each other all our lives. If he'd leaned in and settled those full lips on mine, I wouldn't have had a prayer.

But he hadn't. He'd taken my hand, kissed the inside of my wrist, and turned for the door. He had respected the kids' wishes.

And thank God for those cock-blocking teenagers, or this morning I'd have another notch in my Belt O' Mistakes, and he'd be gloating over his victory.

"Do Jack and the guys have a key?" I asked Daisy, shrugging into a sweatshirt in case we'd have to run for it. I slid up to my partially open bedroom door.

She scrambled up beside me. "Not that I know of."

Metal jingled—the sound the front doorknob made when it was turned.

"What about your soul-ripping magic?" she asked. "Can you do that yet?"

"Who told—Kieran, that big-mouthed…" I gritted my teeth as the front door whined, opening slowly.

"He said the name," she whispered. "I looked it up while you two were ignoring us. Can you do that yet?"

"No. I don't have the first clue."

"Dang it…" She shifted from side to side with fisted hands. "It has to be someone we know, though, right? Kieran has people on guard. They would've stopped an intruder."

"Unless they're dead. If a pack of shifters rolled through, what good would one sleepy guy be?"

"A pack of shifters would make more noise."

I shook my head. Not the good ones. Not the ones

who would come for Mordecai.

But only a week had passed since the procedure. The shifters would want to assess the situation before sending people to break in, and with Kieran's name involved, it seemed unlikely they'd move this fast.

"What if dirty cops know you called about that mobster?" Daisy whispered.

"I called anonymously. Besides, where would they get a key?"

A footstep hit one of the many loose floorboards, squeaking. Sound ceased, the intruder listening. It was too dark to see anything.

I put my finger to my lips to make sure Daisy kept quiet.

Another squeak, closer this time, right at the mouth of the hallway. The person had taken a few steps too quietly to be heard.

Without warning, Mordecai's door flew open. He barreled out, fast and surprisingly graceful.

"Wait—" I swung my door open, bumping into Daisy as I did so. She stepped around me, lithe and agile, beating me into the hallway. "Wait! The adult is supposed to go first."

Too late. Both kids were in the hallway, running at the intruder.

Mordecai threw the first punch, his fist swinging through the air. I could barely see the small-statured person on the other end of the punch. As though dancing, the person bent just enough that Mordecai's fist sailed right by.

Daisy reached them, but she didn't lunge in with her own punch. Instead, she took a running step to the side and hurtled herself at Mordecai's back. The impact shoved him forward at an angle, and he fell into the intruder, who wasn't prepared for the sudden on-slaught. The three of them staggered in the direction of the door, limbs flying.

A bang sounded from behind me, like a foot kicking wood. A moment later, the hardly used back door burst open, slamming against the wall. A large man ran in.

Without hesitation, I darted forward, bat held up and ready. A dark mask covered the man's face and black clothes adorned his body. He rushed me.

I stepped and swung. His arm came up to block. As hard aluminum slapped bone, I struck out with a foot. It connected with his inner thigh, next to his balls. Bad shot.

I prepared for his surprised stagger, ready with an-other kick, but he didn't falter. A long arm came from the side, fisted, ready to clock me in the side of the face.

I jerked away, a narrow miss, my reactions rusty from all these years of not practicing martial arts, boxing, or self-defense. In contrast, he had another punch coming, faster than thought. It hit me in the stomach.

My breath exploded out of my mouth, spit flying. I blocked another punch, but his hands moved too fast. His fingers wrapped around the back of my neck and he shoved me face-first into the wall. I met it with my cheek. My hair was yanked back a moment later, and fingers dug into my arm as he flung me.

I ricocheted off the doorframe of Mordecai's room, landing on my side on the carpet. I scrambled to my feet, but I wasn't fast enough. He was on me in a moment, shoving me to the ground and slamming his body on top of mine.

I gasped for breath, struggling with his weight. With his strength. I was badly outgunned, and on the ground I was the weakest.

I struck out as best I could, fingers widened so I could rake across an eye. I hit hard bone, jamming my fingertips. I tried again, poking a mouth. I curled my hand into a fist and punched, that mouth still there, and this strike more effective.

He grunted before capturing my hands and pinning them above my head.

Fear flared. Panic throbbed in the periphery. He had more than the upper hand—he might even have the fight.

I knew one second of contrasting desires: to freeze in terror, and to fight in rage.

I chose rage.

Adrenaline pumping, I pushed away the fear. I pushed away the panic. Then I pushed away emotion all together. It wouldn't help me now.

I swung my legs up and clasped them around his middle before locking my ankles. I squeezed and twisted my body, much stronger with my legs and core than I ever had been with arms.

He groaned before twisting back, trying to weaken my hold. His hand came down to shove at my knees. His breath wheezed.

I stared up at his face, but it was currently bent to look down at my legs around him. Head-butting his forehead would hurt me as much as it would him. I needed to get him looking up so I could head-butt a softer area, like his nose.

He sucked in a startled gasp before convulsing down, curling in on himself. My hands were pulled with him, his grip on my wrists painful. He was trying to cover his middle.

Kieran had once said that my magic felt like I was pulling apart his chest and reaching in. *You don't know you're doing it,* he'd said. *You don't know how to control it.*

Was I somehow working my magic right now? Was that what this man was responding to?

Mind racing, I thought back to the day I'd spent

with Bria. To what she'd taught me about feeling for and identifying souls.

How different could feeling them and grabbing hold of them be?

I slipped into a light trance, then deeper, but the world didn't drop away like usual. The opposite, in fact. My awareness surged, boosted by the adrenaline flooding my body. Or maybe just flourishing in this non-emotional space.

I took in the world around me. The Line pulsed, never far away, welcoming those who would like to cross. Outside, two spirits moved in my yard, one hanging around purposefully and the other drifting through space and time, wandering. Possibly lost.

Finding spirits without a body was easier. There was no solid cage for them to hide within.

The guy on top of me yanked my hands back above my head to keep them secured. He had a loose hand, and soon he'd use it.

I had to move fast.

Gritting my teeth and yanking my legs to the side, I concentrated on the squishy place inside me that held my soul. It fluttered in a sudden breeze, which, I realized, was from the Line.

The guy glanced up at my hands. His face was in reach!

I surged up with my upper body. My forehead

smacked him in the middle of the face. The soft crunch of cartilage rang out.

His nose. Bingo.

Muscle flared within the squeezing grip of my legs, and I knew the pain he felt would soon turn to anger. Trained fighters didn't go down. They got mad, and then they got even.

I traced his body with my mind before sinking any further into my trance. The Line pulsed brightly now, and souls throbbed beyond it. Within this spectacular world of shadows, strange colors, and light, I could feel the soul of the man on top of me, burning brightly inside of him. It fluttered in the breeze but couldn't escape. It was tacked to the walls of his body.

I needed to unstick it.

But how?

"Fuck this," I heard, low and guttural. Primal. Warm liquid splattered my cheek. Blood. His body lifted up, and I saw his fist pulled high, ready to strike.

Fear made my trance wobble. The man's soul dimmed in my sight.

Breathing fast now, I tried to regain my focus. Tried to figure out a way to latch on to the soul and separate it from the host. Bria would probably know, but we hadn't gone into this in practice. I'd only been training for half a day.

His fist reached the peak before starting the downswing. It picked up speed in a hurry, now rocketing toward my face. If he hit me, it would be lights out.

I jerked to the side, mentally clutching at that soul. Trying to envision grabbing it. Slicing it. Blowing it up. *Anything!*

He grunted, and a strange keening sound exited his mouth, but his fist kept coming. It barreled down.

At the last moment, I squeezed my eyes shut.

Chapter 12

ALEXIS

"ENOUGH." THE ROUGH, commanding voice rolled through the room.

Kieran.

Light rained down on us, Kieran having flicked the light switch. The Line dimmed before blinking out. The feeling of souls vanished.

"Thank fuck," the man on top of me said before releasing my hands and cupping his face. "She nearly broke my fucking nose."

Kieran's voice turned vicious. "Get off of her."

"I would, sir, but she has a death grip on my guts."

Dawning realization struck as I blinked into the brightness, seeing the enormous arms attached to the large body.

Jack.

"Let him go, Alexis," Kieran commanded.

A surge of anger rushed through me. What was this, a training exercise? Breaking and entering, battering me around—all a drill?

I didn't sign up for this. Daisy would've told me if I had.

I gritted my teeth and squeezed harder, pinching that thick body between my Trouble Makers.

"Please stop," Jack whined, still cupping his face. "Call her off, sir. She's got a fucking Kung Fu grip on my…my middle or something…"

I needed to figure out how I did that. I could no longer see or feel his soul, but apparently he felt whatever I was doing to it.

"Alexis," Kieran said, and a blast of intense, spine-splitting magic pulsed through the room.

Jack and I groaned together, but I didn't relent. Sexy magic, painful magic—it all amounted to someone messing with me. This girl didn't like getting pushed around.

I squeezed harder, Jack not innocent in all this (he'd battered my face against the wall), as I glared at Kieran, wishing I could kick him in the face.

Kieran winced and his body tightened, solid muscle under form-fitting black clothes. Breaking and entering clothes.

"What the fuck, Kieran?" I asked through clenched teeth, keeping eye contact and hopefully magical contact.

His magic pumped harder at me, as if the tide were washing into the room. Jack curled into himself again, shaking between my legs, but not protecting himself from my magic. It must've relented from him. Pain blossomed deep inside of me and curled outward, blazing through my limbs.

I sank into it. Fuck him. A little pain was worth making a point.

Kieran's fists clenched and he opened his mouth to speak, but a shape dodged in front of him, sliding to the ground next to me like a baseball player.

Bria, with her Necromancy kit and a lighter.

"Hang on to it, Lexi," she said, her hands moving fast. "Kieran's a horrible twatwaffle. Everyone hates him. What a dick. Let's kill him." She rolled her thumb across the top of the lighter and it sparked to life. She put it to one of her incense sticks. "Kieran, blast that bitch."

"Can I leave?" Jack groaned.

Another intense pulse of power filled the room, cutting into my center and setting my blood on fire. It was like what he did with his sexiness, only terrible. Very, very terrible.

"Oh shit, that...hurts," Bria wheezed, her hands shaking as she set up candles. "Can't you localize that to her?"

"I am," he said, his vicious, stormy eyes locked on mine. Challenging. Dominant. "You're only getting the peripheral magic." He stepped farther into the bedroom. "Alexis, let him go. That's an order."

"It's not"—I squeezed harder—"working hours." The pain from his magic sliced my nerves. Crawled across my scalp and laid babies that bit into my flesh. "Asshole."

I soaked in the pain, letting it bolster my determination.

The muscles along his arms flared. His jaw clenched. His matching determination sparked in his eyes.

And then smoke drifted through my line of sight, carrying the fragrance of sandalwood with it. Thick cords of waxy power connected Kieran and I, growing out of a haze around me and burrowing into his chest.

"Holy shit." Bria turned away from looking at Kieran to flash widened eyes at me. "Keep doing that. Hang on…"

"I don't know what I'm doing," I said, staring at the waxy cords without emotion. Those things should've been heinous, or maybe surprising. Possibly I should've been as awestruck as Bria. But all I felt was detached curiosity, comparing what I saw with what I felt. Finding the points of connection.

The Line flashed above me, and a strong wind bore down on the room, making my soul flap. Power infused my body, strengthening me. It felt like I'd tapped into the Line itself. Like I was wielding this soul-wrenching power on its behalf. Doing it without emotion as I was, it became obvious what a danger this power would be in the hands of the wrong person. Someone without morals, without a clear sense of right and wrong, could use it to create unlimited destruction in the world of the living. Correction: someone *had* used it to create destruction. To create nightmares.

"What the hell?" Jack said in a strangely high-pitched voice.

"Alexis," Kieran said, the tide of his intense magic continuing to surge into the room, pummeling me. It felt like I was buried in sand up to my neck with tide water lapping at my chin, threatening to climb higher and suffocate me. And it would. He was stronger than me. I could feel that. When his magic swelled higher, I'd be swept away.

Could I take him with me?

I lowered my brow as more colored smoke drifted into the air. Red, then green, mixed with the gray sandalwood. Eerie fluorescent lights strobed within them. Those thick cords strengthened, then moved, burrowing deeper into Kieran's middle.

I fanned the magic higher, feeling a tremor as it filtered through my veins. I closed my eyes, focusing on those cords. They burrowed in deeper still, moving down to that squishy middle housing his life's essence.

"Hold," Bria said in the background, her voice

weak. It had been directed away. She wasn't talking to me.

The tips of the cords hit a strange plate of sorts. Like a metal barrier. I tapped it, feeling its solidity. I pushed harder, wondering if I could burst through, or if I had to somehow work around...

"Hold, goddammit," she yelled.

The words jogged me out of the moment. The cords blinked out, and so did the strange fluttering in my belly that was so similar to the headspace I entered when pulling someone back from across the Line.

Murky smoke filled the room, hazing my view of a pale-faced Kieran with his hands braced against the door frame.

"Did I win?" I asked, my voice weaker than I felt.

"Yes, because he was just about to blast you, and didn't. You're welcome." Bria put her hand on Jack's back. His hands cupped his face, and he lay twisted so his shoulder could rest against the ground. I still had a hold of his middle. "You're a visual learner. That's why you're mostly clueless. You can see spirits, so you know how that all works. You can see the Line, so you know what that's about. But a bunch of your magic is more nuanced. It slithers through the folds of the different planes, where you can't see it." She grabbed her incense, and snuffed the sticks out one by one on my dingy carpet.

"Hey! Those'll leave marks," I said, finally relaxing my legs from around Jack.

She snuffed the last incense stick. "Who cares? This rug was trampled to death ten years ago." She tucked them back into compartments in her backpack. "Bottom line, you need to learn by seeing." She tugged the zipper closed. "Don't worry." She grinned at me before rising. "I got you."

"Jack, get up," Kieran barked, lowering his hands from the doorframe. His eyes were on me, unreadable like usual.

Jack moaned, now fully curled up in the fetal position.

"I signed up to do a job, not defend myself from a guy twice my size," I said, gingerly touching my throbbing cheek. "He slammed my face into the wall. And where are Daisy and Mordecai?"

Kieran stepped over Jack before reaching his hand down to me. I took it and a delightful hum ran through my arm and zipped into the core of my body. I grimaced against it, trying to hold on to my anger.

"Your wards are waiting on the couch," Kieran said, pulling me up. He didn't let go of my hand, standing too close. "They have a couple bruises, but are otherwise fine."

Bria touched her fingers to her neck before wincing. I belatedly noticed four red parallel lines with little points of blood welling up.

"Bria let the situation get the better of her," Kieran said in disapproval, his gaze drifting to Jack. "As did Jack."

"No one told me she could fight," Jack said, his sides rising and falling with deep breaths. "I didn't expect her to move that fast. She hit me with a fucking bat." His voice dropped into a mumble. "Why the hell did I volunteer for this?"

"You just had the one," Bria said, shouldering her pack. "And she's half your size, I might add. That chick ward is a nut. She doesn't do anything like normal people. She's like a little gremlin. Then the shifter kid plays off of her, and suddenly I'm under siege."

"Like I said." I shrugged Kieran off. I could not let him get to me again. I had to stand strong. "I didn't sign up for people barging into my house in the dead of night."

"It's morning," Bria said with a grin, heading for the door. "And you're working with a Demigod now. What he says goes, regardless of what you signed."

I felt my expression close down as I turned to face the handsomest jerk I'd ever met. "What he says does not go."

Kieran's gaze delved through me. "Mordecai was told this would happen someday. We wondered if he would share that knowledge with you and Daisy. Much to Daisy's dismay, he didn't. It seems he thought the attack would be focused on him. He didn't realize it could affect the whole house. The whole pack, as it were. It was one of many tests."

"Testing you was my idea," Bria said. "I needed to see what you'd do under duress." Bria disappeared through the door. "And see?" she called. "It worked. Now I just need to…"

I lost the thread of her words as Kieran stepped closer, his sweet breath falling across my face. His hand came up to graze my cheek where it had hit the wall, and suddenly I couldn't breathe. Thoughts fled. His eyes burned into mine.

"Are you okay?" he whispered, concern ringing through his words. Through his eyes. "He was not supposed to physically harm you, just scare you. I think the fight got away from him."

"He would've won."

Kieran's eyes flowed over my face as his fingertips traced down to my neck, stroking softly. "This time. But you've progressed in your magic. Usually you splay my chest open for a moment, then withdraw. This time…" A troubled look crossed his face. "This time…I felt you inside of me. I felt you digging in."

"I know what part of the body I'm supposed to reach into, I just don't know how to get in there." I shivered in disgust, pulling my face away from him. I stepped back, letting the cool air wafting through the open doorway wipe away the haze caused by his proximity. "I don't know if I should figure it out. It's a dangerous place to hang around in, Kieran. I felt the power of the Line run through me. It's intense, and just now, I wasn't connected to my emotions while wielding that power. If I disconnect from my emotions, I'll be no better than the Soul Stealers in those stories. I won't have a firm grasp on my morals."

He glanced down at Jack and then back to me. He shook his head. "You underestimate yourself. I know that because I've had those thoughts before—when I was learning my magic. I tested the limits. I was young and dumb and could get away with murder. Literally. I know what it is to be tempted by power, but I've never shied away from feeling the rush of using it."

"We're different. You've been trained since you were young."

"I was taught to rule with an iron fist. I was taught ruthlessness over goodness. I constantly fight against my training. But you're right about one thing: we are different. And that difference is what makes me trust you without hesitation. What makes me fight my primal instinct for self-preservation so that you can threaten my very soul. So that you can learn." He shook his head again, more adamantly this time. "There is no worry of you losing your way, Alexis Price, even for a moment.

Your statement just proved it. The power doesn't flirt with you, as it does with most. It stands ready for your use. You're in control, not it. That distinction will save you from the thing you most fear."

I blew out a breath, not sure about all this. He didn't know me very well. Hardly at all, in fact. He couldn't know how it would affect me. *I* didn't know how it would affect me.

I was terrified to find out.

"Now, let's go. The first shift is fast approaching." Kieran turned, apparently satisfied with his obscure explanation, before stepping over a prone Jack.

"Where are we going?" I asked, wondering if I should help the poor guy up. He just laid there, staring at the ceiling with his hands flopped out to either side and dried blood smeared across his upper lip.

Kieran glanced back before walking through the door. "I took a harder look at my mother's list. It's time to break into the first of my father's strongholds and see what he's hiding."

Chapter 13

ALEXIS

"ALL RIGHT, HERE'S the situation," Bria whispered as I turned down a desolate street between what seemed like intentionally shabby buildings. Trash rolled along the sidewalk, occasionally disappearing beneath a graffiti-covered van or a truck pulled up to the curb. Up ahead, Kieran rode with a shaky Jack (apparently, I'd freaked Jack out with my magic, and Kieran had then pounded him with his. The guy was not having a good day so far), and Zorn in Donovan's car. Boman and Thane, two more of the Six, followed behind me in an identical BMW. Henry, the final member of the Six, had stayed behind to play babysitter to my wards, who were mad as hell that they didn't get to come. "Demigod Kieran is working off of some list that his mother left to him—"

"It's a list of places that are important to Valens," I replied. "She gave me the names earlier this evening. Or...last night, technically."

Bria paused with her finger up and mouth open. She

lowered her finger slowly. "Oh. Do you remember all the places?"

"Most, though some were random names I didn't recognize. Why? And why are you whispering? It's just us in the car."

She continued to whisper. "Oh good. Then pick-pocketing Kieran wasn't in vain. Cool. I overheard him talking about the list before we broke into your house—"

"I was meaning to ask you—why did you knock and *then* break in...using a key?"

She waved her hand at me, annoyed by the interruptions. "To see if you would attack or just wait and see what happened. Anyway, you're obviously here to check for that skin. I'm here to further your training while you do it. They're here to see what this warehouse is, and possibly steal secrets—"

"I know. They told us before we loaded up into the cars, remember?"

"Right, yeah. But why do you think we're in a separate car?"

"So we don't have to wait for them if the skin's not there but there's other stuff Kieran wants to check out."

"No." She ducked under the visor to look at a shiny chain-link fence stretching out in front of us, blocking off a mostly empty gravel yard. Barbed wire topped the fence in lazy circles, the points gleaming in the dawning morning light. The other identical BMW in front of us started the left turn at the T-intersection. "He's used to people waiting on him. He expects it. And if there is trouble, he usually expects his people—including me—to stay and fight for him. He's a Demigod, Alexis. They play by different rules. You need to start realizing that and stop being a good little puppet. No, he's separating you out so that if something goes down, you can run for the hills. I've been put with you so that I can help you escape. Tweedle Dingleberry was left behind with those maniac kids so that he can watch over you when I deliver you to the house. That clown Demigod has taken a liking to you, and when they do that, they basically piss on their item of interest to claim them. They're all the same. It's suffocating. I hate it. But here we are."

"Riiiggghhhtt. Except…I don't know how to fight. Me getting out of there sounds like a good idea."

"Yes, you do, you're just bad at it." She touched her visor to make sure it was all the way down—even though the sun hadn't fully crested the horizon—before slouching down further. "Sure, we'll get out of there. *After we look around.* He'll try to ship you off at the first sign of danger, but dangerous situations are the best learning experiences. I mean, people like us deal in dead people. We're already up to no good. Sometimes you gotta get caught up in trouble to do your job."

I squinted my eyes and cocked my head, seeing

where she was going with this, and not stoked about ending up in her profession. Going back to my quiet life sounded like a nicer, and safer, alternative.

She whistled softly as she looked out the window at the gravel yard that continued to run beside us, the barbed wire atop the fence nonchalantly telling lookie-loos they weren't wanted, and if they trespassed anyway, they'd end up as shark bait in the bay not far away.

"This yard is enormous. How could Valens have kept something like this a secret from Kieran?" Bria asked, her voice so low I could barely hear her. "Or from anyone?"

"It looks like it's in a really bad part of town," I said, whispering now, too, as we slowed. A small driveway broke up the fence line in front of us. A dimly lit booth sat in front of the metal gate, and a man waited inside it, standing in the open doorway. I couldn't see his face, but unless he could sleep standing up, he'd know we were approaching.

"It's still the magical part of town, though," Bria said, hunching even more as we crawled toward that driveway. "Everyone knows everyone else's business in the magical part of town. I mean, Kieran has made Valens his business, and he still didn't know about this. Valens is clearly good at hiding things. Especially big, sprawling things with lots of fencing and new barbed wire."

I pulled a little to the side, watching Donovan's car.

"I'm half terrified to get mixed up with Valens," she said, "and half invigorated. He's a mad man. He'll string us up by our toes and skin us alive if he catches us being traitorous."

"Not to mention he'll trap our spirits in the world of the living."

"Yeah. And that. But still, what a rush, am I right?"

"No." I would absolutely run if things went wrong. Run, cocoon myself in bubble wrap, and then move. Kieran had been dead right to let me bring my own car.

Donovan hadn't yet turned into the driveway before the metal gate shimmied and started a slow swing open. Without stopping, the car continued through it, everyone in it expecting me to follow.

"Oh, interesting," Bria said with a slow release of breath. "Kieran didn't know about this place, yet in half a night he found someone in it who was loyal to him, arranged entrance, and got his whole team coordinated. What do you want to bet he's got schematics for the building, too?" She shook her head as I crawled toward the driveway. "I've got a semi lady-wood. He's nothing but a toddler in the Demigod sandbox, yet it looks like he's able to play with the big boys. Mad respect. Still stupid of you to get involved with him, but mad respect."

I chewed my lip, eyeing the metal bars of the gate.

The barbed wire on the fence surrounding the establishment was just as good at keeping people in as it was at keeping them out. The guard still stood in the open doorway of the gatehouse, the light showering his grim expression.

"Or else… Kieran thinks this guy is loyal to him," I whispered, barely stopping myself from stepping harder on the brake, "but he's actually loyal to Valens, and this is a trap."

"Right." Bria nodded, leaning her elbow against the window ledge and half covering her face. "Or that."

A cold sweat broke out over my forehead. "What did I get myself into?"

"Just keep going." She nudged me with her other hand. Donovan had slowed down, too, and I could see a head in the back of his car turning around to look at us. "There is always a way out of a tight situation. Trust me. Dumping this car and hot-wiring a service car? No problem. Slitting a security guard's throat? Sure. Resurrecting the security guard and making him show us a secret way out? Been there, done that. There's a reason Kieran has me shadowing you instead of one of the Six. This bitch is good at surviving. I got you. Now keep going. You don't want your face standing out in that guard's mind. You gotta learn to be forgettable."

"Forgettable, I got…" I grimaced as I let my foot off the brake and rolled past the hard-eyed guard. "Courage, I'm having a hard time with."

"It's not a courage problem with you, it's an experience problem. One we'll probably rectify sooner rather than later."

I didn't like the sound of that.

The driveway cut through a large parking lot strewn with gravel that mostly, though not entirely, covered up the white lines. Black drips marred the ground in places, and a few areas were flatter than others, as if something heavy had been set down and then taken away. A long warehouse squatted against the backdrop of shimmering water, the location butting up against a lesser-used area of the bay.

"This is a big parking lot for that warehouse," Bria said quietly, still whispering, still hunched behind the lowered visor.

"A big parking lot, with only a few cars." I eyed those cars, either parked randomly throughout the space or grouped together in front of the warehouse entrance. "Why would people park so far away? If this place had a bunch of employees, it couldn't be kept secret, could it?"

"One would assume not, but then, Kieran knew someone that worked here, and he didn't know of it."

"Weird," I said quietly, following the lead car to the cluster of parked cars up near the front.

"Yes, it is. It is definitely weird. Which, in my experience, means fucked up. So prepare thyself for some fucked up shit, lady, because we're headed right for it."

"Have you always been like this?" I asked as I parked.

She glanced over in confusion. "Like what?"

Which was really the answer I was looking for.

Before I could set the parking brake, Kieran was at my door, his hand on the handle, waiting for me to unlock it.

"Ask him if he's going to wipe your ass for you, too, the micro-managing turd," Bria muttered, flipping up her visor.

"Hey," Kieran said as he pulled my door open, scanning the warehouse. He spared me a glance before reaching down and taking my arm, helping me out. "We're running interference with the cameras, but I don't have anyone else on the inside. We're going to have to use stealth on this."

I nodded and swung the door shut. Kieran's hand shot out and caught it before it hit home. He shut it much more quietly than I would have.

I grimaced. Micro-managing was definitely needed for a while. I worried Bria wouldn't manage me enough...

"We have an hour and a half, roughly, before the shifts change," Kieran went on, putting his arm over my shoulders and pulling me close. It wasn't sexual. This was a huddle. "The people in there are security, and they're tired. They're ready to get off work. With the cameras down, all we have to do is keep a low profile."

"Do we know where the lockers are?" Bria asked, at my other side. "I can grab a couple uniforms."

Kieran nodded slowly and Donovan drifted over with a folded square of paper. He handed it off to Bria without a word before drifting away again. The other guys fell in around us in a loose circle.

"I don't think you'll need them, though," Kieran said, pointing at the double door. Black film covered the glass on the inside, blocking visibility. No windows dotted the walls. "Unless there's something to do with your magic, you'll stay to the side. Stick to the shadows. There should be low light in there, so odds are you won't be noticed in what you're wearing."

"Let's just hope there is something to do with our magic in there," Bria mumbled, tucking the paper into her back pocket.

I glanced down at my black turtleneck and black leggings. Kieran had brought a spandex jumpsuit for me to wear, but not trusting he'd correctly gauged my size (because of my height, I looked thinner than I actually was), I'd decided to adhere to my heretofore firm rule of not being caught dead in anything spandex.

"I thought you didn't know about this place?" I asked, feeling his tug to slow me.

We stopped outside of the double door. Thane, a bald brick of a man with a brown beard and light blue eyes, tapped the face of his phone.

"I didn't," Kieran murmured.

"A few seconds, sir," Thane said in a clear voice made for singing. If he paired up with Jack and his deep baritone, they'd have a good start on a capella group.

"Then how do you know so much about it?" I asked.

Bria lowered her head before pacing to the side. I'd seen that look before. She was searching for souls.

Kieran followed Bria with his gaze. "All I needed was a direction. Everything else was easy to uncover."

"Did you not sleep?" I flared my elbow, making some room between us. I needed to follow Bria's lead, if only to practice.

"No."

"Demigods don't need to sleep?"

"Not when they can harness the ocean's power for rejuvenation."

I widened my eyes before nodding, because that was as surprising as it was cool. "And you still smell like a normal guy instead of like kelp. Amazing."

"I showered."

I opened my mouth to reply, but really, what was there to say?

I stepped farther away and sank into a light trance, feeling for souls my eyes hadn't yet spotted. A soft breeze rustled my middle, a very strange feeling since I didn't have eyes on the Line. A moment later, I felt the souls of everyone around me, nestled inside the armor of their bodies, lightly swaying to the force of the Line.

Someone gasped. Feet scraped against the ground as someone else pivoted.

A hand smacked my shoulder and shoved.

I was staggering before I'd even snapped my eyes open. Luckily, Kieran grabbed me before I could face-plant into a wall for the second time that morning.

"We're going to have to work on that," Bria said, whose raised hand identified her as the shover. "It's disruptive."

"It's downright terrifying, and I don't mind saying so," Donovan said, rubbing at his chest.

"Told you I wasn't exaggerating," Jack said to him.

"Sorry," I muttered, wishing I had pockets to put my hands in. "Clearly I'm doing something wrong."

"We're good, sir," Thane said, dropping his phone into the pocket of his black cargo pants. Kieran hadn't tried to dress him or any of the other guys in spandex. I sensed a double-standard. Then again, Thane had a bunch of stuff, like rope and cable and tools. The only thing I had was a faulty understanding of my magic.

Bria drifted back in beside me. Kieran stepped in front. The guys fanned out around us.

"Don't search for souls," Bria murmured to me as

Donovan grabbed the door handle and pulled it open.

"I just learned that lesson, yes," I said dryly.

She didn't seem to hear me. "Use the ol' peepers. Unless someone corners you, in which case, search like hell for that soul. Real hard-like. Reach in and yank that motherfucker, got me?"

Kieran's deep voice rumbled. "No one will be cornering her."

"Clearly you're used to things always going right." Bria put her hand on my arm, staying close. "In my life, things going right is cause for alarm. Stay vigilant. We're walking into enemy territory."

Chapter 14

ALEXIS

RIGHT INSIDE THE door, large moveable walls draped with shadow sectioned off an entryway. The ceiling loomed high above, with industrial lights dangling down, most of them off. As Kieran had anticipated, the interior was murky and dim.

Donovan paused beside the shadowy entrance before melting into it. Thane scooted around Bria before doing the same. His upper body ducked back out into the dim light before disappearing for the second time.

Bria drifted forward, her hand still on my arm. I followed, but clearly not quickly enough. She yanked me behind her.

Hello pot, calling the micromanaging kettle black.

On the other side of the moveable wall, the space opened up with clusters of tables dotting the floor, many of the surfaces speckled with neat piles of papers or other items. None had chairs pushed up to their sides, and only one that I could see had a stool. Nothing marred the clean floor, allowing plenty of standing room around the tables, plus clear walkways for free movement.

Halfway through the warehouse, the landscape of tables shifted into rows of industrial shelving organized into cubes. The cubes were full of boxes, each box affixed with a white piece of paper. Thick shadow lined the ground and hung off of the shelves, most of the lights off in the back.

"This place is ripe for thievery," I whispered, staying close to Bria. Kieran followed right behind me, reaching out more than once to touch the top of my shoulder. I had no idea why, because he didn't do it to steer me. "All that shadow?"

"They have night-vision cameras," Kieran said quietly.

Ah. That made more sense. And was one of the reasons why I was terrible at stealing—I tended to take things at face value.

Thane and Donovan peeled off to either side, glancing back at Bria. She nodded minutely before capturing my forearm.

"We're up. I'm sensing for souls," she said. "You just...look around."

Miss Powerful over here, and all I could do to help was glance around a mostly empty warehouse.

"Isn't anyone physically in here?" I asked.

"There probably was. That's why we were waiting

on Thane's all clear." Bria slowed before stopping, her head down. "They rely on cameras, but Kieran's got that taken care of."

There I went, taking things at face value again.

I didn't want to look around. I wanted to help.

Bria had told me that my magic was nuanced, threading in between the planes. There had to be a way for me to feel it, to use it, without punching into everyone's chests.

The buzzing from that ghost neighborhood tickled my memory. I remembered the vibration of the spells snaking along the walls. I'd automatically felt the magic when I was close enough. I hadn't tried—it had just happened.

What if I did try? Would I be able to sense it from farther away?

Focusing on what I remembered from the ghost neighborhood, I let the world slide sideways. I felt the souls pulse from beyond the Line. I felt the Line itself, but didn't see it. Didn't feel its breeze. My soul was undisturbed.

My senses were not.

Almost immediately, that soft vibration I remembered lightly traced my left side. A tiny buzz drifted through my body, originating from the same direction.

I yanked my arm out of Bria's grasp and turned toward the buzzing, eyes closed.

My feet moved of their own accord, just like they had in the ghost neighborhood. A large hand grasped my upper arm. Kieran's. Pressure directed me left, probably around a table. There was a sea of them, after all.

When the vibration and buzzing reached a peak, I opened my eyes. And then blinked at the dark gray wall rising up in front of me. Hand held out, I felt the warning for souls to stay away. That must've meant there were specific souls barred in beyond it.

"Bria," I whispered, registering the pulse of a soul beyond that wall. No, several pulses. A handful, at least, their movement jiggling my stomach uncomfortably.

Without warning, they all paused in whatever they were doing.

Became alert.

A shock of fear bled through me and I shut it all down. What if the souls I'd felt inside were living people, and I'd just grabbed someone by the middle? I might've alerted the masses to our presence.

"I feel it," Bria said, hurrying over to me. "Oh yeah. I feel that. There is some serious power in there." She unslung her backpack before looking from side to side. "How the hell do we get in?"

"Thane," Kieran said, and though his voice was soft, his tone was a whipcrack of command.

Without further instruction, Thane moved along

the wall, hands held out and eyes moving.

"They're locked in," I said, resting my palms against the wood. "I can't tell much more from here. But I'd bet the Line is blocked off. I'd also bet…" I gritted my teeth, realizing the feeling of the magic had started seeping into me again. It had almost happened by accident, proof that I used my abilities without thinking about it. "Based on what I felt before, I'd bet these are healthy souls."

"What does that mean?" Kieran asked.

"Valens isn't trying to cut them down slowly, driving them to hysteria and madness."

Bria elbowed me. It dawned on me what I was saying. Who Kieran would inevitably think about. I hadn't intended on sharing that aspect of the haunted house with him.

"He is keeping them here, but not punishing them," I said.

"You can punish souls?" he asked.

"It appears so." I tried to keep my tone light as I tapped the wood with my fingers, impatient. I wanted to see what sort of setup Valens had going inside that wall.

Thane extracted a small bottle from one of his pockets before puffing powder into the air. An unseen current of air caught the white mist, diffusing it. He continued down the wall, puffing every so often.

"You can dissipate a soul, too," Bria whispered.

"Like acid. You can make sure it never comes back. I get called in to do that, occasionally. It keeps the real nasty bastards from being called back and stuffed into a body."

Kieran shifted uncomfortably.

"He won't do that to your mother," I said, feeling the truth of those words as I said them. "He has her under his control. He's using her sk…" I turned away from the wall, looking out over the tables without seeing them. "He's using the thing connected with the sea to rule her," I murmured. "Like how he ruled her in life. He kept her on a small island, surrounded by the sea." I nodded, now gazing at the exit. "A cage by the sea. Or in the sea. That makes sense. That's where he'd keep it."

"None of the locations on my mother's list were in the sea," Kieran said. "One was near it, but on a cliff. High up."

I shook my head. "No. That wouldn't do. He'd need it in the tide. In the surging waters. Her sea-faring form would be in its natural habitat, but she wouldn't be able use it. What a shitty bastard."

"For the record, this is guesswork, right?" Bria asked quietly.

"It is guesswork, yes," I answered. "Guesswork from years of sitting on a rickety chair in front of rug-covered TV trays, listening to people describe their interactions with ghosts and vice versa. Hear enough of those horror stories, and you get a sense for how people inflict hurt on one another. How they push their will on to spirits. I could be wrong, but man...I sure sound right."

"The last time you definitely did. This time...mostly," Bria said as Thane said, "Sir..."

He puffed the powder down the way, showing us what he'd found. The air current sucked it through the wall. The door.

"The cargo pants make sense." I nodded, following the others. "I get it now. And someday, I'll graduate to those instead of being offered spandex."

"Why don't you focus on graduating to some leggings that go all the way to your ankles?" Bria mumbled. "Baby steps."

"Bria?" Kieran said, a command disguised as a question. I had no idea how everyone knew what the commands meant.

She put her palm to the hidden door. Even up close, I could barely see the cracks outlining it. Then again, shadow swathed the surface, hiding the details. Like how to open it.

"A handful of souls. Loose," she said, her eyes closed. "No hosts. No people inside."

"Are you sure?" I asked, gritting my teeth. I'd almost reached through again and checked it out for myself, but I couldn't risk it if the souls I'd sensed were living people.

Her eyes drifted open. Her eyebrows rose and lines marred her forehead. "About which part?"

"That no one in there's alive."

"I see a latch," Thane pointed. "Should I open it, sir?"

"Wait." Kieran stared at Bria, awaiting her answer to my question.

"No people. I'm positive."

At Kieran's nod, Thane bent to the ground and his finger disappeared into a little hole in the wall by the floor. A click sounded, the cracks turned black, and the door popped open. Thane straightened up.

"He's good," I said, stepping back.

"That's why he's one of the Six. C'mon." Bria pulled the door open slowly before peeking into the room beyond. Her body slowly disappeared from view. Thane followed her, ducked back out like he had upon entering the main body of the warehouse, and then disappeared a second time.

I took a step back.

"What's the matter?" Kieran said, checking the sleek little watch at his wrist. I wondered if he knew my birthday was coming up...

"The souls in there are powerful. They felt me feel them out. I'm worried about what I'll see."

Kieran looked behind him. Zorn, Donovan, Jack, and Boman took off walking, their phones out, headed for the tables. He turned back to me. "I'll be right beside you. Nothing will happen to you."

"I know they won't hurt me, but that doesn't make what's about to happen any more pleasant."

Chapter 15

KIERAN

KIERAN FOLLOWED ALEXIS as she hesitantly stepped into the room. She'd sensed the souls, but hadn't been able to discern if they were spirits or people. Nor could she sense a living person's soul without plunging her mental grip into his or her chest. She was so far behind in her magic, even the most basic things were foreign to her.

If his father got his hands on her, she'd be entirely vulnerable. Putty in his father's experienced fingers. He could ruin armies with her on his arm. Ruin cities. Alexis had the power. His father had the drive.

Kieran forced the thought away. That was never going to happen. He'd tear down the world before he'd let his father, or anyone, mistreat her. He protected what was his, with his life, if need be.

"That smell is...unpleasant." A look of disgust crossed Alexis's beautiful features as she edged farther into the room.

A musty, sickly sweet sort of funk accosted his senses. Bria identified the source immediately.

"Cadavers," she said, cutting across the medium-sized room to two rows of what looked like raised flower beds.

"Cadavers. Like…there are dead bodies in here?" Alexis weaved after her, occasionally jerking away from something unseen. "No touching," she mumbled.

"Preserved—wait." Bria stopped beside one of the barren flower beds, and Kieran had to admit the shape did compare to a grave. "This is legit dirt. Are these bastards fresh? Let's have a little lookie and find out, shall we?"

"Part of your job is digging up dead people," Alexis muttered, picking at her thumbnail. "That didn't really register until this exact moment. And here I thought seeing spirits was…unfortunate." She rolled her eyes. "You know I can see you. I just walked around you after the other lady cut through. Use your head."

Kieran caught Thane's eye and received a jerk of the head. Two tables hugged the back corner. Various items were spread out along their surfaces, much messier than the highly organized tables in the main warehouse. Whoever labored in here didn't have a direct working relationship with Kieran's father. Valens subscribed to the theory that a messy workspace denoted a messy mind.

"Necromancer supplies," Thane said as Kieran reached him.

"What's that?" Bria called.

"Necromancer supplies," Kieran answered, picking out the few things he could identify. "Two sets of bells with scrollwork along the side, candle stubs of various colors, packets of incense, some sort of…meditation tape, I think. A cassette tape player—"

"A cassette tape player?" Bria looked up. "We're dealing with someone old and set in their ways. Probably highly experienced. Likely a real shithead."

"He'll be at the top of his trade," Kieran said, thinking of the many ways he could find out who it was.

"Why *he*?" Bria asked.

Thane smiled and flicked a packet of Viagra resting at the corner of the table. "Either a guy, or a woman who dates guys with performance issues." He scratched at a couple brown rings marring the surface of the table. "He doesn't clean, and he's been in this work station for a while. Ten to one, Valens keeps him hidden just like he does this warehouse."

"Doesn't matter," Kieran said, turning away to survey the room. Barren white walls led up to an industrial ceiling, with beams and wires on full display, just like in the rest of the warehouse. Only one light of the dozen was on, casting the space in gloomy light. Shiny tile, clear of scuffs and not matching the desk, covered the whole of the floor. "Thanks to my mother, I've been able to glean a couple of new insights about the ways my father hides information. My father will have grouped him with this compound in his records. I'll be able to figure out who he is."

"Then what?" Thane asked quietly.

Kieran glanced at Alexis, her hands on her hips, staring hard at a fixed point in empty space. "We give the information to Alexis," he replied in an undertone. "She might not be trained on most of the powerful facets of her magic, but she has excellent instincts. She's goal orientated. Give her an end-game, and she'll figure out the best way to get there."

"But the end-game is freeing your mother. If this isn't directly related…"

Kieran shook his head. "She's got a big heart. The end-game *was* freeing my mother, but she can't stand to see all of these trapped souls. I can hear it in her voice when she talks about it. In an effort to make the situation morally correct, she'll release them all, if she can. She won't be able to help it. And in the process, she'll help *my* end-game."

"Whatever's going on in this warehouse is far from morally correct," Thane murmured. "Valens has something wicked up his sleeve."

"Yes, he does." Kieran glanced at the door leading out into the larger portion of the warehouse. "Magically wicked. He's prepared for war. Has been prepared for a good while, I'd guess. He's ready to defend his territory against a hostile takeover."

Chapter 16

ALEXIS

"YOU AND YOUR derelicts aren't supposed to be in here," the man with the fierce gaze said, staring me down. "This is a government facility. Authorized personnel only."

"Dude. You're dead. *You're* not supposed to be in here." I pointed at the color-shifting wall blocking off the Line. "But they locked you in. Doesn't that piss you off?"

The man puffed out his muscular chest. "I'm here because I want to be. I'm here for the greater good."

"Were you this stupid in life?" I held up my hand. "I already know the answer. Clearly you didn't grow out of the habit of blindly following authority. You're the worst sort of soldier."

"I'm the best soldier," the man said, and his bushy mustache wiggled as if he were swishing his lips under it. The other hard-bodied, grim-faced men around us nodded in agreement. "Decorated on three different continents. Active duty for ten years. Retired to special forces." He pointedly looked around.

"Retirement...as in death?" I asked incredulously. "You were so good they killed you when you hit middle age instead of letting you live out the rest of your life in peace, which you'd clearly earned?"

"We were retired to glory," the mustachioed man said. The rest nodded.

"You gotta stop believing what people tell you." I pinched the bridge of my nose. "I mean, it's probably too late now, but I bet someone told you that mustaches looked good, right?" I put up a finger. "And maybe they do on some people. You, sir, are not one of those people."

"How many are there?" Bria asked, still crouched by the graves masquerading as flower beds.

I counted them up really quickly, easy to do with such a small number. "Eight. All hard soldier types."

"Magical?" she asked.

I lifted my eyebrows at Mustache. He stared back at me.

"Are you magical?" I relayed. "Honestly, I know you can hear her. Let's move this along."

"I don't have to answer your questions," Mustache said. His groupies shifted, advertising their confidence in him.

"Bria, can you make spirits answer questions?" I asked, not looking away from his defiant, annoyingly arrogant stare.

"We both can," she answered. "You just don't know how yet."

I gestured at her, lifting my eyebrows at Mustache again. "So?"

Mustache's jaw tightened and uncertainty crossed his expression for the first time. It disappeared so fast I wondered if I'd imagined it. "We are all magical."

I relayed the info.

"And they're all getting stuffed into fresh bodies." Bria rose, leaving the exposed torso of a dead man in the raised grave as she crossed to Kieran and Thane. She looked over the items strewn across the surface of the tables. "How long have they been here?"

"They won't be able to tell time like that," I said.

"Right, right. I always forget that." Bria shook her head. "How many times have they inhabited different bodies?"

I repeated the question.

Mustache's brow furrowed, and uncertainty crossed his features again. He didn't answer. A quick look around revealed he wasn't the only one who wasn't sure. I let Bria know.

"Huh," she said. "Their brains must've been scrambled before they were killed. It's a way to keep someone's skill set but erase their short-term memory, including some of the memories that drift with them into the spirit world. I've seen the practice used in the field. It makes dangerous, powerful spirits easy to control, but it dumbs them down. They go from extremely skilled and great in the field to nothing more than blunt instruments who need simplistic instructions."

"But if those instructions are to simply kill…" I said.

She shrugged, turning around. "You said they were soldiers, right?"

I nodded. "Highly decorated, apparently."

She crossed to a chair tucked in the corner of the room and sat down with a sigh. "There are a million spirits you can call back to use as killing devices. Dumb, easy-to-manage spirits. So many. They practically wait by the gate for a chance to do what they love. But soldiers have a higher-level skill set. They have an increased functionality due to their adaptability, their ease in problem solving. You'd want them for more advanced tasks. You wouldn't want to waste their potential by scrambling their brains."

"Then why did they do it to these spirits?" Kieran asked.

"My guess?" Bria waited for his nod. She gestured at the table. "Because our Necromancer is old. He's tired. He doesn't have it in him to wrangle pushy spirits. That's a young man's game. I'm not even thirty and it exhausts me. I charge an awful lot to do it."

"Why wouldn't someone replace him?" Kieran asked, giving her a sharp look.

She spread her hands. "Did you know the information I just told you? Would you know what this guy was doing if I hadn't told you?" She didn't get an answer, and smiled. "No. You wouldn't. He'd say the brain scramble is a necessary step for transferring a spirit to a new body, and his bosses would believe him. He's the expert, after all. Then he'd give the bosses the parameters the scrambled spirits could work within, and the bosses would adjust their expectations accordingly."

"With work this touchy, why not bring in a second opinion? Someone to monitor your staff?" Kieran said.

"That happens, but Necromancers don't directly rat on each other. It's a community, and if I get old and need to hedge, I don't want some young asshole ratting me out. In turn, I'll use my established position to help the young people get placement. Give and take. You do get jerks who try to steal jobs, but they die early. Usually by a newly filled cadaver murdering them."

"But you're ratting this guy out," I said, fixing my hand to my hip. I wasn't in the habit of lying, and would be damned if I join a dishonest community.

Kieran smiled, as though he'd read my thoughts.

"I'm a black sheep, number one," Bria said, clasping her hands in her lap.

"Snitch," Mustache spat.

"I'm saving up super hard to retire early, number two," Bria went on. "And three, I don't know who this guy is. I'm just telling my employer hypothetical information. I have a hunch that I'm right, but I could be wrong. Look, I schmooze just enough in the Necromancy community to keep from getting killed. It's a tight rope, but I walk it with aplomb."

"You're saying it's likely that the employer of this establishment—"

"Valens," Bria said.

"—doesn't know that his staff of spirits is operating at a reduced capacity?"

"Correct," Bria said, nodding.

"Is the guy who puts the spirits into the bodies the same guy who's been trapping the ghosts?" I asked.

Bria stared at me for a moment, her eyes slightly narrowed. "The short answer: I don't know."

"Long answer," Kieran said.

"Until recently, I'd never heard of trapping spirits," she said, looking at the graves at the back of the room. "I didn't know it was possible, but it is a fiercely handy tool. If you try to call someone from beyond the Line, you're not guaranteed to find them. Many spirits are downright difficult to bring back. Some are impossible. If a spirit doesn't want to make the trek, they can burrow deep into the beyond, and you'll never reach them. I wouldn't mind having a setup where…" Her words drifted away when she caught sight of my angry expression. "I…wouldn't mind…finding out more about it, but never using it for my own benefit, because that would be wrong…" She paused before muttering, "for some reason."

"They are still people, and they shouldn't be trapped in the world of the living," I said, lifting my other hand to my hip. "They died. That's the end of it. Keeping them in the world of the living is either bullshit for them, or if they are really bad people, their presence and negative energy is bullshit for the living. The dead are supposed to exit stage left. That's the design. I didn't make the rules, I just… Well, I don't really enforce them, but maybe I should start, know what I mean?"

"No, I do not," Bria said. "But that's cool. You do you. Go on with your weird self. Anyway, it's possible this Necromancer discovered a new trick, but not likely. Old dogs, you know. Maybe he learned the trick from someone else, but there's a lot of ground to cover so far, and like you said, this guy's home residence is this unfortunate room. If I had to guess, I'd say he's not our guy. That is a guess, though."

So far, that's all Bria and I had. Guesses.

"Spirits lose a portion of their magic when brought back into a foreign body, isn't that right?" Kieran asked.

"Yes," Bria replied. "That's why it's attractive to use

extremely powerful spirits. You get more bang for your buck. You just need someone powerful enough to control them."

"With a brain scramble, are their magical abilities reduced further?"

"It depends on how the scramble was performed," Bria replied. "Working with the brain is always dicey."

"What are their magics?" Kieran asked me.

I went around the room, surveying the spirits and threatening the ones who weren't immediately forthcoming. Thane wrote down what they said and descriptions of each of them on a notepad he kept in one of his many pockets.

"Okay." Bria clapped her hands and rubbed them together. "What's next?"

Kieran checked his watch before meeting my gaze.

"Her...thing is not here," I said without preamble. "And if Bria's right, we still don't know who's creating the spirit traps, or how. They all look and feel the same, though, and I have the might to break through them. But how many exist? What if I can't find them all?"

"Are the traps self-sustaining?" Bria asked.

I shook my head while shrugging. "I don't think so, but I can't be sure until I check back in with the ghost in the government building."

"Okay. Well, first we find that out, obviously." Bria stood and wiped her hands on her black jeans. "And if the person does need to periodically reapply the trap, then the answer is simple—"

"Kill 'em," Thane said softly.

Bria threw up her hands. "Thanks for stealing my thunder, Thane. But yeah. We just have to find the guy, and kill him. Problem solved."

Kieran checked his watch. "Tell me what I'm looking for. I'll post people to watch." He moved toward the door.

I chewed my lip, remembering what the teen had said when I'd spoken to her in the government building. "He should be easy to spot. He has long frizzy white hair and white eyes."

"Anything else?" Kieran asked.

I hesitated before shaking my head. That's all I could remember. So far, that teen seemed to know more than anyone else about this situation. If anyone could direct me, it was her.

Unfortunately, the best way to get found out was to turn up at a large magical hub...and start asking damning questions.

Chapter 17

ALEXIS

L ATER IN THE day, after going home and falling face-first into my bed for a much too brief nap, I summoned the will to take a shower. When a firm knock landed on the door, it was afternoon and I was standing in my bedroom, wrapped in a faded pink towel wet from my shower, staring out the window at the trees swaying softly in the billowing fog. Fatigue clung to me, muddying my thoughts and making me obscenely slow.

"Door," Daisy shouted from her bedroom. She and Mordecai had kept the same schedule as me, but instead of visiting a warehouse in an empty part of town, they'd sat at home and worried. By the time I'd gotten home, they'd been too wiped out to do much besides go back to bed.

"I'm in a towel. You go get it," I hollered, wondering why Frank didn't announce who it was. Maybe he'd taken off. He had seemed awfully leery of Bria. Maybe he sensed she could slap him into a new body, which would make him confront his demise. It couldn't be a nice thought, knowing that the only way to properly come back to the world of the living was in someone else's previously discarded skin.

"You're in a towel with your door open?" Mordecai asked disapprovingly.

"I was going to close it. Give me a break."

"Your shower ended ten minutes ago," he said.

"Yes, time keeper, thanks for the update." I slammed the door.

"Jeez." Daisy's voice was muffled through the thin walls. "What crawled up her butt?"

"She doesn't know what she's doing with the Demi-god's mom," Mordecai answered. "I think it is stressing her out."

"Does she need to take it out on us?"

"Do you need to be so loud through the paper-thin walls?" I shouted.

Their voices cut off and I figured they were getting the door. I dropped my towel and pulled out some jeans and the nicest blouse I had, a scoop-neck with pastel splotches in a lovely deep purple. As much as I didn't want to admit it, Mordecai was right—the situation with Kieran's mom was stressing me out. I'd only been on the job for a day, but I felt completely lost. The situation was much more complicated than I'd thought, and new facets of the problem kept cropping up. Valens clearly had a lot of pokers in the fire. Though we'd found plenty of evidence of him tampering with spirits, we were no closer to helping Kieran's mom.

I felt like I was failing.

I hated failing. It really ruined my mood.

I grabbed my hairbrush from the dresser top and headed to the bathroom, only to hear another firm knock on the front door.

As I paused in the hall, Daisy and Mordecai each stared at me from their beds, their faces expressionless.

I gestured toward the front door with my brush. "Aren't you going to get that?"

"If we wait long enough, they'll probably go away," Daisy said. Mordecai nodded.

I curled my brush hand under and propped it against my hip. "Do you two have short-term memory loss? Last night there was a knock on the door...*and then they broke in.*" I pointed at my face. "See this big purple bruise on my cheek? See this thing? It's all fucked up. I thought an intruder was trying to kill me." I made a circle with my finger over my temple. "That's what happens with Kieran's crew when you don't open the door."

"That was this morning," Mordecai said, attempting to be helpful.

I held up my brush. "Do you want this up your ass?"

"Okay, let's get real." Daisy sat up laboriously. Her

hair, in a loop at the top of her head, flopped around. "They broke in to suss us out. They won't try that again until we have more training under our belts. You're overreacting, which means something else is wrong."

"She needs our help," Mordecai said.

Daisy nodded, her hair loop waving. "I agree. She's floundering." Daisy clasped her fingers, her face the picture of professionalism, her pajamas swimming in angry unicorns. "What's the plan of attack?"

"She has on that shirt she thinks is nice." Mordecai squinted through the gloom of their bedroom, made cave-like by the tightly drawn shades. "She's going somewhere upscale."

I sighed, stalked forward, and ripped the shades open. Fog-filtered light illuminated the room. Both kids hissed and covered their eyes like vampires.

"I don't need your help in anything but answering the door," I said, stalking toward the bathroom. "And this blouse, for your information, is the nicest thing I own besides the suit."

"When is that first paycheck coming?" I heard Mordecai ask. He was talking to Daisy. "She needs to go shopping."

The firm knock turned into a hard rap.

"Get the door!" I yelled.

"Someone is very patient," Daisy said, and I heard two feet thump onto the ground.

"Jack or Donovan would've just come in by now," Mordecai said, his bed groaning. He was probably getting up, too.

"Yeah, but the others never bother to chase us out of the house," Daisy said. "Maybe it's not one of the Six." She paused in the doorway of the bathroom. "Did you ever hear back from that detective in New York?"

I paused in brushing my hair. "Is this question on repeat? I didn't leave a name or number. They can't get a hold of me."

"How about the mafia? Has anyone been following you? Hanging around?"

"Oh my God." I pushed past her, cracking under pressure. These two could try the patience of a saint.

At the door, I flipped the lock with too much force, grabbed the knob with a white-knuckled grip, and ripped it open.

"All that, and she opens it herself," Daisy muttered down the hall. "I could've stayed in bed."

"We should've," Mordecai said, and his bed groaned again.

That probably made two of us.

Zorn stood on the stoop, his expression flat and eyes sparkling with aggressive annoyance.

"I'm here for the girl," he said without preamble. "I will be taking over part of her training.

I huffed out a humorless laugh. "Good. Run her

ragged." Without another word, I turned and headed back to the bathroom.

"Me?" Daisy asked, the confidence draining away from her posture. I frowned, pausing. It wasn't like her to react like this when someone wanted to train her.

"Yes," Zorn said. "Come on."

"But…" Daisy's large blue eyes widened. With her pale, porcelain face and dainty features, she looked more like a fragile doll in that moment than the little gremlin Bria had accused her of being. "Why me? I'm just along for the ride in all of this."

"Not anymore. Let's go." Zorn's tone was rough, his words clipped.

"But…" Daisy gave me a solemn-eyed stare.

"Since when are you wary about training?" I asked, genuinely confused.

"It's Zorn," she said, as though that was supposed to mean something.

"He's not going to hurt you. Not any more than any of the others would. Kieran knows better." I shooed her away. "Off ye git. Go learn something and quit annoying me."

She turned toward her bedroom, presumably to get dressed rather than to hide under her covers.

"No," Zorn barked, making her jump. "You'll train in what you're wearing."

Her mouth dropped open, and red infused her

cheeks. The spell had just broken. She was clearly intimidated by him, but with Daisy, that only lasted until something jogged her out of it.

"You're out of your mind," she said, her voice as hard as his. I smirked. *That's my girl.* "I don't have a bra on. Do you know how much it hurts to run with boobs?"

"Do you?" I asked her, and earned a glare.

"You need to be ready at all times," Zorn said. I slipped into the bathroom and pulled out the blow dryer but didn't plug it in. I wanted to hear this. Zorn had refused to train the kids up until now. I wanted to see what had changed, and if it was a problem that I'd have to deal with. "You'll never know when you have to move. When your cover might be blown. Get used to running with no bra. Get used to wearing enough to bed that you can comfortably slip out of a window in the dead of night. Most importantly, get used to being comfortable in your skin, so that when the situation demands it, you won't worry about little girl pajamas and the comfort of your family. You'll only worry about the task at hand. Right now, that task is a hard lesson. Let's go. Your real training starts now."

I bit my lip, readying for Daisy to blow up, or maybe just call him a lunatic and stalk back to her room. She hadn't signed up for anything. She didn't owe him squat.

Instead, I heard her footsteps moving forward.

"Wait..." I abandoned the hair dryer and peeked my head into the hall, catching a glimpse of Daisy's straight back and head held high as she reached the front door. "What?"

Zorn stepped out of the doorway. I got one glimpse of Bria crossing the grass toward the house before Daisy obstructed my view, leaving the house.

"Is that a good idea?" I asked, stepping into the hallway. "What even is this training? Who set it up?"

Zorn eyed me as Daisy walked by him. "Kieran approves." He reached in, grabbed the handle of the door, and pulled it shut.

Anger simmered inside of me. Kieran approved? What the hell did he have to do with it?

"Really? You didn't see me?" Bria pushed the door open, her head turned toward a departing Zorn. "You didn't notice me coming up the walkway before you shut the door in my face? Oh yeah, keep walking. See how that works out for you tonight. Those handcuffs aren't going to unlock themselves."

Shaking her head, she stepped into the house, then bit her lip. "I really want to slam this door, but I'm afraid the whole house will come down on top of me."

"Likely." I pointed out the door where Daisy was now entering Zorn's car. "What the hell just happened?"

"Why didn't they take me?" Mordecai asked from his bedroom door. He was shirtless and his shoes had been left untied. He'd rushed to get ready, thinking he'd be going, too.

Bria waved the comment away. "Zorn thinks Daisy would make a great spy or assassin. Which is a really big compliment, because Zorn thinks most people are absolutely useless."

Mordecai's face fell and my heart squished for him.

Thankfully, Bria noticed it before I could do damage control. "You have a different calling, kid," she told him. "There'll be plenty of time for you two to train together. But you're about to start shifting and fighting like your kind. Daisy wouldn't be able to keep up. You each need to hone what you're naturally good at, get it? She needs Zorn for that."

Fear and excitement crossed his face. His lips pressed together.

Once again, Bria easily picked up his mood, and this time she met it with sarcasm. "Yeah. You'll be shifting soon. Happiness reigns." She zeroed in on me. "What the fuck is with that top?"

I looked down. "It's a blouse."

She ran her hand across her face. "What a strange circus I've found myself trapped in." She leaned against the wall and sighed. "Right. Fine. Wear Bobo's painting frock if it makes you happy, but let's go. Our window is small."

I plucked at my shirt. "It's the nicest thing I have besides that suit."

"Which is a real damn shame, but it's not my problem at the moment. Come on."

I went back to the bathroom and grabbed the hair dryer. She followed me in. "I want to look presentable."

"Why? He won't be there. It's a quick get in, look around, and get out situation. Hopefully we won't see a soul. Or...you know, a human. You might see a soul. But they can't tell on us, so who cares."

I paused with the plug of the blow dryer an inch from the socket. "But I was going to head to the government building."

"That's not on the list. We can head there and talk to the girl if we run out of leads. We're headed to Valens's house. Three of the rooms made Kieran's mother's list. We're going to check them out while he's in a meeting. Don't worry about Jack." She motioned to the front door. "I stopped by to say hi, then jabbed him with a needle filled with a liquid roofie. He'll be sleeping for a while. Zorn didn't even notice. *That's* why you play head games with boys. It helps your misdeeds go unnoticed. I don't advise that with a Demigod, though. That would just make him more unpredictable. Nothing worse than an unpredictable Demigod." She paused in her babbling. "*Well*? Let's go!"

I batted away all the crazy information she'd slapped at me and latched on to the most salient bit. "You want to go to Valens's house?" I paused, wrapping my head around this. "You want to go to the house of the Demigod of San Francisco—uninvited—and have a look around? Bria, he kills trespassers. And then traps them on Earth so he can torment them forever."

"Yeah. He's a real piece of work, isn't he? Fucking nuts." She motioned me forward. "Come on, let's go. We're wasting our window."

"I feel like you're ignoring me. Bria, *he kills trespassers.*"

"Don't worry about that." She waved the thought away. "We won't get caught."

"But…we might."

"Nah." She shook her head. "We won't. We're good. Come on. It'll be a quick little peek, and out we go. He's not even there. Neither is Kieran. I checked, and they're both in a budget meeting. Those things go forever. We're good."

Nervous tremors raced through my body. Adrenaline pumped into my blood stream. I'd guessed I might have to enter the den of the beast, maybe even a likelihood, but I'd half hoped I'd crack the case before the need arose. I'd more than hoped Kieran would be with me.

Valens was ruthless. No, beyond ruthless, he was

possibly unhinged. If he found us, even without figuring out what we were doing, or what I was, no one would be able to save us.

"You're out of your mind," I said, sticking the plug into the wall. "We should wait for Kieran. He'll flip if we go without him."

"Kieran is watched whenever he's in the magical area. Valens doesn't trust him, and for good reason. Having him along would bring even more heat down on us." She shook her head. "No. That's a terrible idea. Trust me, I'm a master at breaking and entering. I've even got a cadaver in my trunk for distraction. Worst case, I load up that cadaver with the soul of a madman, set him loose, and we run like hell. Crazy souls in an unfamiliar body wreak havoc. They really steal the show. This'll be a piece of cake."

I put my hands out to the sides. "Breaking into a Demigod's house is suicide, Bria—"

"Only if you get caught."

"—and don't even get me started on carrying dead people around in your trunk."

"He's dead. He doesn't care. That body is just bone and tissue at this point. It's fine."

I could only stare at her with my mouth hanging open. How could she possibly be this blasé about something like this.

"I'll guard the front," Mordecai said, his patchy

head suddenly stuck in the doorway of the bathroom. The hair that had fallen out in his illness was just starting to grow back.

"There." Bria shoved her finger through the air in triumph. "He'll guard the front. Case closed."

"No." I pointed at him. Then her. "No! Mordecai, you're supposed to be the voice of reason. This is madness."

"Despite your theory about the water, it makes sense that the you-know-what would be in his house," Mordecai replied. "Valens would probably want to guard it. And Bria said Demigod Kieran is watched at all times. If you have to go, better to do it now, at the beginning of the investigation, when there is no suspicion and both of them are engaged elsewhere."

Bria's eyebrows lifted and her lips pulled down at the corners. "Wow. You're really level-headed."

"Thank you," he said.

"It wasn't a compliment. This is probably the only situation where you'll be any fun."

Mordecai frowned at her.

I looked between the two of them. The gravity of the situation weighed on my shoulders. Mordecai's serious expression flipped my stomach.

Fucking hell, I was going to do it. I was going to go along with this outrageously stupid plan.

Chapter 18

ALEXIS

"OKAY, HERE'S THE situation." Bria slouched in the driver's seat of her Mercedes with the visor down, parked against the curb, looking ahead at the ritzy, quiet street. Huge houses backed up to nothingness, high on a cliff overlooking the sparkling blue, seemingly limitless ocean. Sun showered down on the perfectly kept lawns and artfully cut shrubs lining the sidewalk. Off in the distance, the majestic orange of the Golden Gate Bridge spanned the inlet into the bay.

"This is paradise," I said in Bria's pause. "Deep blue sky, gorgeous houses, and that *view!*" I sighed, in rapture. "What must it be like to live in a house like that?"

"Considering you'd have to live with a batshit crazy Demigod who has more power than sense? Terrible. Now..." Bria rested her elbow on the edge of the window and covered half her face with her hand. "...we're going to grab those Bibles in the back seat and make the short walk to Valens's house. His is the big one at the point there." She fluttered her eyebrows instead of pointing. "We'll go up to his door, holding our Bibles out so people can see them, and pretend like we're trying to get money for charity. Dressed like you two are, that's totally plausible. Then we'll slip off to the side and go around back. Valens thinks just being Valens protects his house (gotta love huge egos), so we won't have any wards to worry about, and I can pick a lock, no problem. We'll be inside in a jiffy. Mordecai can hide in a bush at the edge of the property and text us if someone is coming."

"I don't have a phone," Mordecai said, passing up one of the Bibles. "And this isn't a Bible."

I took the proffered book, an old volume with *Bible* written on the cover in sparkly gray Sharpie.

"This isn't right," I mumbled. "Or believable."

"What'd you think I was going to do, bring actual Bibles?" She scoffed at me. "I don't need God pissed at me. I got enough problems." She turned back to stare at Mordecai, sitting in the middle seat and staring down at the other two books. One was a light red, faded with time. The "e" in bible bumped up against the end of the cover. "What do you mean, you don't have a phone?" she demanded. "How old are you?"

"Fifteen," he replied.

She glared at me. "Fifteen is plenty old enough to have a phone, Alexis. I know you're not a real mother, but surely that has occurred to you..."

"This is my first well-paying job," I said in between deep breaths. The beauty of my surroundings slowly eroded as I considered everything that could go wrong with our non-plan. "I haven't gotten my first check yet. Funds are low."

Her expression crumbled into anger. "He fawns all over you, suffocates you, helps you in and out of cars like you're broken, and he won't give you an advance to cover the staples of life?" She shook her head and blew out an aggressive breath. "If he wasn't a Demigod, I'd punch him right in the dick."

"A phone isn't really a staple," Mordecai said. "Demigod Kieran is supplying all the food we could ask for. That's—"

"No." She held up her hand. "This is depressing me." She huffed and fitted her hands into black gloves. "One thing at a time. First, we need to get into that house and have a look around. *Then* I can sort out this phone issue." She shook her head. "Now. If the house staff finds us out, pretend like you were trying to steal something and run like hell. If the worst happens, and Valens comes home, then we need to sneak out. He can feel magical power." She tapped my arm, looking at the brick red house standing proudly at the turn in the street. "Give the kid your phone."

I did as she said.

"Now. Kid." She vaguely waved her finger in the air. "You text us the moment you see his car. He's driving a lime green Lambo today. You see that, you text us. Then you need to head back to this car pronto, got it? You'll open the trunk, haul out the cadaver, and run back to the house—"

"No." I pushed her hand out of the air before glancing at a slack-faced Mordecai. "No. You won't be carrying a dead body down the street. We've parked too far away to make that look in any way believable."

"It's fine." Bria waved her hand this time. "I dressed the cadaver up. This area is home to some serious alcoholics. Throw him over your shoulder and people will think a son or young helper is carrying some rich drunkard home. It happens."

I shook my head. "I think you're making things up at this point—"

"Only mostly."

"—but it doesn't matter. We need to get moving. This car might fit into the neighborhood, but three people sitting in it surely won't."

"Okay. Then only grab the body if I say to." Bria put her hands up to stall my reaction. "It'll be our fail-safe if things go totally wrong. Trust me, you'll be glad for a dead guy running rampant through the house."

We climbed out of the car and set a quick pace down the street. As we walked between the houses, my jaw dropped at their sheer size. The majority were three stories tall and wider than three of my houses put together. Two large families could probably coexist in one of them without ever seeing one another.

"I got the impression you were into frugal living for some reason," I said conversationally, fighting my tight vocal cords and rampaging heart.

"I am," Bria said, her voice even and calm. She strolled along, seemingly not a care in the world even though she was on her way to break into a ruthless Demigod's house. "I'm saving everything I can. My studio apartment is tiny. Not tiny like your house, but nearly."

"Then what's the deal with the Mercedes?"

"Oh, that's not mine"—she snapped—"I forgot to mention. If we have to run for it, don't run back to the Mercedes. Especially if you grabbed the cadaver, Mordecai. That car is hot. My car is parked four blocks away next to—"

"It's hot...meaning you stole it?" I asked her incredulously.

"Yeah." She gave me a look that said I was dense. "I'm not going to bring a five-year-old Mazda into this neighborhood. It'd be noticed. Not to mention someone might write down the plate number. That'd lead them straight back to me." She huffed. "Madness. No, I grabbed that Mercedes from a sleepy little retirement community on the other side of town."

"Which car to run to is a very important part of the plan. It's worrying that you forgot to mention it," Mordecai said in a wary voice.

"Wow. You are definitely a buzz kill for a fifteen-year-old." Bria glanced back at Mordecai. "I'm not used to coordinating with people on this scale. Anyway, don't head back to the Mercedes unless you need the body. Head down the hill, hugging the cliff. Four—no, five—blocks away, soon after the neighborhood ends and the road splits away, there's an old motorhome parked in an outlet in front of a burnt-out building. The people in that motorhome are probably making drugs or something. I'm parked in front of that. Hopefully the cops will think my car is part of the motorhome's outfit."

"You want them to think you make drugs?" Mordecai asked.

"For a little while, yeah. Have you ever seen what happens when you burst into a meth lab? The thing goes up in flames. Cops don't rush into those. It'll buy us time."

Mordecai didn't comment, and I assumed it was because he was just as gobsmacked as I was. I'd known Bria was a nut, but I hadn't realized it was to such epic proportions. What had Kieran been thinking, pairing her with me?

Too late. This was happening whether I was ready or not.

The brick red house rose up in front of us, easily the largest and most extravagant in the neighborhood, with the best positioning for a scenic view. Flowers bloomed in a cascade of color along a walkway leading from the sidewalk to the house. Perfectly manicured bushes and vibrant green grass decorated the front yard, surrounding a large fountain with a beautiful woman dancing amid splashing waters.

I almost tripped over my own feet when I noticed the face of the woman.

"That's Kieran's mom," I said in a breathy whisper, touching my fingertips to my chest. I needed to get some pearls so I had something to clutch in times like these. "Her likeness, I mean."

Bria squinted at the statue. "Are you sure?"

I studied that face, so similar to what was stored in my memory. Young and vibrant and shockingly beautiful. "Yes. That's the form she takes as a spirit. It must've been her in her heyday."

"Huh." Bria grabbed my elbow and directed me onto the front walk. "Was she full of herself?"

"Not now, but she had a kid and a downhill spiral of a life. There's no telling what she was like before all that."

"Even still, Valens doesn't typically worship anyone

but himself." Bria slowed as we passed the fountain, taking it in. "He might've actually loved her. And when Demigods love, it is *way* overboard. They lose all reason. You think Kieran is possessive? That's just attraction. That's nothing. As you can see."

"Which is why he's holding on to her, even in death," Mordecai said, his gaze scanning the woman's face, then body. Water splashed up from little shoots, like sea foam spraying from a crashing wave. Her stone dress swirled around her legs, and her arms hung in the air, floating as she danced. "He knows she's trapped in this world. She's still with him, even though she's not."

I shivered. "That is so fucked up, I can't even."

"Yeah." Bria nodded and nudged me to get walking. "Very."

"Let's find that skin and put an end to this." I clenched my fists as we stepped onto the huge porch, facing the intricate metal door knocker featuring artful swirls and a weird face with the ring sticking out of its mouth. "At least the door knocker isn't her face."

"Maybe it's someone else. Someone he didn't like as much." Bria shifted like she was impatient before looking behind her, her eyes shrewd even if her bearing seemed peaceful and compliant. "Okay. Let's work around to the back. Any neighbors who noticed us have probably hidden in their bathrooms by now, clutching their pocketbooks, scared we'll pry ten dollars out of their miserable hands. Shitheads. I hate rich people."

I pointed at a big leafy bush at the side of the property line, pushed up against the neighbor's competing big leafy bush. "Mordecai, get between those. You should be able to see the street just fine. Let us know if anyone comes. Then get out. Above all...don't get caught!"

He nodded with worried eyes before slipping away, light and graceful. The branches barely shook as he slipped into their depths.

Regardless of what happened to me, at least he'd be able to run.

Chapter 19

ALEXIS

"He's going to be really good someday," Bria whispered as she yanked me forward, really handsy for someone who didn't like micromanaging.

We wove between bushes not indigenous to the area before reaching a freshly painted wooden fence separating the front yard from the back. She hunkered down to the side, dragging me with her. "I don't know the layout of the house. There wasn't much time to plan, and even if there had been, I still wouldn't be as good as Kieran. There's the question of training—"

"What's your point?" I made a *get on with it* gesture.

"I know we need to get on the other side of this fence, but I don't know if we should climb or open it."

"Why wouldn't we just open it?"

"Because there might be a kitchen window on the other side, or some other door or window from which someone would notice a gate moving."

Scowling, I grabbed the top of the fence, doing a small hop as I pulled myself far enough up to get a good look.

"It must be really fucking nice to be tall," I heard Bria mutter.

A stretch of wall greeted me, followed by a glass double door down the way, currently closed. Shining glass hinted at windows beyond the doors, dotting the side of the house. Bright blue shivered in the distance. Valens didn't have a fence blocking off the cliff face. At least not a tall one that would obstruct my current view.

"We're good to open the gate." I lowered down before moving to the other side and reaching my hand over to grab the metal clasp.

"Really fucking nice to be tall," she repeated. "Look at you. So easy."

"I don't think I've seen a wooden fence painted this color blue," I murmured as Bria pushed through ahead of me.

"Of course you haven't. You don't hang out with ridiculous people. You stain or whitewash a fence. Everyone knows that. You don't paint the thing like you would a house." She trotted along the side of the house, her shoulder skimming the wall. "Some overpaid landscaper or designer probably wanted to be different. Morons."

She paused next to the double door before leaning forward ever so slightly and catching a peek inside.

"Curtains, nice," she said, glancing at the neighbor's

house. Sunlight glanced off the windows, the reflection masking anyone potentially looking out. "Way retro, but great for breaking and entering."

"You have strong opinions on house design," I whispered.

"I've been in and out of a lot of rich people's homes. Trust me, there's a right way to do things, and then there is too much money and overpriced help." She unslung her backpack and pulled out a small black kit. Metal jingled as she opened a flap, extracting two thin rods with smaller straight or slightly bent ends. "Let's see what's inside, shall we?"

I watched the neighboring windows for movement, but it didn't take long before a metallic click pulled my focus. Bria curled her fingers around the long, gold-colored (and possibly real gold) door handle before pushing down. Air disturbed the curtains as the door cracked open.

We listened. The crash of the ocean waves far below blocked out any subtle sounds we might've heard from inside the house.

Bria ducked farther in, parting the curtains slightly so she could have a look. She poked her face through the slit in fabric. A moment later she was back, a surly expression on her face.

"A glass double door leading into a fucking laundry room? Are you kidding me?" She shook her head. "This is what I mean. What a dumb fu—whatever. It doesn't matter. Come on."

I followed her, moving slowly through the curtains. For once, I was in wholehearted agreement with her about a design flaw. A small cream couch sat opposite us with a cream cushion resting against the back. A gossip magazine featuring two famous people wearing grim expressions lay in the middle of a cushion. White cabinets lined the left wall and a space-age-looking washer and dryer rested on two pedestal looking things across from it. Beside them sat three rolling hampers and a larger canvas one. A nondescript doorway beside the sofa housed a plain white door, currently closed.

"I need sunglasses for the amount of white in here," Bria whispered, moving quickly through the room. She paused by the closed door. "Okay, we need to visit the trophy room, the west sitting room, and his private quarters. I'm betting on the private quarters."

"And you have no idea where any of these rooms are?"

"No. I tried to pull it up on Zillow, but this address wasn't listed."

Nervousness swam through my body. "Shouldn't you check if people are inside or not? Aren't you feeling for souls?"

She shook her head, placing her hand on the door knob. "If he has some high priority guest who can feel magic, I don't want to go prodding around with my magic."

"You don't know if he has a freaking guest over or not?"

"He doesn't." She shook her head confidently. "Definitely doesn't. It's just a precaution, is all."

She didn't take precautions. And this situation was terrible.

"Come on." She turned the handle before slowly opening the door. Without warning, she slipped out and was gone, leaving a crack for me to go after her.

My feet glued to the floor. My stomach somersaulted.

Her anxious face appeared in the crack. "Come on! The faster, the better. In and out. We don't have time to be scared."

We did have time to run away right now. We could just sprint back to the stolen car and forget this had ever happened.

But when my feet started moving, it wasn't in the opposite direction.

Nearly holding my breath, I followed her through a small hallway with a bathroom on one side and a closed door on the other and into a long kitchen with a really freaking cool reclaimed wood table that would go perfectly in the dream house I would build when I married a prince. At the other side, an open doorway led into an equally empty small (for the house) sitting room with lovely dark wood floors, not so lovely white chairs and couches, and a shit brown rug that someone should've been fired over. An older man stood at the window with his hands clasped behind him and a slight hunch to his back.

"Excuse me," I whispered, tip-toeing in his direction. "Sir?"

The man slowly glanced at the other entrance of the room. When he didn't see anyone, he finally found me.

He started when he caught me looking directly at him.

"Yes, I can see you. Listen, can you tell us where the trophy room is?"

His shoulders swung around, the movement *painfully* slow. He'd clearly died of old age and never left his house. Nor had he embraced a younger body. Or even an older body that moved at normal speeds.

"You can see me?" he asked.

"Yes, yes. And I'd love to talk to you about that, but if the owner of the house catches me in here, he'll turn me into a walking nightmare. I just need someone to direct me to the trophy room." The old man's face closed down and I realized how this must've looked and sounded to someone who used to inhabit these walls. I put my hands up. "I won't be stealing anything. I'm just trying to find a spirit who might be trapped here."

"You mean that lovely young woman with the dark"—he lifted his hand to his head before making a waterfall gesture—"dark, dark raven hair?"

My mouth dropped open. "When did—" I gritted my teeth. He wouldn't know how much time had passed. "Do you see her often?"

His brow furrowed. "No. Not often. A couple times, I think. She reminds me of the woman who lived here once. She was a lovely creature. Like gently rolling waves on a—"

"Yes, yes. Sure, sure." I hopped from foot to foot, impatience gnawing on my guts. "She's trapped in spirit form in this plane. Do you know anything about that?"

"Is that right? Well that's sad. I stay here because I like it here. It's comfortable. I see the comings and goings, the busy bustle. I watch from my window—"

"Yes, yes. Okay." He didn't know anything. Even if she'd spoken to him directly, he probably wouldn't have retained any information. His fixation was on the house. "The trophy room. Where is the trophy room?"

His directions took forever, because he kept forgetting how space and time worked. How this house had changed while he'd been squatting there. He'd been here for a *long* time, and it showed. He room-hopped without even knowing he was doing it.

The trophy room was on the second floor, the same floor as Valens's private quarters. It would make more sense to hit up the west sitting room first, then continue on to the stairs, so we took that route, racing across the shit brown rug to the dining room and then flitting through the hallway that could be seen from the front door.

"He says they have two maids who come in the morning," I whispered to Bria, out of breath. "One butler, who keeps a room upstairs—that's why the alarm isn't set—and an on-call cook. Just the butler is here right now. He thinks. But he might not know what *right now* actually means anymore. He might not even be talking about inhabitants from this century."

My breath caught in my throat as we arrived at a large entryway to a *gorgeous* sitting room with enormous bay windows facing the sparkling ocean. The deep blue sky reached down and grazed the dark blue of the sea, the color so similar to Kieran's eyes that a strange pang unfurled in my gut. The sun highlighted the red-orange of the Golden Gate Bridge, and little dots of white—sailboats—drifted along the waters of the bay.

"This is…" I didn't have words for the beauty on display. How lucky to be born into a house like this. To see this every day as a birth right.

"This is a goddamned shit show. What is up with that fireplace? It's stuffed with wood." Bria shook her head angrily as she took off to the right corner of the room.

Again, she wasn't wrong. It sounded like a nonsensical complaint, but she was right. The entire fireplace was stacked with wood, from the bottom to the top, left to right. It looked as if someone had stacked it for later use, except they'd chosen to store it in the place they would use it. So weird.

"The view, though," I said, grimacing at the gaudy mirror above the marble fireplace, the mauve walls, and the cream and glass furniture, which I hadn't noticed at first glance. "Okay fine, in this instance, their decorating skills could use a little work."

"Not in this one instance, trust me. Now hurry up, we need to get out of here."

With a last glance out the window, my heart sinking at the thought that I'd never find a prince who'd build me a dream house like this one, I let my eyes drift closed and felt around the room for a spirit trap. The Line materialized almost immediately and a tiny breeze flowed along my skin. Nothing obstructed it, however. Nothing buzzed, calling my attention.

"It's clear," I said, letting my eyes drift open. "Kieran's mother obviously thought this room was special because of the view."

Bria nodded, doing her own sweep. "I agree. Next. And move faster. We only have a half hour before we should mosey."

"Why a half hour?"

"That's when the meeting ends. Then Valens will have to drive home. We've got time, but not that much time, get it?"

I swallowed my fear and picked up the pace, crossing to the wide hallway and nearly jogging toward the stairs.

"That ghost was right—there's one person in an upstairs room," Bria said quietly, grabbing the white banister and swinging around to the steps.

"Can people hide their souls from you?"

"I didn't think so until I met you. You do it occasionally." I frowned in confusion. I didn't have the foggiest as to when or how. "I'm learning lots of new things lately. I'm not sure if I hate it or love it."

At the top of the stairs, a wood-paneled double door stood open. I stepped in—and immediately backpedaled. "What in the holy fuck?"

Bria stepped around me, once again veering to the right to start her inspection. "Come on."

"I thought they were trophies, as in...awards." I swallowed the acid rising in my throat.

Though the room was beautiful, with high, wood-paneled ceilings, rows of bookshelves laden with books, and rustic wooden floors, the items in the room were god-awful. Stuffed elephant feet balanced the pool table, the sides of which were made out of ivory. A unicorn head hung on the wall, its golden horn gleaming in the mood lighting. A stuffed phoenix perched on a wooden stick, its days of rebirth stolen. A skin of some kind stretched across the floor.

"Hunting these magical animals is illegal," I said, a strange and uncomfortable feeling washing over me. "They're endangered."

"He's above the law."

"No one is above the law." I clenched and un-clenched my hands, my ire rising. "Kieran really did yank down the freak show to stop me from participating. If he cared about the animals, he wouldn't live here."

Bria glanced up as she moved locations. "He does that in every city he visits."

"But…" I spread out my hands, indicating the room at large.

"This isn't his." Bria paused at a desk made out of colorful dragon scales. "Valens is known for his hunting. Of people, of animals. No one gets away." She paused. "Literally, I guess, right? The magical animals end up in this room, and the people end up in spirit traps. Man, that guy is fucked up."

I clenched my jaw. Acid bit the back of my throat. "I want to help Kieran. Help him take on—"

Bria made a shushing gesture. "Best to stay on light topics, like what a dick Valens is," she said quietly. "I'd hate to find out my intel on this place is wrong, and there is actually surveillance besides an old butler and a few cameras on the expensive cars. Come on, search. We haven't got all day."

I let out a breath, trying to regain my focus. A dragon head with glittering golden scales stared at me from the wall, making it difficult.

I drifted into the middle of the room, careful not to touch anything. Before I even closed my eyes, a very slight buzz permeated my body, followed by a surge of adrenaline. A spirit trap in this room. "Bingo," I whispered, following the feeling to the back of the room. There, sitting on the middle shelf, sat a little gold box with a tiny lock fastening the cover.

"Bria," I said in excitement, nearly reaching for it. "I found it!"

Chapter 20

ALEXIS

S HE HURRIED OVER, her footsteps light despite her haste. Her shoulder bumped mine as she surveyed the box.

"The spirit trap...thing is on that?" she asked, pushing up on tiptoes to get a peek at the top.

"Yeah."

"It's too small for a selkie skin." For the first time I could remember, sadness dragged down Bria's expression. She turned away. "Besides, it wouldn't make sense to keep a skin in a fairy box."

"What do you mean, a fairy box?" I pushed in closer. Intricate words and designs were etched into the gold. Spells, maybe.

"It's a box to trap fairies," she said. "You can make them yourself, or buy one that's already set up. They aren't foolproof, though, and the rate of failure if you do it yourself is high." She moved to the other side of the room. "It looks like he did it himself."

"But..." I let what she said sink in. "Killing a fairy is

murder."

"The most interesting game has the intelligence of the hunter." Bria bent to a case with a glass top. "See if you feel anything else, but don't look around. You won't like what you find."

Disgust ate at me. "Are there more like this?"

"Like I said, you won't like what you find." Bria straightened up and glanced back at the fairy box. "But you know what, that fairy box looks pretty new. What do you think, ten years? Less?"

I shook my head, hardly able to bring myself to look at it again. "Yeah…"

"See if you feel anything else. I have a theory."

I didn't. The only buzz came from that box, where the fairy's spirit was trapped inside a space so small it would barely be able to move.

"I don't feel any souls." Bria lifted the top of a gold and white urn, peeking inside. "He used to keep their ashes, it looks like." She lowered the lid and bent to the side. "This was a mermaid, and the urn is dated fifteen years ago." She straightened up and tapped her chin. "The fairy box has a spirit, but the mermaid is ashes. It means trapping spirits is a newer process. Given that I really don't think our old Necromancer would be up for it, I'd hazard a guess that the person doing this is a newer staff member. As in, hired in the last five or ten years." She walked toward the door and gestured for me to follow. "Come on. Let's check out Valens's room really quickly."

"We should find out if anyone else has heard of the ability," I said, trying to move as silently as Bria. Unfortunately, it made me slower. "If it's a rare ability, surely there's a record of it somewhere. I mean, I would've thought you'd know about it, given your profession."

"I know, right? Color me surprised."

"If this spirit trapper is handling some of Valens's key...possessions, he or she is probably a high-dollar employee."

"At least medium to high, sure. Valens typically underpays people if at all possible."

"Right. How many high-dollar employees do you think Valens has brought on in the last five or ten years? Can't be *too* many, can it? Payroll would have that info. We can check it out."

"Kieran will handle all that." She waited at the doorway. "Honestly, what do you have, lead feet? Hurry—"

She cut off and her body stiffened. In another moment, she darted back into the trophy room. Realizing something was wrong, I broke off in the other direction.

A door closed down the hall, wood softly bumping against wood. Fabric swished and footsteps thumped. The butler was active.

I slipped behind a large wooden chest, peeking

around the corner. A tall, thin man with graying hair and loose jowls drifted into the hall, visible from the doorway. He was nearly out of sight when he slowed. A loud sniff invaded the dense silence.

The floor creaked and his confused face edged into the doorway.

I pulled back slowly. Fast movement would attract attention. Thank God he couldn't see my racing heart.

Another sniff. He had a superior sense of smell.

Fabulous.

Rhythmic, soft buzzing rattled my bones. Bria's phone.

I squeezed my hands into fists, hoping to God it was a booty call, or a telemarketer, or anyone else but Mordecai telling us to get out. Nervous anticipation of being found weakened my bladder, a horrible side effect to my trying for secrecy. I would make a terrible spy.

A careful footstep entered the room and my bladder threatened to give out. The buzzing cut off abruptly. I held my breath.

Murky silence filled the room with expectation.

Then a deeper buzzing began to roll through the floor as a soft hum permeated the walls. The feeling crawled up through my body. Was it magic? A trap being set somewhere?

Leather shoes squeaked and shoe soles squealed as the man turned. His footsteps retreated from the room.

I held my position. He might have pretended to leave to draw us out. Daisy did that all the time.

"Come on," Bria whispered, hurrying to the door.

Clearly she didn't have a Daisy in her life.

"What if he comes back?" I rose up just enough to look over the chest.

She braced her hand on one half of the double door and leaned out. She shook her head slightly and stepped farther out.

Movement from the other end of the room caught my attention. The older man who'd given us directions earlier stood at the back wall in the corner, his hands at his sides.

"The owner is home," he said. If only the words were attached to a string, I'd rush over there and give them a yank to get them out faster. "He will change in his quarters before taking a brandy in the parlor. Often he stops in here to marvel. I suggest you get out."

"I would love to get out, but he's downstairs, and we're upstairs," I whispered. "I can't fly."

I repeated his warning to Bria. "This is okay. This is fine." She held her hand out to still me, or calm me, or maybe stop the world from turning, I couldn't be sure. "There are a million rooms in this house. We'll hide in a guest room. Mordecai can bring the cadaver to the window below us. I'll slap a soul in it, turn it loose, and we'll escape while Valens is looking into the commotion."

It was bad when animating a dead body sounded like a great course of action.

"There's one problem…" I bit my lip, my mind racing. "If he gets even remotely close to me, he'll sense my magic. Kieran could."

Bria's head turned slowly until she was staring at me with *oh shit* eyes. The expression cleared in an instant, replaced by determination. "That's fine. That's okay. There's a third floor in this beast. You go up there and hide in a freaking broom closet, if you have to. Go way to the back and wish for Narnia. I'll find a room with a window somewhere on this floor. Any higher, and I won't be able to work with the cadaver. I'll get that dead body tearing up the flower pots and draw Valens out of the house. You get to the backyard. Jump the fence into another backyard—you're tall, that's in your wheel house. Hey, go crazy and jump a few fences. Get out to the street and *run like hell*. Yes? We got this. I've been in worse situations. Not with a Demigod, but hey, I'm open to upping the stakes."

It was a shitty plan, but my mind went blank to any alternatives.

"Crap," I said, standing. The first stages of panic shook my limbs. I licked my lips and forced away the fear. "Okay."

She nodded. "Okay. Have faith."

She darted out of the room, hurrying left, away from the stairs.

I was hurrying to the doorway when I heard, "This way is safer."

The man pointed at the bookcase. I slowed, because even though he was operating at half normal speed, his brain seemed to be functioning fine.

"Which way is that?" I asked.

"I don't have the energy to open it. This room used to be bigger. Somewhere along the way, they cut it up to allow for a larger hidden chamber. I never understood why, myself, because it's awfully dark in the hidden halls, but—"

"What hidden halls?" I made circular motions with my hand. "Get to the point, man!"

"This house is riddled with secret passages. Magical people have been persecuted for centuries. Burned, staked, left for dead—"

"Yes, yes, what about the halls?"

"You can enter the passages here. One leads to the carriage house, but a cabinet blocks the way now. It's a large—"

"Do you mean the garage?"

"I'm...not sure."

"Just..." I flapped my hand, trying to get this conversation to move faster. My heart set a fast drumbeat in my chest. "Does Valens—the owner of the house—use it very often?"

"Oh no, why would he? Magical people are out in the world now. It's a whole new day. I wish I'd lived to see it. Lived to *live* it—"

"Right, right. Yeah, yeah."

"People have come and gone. Come and gone. I don't think I've seen anyone use the halls in…" His face closed down in confusion. The thought of all that passing time had shut down his train of thought.

"Cool. Awesome. How do I get into the halls?"

"Oh. Well…" As he turned toward the bookshelf, deep voices echoed down the main hall.

Valens was coming.

"Hurry, hurry, hurry. Go, go, go!" I pushed in right next to the man, willing his hand to go faster as he moved it through the air, stretching a finger out to point. Finally, it stopped in front of a slight groove. Beside it ran a larger than normal crack between the bookshelves.

"I'll be damned," I said, ready for him to push aside so I could get to work.

His pointer finger was on the move again, though, dropping through the air and drifting left, toward the opposite side of the shelf with the groove. Down near the bottom, on the end next to the tighter crack, a tiny inlet allowed enough room for three fingers.

"Push, and pull," the man said. "You push…" His

finger started back to the other side.

The voices in the main hallway increased in volume, two men talking. They were climbing the stairs. Coming this way. "I got it," I whisper-shouted. "Move. Move!"

With shaking hands, I slid over and stuck my thumb on the groove, reaching into the small hole with my other hand to feel around for something that screamed "open the secret entrance this way!" My middle finger slid across a raised area that moved slightly when pressed. A button!

"I got it," I whispered, adrenaline pumping through my blood.

The loudness of the voices increased, and through the tangle of words I could swear I heard "smell."

"Shit, shit, shit, shit…" I pressed the groove as hard as I could and a little slat in the wood that I hadn't even noticed toggled downward.

"That is not proper language for a young lady…" the old man said in disapproval.

"When my life is in danger, the very last thing I am is a fucking lady." I jabbed the button as hard as I could. My nail bent back painfully. The voices increased in the hallway.

"Bugger fuckballs, *come on!*" I contemplated abandoning my efforts and diving behind one of the many horrible attractions in the room. The voices were right on me, now, nearly at the top of the steps. A deep baritone rolled down the hall.

The man moved in to help. "If you'll just—"

The button clicked. The hidden door popped. The crack grew wider.

Heart in my throat, I yanked it open, grimacing at the mournful wail of old, unused hinges. When the opening was big enough, I slipped in, scraping myself against a jagged piece of metal.

The voices paused, possibly because they'd heard the noise. If I'd had more time, I would've waited to close the hidden door, but they were right down the hall.

Gritting my teeth, I pulled the door toward me, my hand brushing against cold metal. A handle. I gripped it and pulled harder, the squeal raking across my bones. Wood groaned. Something clicked. Darkness enveloped me.

Chapter 21

KIERAN

KIERAN STOOD AT the windows in the west sitting room, staring out at the sparkling ocean. The view took his breath away, easily the very best thing about his father's house. It made the odd choice of décor almost bearable. It also had a way of melting his stress and loosening his shoulders, allowing him a few quiet moments of harmony.

His phone vibrated once in his pocket, a text or email.

Jogged from the quiet moment, he pulled the device out of his pocket and glanced at the screen. Jack's name came up—*That hellion dosed me. I just woke up face-first in the weeds. The girls are on the loose and the shifter kid is with them.*

He felt his eyebrows lower. Why would Bria want Jack out of the way? What was she planning?

Fear seized his heart.

Had his father gotten to Bria? Did he know what Alexis really was?

He turned from the window, but before he could take two steps, his phone vibrated again.

Bria: *I hear you're in your father's house. What a strange coincidence. So am I.*

All Kieran could do was stare for a moment. Another text came in.

Bria: *I was just about to animate a cadaver. Should I still do that, or are you going to lend a hand, or...*

He started toward the stairs immediately, fear and violence pulsing through him in waves. His father had just gone up with Sodge to check out some strange smell in the trophy room. Sodge was a retired Elite, something like Kieran's Six, and had been blessed with a sliver of his father's power. The older butler couldn't feel magic or power level, but he had heightened smell, one of the few things age hadn't stolen.

Alexis had wanted to check out the trophy room. That and a few other rooms were on that list his mother had given her.

Jack never would've let them into this house without Kieran.

He clenched his jaw. Bria and Alexis had gone too far this time. They were endangering their lives, his mom's future, and his intricate plans. If his father caught them...

Where are you? Kieran typed out to Alexis, rounding

the bottom of the stairs.

A return text immediately appeared on the screen. *This is Mordecai. I have her phone. Lexi is with Bria.*

Where are you? he typed again, to Bria this time.

Second floor. Some sort of orgy room or something. There are pillows and sex toys everywhere.

Kieran stilled, halfway up the stairs. His father only used that room when entertaining his revolving harem. They'd be safe in there until Kieran could distract his father and send them out.

He flicked through possibilities as another text came in.

I sent Alexis to the third floor.

Kieran's fingers tightened on his phone. Why the fuck would the paid protection send her mark to another location?

He started forward again. There were two creaky steps on the stairwell to the third floor. He'd cultivated those warnings himself. If they'd been disturbed, he would've heard it from his current location.

She was still trapped on the second floor.

Hold, he typed as he walked, sweat coating his forehead. *Let me assess the situation.*

He slipped the phone into his pocket and picked up the pace.

His father and Sodge stood at the dragon scale desk, glancing around at the various disgusting displays of misspent power. Kieran loathed the trophy room, which made him want to tear his father's head from his shoulders and add it to the other hideous things hanging on the walls. To keep from telegraphing an unusual interest in the room, he stalled in the doorway like he always did.

His father glanced up with a perplexed expression.

Kieran looked around, as though reading his father's confusion and trying to discern the problem. He dropped his gaze when he didn't see anything. It was unwise to appear too interested in his father's activities.

"I was thinking about going for a swim," Kieran said, taking a risk. Before the budget meeting earlier, his father had mentioned he wanted to speak with him. Valens had left work early to head home for their discussion, so Kieran figured he had pressing items to discuss. Hopefully that would keep his focus now. "Did you need to talk to me about something, or can it wait until after…"

"Kieran, come in here for a moment, if you would." His father gestured him closer, the perplexed expression sticking firm.

In keeping with his normal behavior, Kieran glanced behind him at the hall before taking a few nonchalant steps farther into the room. His phone vibrated in his pocket.

"What's up?" he said, taking out his phone and glancing at the screen.

Jack: *I've got a lock on Bria's car. It's five blocks from your father's house. Are you home yet?*

He fired off a reply. *They're in the house. Bria is covered for now. Alexis unaccounted for. Get the team closer.*

"Do you smell anything...odd?" his father asked, walking out from behind the desk. He paused by an old chest that held heavens knew what. He glanced at the floor and then turned toward the back of the room. "It's faint. I only get it occasionally."

Kieran shook his head before taking a few steps in his father's direction. His stomach curdled as the tantalizing aroma of Alexis's magic seeped into his body and energized his tired mind. He loved that smell—entrancing, strangely intimate, and desperately addicting.

He took a step toward the back of the room, catching another whiff. Pretending he didn't know what it was, he glanced at the ground and looked at the surfaces around him. "Did the maids put in an air freshener?"

"Oh..." Sodge put out a finger as though he were remembering something from long ago. "Priscilla was complaining about the stale smell of a few rooms the other day." He looked at the baseboards. "I had forgotten, sir. Excuse me. That must be it."

Valens's expression withered, but he didn't react. He had a soft spot where Sodge was concerned, one of his few.

With a last glance around, Valens turned toward the double doors. "It's nice, at any rate."

"It is. Faint, though," Kieran said, going back to his phone. He tapped into his email as he followed his father out, doing everything he could think of to feign disinterest.

He hadn't lied—the smell was faint. Alexis had been in that room, but she wasn't anymore.

He had to find her before his father did.

Chapter 22

ALEXIS

"FOLLOW ME," I heard as I waved my hands in the air in front of me. Inky darkness filled my vision and stale air clogged my throat.

"How the hell can I follow you when I can't see anything," I whispered. The words drifted out into the nothingness before dropping away. They didn't echo. "There aren't stairs in here, are there? Or a big pit with spikes at the bottom?"

"Turn on the ultra violets and then you'll be able to see just fine," the man said. He was talking about the plane where the Line beckoned. "That was my greatest discovery. The pull of the afterlife was compelling at first, I will say, but eventually you learn to ignore it. You'll move faster if you stop dragging your feet."

"I don't want to move faster," I said, stopping. "You never answered my question about the pit."

I slipped into a light trance, and the Line materialized almost immediately. A light breeze fluttered my soul and the colors morphed into strange fluorescent hues, like an overexposed photograph.

"You're not quite there," the man said. "You have to go a little closer…"

But I'd never gone closer to the Line, I'd always pulled the Line closer to me. The distinction was a small one, but it was telling, too. Kieran's words drifted into my memory—I used the power, it didn't use me. Apparently, I always had.

The walls around me flared into view, a foot beyond my fingertips on one side, and two on the other. The low ceiling pushed down on me, and smooth cement stretched out in front.

"Wow." I dropped my outstretched hands. "That light is incredibly handy, and this is an impressively large hidden passageway."

"The owners of this house have always been afflu-ent," the man said, leading the way. "I, myself, increased the size of the passageways in one of the areas. Where I could, you know. You have to tear out walls, and re-size some of the—"

I let the drone of his voice ebb and flow around me as we reached a T junction. He turned left without skipping a beat, but I paused in the middle, trying to get my bearings.

"We're going up to the third floor, right? Some-how?"

"The third floor…" He glanced back in confusion.

"Keep it together, man. Now is not the time to forget your whereabouts. This is your house, remember? You live here. You know it like the back of your—"

I cut off when a woman with long blonde hair and a glowing blue dress drifted toward us. Her feet stayed perfectly still, sliding against the smooth ground.

"Marlene," the man spat, his confusion dissolving instantly. Irritation took its place. "She always turns up when I use these hallways. One moment of weakness and she haunts me forever."

"I heard that," Marlene said as she drew near. Her liquid brown eyes settled on me. "One moment of weakness..." She laughed, a shrill sound. "Is that what you're calling it? Weakness?"

"You have to understand," the man said to me. I grimaced and edged around him. I didn't want to get involved in a really old domestic dispute. "My wife was away visiting her sister. A man has needs."

"So does a woman, but we don't drop our pants whenever a hot guy comes along." I picked up the pace. "Self-restraint, look it up."

Maybe I did want to get involved in a domestic dispute, just a little. Honestly, I was not a fan of cheaters.

"You said you were going to run away with me," the woman said, following us now. "You said we could start a family. Remember all those nights, lying in those sweaty sheets..."

"Good God," I muttered, wishing her voice would ebb and flow as well.

"You ruined my marriage," the man said, stopping with me at the next junction.

"You ruined my life," the woman retorted, unfortunately stopping with us. "You left me without a home. Without a job—"

"Please don't say pregnant. Please don't say pregnant," I muttered, looking at the dead-end up the way. "There are stairs somewhere, right?"

"The ladder is just up this way." The man continued on, moving slightly faster than before, which was not to say he was fast. Maybe the lady was actually good for the situation. If only she'd stop talking...

"If it wasn't for Lord Stockbridge, I would've died on the streets," she continued, plaguing our steps. "He was kind and gentle..."

"Ugh." I turned left when the man did, doing my best to ignore Marlene's attempt at making the man jealous. Up ahead, a metal ladder clung to a sheer wall.

"Well, that's clearly too high to go to the third floor," I muttered, looking up as I got closer. "A fall from that would break a bone or two. Maybe crack a head. Where does this lead—"

"For the last time, you preyed on me," the man said to Marlene. "I was having my brandy when you sauntered in with that clear negligée. What was I supposed to do?"

"Fire her, is my guess." I ran a hand in front of his face. "Hey. Where does this—"

With a scoff, his body winked out. I stared at empty space for a beat.

"He always does that, the coward," Marlene said, before tossing her hair, styled in an old-fashioned cut, and turning back the way she'd come.

I faced the ladder again. "I guess beggars can't be choosers when it gets you out of a jam."

Taking a deep breath, I grabbed a rung. Metal was tough. Much tougher than wood. It could stand the test of time. Right?

I shifted my weight and pushed off my foot, bracing myself in case the rung broke. Then I climbed up to the next rung, doing the same thing. The metal didn't bow. It didn't give in.

Halfway up, at a height where I'd hurt myself if I fell, I climbed faster, wanting to get this over with. Lord help me if I'd eventually have to go back down.

Nearly there, and a sickening *crack* made me freeze.

My breath was loud in the thick silence.

Another rung and metal whined. The ladder shook against the wall.

It wasn't a rung making that sound. It was a brace, the thing attaching the ladder to the freaking wall.

"If I make it out of here, I am going to kill you,

Bria," I said through clenched teeth as I quickly debated going up or down. Up meant a larger fall. Down meant I'd be stuck on the same floor as Valens. Being that I couldn't permanently hide in the darkness, I'd have to randomly pick a room and hope he wasn't in it. With his ability to sense magic, how long would it take for him to find me?

"Mother trucker biscuit fucker," I ground out, grabbing the next rung and hefting myself up. Metal whined again, but I kept going, moving as fast as I could. The brace clattered against the wall. I moved my foot onto the next rung, reaching up, the lip of the floor only five feet away. Another rung and I might be able to reach it.

The right side of the ladder broke away from the wall, sending me careening. I barely held on as my body whipped around. A foot slipped and then I was dangling, pulling harder on the old braces.

"Go, go, go," I urged myself, scrambling back onto the ladder and climbing like my butt was burning.

Metal screamed now, the left-hand brace ready to go. Pieces of the wall kept dropping away like powder, releasing the screws holding the ladder firm.

Chest tight and breath coming fast, I grabbed the next rung, then the next, keeping my focus on holding on. If I balked now, I might find myself plummeting to the floor with the broken ladder.

Another screw pulled free. My foot hit the next

rung. I hefted myself up, reaching over the lip, and found a metal handle in my way. I grabbed it and pulled, lifting my body. Another screw gave away and the left-hand brace quickly followed. The ladder pulled back from the wall.

I held onto that handle for all I was worth. If it gave way, I was done for.

Laboriously, I heaved myself up over the edge, finding another handle on the other side, and dragged my body against the loose ladder. Once up, the ladder tipped backward, the very top hitting the opposite wall with a loud clang. It vibrated, but since the bottom braces were still intact, it didn't fall.

I wouldn't be using the tunnels to get back down.

Arms and legs tired, I dusted myself off and looked around, taking in my three options: right, left, or straight ahead. It all looked the same.

Shrugging, I went straight ahead. At the end, I found a horizontal bar affixed to what I hoped was another secret door. The only direction the bar would go was down. I had to use both hands and all my weight, but finally earned a loud *clung* for my efforts. The door popped out toward me, a rectangle misplaced from the wall, but it didn't go very far.

"What the hell…" I whispered, pulling on it, feeling a little give. I yanked, then braced my foot against the wall of the tunnel and gave it all I had. Nothing.

"Bugger," I said through a panting breath, moving to the side and glancing through the crack. Only a small sliver let me view the low-lit space beyond. I could barely make out a couple of sleeves.

I smiled. It was a closet. Maybe not a broom closet, but close enough that I'd followed Bria's instructions…though I'd never forgive her for landing me in this mess in the first place.

We wouldn't get caught, my left toe.

Frowning, I looked at the door and pulled it toward me again. When that didn't help, I leaned against it, thinking.

Old wheels cried out. It was on a track.

"Ah ha. I've got your secret, you dirty bastard." I shoved the door harder. Metal protested as it scraped. Wheels howled.

Without warning, something gave loose, though the horrible racket continued unabated. The door ripped to the side.

A large hand grabbed me by the blouse and roughly yanked me through the doorway.

Chapter 23

ALEXIS

I LASHED OUT, first with my fists and then with the strange power I was still learning. I punched a hard cheekbone and burrowed my power into a solid chest, ramming against the metal plate in the middle. Colors burst to life, vibrant and refreshing, as the Line sprang back into view. Power rushed through me. All I had to do was focus my strength, and I would have my attacker's soul in my unyielding grasp.

Without warning, I was blasted with power so strong it hauled me under the surface and held me down, drowning me with its potency. Pain burned across my skin before boiling in my middle. Agony blistered behind my eyes and within my mind, blotting out thought.

"Yield." The voice was barrel-deep and raspy, and extreme relief surged through me.

I dropped my hands and closed off the Line, sagging within Kieran's hold.

"Thank God," I said, my words thick and tears embarrassingly filling my eyes.

His grip on me relaxed, though it probably shouldn't have. He clearly didn't know me very well.

Anger rose up to burn through the despondency. I never stayed down for very long. I couldn't, not with the life I led.

I jerked up my hands, throwing him off me. Then I slapped him right across the face. That would get his attention. "What the fuck were you doing, yanking me through the door like that? You could've hurt me."

He knew one moment of obvious confusion before he burst into action.

He grabbed my upper arms and muscled me out of the closet and into a large bedroom, clearly just as angry as I was. Light fell across his gorgeous face, drawing my attention to the rage and fear sparkling in his deep blue eyes.

"What were you thinking, coming here without me?" he demanded, pushing me against the wall. "Thank heavens I came up here to follow normal protocol and change, or I would've been looking for you in the wrong part of the house."

His hard, dangerous stare set my legs to trembling and cold crawled up my spine. The limitless power of the ocean raged within those eyes, like a storm charging the air before lightning zapped down. He could unleash terror, and flay me alive.

I lifted my chin in defiance, refusing to cower.

"You're watched," I said through gritted teeth, fighting the desire to run. Fighting the intense need to submit. "They'd know you brought me here. They'd have my face, and soon they'd connect the dots. Me in that ghost neighborhood, me in that warehouse, me…the next place I'll have to go to find a spirit trap."

My bluffing was starting to come apart, but I'd be damned if I ratted Bria out. I'd agreed to come, after all. I was now part of the crime.

"You drugged Jack." Fire danced in his eyes.

"He would've gotten in the way. Or he would've snitched, and you would've done something stupid."

Kieran leaned toward me, his face inches from mine, his anger a palpable thing. "*You* did something stupid. You're in incredible danger here, Alexis. *Incredible* danger. If my father—"

"I know," I said. "Your father was supposed to be in a meeting. Things don't always go as planned. But we had to take that chance, Kieran."

"No, you didn't. I could've—"

"Done what? Looked around aimlessly? You've had your chance. For six months, you've had your chance. You hired me for a reason."

His fingers squeezed my upper arms, edging up to the line of painful.

I shifted, edging up to the line of kicking him in the

balls.

His eyes bore into me, full of lightning and intensity. Fear flipped my stomach, my primal response to his power and strength.

Fire kindled in my core, my equally primal response to his proximity. Heat rolled off of his body and caressed my skin. He was raw and vicious and powerful, and something in me craved the force of him.

My breath sped up as his eyes roamed my face, settling on my lips. My lips tingled in response, feeling the memory of his kiss.

"Don't ever do something like this again without checking with me first," he ground out, his body inches from mine. His grip tightened on my arms. His fervor sent a wave of heat through me as powerful as the tide.

"Or what?" I asked in a breathy whisper.

His lips crashed down onto mine, needy and persistent. His taste, salty sweet, washed through me.

I meant to resist. I meant to push him away. I didn't want to give him what he wanted. But I couldn't help myself. I couldn't stop my hands from sliding up his hard chest and hooking around the back of his neck.

I fell into that kiss. That sinfully decadent kiss.

His hands dipped under the hem of my blouse and ran up my fevered skin. His large palms drifted over my breasts and his thumbs dipped into my bra and circled my sensitive nipples. I moaned into his mouth, not wanting anything else in the world more than I wanted him right then.

Decision made, reason fleeing, I pushed my hands between us and ripped open the front of his slacks. I shoved the fabric down as his hands worked around to my back, aiming for my bra clasp. His enormous length sprang up, ready and eager.

Unable to help myself, I made room with my hands and sank down to my knees. I took his hard shaft by the base and circled the head with my tongue. His hand curled in my hair and a deep moan urged me on.

I pushed my lips over the tip and sucked in as far as I could, taking in more than normal just to cover some ground. My gag reflex wasn't pretty, but when his moan turned into a heady groan, it was clear it didn't matter. I stroked with my palm and backed off with my mouth, sucking so hard I knew the sensation would be just on the edge of pain. I hadn't forgotten getting yanked through that door.

"Oh Lexi," he said, using my nickname for the first time.

Something warm unfurled in my middle, soft and deep. I sucked in again, pushing even farther, my eyes watering now. He gave my hair a tiny yank, a little aggression to go with his pleasure.

In the mood I was in, I fucking loved it.

I increased my pace, needing him. Needing the taste

of him, the feel of him, steel covered in velvet. I cupped his balls as I pulled off his cock, my suction making a *pop*.

"Yes," he breathed, hardly more than a sigh.

I stood in a rush, grabbed two fistfuls of his dress shirt, and ripped. Buttons flew and fabric parted, revealing a torso made in heaven. Perfectly defined pecs led down into the six going on eight pack that had haunted my dreams since the last time I'd seen it.

He shoved me against the wall, his hips pulled away just enough to get at my buttons. He shoved the fabric down, panties included, before skimming a surprisingly delicate touch up the inside of my thigh.

Goosebumps washed across my skin and anticipation choked the breath in my throat. His kiss was hard. Demanding. His feather-soft touch ever so lightly traced up my center and flicked my clit.

My world slipped sideways and any thoughts other than his touch fled from my head.

His other hand cupped the back of my neck—possessive, controlling, and strangely erotic—while his finger circled my clit, still so lightly. No relief. He was playing me like a master played an instrument, and I could do nothing but hang on to his thick shoulders for dear life.

My eyes fluttered as his finger traced down my wetness, still finding no purchase. With his chest he pushed me harder into the wall, leaning his size and strength against me. Making me feel fragile and delicate, but utterly protected by this robust and intensively powerful man.

"Just fuck me already," I groaned against his mouth. So keyed up. Past the point of sanity.

I earned a dark chuckle.

He pulled my legs up to his hips before gyrating against me, his cock rubbing up my wetness and over my clit before retreating, sending delicious shivers through my body. His tip just barely kissed my opening, and stalled...before he thrust.

Colors sparked behind my eyes. Pleasure coursed through me. My body stretched to the point of pain.

"Oh Kieran," I sighed, letting my head fall back to thunk against the wall. Everything stopped for a moment as my focus reduced down to the gloriously consuming sensations. He filled me up and then some, sending me higher. "Oh God."

He pulled back before unceremoniously thrusting again, ramming into me. And again, no mercy. I held on with everything I had, unable to think. Unconcerned about decorum. I swiveled my hips, heightening the sensations.

"Yes, baby," Kieran said, his accent seeping through.

The soft breeze of the Line drifted down, fanning my power. Both types of his magic swirled around and within mine. As magic boiled and pleasure throbbed, expanding with each hard thrust, I felt myself losing control.

"Oh God," I cried. "Too much."

"Can't…" he grunted, ramming ecstasy into me. "Can't…stop. No…control."

My body wound up, tighter and tighter. His muscles flared. Our magic mingled. I could barely breathe through the intensity. I needed it to end while wanting it to go on forever.

"I…need…to…" He thrust into me with every word. I pushed against him, animalistic. "…have…all…of…you."

Movements got smaller and ten times more intense. The tide of pleasure rose as he pounded into me.

"You're…*mine!*"

An orgasm blindsided me. I cried out, lost to the feeling of him. Wave after incredible wave of pleasure tore my body apart and blasted it into a million pieces. I shook as he groaned, the two of us finishing together.

"Holy fuck," I said through clenched teeth, riding the climax. The waves kept coming, frazzling my wits.

"Oh God," I said again, finally coming down. An aftershock made me shiver. "Holy fucking God."

He wobbled, taking an arm from around me to brace himself against the wall. His chest rose and fell quickly, out of breath.

"I told you," he said before kissing me languidly.

"What?" I asked against his lips, floating in the sublime afterglow.

"Hate sex can be fun."

I nibbled his bottom lip. "Except I don't hate you."

"Angry sex, then."

"Hmm." I let my legs slide down from his hips. My feet hit the floor, but my knees instantly buckled.

"Uh-oh. Here." He reached for me before wobbling again, hitting his shoulder against the wall. "You've done a number on me." He braced an arm around my back and swung my legs up, cradling me against his chest. "My father will be going swimming with me. You'll need to get out while he's out of the house. You can't stay." Regret crossed his features, but the expression was gone so fast I second-guessed whether I'd seen it at all. "Do you understand?"

"You mean I *can't* hang around the house of a guy who might turn me into a mindless zombie hell-bent on ripping souls out of people's bodies? What bullshit." I laughed and leaned my head against his shoulder, utterly and blissfully content.

I'd wait until I made it out of the house in one piece to reflect on what an absolutely terrible idea this had been. On his repeated declaration that I was his, and how delicious it felt to hear him say it. I'd certainly wait to think about how completely fucked up our working relationship was bound to be now that I'd given in to him.

And how much I already wanted to do it again.

Chapter 24

ALEXIS

"WHAT IN THE actual fuck—" Bria cut herself off, cocking her head at me. She dragged her gaze down my body as she edged a little more out of the second-floor room she'd been hiding in. "What…"

I smoothed the high-fashion shirt that currently draped my body in elegant sheets of expensive silk and…other stuff I couldn't put a name to because I'd never owned any nice clothing before.

"He had a drawer of clothes for me," I said as heat crept into my face.

"He had a drawer of clothes for you," she repeated in a flat tone. "And why, pray tell, did he have a drawer full of clothes for you?"

I glanced down the empty hallway. Kieran had granted us a short window in which to get out unnoticed. He'd gone swimming with his dad—I assumed their pool was the ocean—and ordered their butler to arrange drinks and snacks for them upon their return. Before leaving, he'd described the best way out of the house, and grilled me about the hidden tunnels.

I had a feeling that someday I'd be back here, and I'd need to chat with Mr. Cheater and his miserable mistress about all the entrances to the hidden hallways.

"He stole some of my clothes a few weeks ago, and from that, and his clearly detailed eye, he figured out my measurements and arranged for clothes to be purchased for me." I flicked my hair, pretending like that was totally normal. "He has always assumed he'd get me in his bed, and clearly he was ready to lord his conquest over me. It's no big deal."

"But you didn't end up in his bed?"

"No!" It wasn't lying, simply omitting that I'd ended up against his wall.

Heat washed through me. That situation had been so incredibly hot that now I was pretty sure beds were overrated. I might never want to bang in a bed again. Not when a wall was present, teamed with a man strong enough to hold my weight and then some.

Bria shook her head. "Dare I ask how you ended up in his room in the first place?"

I followed her down the hall, flustered. "That ghost from earlier got me into a secret hallway, and I ended up in Kieran's room. His room takes up half the top floor of the house."

"Uh-huh. So he found you in his cavernous room and then happily showed you your drawer?"

"Not happily. He tried to push his weight around, and I gave him a piece of my mind."

"Uh-huh." I could tell by her tone that she knew exactly what had happened.

I clenched my fists. "And then I had sex with him. Okay? Happy? I slapped him across the face, then gave in and banged him."

"Well. You sure showed him." She raised her hand and grabbed something imaginary. "Toot, toot."

"What are you doing?"

"All aboard for the train of bad decisions." She tugged what I now realized was a chain again. "Toot, toot."

"It was just this once," I said, trying really hard to believe it. Maybe if I said it enough, it would be true. "Now I know what it was like, the question was answered, and I'm done. It's out of my system. Besides..." I wiped my hand across my suddenly flushed face. "Guys like him just want the conquest. He got it, and now he'll get bored. It's finished."

"Guys expecting to get bored don't give a woman her own drawer." She glanced back at the large canvas sack I'd stolen from his closet and stuffed nearly full. I dragged it along the hall behind me. "And they surely wouldn't expect the object of their affection to then steal everything out of said drawer and take off."

"That's his fault. Clearly he doesn't know me very

well."

"Clearly." She stopped at a double door, one of the doors slightly cracked.

"Wait…" I blinked and looked around. In my Kieran-induced haze, I'd shut off my survival instinct, thinking wrongly that Bria would lead me out of the house. Kieran had texted her the instructions, after all.

Stupid me.

"Where are we?" I asked in hush.

"Valens's room. Probably. Come on, let's have a quick look."

"Wait, what? No!" I looked down the empty hall, half expecting Valens to come strolling along at any moment. "We need to get out of here."

"We will. Right after we have a look."

"Bria, no. Wait." I grabbed her arm and pulled her back, rougher than I'd intended. "We just had a narrow miss. We can't chance another run-in."

Bria faced me, her bearing confident and mood calm. I had no idea how she did it. Or how she was still alive.

"We've been through all this…to give up in the final hour?" she asked, her tone disappointed. "We're *right here,* Alexis. We're right outside his door, and we've got time. Time that we're wasting right now. That trophy room gave us a couple great clues. Maybe this room will give us another. Or hell, maybe he's got the skin in there. I wouldn't doubt it, as fucking nutty as he clearly is. You think a drawer is a bit much? This guy built a fountain. A fucking fountain, Alexis. It would stand to reason that his room would have *something* of interest. And if it doesn't, I bet his office would…"

I held up a finger while pressing my lips together, matching her disapproval. "I might be convinced to duck into this room for a moment, but I am *not* going into his office. I am drawing a hard line on that one."

A smile spread across her face and she winked. "I figured that would work. Come on."

She pushed open the door and dashed into the room.

She'd just played me. I needed to stop being so damn gullible.

Light greeted me as I stepped into the large room, a tiny bit smaller than Kieran's, but twice as plush. Half of the view was a sparkling blue expanse, and the other half appeared to be the corner of the neighbor's beautifully cultivated yard and the glittering orange of the Golden Gate Bridge in the distance. In keeping with the rest of the house, a cream rug spread across the hardwood floor and a gaudy mirror and some crappy abstract paintings decorated the walls. An enormous bed jutted out in the middle of the room, and a little sitting area comprised of a cream couch and a white-topped coffee table had been arranged beside the windows. An uncomfortable looking chair pushed back against the wall next to the dresser.

"Clearly someone was just trying to fill the room," Bria said, already scanning the bookcase in the far corner. "What stupid little knick knacks in front of a useless shelf of books. I mean, if he's some great reader and didn't want to walk down the hall to get—"

I let her words drift away as I closed my eyes, slipping smoothly into that light trance. The more I did it, the more natural it felt.

No magic buzzed through my body. No vibration beckoned to me. The room was clear.

"Nothing," I said, opening my eyes as disappointment dragged at me. It would've been so much easier if he'd been keeping the skin in his closet. Or under the bed. But he wouldn't have stowed it somewhere and left it unprotected.

"Are you sure?" Bria asked, moving toward the closet as though she'd heard my thoughts.

I nodded, looking over a weird statue on the dresser, and then a picture of a little boy, four or five, with a tiny fish on the end of his fishing pole. Wild weather whipped the boy's hair and boiled in the sky. White points capped the waves in the body of water behind the boy—a lake or a bay. The bow of a simple wooden boat could be seen in the corner of the frame.

"Kieran," I said, leaning closer. I could see the resemblance of this little face to the man he was today, his triumphant smile making those stormy blue eyes glitter with pride. His cheeks and the tip of his nose were red, the biting cold leaving its effect. "Kieran in Ireland. Must be. We don't get weather that extreme here, not even in the magical zone when Valens is in a bad mood."

Bria stopped behind me. "You must be right. Wow. I wouldn't expect Valens to be a proud papa."

"Me neither. But then, I wouldn't have expected him to have a big fountain of his dead wife, whom he basically tortured. Just goes to show…"

"That he's a nutter, I know." Bria nodded as I moved away. "Jump off that train, lady. This isn't a family you want to join."

I did a quick scan of the other surfaces. I didn't really know what I was looking for… until I found it.

On his nightstand, the last thing he saw before he rolled over and closed his eyes, was a photo of the subject of the fountain.

"Where is this?" I pointed at the photo of Kieran's mother on a beach, her raven hair ripped to the right by a gust of wind, her smile wide and gorgeous on her beautiful face. Her cream dress billowed, alive and electric. She looked young and free and without any worries. White foam crawled up the wet sand behind her, a wave coming in and reaching for her bare feet.

Far in the background, a violent wave had just crashed against a jagged cliff, throwing spray into the air. The effect framed the photo, setting her off perfectly.

The photo was stunning. She was mesmerizing.

"Where is this?" I repeated, tapping the glass with my finger.

Bria leaned in and an *oh shit* expression crossed her face. "It's the edge of Ocean Beach. Just down the way." She grinned triumphantly. "You were right all along. Look at you, reading people. Come on! Let's unleash the Kraken."

Chapter 25

ALEXIS

MORDECAI JUMPED OUT at us as we ran across the front yard of a neighbor's house down the street from Valens's. Kieran told us to hop fences until we reached the blue house, and then go out through the side of their yard—they were rarely home.

"I was worried sick," Mordecai said, his eyebrows lowering in confusion as his eyes shot from my attire to the sack I lugged behind me. "Did you steal something?"

"Is it stealing if it was bought for you by a misguided Demigod who wants his way?" I returned.

"No, it is not. It is reclaiming what is yours. You are totally in the right." Bria stopped up short when she noticed the Mercedes was gone. "Well shit. We have to hoof it."

Without skipping a beat, she pointed down the hill and picked up the pace.

"No, no. Wait—" Mordecai cut off as a black BMW rolled toward us from the opposite direction, stopping by the curb. The tinted window lowered, revealing an angry-faced Jack.

"Good thing he holds grudges," Bria said, changing direction. "He's the one we need."

We climbed into the car, Bria sitting in the front passenger seat to take the brunt of Jack's anger. I'd already been yelled at by Kieran—it was her turn to take some heat. Besides, she was the one who'd actually dosed him.

Jack slammed the car into gear before easing pressure onto the gas pedal. If it had been a different situation, I was sure he would've stomped on it and peeled out. But we had to maintain a low profile.

"What happened to the Mercedes?" Bria said, pulling out her phone.

"Zorn dropped it in another part of town," Jack said, fury simmering just below the surface. Either he was terrible at hiding his anger, or he didn't want to. "Kieran didn't want it drawing attention up here."

"Cool," she said, not affected by the intensity of the large man next to her. "We need to head to the top of Ocean Beach by the cliffs." She showed him a picture. "This end. Just down the hill."

He didn't glance over. "Like hell we do. I'm taking those two home, and you—"

"We might know where the skin is," Bria said, before explaining what we'd found.

By the end, Jack had let off the gas.

"You're sure about all this?" he asked, his dark eyes boring into me through the rearview mirror.

I shrugged. "I can't be sure of anything until we check it out, but it makes sense. It fits."

He nodded slowly, pulling over to the curb. His fingers tapped against the steering wheel and he gazed out the window. "Did you tell Demigod Kieran?"

"It clicked two seconds ago," Bria said. "He's out with his dad. I figure it's worth checking out. We can text him if we find something. Unless you think they swim around that area?"

He pulled away from the curb again, back to full speed. "When they're together, they swim way out. They test each other. A gentleman's competition."

"What's a gentleman's competition?" I grabbed the corner of his seat and leaned forward so I could hear better.

"It means they silently try to outdo each other while pretending it's a normal day," Bria said, stowing her phone. "Ego at work, if you will."

"What happened in there?" Mordecai asked as we left the neighborhood and turned onto a road that would wind down the hill, hugging the cliffs.

I quickly went through everything, trying to skip the part in Kieran's bedroom. I should've known Bria wasn't finished with me yet.

"Did you use a condom?" she asked suddenly.

"*Shhh*," I said, my face flaming again.

"Why? You don't want Jack to know?" Bria glanced back. "Trust me, it's obvious. You've got that glow of a good lay. You can't hide that shit."

"Would you stop?" I lightly jerked my head at a wide-eyed Mordecai.

Bria laughed and turned back around. "That kid is edging into the Wild West of hormones. If he's not already thinking about sex daily, he will be soon. The best thing you can do is keep everything out in the open so there are no secrets, and so he'll know to use protection. You used protection, right?"

"Talking about sex is not the problem," I muttered. "It's him knowing I gave in when I really shouldn't have."

"What did you do?" Mordecai asked me.

"Well, the cat is out of the bag now." Bria glanced back again, and I swear I wanted to throw myself from the moving car out of pure mortification. Or maybe I wanted to throw her out of the car. I'd never been shy when talking to the kids about these things, but in the past, I hadn't been talking about *my* life.

I sucked it up. I was a role model, no matter how unqualified. I needed to set an example.

"I'm covered. The pill is free when you're below poverty level, and he's a Demigod—he can't give or receive STDs. It was safe. I was safe."

I lifted my chin, feigning confidence and trying to hide my embarrassment.

"He didn't use a condom?" Jack glanced back, shock written clearly on his face.

We descended the hillside, now overlooking the strip of beach pounded by messy, windswept waves. Swirling fog clouded the sky, promising a crappy beach-going experience. An experience Valens must have purposely cultivated, because back when the picture had been taken, he'd kept this area as clear and lovely as the rest of the magical zone. He didn't want people down here.

Butterflies surged through my belly. That information had just increased the likelihood that we were right.

"Did he ask you if you were on the pill?" Bria asked, cutting through my nervous excitement.

"He might know," Jack said. "He's been thorough when it comes to her."

"Yeah, but...she could sabotage the situation," Bria murmured as we pulled into the sandy parking lot. A small smattering of cars and trucks dotted the lot, most of them pushed up right next to the walkway overlooking the beach.

"He clearly trusts her." Jack put the car into park.

"Yes, he does, doesn't he?" Bria shoved open the

door, and before she was fully out, I heard, "Toot, toot."

I sighed and followed them out of the car. What a mess.

"Right, so..." Jack stopped on the walkway, littered with trash and piled with sand where the sidewalk met the graffiti-marred barrier, a semi-circular wall to keep any extreme swells or rises in tide from washing out onto the street above. At a break in the barrier, steps led down to the windswept beach.

Bria looked first one way down the sidewalk, then the other, before eyeing the barrier itself. "I've always thought this area was neglected because it's right next to the dual-society zone. But now I'm starting to wonder..."

"That's what I was thinking," I said as I descended the four steps onto the rocky, trash-strewn sand. "People rarely come out here for pleasure. They go over to the other side of the point where the weather is good."

"Then what are these cars doing here?" Mordecai asked, gesturing around us.

"Some are fisherman, and some..." Bria glanced at a beat-up motorhome. "Are probably doing drugs. Speaking of which, I need to grab my car."

"Thane took care of it," Jack said with a smirk. "He dropped it at your house. You're at our mercy now." Violence glimmered in his dark eyes. A shiver ran the length of my body.

Bria laughed, chugging through the sand beside me. "Sure, sure. Keep thinking you've got the upper hand. Let me know how that works out for you. Better yet, I'll let you know how it'll work out for you...when you least expect it."

Cold moisture touched my cheeks and slid across my skin, the fog so thick it felt like a sprinkle. Swirling sheets of gray obscured my vision. Large, half-burnt pieces of driftwood hunkered in the sand as we passed. The hard-packed wet sand bore evidence of the beach's desolation. There were no footprints.

"It's like some dystopian scene," Bria whispered, looking out toward the cliffs.

The boom of a wave crashing against rocks inter-rupted the wind blowing against the shell of my ear. A rumble followed, the waves rolling down along the sand break.

"I hit this beach every so often," Jack said, squinting through the fog to the cliff on our right, the one in the picture. "Never this far down, though. The base of that cliff face is really rocky, from what I remember. It gets hit with some hard currents and rip tides. If you got caught up in it, it'll slash you up pretty good. Through the shifts in the fog over there"—he pointed—"it looks like a washing machine. All that white means *keep out, rough seas.*"

"Could Valens get in there and leave a trunk or something?" Bria put her hand up to shield her eyes, as though the sun were the problem and not a thick sheet of fog.

"He could, yeah. Easy." Jack worked at the buttons on his shirt. "He could just still the waters and swim on out there. Or push the water aside and walk. He's a descendent of the god of the sea. He has power over—"

"Right, yes. We got it," Bria cut in.

"Pushing the water away," I said, nodding. "That would make it easy. He could get someone across to refresh the spell on the skin. The treacherous area makes it safe, because even if someone wanted to check it out, they wouldn't be able to because of what Jack said." I blew out a breath and ran my fingers through my hair. "Which means we don't have much but a hunch. Kieran will have to…"

Jack shrugged out of his shirt, displaying his robust chest and huge arms. He unhooked the clasp on his pants and pushed them down his muscular thighs. His underwear quickly followed.

"Whoa." I jerked my head away. "Wow. Warn a girl."

"I'll check it out really quickly." Jack jogged toward the ocean, and I couldn't help getting a peek at his well-formed backside.

"What is his magic?" I asked as he waded into the

water without so much as a shiver. He dove into the rush of an oncoming wave and disappeared below the surface.

"Kraken," Bria said, watching the water.

I shifted so I could stare at her. "Are you serious? Those are real?"

She frowned at me. "Of course they're real. Most of the myths and supernatural stories we hear were originally based off of magical beings. Why do you not know this?"

"No. I mean…" I looked out over the rough water. "I knew *that*, I just…" I shrugged. "I've never heard of a Kraken."

"Clearly you have, since you just asked if they were real."

"No, I mean, I've never heard of them as—never mind."

"Is the dual-society zone a black hole, or something?" Bria asked incredulously. "Because *wow*. You are ignorant."

"Right. Fine." I tried to let it go. And failed. "But I've literally never heard of a real one. Not in society, anyway."

"He's a shapeshifter, then?" Mordecai asked.

"He is a shapeshifter, yes…obviously," Bria said, watching the waters. "A shapeshifter of the sea. There aren't many of them hanging with humans. Most of them stick to the sea. I think Kieran met Jack off the coast of Ireland somewhere. Or maybe it was Scotland. I don't know how long ago—I only care so much, know what I mean? Sometimes when people talk, I accidentally stop listening. My mind is a more interesting place to be."

"That's one way of putting it," I mumbled. "He doesn't have an accent, either."

"He gets that from the blood oath. All the Six automatically speak the local language anywhere they go. It helps them protect Kieran or something, I don't know."

"So…are Krakens really as huge as the myths say?"

"They can alter their size to fit various bodies of water they inhabit. Only the most powerful can get that big. Before you ask, they resemble a cross between a squid and a whale. They're really weird looking, I'm not going to lie. But the strongest of them—like Jack—can take down ocean liners. He's a big deal when it comes to the sea. Which is why he's one of the Six. Each of the Six is exceptional in some way."

"Would he ever think of adding more guys to the Six?" I asked, shifting from foot to foot. The waiting was killing me. I wanted to know if I was right. I wanted to know that if worst came to worst, I could still save Kieran's mom.

"Then he'd have to change the name." Bria frowned at me.

The seconds trickled by, turning into minutes, then handfuls of minutes. Mordecai walked up the beach toward the cliff, then back down. Bria and I stared out at the waters.

"That area couldn't kill him, right?" I asked in a hush, my words drifting into the thick fog and disappearing.

"No. He might come back a little battered, but he won't let himself get into a situation where it'll kill him."

"Is this why he's the one who will be walking me through the change?" Mordecai asked, coming to stop next to us again. His voice quavered just a little, full of excitement and fear.

"Obviously." Bria shook her head. "Wow, you two are about as magically dense as can be. How have you made it this far in life?"

"By not getting involved with magical people," I replied.

"And look where that got you. You're involved with the worst of the bunch." Bria rolled back on her heels before checking the watch on her phone. "What's taking him so long?"

"How will he show me, if…" Mordecai's voice drifted away.

"Don't know, kid. That's not my area of expertise. *Finally!*" She pointed out at the water. Through the swirling fog I could just see Jack riding the top of a wave, his body as flat as a board and his arm held out. Body surfing. The wave crashed down, bringing him with it, and he disappeared under the churning foam. A moment later, he rose gracefully from hip-high water and jogged in our direction.

I jerked my head away, having caught sight of dangling bits I had no business noticing.

"What'd you see?" Bria asked, bending to gather his clothes.

He breathed deeply as he neared, catching his breath. "You hit the nail on the head."

Excitement surged through me. I couldn't help smiling and turning to him. "It's there?"

He ran a hand over his short hair, flinging water. "It's definitely there. It's at the base of the cliff. It really is a washing machine in there. It's fucking nuts. The current rips and tears you every which way, the rocks are extremely jagged, and more than a few spots could catch you and keep you. A human or normal magical creature wouldn't have stood a chance. Not a chance. I barely made it in and out."

I belatedly noticed the gashes along his arms and across his broad chest. Blood oozed down his skin, but he didn't seem troubled by it.

"You're sure it's what we're looking for?" Bria jerked her head back to the car and started walking.

"Oh yeah." Jack nodded emphatically, a huge grin on his face. His energy sizzled, potent and infectious. The water had clearly revived him. "I got right up on it. It's a sort of trunk—really classy—with her fucking name on it, man. And engravings of her in both forms. It's her skin. It is her fucking skin. That prick made a shrine out of the box."

"Sick fucker," Bria said.

I pushed away the uncomfortable sinking of my heart. Kieran's mother had been attached to the worst kind of man. He'd kept her in a living hell without her skin, and the bastard hadn't even freed her from his honeyed trap after death. Yet he still clearly loved her. He had to have with the fountain and the picture. His mind must've been bent toward insanity when it came to her. Regardless, there was one thing I knew, it was that I could set her free.

"Tell Kieran," I said, barely able to breathe. "We'll have to do this on his timetable, but tell him. Whatever else happens, at least he can save his mom from a life in Demigod-made purgatory."

"Freeing her is going to start the war," Jack said.

Bria slapped her hands together and started rubbing. "Let's hope so. I'm so ready to take that fucker down."

Chapter 26

ALEXIS

L ATER THAT EVENING I sat at the kitchen table with wet hair, wrapped up in the coziest bathrobe in existence. Clouds in the shape of slippers adorned my feet, and my skin smelled of lilac. Until today, I hadn't even known what lilac smelled like, but it was the fragrance of the silky lotion I'd shoplifted from my shelf in Kieran's medicine cabinet. The guy had been very prepared for me to sleep over, which was a little surprising given it was his dad's house and that was a no-go. He clearly hadn't been using the ol' noggin, which was good justification for snatching all of it and running. They weren't pity purchases, but I was fine with treating them like they were.

Momma got some brand-new treats.

I took a deep breath and glanced at the phone sitting next to me on the dining table. I'd left Kieran a voice message earlier, giving him a summary of the impromptu visit Bria and I had made to Valens's room, and what I'd concluded after seeing the photo. Then

Jack had taken over and given a first-hand account of the trunk he'd found at the cliff-base.

I hadn't heard a word since. The anticipation was absolutely killing me.

"Hey." Daisy yawned and scratched the rat's nest on her head as she crossed to the fridge, just up from her nap.

"Hey." I leaned harder on the table. "How'd it go earlier? Did you have a good time?"

She pulled open the fridge door and stared into it. "It was fine."

"Fine? Well...what'd you do? You left in your pajamas for crap's sake."

She shrugged. "Not much. We hung out in shadowy areas and watched people."

"Like a creeper?"

She pushed the door shut. "Yeah, kinda. It was weird—women glanced our way the most. Only one picked us out, but quite a few looked around."

"Women are used to creepers hanging in the shadows and staring. It's sad but it's true. So...you're cool with it so far?"

She scratched her butt and slouched against the kitchen counter. "Yeah. When are the guys going to get here with dinner? I'm *starving*."

Mordecai trudged in a moment later, his eyes puffy and dark bruises covering his arms from another bout of hard training with Jack after our jaunt to the beach. He'd also taken a nap.

"You'd think it was eight in the morning with the way you two look," I said, a strange uncertainty filling me. I felt like I'd been pushed out of the loop. Like their lives had taken a turn, and they no longer needed me. It made me want to rush them and clutch on for dear life.

As always, I handled it badly. "Did you get any school work done? Because you can't spend all your time fighting and gallivanting around the city like creepers. You need to work your minds as well as your bodies."

Daisy rolled her eyes at me, and that was so much better than *fine* or one of her shrugs that I breathed a sigh of relief. Attitude I could handle. Indifference made me edgy.

"Yes, we did our homework," she said, glancing at the clock on the stove. "But seriously, where's dinner? It's seven o'clock. They're usually here making it by now."

Mordecai opened the fridge and stared into it.

"You're wasting electricity," I barked. I could only last for so long. "And I get paid soon. We're going to have to get used to making our own meals again."

Mordecai turned toward me as Daisy's eyes widened.

She pushed forward off of the counter, suddenly

alert. "Why would you do that to us?" she demanded.

"Who are we to turn down free services?" Mordecai asked. "Usually we're all for people giving us things."

I stared at them incredulously. "I thought you guys would agree with me."

"Agree with you, after all the hell they've been putting us through?" Daisy glowered at me. "No way. They owe us dinner."

"Besides," Mordecai said, "I think they like it. Even when they show up in a bad mood, they're smiling by the end."

I dropped my head into my hands. "Except we're giving them one more toehold in our lives. Kieran is my boss, his guys are training you—we need an off-switch. We need to get back to our family."

"We're still a family. We're just inviting in more family for a limited time, provided they buy groceries and make us nutritious, delicious meals from scratch." Daisy blinked those giant blue eyes at me, utterly serious.

"Besides, you kind of gave Kieran a bigger toehold earlier, so I doubt a dinner or two will matter," Mordecai murmured.

"Why?" Daisy asked, turning to Mordecai. "What'd she do?"

Mordecai looked at the ground.

Suspicion crossed Daisy's face as she turned back

slowly. "Lexi, what did you do?"

My phone rattled against the wood of the table, giving me a more than welcome distraction. A text message flashed across the screen.

Thane: *You don't have a BBQ, right?*

I snatched the phone as Frank's muffled voice drifted through the door. He'd come back, apparently. I paused to listen, but couldn't make out any words.

No, I typed, my fingers flying across the screen. *Have you heard from Kieran? Did he say anything about his mom?*

Dinner is on the way.

"Why would he ignore my question?" I muttered, staring.

"What'd he say—"

A knock cut Mordecai off. I stood and handed over the phone, ready to badger the Six until they told me something. "No one's told me anything since I left that message for Kieran this afternoon." I crossed to the door. "I have no idea what's going—"

The air left my lungs as I pulled the door open. Butterflies swarmed through my ribcage.

Kieran stood on my porch, surrounded by thick, swirling fog. A dark blue T-shirt, matching his eyes, clung to his impossibly muscular body. Damp hair hung limply across his forehead, giving him a wet look that sent heat blasting through my core. The smell of the ocean flooded my senses as I gaped at the large trunk suspended between his strong hands.

"That's…" My eyes glued to the finely-worked wood and the swirling images etched into the top and sides. A seal frolicked through the carved waves, interrupted by the name Lyra. "Is that your mother's name? Lyra?"

"Yes. May I come in?"

"Yeah. Yes, of course." I stepped out of the way as I heard an appreciative whistle.

"We don't get women around these parts who look like you," Frank said in a strange tone.

A form appeared out of the mists, ethereal and beautiful, with a sad smile and a flowing cream dress. She drifted toward me with her hips swaying and confidence radiating from the perfect lines of her body.

Kieran's mom, Lyra, no doubt summoned by her son's turmoil and the trunk he'd rescued from the cliff.

A moment later, the image was ruined by Frank following behind her, his eyes on her butt and an appreciative smile on his face.

"Really, Frank?" I asked, annoyance dashing my mood. "That behavior is inappropriate."

"What?" he said, stepping onto my porch with his hands out. "She's a beautiful woman. I'm just acknowledging it."

"She doesn't want a dirty old man like you acknowledging anything, Frank. Guys like you are the reason women can't ever relax."

"Oh, come on now," Frank said, attempting to follow Lyra into my house. "I don't mean—"

I slammed the door in his face.

Kieran stood in the kitchen, still holding the trunk, nearly as wide as the doorway and over a foot tall. It must've had a good amount of weight to it, though Kieran didn't show any strain.

"Here." I patted the table, pushing aside a random piece of junk mail that hadn't found its way to the garbage. "Set it here."

Sorrow etched his face and anger sparked in his eyes. He set the box down gently, as though it was the most precious commodity in the world.

"That's it?" Daisy said, giving Kieran a wide berth as she made her way to the table. "You did it?"

I glanced at Lyra, whose sad gaze was focused on her son.

"Yes, that's it. That's the skin." I didn't have to affect a trance to feel the hum of the spirit trap. "Or…the spirit of the skin, I guess."

"It's in there?" Kieran said, his deep voice gruff, struggling with emotion.

I fell into the depth of those stormy eyes, feeling the aching misery beyond the shallow anger. His grief was sharp and fresh, slicing through him. I could feel the anguish in his soul, crying out for a life raft in the turbulent waters of loss.

"The spirit trap is keeping something in there," I said, going to him without thinking. I put a supportive hand on his arm. "I think we can assume it is the skin."

"Can you…" His voice hitched and he clenched his fists.

Daisy and Mordecai both drifted out of the room without being asked, knowing instinctively to give him space. Demigods weren't in the habit of showing vulnerability. They might not like Kieran at times, but they both understood human suffering.

"Can you break the hold?" Kieran whispered, his body tense. Tremors ran through him. I couldn't tell if they were from sorrow or rage.

"Yes. But…" I slid my hand down his forearm before slipping it into his. Without hesitation, he entwined his fingers with mine. "Are you sure you want to do this now? Your father will know. He's…a little off his rocker where your mother is concerned. That fountain, the picture, the placement of the box…"

"The fountain…" A crease formed in Kieran's brow before his eyes went distant. Startled, he glanced down at the box. "Are you sure?"

"Yes. It's the likeness of her when she was younger. Before you. It's the form she uses now." I looked at his mother, waiting beside him.

She met my gaze and tilted her head forward. I

couldn't tell if it was a bow or a nod.

"He revered me, at one time," she said. "He treated me like the most precious thing on the planet. I was too young to know that it was an illusion. That the thing he loves above all is himself. I was a treasure, but only as long as I was under his control. I learned the hard way what it was to defy him."

"Yes, you did," I mumbled.

Kieran started before looking down at me, his gaze so open. His depths laid bare. "Is she here?"

"Yes. She followed you in." I told him what she'd said about his father. I figured he'd want to know, in case she'd never told him of the good times. In case he couldn't understand why she'd fallen for a guy like his father, who'd put her through hell.

He blew out a deep breath and nodded. "I want to do this now. She's waited long enough. Even if you can't find the person who did this for my father, at least she'll be free. But…" He squeezed my hand. "Can I have a few moments with her? To say goodbye."

"Yeah, sure. Of course." I slipped my hand out of his grasp. "Totally. Just let me grab the kids and we'll head outside. Let me know when you're ready."

I left him standing there, a powerful, strong man—a prince of the magical world—in my tiny, run-down kitchen, nearly brought to his knees by the passing of his mother. The image crawled into my heart and settled, bringing tears to my eyes. He did share some of his father's traits—he was possessive, demanding, and downright terrifying. But he also had so much of his mother, like compassion, morality, and a beautiful soul.

Unlike his father, he didn't love himself above all others. If I'd ever doubted, I now saw the proof before my eyes. He would sacrifice his wellbeing to bring peace to his mother. He would let go of the hope of his own throne to make sure she found her permanent resting place.

He would go to war with a more powerful foe to bring her justice.

I wiped a tear off of my cheek and went to grab the kids.

Chapter 27

KIERAN

KIERAN SAT DOWN at the table slowly, pain throbbing through his middle. The front door closed with a soft click, Alexis and her wards leaving him alone. The trunk sat in front of him, magically treated to stay in the water forever.

"I miss you. Every day," he said, speaking to his mother like he had those long months after she'd slipped into a coma. "I miss the good times we had together, when you took me horseback riding or fishing. When we read together or made up stories. I remember when you watched me learn my place in the waters of the lake, then the ocean. I didn't know then how much that must've killed you, land-trapped as you were. I didn't know, because you sacrificed your happiness for me. You hid your pain so that I could live free. You hid the itch, your longing for the ocean, so that I could experience it fully. For that…" He took a deep breath, emotion choking him. "For that, I owe you everything. I'd be nothing without your guidance. I'd be an empty, power-hungry shell, like my father. By sacrificing yourself, you saved me."

He wiped away a stray tear and curled his fists, trying to regain control of his emotions.

"I never would've found your skin without her. Without Alexis. She's a hero. More than a hero…" He bowed his head and re-clasped his hands. "She's putting herself at risk for me. To free you. She's putting you, a complete stranger, before her own safety. She's the best sort of a person. One who sacrifices herself, like you always did." He shook his head. "She's dealt with me—with my…manipulation and manhandling, with my mood swings and prodding into her life—she's dealt with it like a warrior. No fear. No apologies. I've never known anyone like her. I'm glad you got to meet her, even if it was like this."

He put his hand on the trunk, the grief so fresh he could barely breathe. It felt like he'd just lost her all over again. But this time, he was sure he'd be saying goodbye forever. That she'd finally, after all this time, find peace.

"I'm at a crossroads, mother. I'd planned on staying distant from everyone while I carried out my vengeance, but I'm…" He took another deep breath. He hadn't admitted this to anyone. "I'm falling for her. I think it comes from a good place, but that's tarnished by the danger I've put her in, isn't it? Dad knows I'm spending a lot of time in the dual-society zone—he talked to me about it earlier. For now, he's content with my explanation about organizing the magical fair here, but soon he'll want more thorough answers. And when he does, he'll discover Alexis. It won't be hard—she illuminates the world like the noon sun. He'll discover her magic, and if I'm not strong enough to stop him, he'll turn her into her worst nightmare. He'll use her, body and soul." He gritted his teeth, rage flaring within him, and ran his fingers through his drying hair. "Not to mention that I'm already possessive like he is. I would lose my mind if another man touched her. I don't know if I could stop myself from killing him. And I can't help but wonder... If she left, like you tried to do, would I do what Dad did? Would my pain morph into the desire to control her? To punish her?"

He pushed off of the table and stood in a rush.

"I don't know what to do. I'd intended to push her away when this was all done, for her own safety, but now..."

He paused, and in that moment, a soft breath drifted across the table to him. Words barely heard. His mother's soft voice.

"Let her go..."

Chapter 28

ALEXIS

F RANK'S VOICE REACHED around the side of the
house, so much more annoying when it wasn't
muffled through a door. "It's Donovan with dinner.
What is this situation with the weather? I can barely see
out here."

I relayed the message to Daisy, who bounded up out
of the weeds and jogged around to the front of the
house.

"I better go…" Mordecai was bounding after her a
moment later, two savages.

I stared out at the swirling mists, barely able to see
the neighbor's house looming beyond the fence. Kieran
had been in there for about fifteen minutes, and part of
me dreaded what would come next. Breaking that trap
and setting his mom free was a surefire way to get
Valens riled up.

Then again, her trunk had been moved. That would
probably be enough.

"Looks like burgers," Frank called out. "I do miss

the taste of burgers."

I rolled my eyes, then jumped as Lyra drifted around the corner of the house. She was actually going through the motions of walking, but it still looked like she was drifting. I was ninety-five percent sure she'd walked like this in real life.

"You must do as he says." Her voice was sad but firm. My back straightened in defiance. I really did hate being told what to do. "You must follow his guidance. It's for the best."

"Hmm." I sucked in my lips, still not comfortable arguing with this lady. "Mhm."

"I thank you, for all you have done." She stood beside me, and I got the feeling she didn't want to sit down because she'd dirty her dress. Or maybe sitting in weeds wasn't her forte. "You have shown him there is a place in the world for compassion. You have reinforced that there are good people, and if he tries, he can be one of them."

I pulled up my knees and draped my arms around them. I didn't know what to say.

"But respect his wishes, and do as he says," she continued, taking a step back. "It is for the best. For both of you."

Something uncomfortable lodged in my middle. "Why? What is he going to—"

But then she was gone, blinked away into the fog.

"We can go in." Daisy's head appeared around the corner. "Donovan brought a feast. Thank god. I am so hungry I could eat a whole cow. Come on."

Kieran stood at the kitchen sink, looking out the window at gray nothingness. Donovan was unpacking the bags of groceries he'd set down beside him.

"Everything...good?" I asked.

Kieran glanced back at me, a strange look in his eyes. He nodded and turned. "Yes. Do you need help to break the spirit trap? Should I bring in Bria?"

I squinted at him, because he sounded brusque and authoritative (in other words, normal), but his mother's words were rattling around in my head.

"No, I can do it myself. I don't need help."

"Are you able to put the trap back on?"

I hesitated suspiciously. Was this what his mother had been referring to?

"So I can put the trunk back and hope it fools my father until we find the culprit," he continued.

I had intended to think through his mother's request, and the possible implications, but his words stole my focus. *Could* I do something like that? I could banish spirits beyond the line, or pull them back from it, but could I devise something to keep them here?

"I...don't know," I said, examining the trunk.

I heard Frank shout, "It's that grim-faced one. He's got more bags."

"You've got more coming?" I asked.

Donovan glanced over his shoulder. "Yeah. Why?" His gaze hit the table. "Oh. We can figure out a place to sit, don't worry."

A knock sounded at the door.

"Another one!" Frank shouted. "They're really starting to pile up, now. This one is in a van. What are you doing in there? Are you having a party? Why wasn't I invited? Your mother always invited me to parties. Oh, the times we had. Why, one time, in the full moon, we decided we'd—"

"No, no, no," I said hastily, running for the door. I yanked it open. "Frank, don't you dare continue. Shut it down, right now. I don't want to know what you and my mom did."

Zorn stood on the porch. His eyes widened, and he looked around at the yard. Thane, just coming around a big white van, stopped like he'd done something wrong.

"We'd dance near a fire in the BBQ pit and share a bottle of wine," Frank finished with a scowl. "Good gracious, young lady. You'd think I was talking about a pagan ritual or something."

I sighed in relief, opening the door wider for Zorn. "I thought you were about to get lewd," I told Frank, gesturing for Zorn and Thane to get a move on. Frank was in a weird mood—probably from seeing the beauty of Lyra. I was worried he'd start to reminisce about his conquests.

"I would never," Frank said pompously. "My sex life with your mother was our business."

"Gross!" I slammed the door. The guys would just have to forgive me.

"She was a feisty woman in her day," I heard. "An independent, feisty woman. What she did behind closed doors was—"

I ripped the door open again, startling Zorn into stepping back. I allowed my magic to build and then *pushed,* forcing Frank off of my grass and out of my yard. Magic sang through me, but no breeze or pulsing Line materialized.

I stood there for a moment, thinking through what I'd just done. In effect, I'd manipulated a spirit. To do that, I'd had to lock on to him. To do *that*...I'd had to pick him out of the line-up of all the spirits I could feel.

I could feel souls. I'd been able to all along, without the extra power of the Line. I'd just never thought about it that way. My preference for visual learning, combined with my ignorance of how I was making things happen, had definitely hindered my growth. And now I knew.

"Is everything...all right?" Thane asked, stopping on the walkway with a wary expression. He held a black, circular grill.

"Yeah. A ghost was talking about his time with my mom." I shivered. "I'd suspected, but...it's gross when you find out that stuff about your parent, know what I mean?"

"Yes." He took a hesitant step forward. "Is it…still here?"

I laughed and gestured for him to come closer. "No, I just banished him from my yard. What's going on? Are we having a party?"

"You found Mrs. Drusus." Zorn entered the house, and I *almost* didn't notice him furtively glancing back at the fog-shrouded yard. It made me laugh that even Zorn was weirded out by ghosts. "We weren't sure it could be done."

"Ah. Well. You didn't have a couple of crazy girls on the case."

Thane jerked his head to the side. "I'll set up in the backyard."

I nodded and shut the door, turning back toward the kitchen.

"I hear you also discovered hidden hallways in Demigod Valens's house," Zorn said as he stalled at the edge of the kitchen.

Daisy barely glanced at Zorn before going back to slicing tomatoes at the table. Mordecai yanked leaves off of a head of lettuce. It looked like Frank had been right—burgers.

"Yeah. Valens has a really old spirit living in his house," I said, sitting down at the dining table in the chair nearest the trunk. "And the spirit's mistress lives in the hallways. Those two would drive you to drink."

"Were there any others in there?" Kieran asked, his gaze roaming my face, his expression stone-like.

I shrugged. "Not that I saw, but it's a big house. You never know."

"Do you think you could figure out all of the entrances to the hallways?" he asked.

I shrugged again. "If the old guy will cooperate, sure. But I'd probably have to talk to him outside of the actual hallways. Once that Marlene gets after him, things start to deteriorate real fast. He's totally at fault, though. I mean, she's no picnic, but blaming his infidelity on everyone but himself? What a dick. I bet he doesn't want to cross the Line because he's afraid of what his wife will do. I wouldn't be surprised."

Donovan's hands slowed in packing ground meat into patties. "Can…exes find you across the Line?"

I leaned closer to the trunk and closed my eyes, feeling out the magic. "I don't know. I've never asked," I answered distractedly. "Kieran, maybe you should get Bria after all. Letting her spirit out should be easy, but without seeing what I'm working with, I don't know that I'll be able to put the spirit trap back on."

Zorn disappeared from my peripheral vision, clearly having gotten a silent command.

I put my hand on the trunk and closed my eyes, allowing the Line to materialize. Following my intuition, I pulled the Line and its power closer as I gathered my magic, intending to use the lighting of the spirit world as a guide the way I had in Valens's hidden hallways. That had been a handy trick.

A gale-force wind ripped through the kitchen, making my soul flap within my body. Power and electricity surged through my middle and then out through my limbs. The protective cocoon around the trunk pulsed and moved, inviting me to open my eyes and see it.

Like I'd expected, the magic surrounding the trunk moved like oil on water, sliding over the wood in an intricate dance. I pulled more power and heard a groan. A chair fell over. The table shoved to the side. A door jiggled.

Yanked out of the moment, I was just in time to see the whole room fleeing except for Kieran, who was backed up against the corner of the counter with a grim face and hard eyes.

"Oh." I waved my hand at the newly evacuated kitchen. "You all felt that, huh?"

He didn't open his mouth. Just nodded.

"My bad. Why don't I...go into the bedroom." I rose. "Oh. But good news—I don't need Bria. I figured out how to see the magic without the necromancer aids."

"You just have to clear the room to do it."

"It isn't totally practical yet, but…baby steps."

"That felt like baby steps, yes." He was laying on the sarcasm a little thick.

"You're the one who wanted to do this now…"

He started forward. "Let's move this to your bedroom."

Butterflies filled my stomach and I tried desperately not to read into that comment.

Chapter 29

ALEXIS

AN HOUR LATER, I sat on the ground in my small bedroom with sweat rolling down my face, trying to recreate the spirit-trapping spell on my jewelry box while Bria created differently colored billows of smoke by my side. Kieran sat on the bed with his fingers clasped, watching my efforts and occasionally dealing with my surges of power that kept chasing Bria from the room.

I wiped my forehead and sat back, staring at the mishmash of weird that now coated the mostly empty jewelry box. A look at the trunk prompted a sigh.

"I can't make it look the same." I dropped my hands onto my knees. "But I'm pretty sure what I created will do that same job. It's kind of like eternal banishment."

"What does that mean?" Bria asked, wiping her nose. One of the lit incense sticks had apparently given her a runny nose. She didn't volunteer which one, or accept my offer to put it out.

"Well…" I chewed my lip, thinking it through. "It's

essentially a banishment spell. Something I use to send spirits packing. Not across the Line, just *away*. I erected that into a sorta standing situation, one on each side of the box. Each wall repels the spirit away. In this tiny box, the spirit would be pinging around inside of there all the time. A real shitty situation. But in a room, it would just be tossed away from the walls or ceiling."

"What about the ground?" Kieran asked.

"The ground acts as a natural barrier," Bria said, wafting more smoke my way. "If you were to kill someone by burying them alive in more than three feet of earth, their spirit would be trapped with the body. It's why cultures typically leave dead bodies out for a least a couple days—for viewings, wakes, that kind of thing. It gives the spirit time to figure out what they're doing."

"I didn't know any of that," I muttered.

"Do you think another magical worker would know you switched out the spells?" Kieran asked.

I pulled my lips to the side in disappointment, knowing when I was beat. "Unless it was a real idiot, yeah, they'd know."

"They'd also know someone with a pretty unique skillset was *banging* around," Bria said with a sly glance at Kieran. It wasn't hard to miss her double entendre, and unfortunately, she was too far away to smack without being seen.

"I agree," he said, either missing her jab or not car-ing. "Take off the trap and leave it as is. Possibly the magical worker will think his own carelessness was to blame."

"It's not like he would say anything." Bria pulled a crumpled-up tissue from her pocket. "Valens wouldn't know one way or another, and the magical worker wouldn't want to admit to letting the most important spirit get away."

"Unless he intended to stuff her in a body down the road…" I let my words trail away.

"We can find this S.O.B. before then." A determined look crossed Bria's face. "We're on to him now. A tiny bit of digging and—"

"No." The word came with a crack of command, the effect snapping my back straight and sending a jolt of fear racing through me. Kieran was intense, there were no two ways about it. "You'll leave him to me. This is the end of it. Bria, you will continue training Alexis, but Alexis, your task is at an end. After tonight, there will be no more investigation."

My mouth dropped open, and a different sort of fear crawled in. Memories of job searches, crappy positions, and starving kids raced through my head. The kids were working their tails off, but they were happy now. They had full bellies and a purpose. *I* had a purpose.

If that was coming to an end…

"I will pay you a year's wages, Alexis," Kieran said softly, clearly reading my expression. "Never in my wildest dreams did I think you'd solve this so quickly. Additionally, you have a bonus coming for your quick work, written in by your business manager."

"And after that, I can get you work, no problem," Bria said, winking. "We can get out of this murky pit of despair, too. Maybe hit up Australia or something—"

"No." There it was again, only this time, something in his tone sounded tortured, pulling my gaze to him. He gritted his teeth and clenched his fists, like he was stopping himself from commenting further. He gestured stiffly at the trunk. "Release her skin. Let her go."

"Whoa, whoa." Bria hurriedly gathered up her supplies. "That's too personal for me. I need to get out of here."

After she was gone, I stared at the trunk for a moment, uncertainty rolling back in. The termination of my job should've been a good thing, especially since I was still getting paid. I would totally take that check and nod in thanks. Who was I to say boo? I mean, Kieran was a nightmare of a boss: possessive, controlling, and he often stuck his nose in where it didn't belong. And then there was the danger from Valens. It would be way safer to distance myself from the lot of them. I could move somewhere nice, with better weather and cleaner streets. We could start over, with the money to do it right.

So why did my chest ache like I was about to go into cardiac arrest?

"Is she here?" Kieran's voice was quiet and thick, ringing with emotion.

I startled out of my daze, worried about what I was feeling. Worried about letting go of it.

"Yeah, sure. I mean..." I shook my head and glanced around at the empty room. "Uh...no."

Confused, I met his eyes, recognizing the sadness there. Usually that was all it took to bring his mom floating in.

"Is there a way to call her?" he asked, his focus on me intense.

"Well..." I patted my nonexistent pockets for my tarot cards, as though I just carried them around constantly. "How do you usually call her?"

"Think of her, I guess."

"Well..." I frowned, still confused. "Aren't you doing that?"

He blew out a breath and shook his head before looking away. His brow furrowed, which probably mirrored my expression, and silence descended in patches as conversation rose and fell from beyond my closed door.

A few moments later, Lyra drifted through the wall, her expression sublime and her dress flowing without a breeze.

"No one usually looks that good as a ghost," I muttered, turning toward the trunk. "It's unnatural."

"Is it time?" she asked, taking a seat beside her son.

"Yes," I answered.

"I meant to ask…" She paused and I lifted my eyebrows at her. Kieran continued to stare at me, so I pointed at her. "She's here. In case you thought I was talking to myself."

He nodded, but his eyes didn't leave mine. Not like there was any reason for them to, I supposed. He had to take my word for it, after all.

"As a spirit, do I have any power in this world?" she asked.

I froze for a moment, because I knew where this was going. She was asking if she could hang around and try to protect her son. Or maybe help her son in some way.

Not only was that mostly impossible, she'd probably just get captured again, and Kieran would be in the same position he just was, only Valens would hide her spirit better.

I took the super blunt approach. "Once you die, you stop being useful."

Her stare was hard for a moment, as though trying to read me, before she nodded in understanding.

"Okay." I closed my eyes. "Here we go."

"Good-bye," Kieran whispered, finality to his tone.

"I'll miss you."

"You were the best son a mother could have," she said, and I relayed the message as I fiddled with the spirit trap. I could crack it open like an egg, but I wondered if I could just fade out one of the little patches cobbling it together and let her spirit slip out the side. If I did it that way, maybe the originator *would* think he'd messed up. It was possible.

Then again, maybe the guy's periodic visits to the government building had nothing to do with strengthening the spell. Maybe he just came there to pick up his paychecks. I couldn't know for sure unless I checked it out...and now, according to Kieran, there would be no need.

"I love you dearly," she said. "Please live your life to its fullest. Break Valens's hold over you, and find happiness. Please."

"I intend to," Kieran said after I relayed the message.

I glanced at his face, and before his stone mask slipped over his features, I saw the lie. The uncertainty.

He planned to go up against his father, and he wasn't sure he would win.

Which was crazy, because he always sounded so confident. So in control.

That's how he was trained.

The ache in my middle grew, responding to my

worry of what he faced, as I peeled away part of the slippery spirit trap. There really wasn't anything to it when I embraced the power of the Line.

A gasp made me jerk my head around. Lyra laughed like a girl and jumped on the bed, putting her hands into the air in an expression of joy and bliss. A strange wetsuit looking thing drifted through the air to her, and she grabbed it and held it close. The Line pulsed above us, all around us, beckoning to her.

I described everything I saw in as much detail as I could muster—describing the Line didn't make much sense if you couldn't actually see and feel it.

A boyish smile crossed Kieran's face. Relief.

Lyra hugged her skin and headed for the wall of the house.

"Wait, wait—whoa. Where are you going?" I asked.

Her smile was serene. "For a proper swim, and then to eternity. I am finally whole again."

She disappeared through the wall, leaving silence in her wake.

"She's gone?" Kieran asked.

I stood slowly and pushed back my hair. "Yes. She'll probably cross over in the ocean. That seems fitting." I turned my attention to Kieran, sitting on the bed with his hands clasped, that extreme focus on me again. Sadness creased his features and lingered in his eyes. "She was blissful. She's finally at rest, Kieran. You gave her peace."

"No," he whispered, rising and stepping closer. His breath dusted my face. "You gave her peace. I gave her you."

He grabbed my cheeks with both hands. Passion flared within me and fire licked at my core. I expected a hard kiss, like earlier, rushed and frantic. Instead, electricity jumped between us as his lips slowly grazed mine, savoring the contact.

I closed my eyes and opened my mouth, inviting him in. His tongue probed before he backed off to nibble on my bottom lip. His hands slid down my sides and hooked around my middle.

Warmth spread through me from deep down as I sunk into the feeling of his arms wrapped around me. Of his strength and power. Of his gentle touch. He was what I'd always longed for in my quietest moments—the rush of desire wrapped up in a blanket of safety.

In that moment I knew...I had to ride the train of terrible ideas one more time. Just once more to thoroughly get him out of my system. Right after that, I'd go back to being a logical adult who didn't get mixed up with dangerous men filled with all the strength and power of a god.

Just one more time.

Toot, toot.

I slid my hands down his front and stopped at the

base of his T-shirt before slipping inside and putting my palms flush with his hot skin. His thumbs stroked my chin as he deepened our kiss. I pushed my hands up and the shirt with it, grabbing the ends in fistfuls when I reached his shoulders.

He leaned back, his eyes liquid and opened up all the way down to his soul. Without thinking, I reached into his chest, only needing a trickle of the Line power to do so this time, and stroked the edge of that hard plate protecting his essence. He sucked in a breath and tensed, but didn't fight it. Instead, he lifted his arms so I could pull off the shirt, and then looked down at me again.

"It's terrifying when you do that," he said softly, the corners of his lips tweaking upward into a sheepish grin. "It's one of the rare times I feel completely vulnerable. I know one heart-stopping moment of thinking I can't protect myself before I feel my magic build. It's so primal, the response. I can see why people with your magic have been feared through the centuries."

Doubt bled through me and heat prickled my eyes. But before I could pull back, he shook his head and gripped my upper arms. His smile melted and eyes grew serious.

"I wasn't trying to make you feel badly just then, Alexis," he said, putting one warm hand to the side of my neck, and using the other to capture my hand and place it on his heart. "I'm in awe of you. There is only one other thing that makes me feel that sort of vulnerability. It speaks of your power, and your rare gift. It's a treasure. You're a treasure. I trust you implicitly."

"You didn't trust me so well when you blasted me with your magic in your bedroom." My voice quavered, a result of remembering the horror I could become. Amazingly, however, I didn't lift my chin to offset it. I didn't reach for anger to cover the moment. He'd admitted to a vulnerability, and so I let him see mine.

His lips quirked upward again. "Usually I can control my reaction. That time I couldn't. You blindsided me, what can I say? In more ways than one."

I leaned forward, wanting to steal a little more of his heat. "Where's the other place you feel vulnerable?"

His eyes dulled and his smile melted away for the second time. "When I'm at sea with my father."

Chapter 30

ALEXIS

I'D BEEN RIGHT. Kieran was unsure if he could handle what his father would throw at him.

"Then why will you challenge him?" I asked, worry rising. I slid the fingers of my free hand over his slight raven stubble. "Your mother is free. Why not leave it at that? He can't know it was you."

Kieran shook his head, and a sudden burst of his magic sizzled across my skin and booted me out of his middle. "My father won't let something like that go. If he figures out what happened, he won't rest until he knows who was responsible. Until he punishes them. Look at what he did to my mother. He won't be any easier on his son."

I let my hand fall until my fingertips were digging into his shoulder, my aggression matching the feeling of his magic. "It just so happens that you have a holy terror working for you, one that can clear a room in ten seconds flat. A whole room. Ten seconds. As soon as she learns her magic, she might be useful."

The mood shifted and his tone deepened. "You will stay as far away from this as humanly possible, is that clear?" Shivers crawled up my skin and fear made my legs quake. Talk about a primal reaction. "You will go nowhere near this. You've done what I needed you to do. You found my mother's skin and set her free. She is no longer a liability, and neither will you be. I'll take it from here."

I frowned and took a step back. "Okay, but what about all those other trapped spirits?"

"I have the information you found, and I have Bria to help lock down the person who did this. I'll find whoever it is, and I'll make him disappear. His magic should be ripped away with him. Worst case, it'll seep away in time. My father will lose that asset, and with it, his access to the captured souls."

"Bria—" I clenched my jaw in outrage. "You can't involve her and not me. I helped bring all this around."

"Lexi," he whispered, and his eyes softened. The warmth in my middle expanded a little more with the sound of my nickname on his tongue. He lightly trailed his fingertips down my cheek. "Please. Bria has lived this life for years. She's hardened to it. Trained for it. And if she is caught, she can't be scrambled and turned into a war machine. You could be." He traced a thumb across my lips before leaning in and touching his lips to mine. "Please, let me protect you. I brought you into all of this. I shattered your peaceful, quiet life. Let me try to restore a little of that. Please do me the favor of letting this go. Of going back to hiding yourself from the magical world." He paused, staring at me with pleading eyes. "For me."

I read his concern clearly, his worry that something might happen to me. *This* was what his mom had meant when she'd told me to listen to him.

My heart squished, and before I knew what was happening, I was nodding at him. "Okay."

He kissed me deeply, and the room fell away. The uncertainty of my magic and my future vanished. All I knew was his lips moving against mine, his hands slowly drifting down my body.

"You're beautiful," he murmured against my lips. "When I first saw you, I thought you were trying to disguise your beauty with the rough clothing. Trying to blend into your surroundings. It seemed so daft. A creature like you was not made to fit in, you were made to stand out. To draw notice. Your angelic face, your easy confidence, your incredible magic—you are one in a million, and it pains me that you have to be hidden away from admiring eyes."

My body felt as light as air. I hadn't thought my heart could swell any more, but he'd just proven me wrong.

I unbuckled his jeans, not able to stand it. Needing

him with a fire I could barely understand.

Clearly sensing my urgency, he pulled my shirt over my head, ripping a clasp when it got caught, and threw it to the floor. I pushed down his pants as he took two fistfuls of mine and ripped them apart. Fabric screeched and a zipper tore before he spun me around and backed me against my bed. He wrapped a strong arm around me before kneeling onto the mattress and lowering me to my back.

I reached for his hard length, only to miss as he pulled my pants off the rest of the way. He stepped out of his without ceremony, and I took a second to feast on the marvel that was his body. Thick shoulders and cut pecs reduced down into an almost eight-pack before ending on that large cock straining for me.

I pushed the blankets back and scooted more thoroughly onto the bed, feeling a jolt of anticipation when he crawled after me slowly, passion burning in his stormy eyes. He pushed a knee to the side and bent over me. I gasped, arching as his hot tongue licked up my center. He swirled around my clit and then sucked it in, sending my eyes rolling to the back of my head.

"Hmm, Kieran." I dragged my fingers through his unruly black hair. A finger plunged into my wetness, followed by a second, and his mouth created a pulsing suction to match the pace of his fingers. "Holy—shit." I gyrated upward into his mouth. Sensations coursed through me so hard and fast I wasn't ready for them. "Holy crap, no. Yes. Oh God."

His dark chuckle spoke of sex and fire and writhing bodies. "Do we need a safe word?"

"I don't LIKE—oh! Pain. No PAIN—*hmm.*" I closed my eyes as his sexy magic rolled over me, kissing every inch of my skin. "Oh yes…"

"There is pain, and then there is being right on the edge of the precipice, begging to come, and not being allowed to."

"Too many words. Stop with all the WORDS—holy shiii—"

He stroked my clit with his tongue in a way I hadn't even known was possible. Pleasure pounded through my body, making my jaw clench shut for a moment. He worked with his fingers, then sucked again, before going back with his tongue. If oral sex was an art, Kieran's rendition would be priceless.

I couldn't speak. I couldn't move. My back arched and my whole body tensed, drowning in ecstasy. I hit a wall before he switched it up, and then I blasted through it. Climbing past heights I'd never before reached, and rocketing higher still.

Sounds with no shape exited my mouth. Moans increased in pitch. The waves of pure pleasure increased in intensity.

"Please, no," I begged, strung out. At that edge he'd

warned me about. Needing to jump off. "Please, yes!"

Without warning, the suction stopped and his fingers disappeared. My sex pounded so hard I couldn't think straight. I ached with wanting.

His body slid over mine, my skin so sensitive that it felt like a thousand little electric shocks of pleasure. I moaned and slid my hands down his muscular back, marveling at the definition. His large cock prodded my opening, and my body jumped out of my skin.

"You should've picked out that safe word when you had the chance," he said softly, his voice silky smooth, his magic mixing with mine in an exquisite cocktail.

"Please," I begged, my body burning me alive from the inside out. I deepened the kiss, wild now. Desperate.

"Hmm." He pushed up onto his elbows and reached in to grab his cock by the base before running it along my slit, getting everything wet. His body lowered onto mine before he dragged his tip against my slit and stopped at my opening.

I braced, and without meaning to, reached into his middle with my magic. When I felt that hard plate this time, I didn't try to push through. I soaked into it, easing down into him like I envisioned his cock easing down into me.

He gasped right before his magic slammed into me, flaying me open. Strangely, it didn't hurt. He wasn't forcing me out. He was allowing me in.

I finished burrowing through that inner wall and

there it was—his most sacred possession, the very essence of him. I stroked it with a feather-light touch, marveling at its pureness and beauty.

He gasped again and grabbed the bed to either side of me. I slid my legs up his sides, not sure what I was doing, but knowing it felt right, and dragged him back down on top of me.

He didn't hesitate this time. He didn't have the ability.

He thrust into me with everything he had, filling me to the point of pain and making me call out his name. I grabbed his shoulders and opened myself up in a way I hadn't before, not to anyone, connecting his middle to mine in a straight line, soul to soul. Whatever I'd done to his soul, he would in turn do to mine.

His magic slid across my body before soaking in, a million pricks of lava buffered by his sexy magic. I groaned, the feeling just on this side of pleasure, heightening the experience. Our magics mixed together before converging on the line connecting our souls, strengthening the bond.

He pumped harder, animalistic. I met each thrust with a wild upswing of my hips, taking him deep. Pleasure pounded. My body wound tighter. Thoughts fled and nothing existed but the connection between us. The little tugs of our connection sent glorious shivers through my body, pumped higher by the sensation of him moving inside of me.

"Oh God, Kieran," I said through clenched teeth, unable to stand it. "I can't. I…can't."

He grabbed my hands and pushed them above my head before entwining our fingers, his chest flush with mine. Ours souls connected. Our magic fused.

With his one last thrust, deep and hard, I blasted apart, flying to all points of the universe. Magic coursed through me, then ran through him, before coming back, like a wave in a bathtub.

I trembled under him as he shook, groaning with his release. Another orgasm took me, this one still better than any before it, but just an aftershock. He shook again, his groan almost anguished this time. Once more and I went limp, bliss sparkling in my bloodstream.

"Huu." I wasn't sure what I'd been trying to say, but I left it at that, closing my eyes with the solid weight of him pushing me into the mattress.

"Truan," he replied, and I figured he had the same problem I did.

He rolled to the side and dragged me against him, fitting my head to the hollow between his neck and arm. I closed my eyes in contentment, still feeling that weird line I'd drawn between us. Still feeling our fused magic running back and forth through it.

I had intended to figure out how to tear it down, but before I could un-fog my mind enough to think, sleep pulled me under.

Chapter 31

KIERAN

A LIGHT BUZZING brought Kieran out of a deep sleep, making him hover on the edge of consciousness. His body felt blissfully sated, warm and content. He couldn't remember ever feeling this good, or this relaxed.

The buzzing tugged at his awareness until he finished the climb up to wakefulness. He blinked in the low light of Alexis's tiny, decrepit room, with the faded paint and stained carpet. The shabby curtains hung at odd angles beside the single-paned window. Old furniture, some on its last leg, dotted the space, her possessions all fitting comfortably because she had so little.

If he'd seen this place before knowing her or her wards, he would have grimaced and quickly extricated himself from the situation. He would've thought she was a criminal or shady magical worker, hiding from the law. His perception would be that she wanted to live in this squalor, having no respect for herself or her surroundings.

How blind and judgmental he'd been. How prejudiced against the people who lived outside of their clearly defined zones. He'd been as closed-minded as the Chesters regarding why someone would have to live in a place like this, outcast from both societies.

Alexis's soft breath dusted his chest. He turned his head and kissed her forehead. She'd opened his eyes to so much. Without trying, she'd forced a different way of thinking on him, and it had made him a rounder person. A better person. Through her, he was becoming less like his father, and more his own man.

Let her go...

Something hot and tight coiled in his chest, and his arm contracted, jerking Alexis closer to his body. She moaned lightly and curled tighter around him, sliding her leg over his and her arm up his chest to rest on his heart. He took it, fighting the overpowering desire to assume complete control of her life. To ensure that she stay safe, through overbearing means if necessary.

That was why his mother had told him to move on. He knew it in his heart. Try as he might to fight it, he couldn't escape the extremely possessive personality traits most Demigods were known for. He latched on to what he deemed his, and through hell or fury, he protected that thing—or person—with everything he had.

In the process, he'd surely smother her, making her less than herself.

Alexis deserved better. She was a wild spirit, most beautiful when she was free. She deserved a man who would be her partner—the air to her fire, and not the water that would douse it.

Besides, Kieran's father thought of magical San Francisco as his. If someone tried to take it, Valens would destroy that person mercilessly. Valens had protected his claim for decades. Nearly the full lifespan of a non-magical human. He'd know how to combat his son, someone whose training he'd organized and progress he'd monitored. Someone whom he'd always watched. Even now, people would be out there trying to figure out what was taking Kieran's time.

If Kieran dragged Alexis any further into that, she'd die right alongside him. He was doing everything he could to prepare, but as the inevitable neared, he had to face the facts. She couldn't be a part of what came next.

He released his arm and pulled it away, gritting his teeth against the overpowering urge to stay where he was. He took one last moment next to her, listening to her breathe and feeling her heart beat against his chest, and then eased out from under her and climbed off of the rock-hard mattress that wasn't fit for a dog.

As soon as he could figure out how to mask his efforts, he would gut this house and build it up anew. She deserved the very best, and he could still provide her with material things. Even in death, if he set it up beforehand.

A soft buzzing drifted through the room again. He found his pants and patted the pocket, finding his vibrating phone. Zorn's name appeared on the screen, along with the time. Four in the morning. Kieran had never spent so long with a woman. Not in his entire life.

His father would know that.

"Bollocks," he muttered, stepping into his pants and pulling on his shirt. He needed to figure out a good cover.

He glanced down at his mother's trunk and a surge of sorrow punched him in the gut. This time, though, a soggy sort of peace drifted up to ease the pain.

She was in a better place. Because of Alexis, his mother was finally free. She was free to ride the waves of the sea, to dive down into their depths, and to find peace.

Alexis needed to keep her own freedom.

Hardening his resolve, he hefted the trunk and made his way out to the kitchen. Zorn waited in one of the chairs, as quiet as death.

"I wondered if you'd leave her," Zorn said in a flat tone. He knew the score.

Kieran didn't say anything as he gently set the trunk down on the table. He noticed a white notepad with a vet's name at the top. Next to it was a promotional pen from some cafe. This house used whatever they could get their hands on. True survivors in a hard life.

A handwritten note lay detached from the pad. He angled his head to read it.

I was in your house. Standing over your sleeping body. I could've killed you. Next time I will try.

It was clearly meant for Daisy.

"Creepy," Kieran said, taking up the pen.

"She thinks like me. She responds in ways I usually do. Anything less than extreme threats will roll right off of her."

"So then…she's perfect for your teaching methods."

"The first to be so, yes. She's had a unique upbringing."

"Haven't we all." He wrote a note of his own and ripped it off.

"Valens will wonder where you are." Zorn stood before picking up his note. They walked silently down the short hall together, separating to deliver their notes. Kieran put his note on the pillow next to Alexis's head. It was for the best. Otherwise she'd probably try to stab him in the chest again. And after last night, he had a feeling she could. She'd figured out how.

He frowned as he made his way back out. Zorn was in the hall, too, slipping a roll of tape into his pocket. He'd taped his message to Daisy and Mordecai's door.

"You're going to steal their tape?" Kieran asked, rubbing at his chest as he made his way back to the table. Now that he was focusing on it, a strange weight had lodged there. It didn't press on him in any way. It just sat in his middle, deep within his person. It was strange and foreign, though comforting, and for some reason, he got the impression it was a remnant of whatever she'd done to him last night.

"I didn't see any tape when I was rifling through their drawers earlier this evening. Or yesterday evening, I guess I should say. I figured I'd better bring my own."

Kieran hefted the trunk again. "And you're not going to leave it for them?"

"Why should I? It's my tape. Alexis has a job now. She can get her own."

Kieran huffed out a laugh and headed for the door. "You and Daisy definitely have similar outlooks."

Zorn opened the door for him and stood to the side, waiting for him to go through. The weight in his middle intensified. He frowned, wanting to swipe at his chest, as though that might dislodge it. On the porch, when the tug increased, he glanced down, half wondering if a magical string of some kind was attached to his middle. He couldn't sense any power, though. He couldn't sense any residual magic drifting from or attached to his body.

"Are you going to drop off the trunk this morning?"

Zorn asked, stepping off the porch before him.

"Yes. I want to put a camera on the area. If we can get a satellite on it, that'd be best, but a stationary camera will do if that's not possible. There must be a place we can hide a monitoring device."

"Navigating that fog will be—what is it?"

Kieran stared at a solitary figure standing in the middle of the struggling greenish-brown lawn. A gray comb-over adorned an otherwise shiny scalp, and wrinkles layered a pair of watery brown eyes. He wore a plucky suit from yesteryear, and slouched in a way that made an otherwise small stomach appear larger.

His outward appearance and obvious trespassing wasn't what made Kieran stop and stare. There was a weird feeling about him, almost as if his solidity could dissipate into nothing at any moment.

"Do you see that guy?" Kieran asked in a hush, sudden anxiety making his heart race.

Zorn looked around the front yard. He was a man who missed very little, so certainly he'd notice a man in his sixties hanging out in plain sight.

"Tell me you can see that guy," Kieran said, a cold sweat breaking out.

"Where?" Zorn said, his body loosening, preparing to react violently.

"She gave me her power." Kieran started forward, his body stiff and adrenaline surging through him. "She

307

gave me the ability to see spirits."

"What?" Zorn took the trunk from Kieran, studying his face.

Kieran moved down the walkway, stopping when he was even with the man. Staring at him.

The man looked behind him, then around the yard, then finally back at him. "Can you see me?"

A wave of dizziness hit Kieran, his mind reeling. "You're not..." He swallowed. Of all the things he'd been through, all the things he'd done, seeing the spirit of an old man was the thing that gave him pause? "Are you Frank?"

Zorn startled and pushed in beside Kieran.

The man put a finger to his chest and lifted his gray eyebrows. "You can see me?" he repeated.

Kieran wiped at his chest, feeling that tug again. It was trying to draw him back to the house. Back to her.

"Somehow, she gave me the ability to see spirits," Kieran said again, mystified.

"How?" Zorn asked as Frank said, "Well, I'll be damned. That's great, actually. I know you're the one who organizes security around these parts, and I have been keeping an eye on things. It'll be great to discuss the situation firsthand, with—"

Kieran swung his gaze back to Frank, his patience quickly wearing thin.

The ghost cut off. His mouth closed and his lips

turned white.

"I don't know," Kieran answered Zorn, thinking back to the night before. To the feeling of her lightly stroking the very center of him, an insanely intimate and erotic moment. She'd opened herself to him, too, in a way that had drawn him in, body and soul.

...body and soul...

"Will it last, do you think?" Zorn asked, moving on toward his car and much larger trunk.

"I don't know," he repeated, his tone harder this time.

"Do you think she did it on purpose?"

Kieran shook his head. He had no concrete answer, but it seemed unlikely. She didn't have enough working knowledge for that.

"I think she was just reacting to the moment. The question is, if this lasts, will it help or hurt?"

Kieran stopped beside the car and waited for Zorn to open the back. He did so as Frank the Ghost drifted toward the sidewalk, watching their progress.

A flare of territorialism stole over Kieran, making him grit his teeth. He moved to the car with stiff legs, but couldn't contain a surge of aggression.

"Get off of her lawn," he ground out, turning. A wave of power swept the yard, cutting into the center of the ghost. Zorn staggered against the car. The ghost's face contorted into a look of fear, then terror, before he sprinted to the sidewalk and bowed.

"So sorry, sir. I see my error," the ghost groveled. "Lawn is a sacred thing. Trampling all over it is rude. That was my fault. I'll stick to the hard surfaces, weeds, and dirt from now on. Thank you for showing me the error of my ways."

Kieran let his gaze linger on the repeatedly bowing ghost, driving home his point, before reaching for the car handle. Zorn strode to the driver's door, his gaze speculative and face pale.

"That was Alexis's magic," Zorn said conversationally.

"Appears so."

"It wasn't as nuanced or terrifying as hers, but it still fucking hurt."

"That'll be helpful," Kieran said lightly, hiding the strange uncertainty tickling the pit of his stomach.

"Yes. Unless you do it without thinking and alert everyone of this new, extremely potent magic."

"Unless that, yes."

"You'll have to control your moods a little better."

Kieran headed to his Ferrari. "Or learn to control which of my magic goes into which command."

"Or that, sure."

"If it lasts."

Zorn nodded. "If it lasts."

"It would sure be helpful if it did."

"For all of our sakes, yes." Zorn opened his car door, then paused for a moment. He tilted his head and a very rare grin twisted his lips. "I find myself incredibly jealous, sir. Incredibly jealous. And you likely have only a sliver of the power Alexis has within the spirit realm. Just think what she will do when she reaches her full potential."

Chapter 32

ALEXIS

THE FIRST INDICATION that something was amiss: light drifted through my window, not hindered by thick blankets of fog.

The second indication that something was amiss: the lack of the comforting warmth of the large Demigod who had given me the best sex of my life.

The third indication that something was amiss, which didn't materialize until after I'd propped myself onto my elbows and looked around my empty bedroom in bewilderment: a small square piece of white paper had been left on my pillow.

With a falling brow, I sat up and grabbed the note. Written in a surprisingly delicate scrawl was: *Goodbye. I'll miss you.*

My heart sank.

I knew at once he was telling me goodbye forever, like he'd told his mother last night. He'd been serious about trying to protect me, and to him that meant pushing me away.

A strange hollowness ached in my middle, followed by a tug to hurry up out of the room and go...

I didn't know where I wanted to go. Just...*out.*

Out there....

Out there somewhere...

I frowned in confusion, processing. The memory of stroking his soul came back to me. It had been so easy to get into that protected cavern and find the treasure of his person. I hadn't forced my way in, I'd seeped in. The difference had been in the approach.

Or maybe the difference had been in his openness. He hadn't put up his usual blockade, and when he'd used his magic, it hadn't torn me apart like it usually would.

Now, he and his mother were out of my life.

I sat in the stillness of the room, deciding how I felt. Deciding what I wanted to do.

He'd left me in peace—in the safety of anonymity. He'd pushed me out of his controlling sphere, and out of danger. He'd given me back the life I'd lived before him, but with a bunch of money to make things easier.

He'd set me free.

He'd also given me unbelievable sex, filled with passion and yearning. Filled with respect and mutual pleasure. He'd been better than his sexy magic felt, something I hadn't thought possible. It would be hard to let go of that.

It would be hard to let go of *him*.

Really, I should be thankful he'd relieved me of the need to extricate myself from the situation. The man was bad news. He'd had his people barge into my house in the middle of the night and knock us around, for goodness's sake. Maybe we were on equal footing in bed, but in life he'd always been in charge and three steps ahead. Bria was right—I needed to steer clear from that sort of nonsense.

Besides, Kieran was a product of Valens. That guy was whack. He'd imprisoned his love in life and in death. He'd made shrines for her while basically torturing her. That was so far from normal it was in a league of its own. Kieran wasn't just protecting me from Valens by pushing me away, he was protecting me from himself and his crazy heritage.

He's trying to protect me…

I dragged my teeth across my bottom lip and stared out the window.

That's what it always came down to. He was trying to protect me.

I'd never been in any danger from Kieran Drusus or any of his people. He'd inherited some of his father's traits, but he was no Valens. He'd healed Mordecai without expecting anything in return. He'd hoped for something, sure, but he'd left me free of obligation. His men were training Mordecai and Daisy on his orders, and he also paid for our groceries and ensured someone made us dinner every night. He'd bought me extremely expensive clothes and hadn't even mentioned the fact that I'd stolen them from his house. He was training me. Leaving me with a year's salary plus a large bonus...

The first thing he'd ever done for me was give a sick kid a blanket.

He had a lot of faults, that was clear, but I believed in my soul that he was a legitimately good person. He tried to do his best, even if he sometimes fell short.

So maybe I *should* cry?

Anger rose up out of nowhere.

Silly rabbit. Crying in these situations isn't your speed. Ignoring manipulative buttheads and doing as you please is more your style. Do you, girl.

I clutched the note in a fist, ripped the covers away, and swung my feet over the side of the bed.

I would do me. I would catch the sonuvabitch who'd been trapping souls, I'd learn how to wield my magic as a weapon, and then I would wreak havoc in the magical world to protect the guy who was trying to protect me.

I strutted to the door, almost forgetting I was butt-naked. I quickly shrugged into some ill-fitting sweats and resumed my strut. When I opened the door, I caught Daisy coming out of her room, wiping the sleep from her eyes. The square of white on her door caught our attention at the same time.

I stepped closer, my skin crawling. "What in the holy fuck?"

Daisy read the note, not signed. Thank God it wasn't written in Kieran's scrawl, or someone else would need to do the protecting while I rained hell on him.

"He's full of shit," she said, clearly knowing who'd left the creeptastic note.

"If you keep swearing, I'm going to punch you in the face for each infraction."

Her sleepy eyes blinked at me. "Okay."

I pointed aggressively at the note. "Who wrote that, and do I need to go on a killing spree?"

She rolled her eyes. "Ew. No. Zorn wrote it, obviously." She trudged down the hall toward the kitchen. "For some reason, he thinks that after just one day of training I should know when a stealthy intruder at the top of his game lets himself into my house with a key he probably got from your possessive boss and enters my room. He probably went through my shit, too, trying to find something that would press my buttons. I would've."

"So..." I shifted as Mordecai sat up from his bed and rubbed his eyes. I pointed at the note again. "He *did* stare at you while you were sleeping? Because that is incredibly messed up, Daisy."

She shrugged. "He was probably trying to see if I would feel his presence. But dude, I've only gotten *one* lesson from him. And he's a master at stealth, like I said. Obviously I wasn't going to wake up. Come *on*."

"So then…" I put my hands on my hips, really unclear as to how she was so blasé about the note. "Which is the part that's full of shit?"

"He won't try to kill me yet. Give me a break. If anything, my not waking up is his failure as a teacher. He needs to try harder." She continued into the kitchen, leaving me standing there with my mouth open.

Mordecai met me at the door and read the object of our discussion. A tremor moved through his body and a strange look sparkled in his light eyes—a mixture of rage, wariness, and aggression. Intense aggression, like an alpha animal sensing danger in its territory.

The shifter was blossoming in Mordecai. The guys were right. He'd need to learn to change into his animal soon. Very soon.

"Who did this?" His deep, threatening voice was only slightly ruined by the crack halfway through. Puberty was a dickhead.

"Zorn. Apparently, it's a training exercise." I shook my head and continued down the hall. "He forgets, though. He was in *my* house uninvited, not hers. And that motherfucker will answer for it."

"Yes, he will."

My small hairs stood on end and I grinned. Zorn was shortsighted. He was focusing solely on one individual in the household, clearly forgetting that we were a family. A unit. You fucked with one of us, you fucked with all of us. And we were crazy.

"Leave it alone for now," I said, stalling near the kitchen. "I want to see how this plays out."

Daisy stood at the kitchen sink eating a leftover piece of watermelon. The juice dribbled down her chin and into the kitchen sink. I probably should've encouraged her to sit at the table like a normal human being, but then I'd also have to encourage her to clean up after herself... Too much effort.

"What're your plans for today?" I asked, feeling a wave of anticipation about my own plan. I grabbed a Pop Tart and sat down at the table, breathing through my nerves. Working up my courage. This time, I'd be defying two Demigods. Talk about crazy.

"Zorn will probably try to kidnap me or something," Daisy said, opening the cabinet at her knees with sticky fingers and throwing the rind in the compost bin. I thinned my lips at the thought of the mess on the handle. "He thinks shock value is the only thing that'll get through to me. I'll go with it until I'm good enough to get one over on him."

"Or maybe he's setting you up to think that."

She grabbed another piece of watermelon out of the

tub. Mordecai sauntered in wearing faded sweats with holes in the knees and a shirt that was barely holding together. He had other clothes, but he wore his favorite things into the ground.

"I thought of that," she said. "And I'll definitely look out for it. But I really think he latched on to one element of me, and disregarded the rest. Like I'm some ape with a one-track mind."

"That's sexist," Mordecai said, eating a muffin as he leaned his butt against the counter.

"No, no." I pointed at him. "No. You lean over the sink like your sister or you lean over the table. The floor is way harder to clean than wiping off a surface."

"Or get a plate, idiot," Daisy said, smacking him with a dish towel.

"Then I'd have to wash it, *idiot.*" Mordecai crossed to the table.

"What's sexist about it?" Daisy bent over as more juice dribbled down her chin. "I didn't say anything about guys."

"You always call me an ape," he said, "because you don't think men have evolved beyond them."

"You are an ape."

"See? It's sexist. You don't call women apes."

"Fine. Would you prefer I called you a cu—"

"Don't you do it," I yelled. "No swearing."

Daisy narrowed her eyes at Mordecai. "I only didn't

finish that sentence because I believe, in my bones, that she would punch me in the face."

"All right, all right," I said putting up my hand. The note crinkled between my thumb and palm, reminding me of what was on it.

The ache in my middle intensified and I dropped my hand again, swallowing the lump in my throat.

The door burst open and I jerked around to look. Mordecai pushed up from the table, half-standing. Daisy barely flinched. I couldn't remember if that was normal or not.

Bria winked at me before shutting the door and strolling in, her heavy boots thudding on the floor and her camo backpack hanging from her shoulder. "Yes, I will just walk right in, thanks for offering," she said, then frowned at me. "Why aren't you ready? Let's get going."

I braced, confused. "Where?"

"What do you mean *where?* The government building. Didn't you say you needed to check that place out?"

"Yeah, but… Didn't Kieran tell you that he pulled me off the case? He wants me out of the picture now."

"Yes," Bria said patiently, and sat at the table. "He did tell me that." She frowned harder. "You weren't actually thinking of listening to him, were you? Because if so, I seriously misjudged your personality."

"Wait, wait, wait." Daisy hurried to the last chair

and sat. "We have to start at the beginning. There are issues we need to discuss regarding that stalking S.O.B."

"We were supposed to do this in a private family talk," Mordecai mumbled, and a different sort of anticipation jiggled my stomach. They were going to bring up what had happened between me and Kieran.

I hated when they were disappointed. It always cut right through me.

"Don't mind me," Bria said, crossing her arms over her chest and leaning back. "I'm just a fly on the wall."

"Lexi, honestly, what were you thinking?" Daisy demanded. She leveled a finger at me. "And don't say it was just the one time, and you had to get it out of your system, and blah-bidy-blah. I know about his dad's house. That excuse won't work this time."

"This time?" Bria beamed in pride. "I knew you were my kinda girl, Lexi. Except, if you were ever to love and leave a guy, the entitled Demigod would be that guy. Remember what I said about the train? You need to get off that train. I know I just said it yesterday, but clearly it bears repeating…"

"I know, but—"

"He has been manipulating you since he met you. He's been aiming to get this one exact thing," Mordecai said. "He stalked you, remember? Decent guys don't stalk people."

"No, but he was stalking me because of my magic—"

"And he was crude about the nasty business." Daisy's eyebrows lowered. "Nice guys aren't crude."

I barely stopped myself from saying that the crude language had been extremely sexy, and while Kieran was respectful of me, no one could call him nice. He was a powerful sort of dangerous. Crude worked *very well* for him.

"You finished the job he hired you for," Mordecai said, "so you have no reason to stay on. If you do, he'll probably just try to use you again."

"That's what Demigods do," Bria murmured.

Mordecai nodded, validated. "I think you should sever the connection, Lexi. You helped his mom, and now you should get on with your life. He can't ask any more from you."

"But we'll still bring down the guy that is trapping souls, right?" Bria asked. "Because that should be our thing. He doesn't need to play any part in that. I mean…except if we get caught. Then we'll throw him under the bus and skedaddle."

"Right." Daisy nodded, as though expressly ignoring the order of a Demigod wasn't a big deal.

I remembered the last time I had angered Kieran. The intensity with which he'd ripped me through the closet door, and then—

My core tightened and my face heated. I rubbed my hand over my face. I definitely hadn't gotten him out of my system. The opposite. I wanted him more now than I ever had.

"We can find a way to earn a living," Mordecai was saying, cutting into my reverie. "We made do before him, and we'll make do now. We have the bonus for completing the job early, and you have some nice clothes, so we have time to get situated."

"He said he'd pay me for a year," I said. "He didn't expect me to find his mom's skin so quickly."

Bria raised her hand. "Um, can we say rock star? Because Lexi found that skin *incredibly* quickly. She could get a job in any investigative firm featuring dead people."

"She has priors," Daisy said.

Bria furrowed her brow. "Who doesn't?"

"Before you say anything—when you get back to the topic at hand—I'm totally going to accept his offer. Don't even try to talk me out of it."

"Ew." Daisy gave me a teenager's disgusted look, which threw in not-so-subtle shades of *you're an idiot.* "Like we'd try to talk you out of some rich guy's free money."

"So that settles it." Mordecai slapped his hands on the table. "We'll live cheaply, like we have been, and use most of the money from the stalker to get a business going for you, like we were originally planning. We can save the rest. Daisy and I can get jobs when we're sixteen to pay the Six to continue our training."

Bria leaned forward on the table, her mouth open, looking at Mordecai like he was an insect under a microscope. "Are you for real?"

His brow lowered. "What? That seems like a sensible plan."

"That is an extremely sensible plan, and if my skin weren't crawling, I'd be incredibly impressed that you're so practical at fifteen."

"Yeah. I know. It can get annoying." Daisy rolled her eyes again.

"Well…" I flicked the note onto the table and another wave of butterflies fluttered through my belly. It was time to get going. I couldn't stall any longer. "Severing the connection has been taken care of. He has locked that down."

Bria dropped two fingers onto the note and slid it closer.

"I got hit, then quit." I leaned back. "What he wrote on the note is what he said to his mother when she left my bedroom. To him, it's over. He doesn't want me near the job, he doesn't want me going after the spirit trapper, and he doesn't want me in his life at all. He'll pay me, but that's it. You guys got your wish."

My throat burned and my chest felt tight. The weird new feeling in my middle started aching. I swallowed down the emotion, but before I could say anything else,

Daisy slammed her hand down on the table.

"That's bullshit! No way. Am I right, Mordecai? He can't just"—she swung her hand over the table—"waltz in here, mess with her mind, and then take off. That's fucked up." She put her finger in the air and looked at me with raised eyebrows. "I know the new rule is no swearing—"

"That's always been the rule—"

"—but this warrants it. He stalks you, gets his mom freed, gets some punani, and then he walks?" She stood from the table and paced the kitchen floor, acting the part of the scorned woman on my behalf. "He needs his dick cut off, that's what he needs."

A smile emerged on Bria's face as she watched Daisy. "This kid is my spirit animal."

"I thought you wanted this," I said to Daisy. "He's severing the connection."

"No." She rounded on me. "He is playing you like a chump. No guy should get away with emotional sabotage. Am I right, Mordecai?"

Mordecai watched Daisy for a second. "Well...he shouldn't, but at the same time, this means he won't bother us. It actually works out. We can egg his car like we were planning that one time, and maybe try to get something of his so we can burn it on his lawn. Other than that, it's probably a good thing."

"Yup." Daisy pointed at him righteously. "Burn his

motherfucking shit. Burn it. No one messes with *my* girl and gets away with it."

Bria leaned against the table, looking at Mordecai again. "I half take it back. I might like you after all."

"Okay, okay." I put up my hands. "All right. Let's tone it down." I sighed and pinched the bridge of my nose. "Bria, let's go find that girl in the government building. We'll talk about this later." I leveled a finger at Daisy and then Mordecai. "Do not throw eggs—because they're expensive and we might be buying our food again soon—and don't burn his shit. Okay? Chill."

Daisy crossed her arms over her chest, her expression sullen. "What about throwing rocks? Rocks are free."

"Daisy…" I lifted my eyebrows in warning. Bria's smile burned brighter.

Daisy looked away. "Fine," she muttered.

After a nod from Mordecai indicating he understood, too, I stood. "Come on, Bria."

"Sure, yeah." She didn't get up.

I scowled down at her.

She looked pointedly at my clothes, her smile still going strong. "Did you want to get dressed first? In a pair of pants that actually fit?"

Chapter 33

ALEXIS

"**Y**OUR KIDS ARE rock stars," Bria said, driving a Range Rover. It seemed unlikely she owned two vehicles, but I didn't ask. If I got clarification, I'd be an accessory in the crime. Ignorance was probably my best defense. "Now I get why you saddled yourself with them."

"That wasn't why," I muttered, looking out the window. I felt weird. Like I should go for a swim.

No, that wasn't quite it—or at least it wasn't the whole of it. I could feel the power of the tides, the pull of the moon, and the building blocks of the air around us. I could sense Bria's power throbbing in her core, bright and strong. And above all of that, I felt the ache in my chest lessened with each passing mile. I was headed to that *somewhere* I'd wanted to go when in my room.

In my gut, I had a strong suspicion of who was at that *somewhere*.

"He's got a hold of you, huh?" Bria asked, her voice

as calm and even as ever, but with a new gravity that drew my focus.

I considered lying. Or evading. But at some point, I had to be honest, with myself more than anyone.

"Yeah. He's got a lot of faults, but…I've seen a lot of goodness, too. He kinda wears on a person."

She slowed as we reached the magical check-in gate. She used the lower-level line.

"Kieran didn't get you a pass for the other lane?" I asked.

"Yeah, he did. But if I used it, people would know I was coming and going. This way…" She handed the guy her card and smiled up at him. "That hat looks stupid on you."

He scowled as he scanned her through. He didn't comment as he handed the card back.

"This way," she continued as she started forward, "they think my fake alter ego is coming and going, and a search on it will bring up bupkis."

She handed me the card, which bore a completely different name.

"You can get fake IDs for the magical side?" I asked in a hush.

"For both sides, and everything in between, if you know the right people. I know all the right people."

"Can you get me one?"

"Sure."

"And Daisy and Mordecai?"

"Yeah, why not." She turned the corner, letting silence descend. Music played softly in the background, competing with the car's motor. "Valens wouldn't have walked away from you," she said finally. "Not from your allure, and certainly not from your power. You could really help Kieran. Fully trained, you might be able to turn the tide. I've been reading up on your power. You're no Demigod, but your abilities don't register in most of Hades's heirs. You've inherited a specialized skillset, which, paired with your power, could cut an entire army at the wick. You could be his savior." She tapped her thumbs on the steering wheel. "No Demigod I've ever heard of—hell, no extremely powerful guy with a huge ego and bigger agenda—would turn away from you. He would get two for one: someone he is clearly *very* into, plus someone who could greatly help his cause. He'd be a moron for walking away."

"He says he's trying to keep me safe."

"Yeah. And you know what..." She laughed and shook her head. "I actually believe that. In this one instance, I *actually* believe that. Somewhere, pigs have sprouted wings, and are taking to the skies. A Demigod is thinking of someone besides himself."

I tapped on the arm rest, my other little secret on the tip of my tongue.

"Go ahead and spit it out," she said, reading my

mind.

I exhaled a breath I hadn't realized I was holding. "I'm not going to let him push me away from the fight. I could be wrong, but I think he has doubts, and I get the impression that he thinks this is an impossible battle—"

"He'd be stupid not to."

"I could help," I said. "I'm learning really fast—"

"Lightning fast."

"—and I can clear a room already. Like you said, maybe I can turn the tide." I leaned my forehead against the window as we parked in the farthest available spot in the corner parking lot of the magical government building. "He is trying to do the best thing for me by keeping me away. But…" I shook my head, rolling my forehead against the glass. I pulled back. I would draw attention if I had a big red spot in the middle of my forehead. "He needs the help, and I can't in good conscience do nothing. I believe in his cause. Valens is a big dickhead. He needs his day of judgment, and I want to bring it to him. Not to mention that I want to help Kieran. This is my fight, too."

"Amen, sister. Put 'er there." She threw up her hand for a high-five. I frowned at her, but it would be unthinkable not to follow through with a high-five. "I hoped you'd say all that. Well, not about falling hard for Kieran, but about sticking with the fight. I'm excited to see what you unleash. It'll be awesome."

She got out of the SUV.

"Wait…" I nearly tumbled down after her. The SUV was a little higher than I remembered from getting in. "I didn't say I'm *falling hard* for him, just that he's gotten to me. It's different."

There were limits to my honesty.

"Sure." She put a hand up, stilling me.

The parking lot gently sloped down to the large magical government building. The bay beyond it sparkled in the sun, all the fog cleared away from this area by Valens. Anxiety unfurled in my middle, knowing the might that awaited inside those walls. There was no reason for the top tier to notice me, not yet, but that didn't mean they wouldn't. There was no telling what they'd gleaned of Kieran's plans, and who was helping with those plans.

Hell, there might've been cameras overlooking the beach. They could have my face on wanted posters. Anything was possible, and I didn't have a clue about any of it. I was walking in blind.

"Okay," I said, expelling a breath and trying to calm my nerves. "All we need to do right now is go in there, talk to the ghost, and get out. We're looking for information. We don't need to cause a scene."

Bria nodded, pointing at a little trail cutting across an undeveloped area and curving down the hill toward the building. "I'm pretty fluent about the positioning of all the cameras in this joint. There are quite a few outside, but not as many inside. Definitely not a lot in the common areas. Valens's office will be dicey, but that's what ski masks and fire alarms were made for."

"What? No—" I followed her onto the trail. My foot slipped on loose rock and dirt. "Did you hear me? We're just here to contact the ghost."

"Yeah. And then we should check out Valens's office. We found stuff in his house, so we'll probably find stuff in his office, too."

"No, Bria…" I put out my hands for balance as the trail ran down the hillside, much steeper than it looked. Only a few pieces of driftwood haphazardly cut into the dirt provided any sort of foothold. One slip and I'd be rolling ass-over-end. "If we want to break into his office, we need a better plan. We certainly can't go in the middle of the day."

"There is a lot more security at night. That's when they've had all the break-ins in the past. Don't worry, though. I got this. We won't get caught."

"That's what you said about his house!"

"And look, we didn't get caught. But seriously, it's fine. I brought supplies to start a fire."

"Wha—whoa." I flailed my arms to keep my balance as my feet slid. My toe hit a rock, tipping me toward Bria. I jogged down and clutched her shoulders to stay upright.

Somehow, she wasn't having a problem managing the path.

"No fires. No breaking in. That ghost seemed to know what our guy looks like. And while spirits aren't good with the passing of time, I can probably work with her. I can figure out a way to pinpoint how often the spirit trapper comes around."

"All of that sounds very logical," she said, and though I couldn't see or hear it, I got the distinct impression she was laughing at me.

"No fires," I reiterated.

We finally reached the wall of the building, and she turned right toward the back corner. Once there, she glanced around the side. A black orb clung to the underside of the overhang, above a nondescript gray door. A small red light blazed from its backside.

"Okay," she said quietly, watching that orb. "When that light goes off, we're going to—"

The light clicked off and she sprinted forward, pulling her backpack from her shoulder at the same time. I jolted after her, my heart jumpstarting as adrenaline dumped into my bloodstream.

She came to an abrupt stop at the door and I barely kept from slamming into her back. With economic and lightning-fast movements, she pulled out a card with a cord attached and flashed it in front of a black pad stationed on the wall. After a metallic click, she yanked the door open and dashed inside. I jetted in after her, peeling off to the side and breathing heavily. The door swung shut behind us and another click announced it was locked again.

"Okay." She stashed the card into her backpack, zipped it up, and swung it over her shoulder. "Sneak in through the back. *Check.*"

Without another word, she started off down what looked like an off-white service hallway, with a couple of large canvas bins on wheels and racks of cleaning supplies.

"Why does the camera turn on and off?" I whispered, checking behind us periodically to make sure the coast was clear.

"The feed rotates back and forth between two entrances, and the rotation moves pretty fast. Fast enough that the idiots in charge think it's secure. Okay, where are we going?"

"Either the lobby area, or the hallway near the medical area at the top of the front stairs."

"Got it. Upstairs is a little more sheltered than the lobby, so we'll hit that up first."

"No fire," I reminded.

She navigated the hallways with ease, somehow dodging in and out of people without drawing their notice. I, on the other hand, drew eyes constantly. Some people smiled, some scowled, and one had the fiercest resting bitch face I'd ever seen. I was the one staring at her, that time. She looked like she was about to kill someone. If not for her bored eyes, I would've assumed she was on a murderous rampage.

"Do I have stuff on my face?" I asked as we climbed a set of stairs I didn't recognize. The building was large and I'd only been there a couple times in my life. I had very little knowledge of it. It was a stroke of luck Bria had decided to countermand Kieran's demands and bring me here anyway.

She glanced back. "Nope. Why?"

"I seem to get…" A round-faced man glanced my way. His gaze stuck. "People keep staring at me," I whispered, trying not to look back and see if he was still staring.

He was.

"Yeah. You're dressed nicely and your hair is combed."

"So? You're dressed…" I glanced at the side of her Motley Crue T-shirt, a name I didn't recognize. Judging from the big-haired guys with guitars on the front, it was some sort of eighties band. A leather bracelet embedded with spikes wrapped around her wrist, and black cargo pants draped her legs. "Your hair is combed."

"I'm merely good looking, made weird by the punk-rock edge. You are extremely pretty. And with those new clothes, you look polished but not too polished. Fly-aways, no makeup—you're a natural beauty, and you show it off without intending to show it off. It's a real good look. If I cared, like, *at all,* I might give it a go myself. As it is, I'm cursing myself for letting you go out like that. I was so afraid you'd wear pants only useful in a flood that I forgot about the bigger picture."

It was hard to pretend the staring wasn't making my skin crawl. I'd never been noticed this much in my life. In fact, usually I wasn't noticed at all. That's what was so great about the dual-society zone—you could skirt around people with your head down and usually get through a day without anyone glancing at you at all. This was...disconcerting.

"This is the hall, right?" Bria said with a hush, slowing.

I recognized the far end, with the fashionable metal tree climbing the wall and spreading across the ceiling. There was a little alcove over where I'd first seen the girl. She'd pointed out a skulking Jack...

I hadn't even thought about having a tail. "Who was on duty this morning? At my house?"

"No one." We both drifted to the side as a few important-looking businessmen passed us. "Kieran pulled them off duty. I was confused until you showed me the note. It seems like it's true. He's gone. He's out. That means the Six are gone, too. He's leaving you to your life."

A strange rush of pain coursed through me, quickly followed by ol' trusty, my anger.

"Well, fuck that," I seethed.

"Yeah. I agree. What if you were in danger? I mean, the cameras aren't going anywhere, but still."

"What about the kids? Did he just walk away from them, too?"

She shrugged. "Don't know. Though even if he did, I have a feeling the guys aren't going to give up. Zorn definitely won't. They might keep training them on their own time. He could stop them, but..." She shrugged again. Kieran had left some gray areas.

I pushed it from my mind. Now wasn't the time to fret. I needed to focus on the situation at hand.

Two men crested the stairs when we were halfway down the hall. Both were dressed in similar expensive suits that contoured their trim bodies, and I had to bet they went to the same tailor. The fair-skinned, twenty-something man on the left had gorgeous black hair that cascaded down beside his face and over his shoulders in a shiny sheet. His conditioning game was *on point!* The guy next to him, freckle-faced and with rusty orange hair, was probably so jealous he didn't know what to do with himself. I would be.

The freckle-faced guy, in his forties, glanced my way, and his eyes sparkled with self-importance. When he looked away, it was as if his chest puffed out. The other guy must've noticed, because he straightened his shoulders and lifted his chin.

They were trying to advertise their importance. Except they looked like cheap clones of the clearly important people we'd skittered away from a few moments ago. These guys probably had mundane jobs with a teeny bit of clout, and it went straight to their heads. What douches.

Bria's hand hit my shoulder and her foot jutted out in front of me. She shoved me into the wall.

"Ow," I said without thinking, reaching for my banged-up shoulder.

The red-haired man glanced back, momentarily slowing, and a strange spark of power flared in his middle. Small specks formed in the air around him, barely discernible. In a moment, the specks were gone, and he'd picked up his pace.

"Go," Bria whispered, hurrying us along. "*Go!*"

Chapter 34

ALEXIS

I LOOKED AROUND for an attack. "What? What's happening?"

"What do you mean *what*?" She grabbed my upper arm and hustled me along, jerking me to the side at the last moment. The tree climbed the wall not far away, its metal branches spreading across the ceiling.

Freezing cold stopped my breath and passed through my body, sucking at my energy. It passed out through my back, out of sight. Bria had found the alcove I'd been looking for, and it was occupied.

"Crap, no!" I jumped like I'd sat on a cactus, then spun away, hitting the fake tree. I stumbled backward and finally fell on my butt, way out in the middle of the hallway. Thankfully, the guys who were making their way to the end, about to turn the corner, didn't look back.

She darted out, grabbed my arm again, and bodily dragged me to the side. "Get up, you donkey! I swear, I've never seen someone stick out so much in all my life.

It's like you are *trying* to grab people's attention."

"What did I do?" I asked, pushing myself up to standing.

"What did you—" Her mouth dropped open and she widened her eyes as she swung her hand back toward the way we'd come. "Oh nothing, just stared at those clearly well-paid guys with all the confidence and swagger of someone at the top of her game. It's like you were challenging them to prove themselves, you nitwit. Around here, they just might. That's a way to get noticed. We're actively trying *not* to get noticed."

I huffed out a laugh. "Those guys aren't all that well paid, trust me. Decent paychecks, fine, but they suffer from small man syndrome. They have to advertise their coolness to get noticed."

Her glower turned into a confused frown. "How do you know that?"

"It's written all over them. Those nearly matching suits, the forced bravado, the attempted swagger—give me a break."

Her head tilted, her eyes going distant as she probably replayed their images in her head.

I'd never truly appreciated how much insight I'd gained from reading people and their ghosts at the freak show until this moment. And while I could be wrong this time like any other, the ease with which I'd found Lyra's skin had given me more confidence.

"Anyway," I said, "I wasn't staring at them. I was just noticing the one guy's awesome hair. Did you see how shiny it was? I wonder what product he uses…"

"Genetics." She stepped deeper into the alcove, right next to the teen girl I'd been looking for, with her large eyes and her fingers nervously picking at her large buttons. "You're fucking with my chi, Alexis. You are really fucking with my chi, right now." She took a deep breath, collecting herself. At least now I knew one thing could mess with that breezy calm of hers. Me. "Now." She adjusted her backpack. "What are you looking for?"

I pointed at the girl beside her.

"It happened," the teen said in a squeak, who'd clearly been waiting for a chance to speak.

"What?" I asked.

"What?" Bria asked me.

"I've been taking the calendar days," the teen said. "From the desk. Today is the second. I knew you'd come back."

"You've been taking the calendar days?" I shook my head in confusion. "I don't know what that means."

"Shit." Bria braced herself like a spider, knees bent and arms out to the sides. "Is there a spirit around me right now? Why can't I—oh shit, I *do* feel her! Damn it, Alexis." She pushed away and flattened herself against the adjoining wall. "You're taking me out of my game."

"The little…" The teen made a box gesture with her

hands, ignoring Bria. "Calendar days."

Understanding dawned. "The joke-a-day calendar type things?"

"Today is the second," the teen reiterated.

Adrenaline dumped into my body. "Meaning…it happened today? The guy came today?"

A woman glanced at me as she passed, her silk dress swimming around her legs. Another highly paid somebody-or-other, only this one had a shitload of arrogance to go with it.

I curled my lips in and ripped my gaze to the ground so Bria didn't get any ideas about throwing me down the stairs or anything.

"What happened today?" Bria whispered, her gaze darting around. "The spirit trap?"

"I was downstairs," the teen said, "watching people coming and going, and it happened. The white-haired man came. I snatched a calendar day and then came up here to get away from him. He tries to slice off parts of me. He's not strong enough, but it still hurts. I hate it." She shivered and pulled her sweater tighter around her body.

"Is she talking?" Bria asked, watching my face. "What's she saying? Because if the trail is fresh, we can bag this bastard right now."

"Hurry." I gestured at the teen. "Show us the calendar days."

She nodded and pushed forward into the hall. A moment later, she disappeared.

"Dang it," I whispered, hustling toward the wide stairs that led down into the lobby.

"What happened?" Bria asked, right beside me.

"She's an Apporter. She just teleported away. She clearly forgets other people don't share her ability. She's insanely strong. Or she used to be, at any rate. She was going to be in Valens's Elite group but she got pissed off at a trainer one day and teleported him outside. She was on the fourth floor or something. High up. He went splat."

"Oh shit," Bria breathed. "I heard about that. That was like...four years ago, I think. She was extremely powerful and rare, but uncontrollable. Valens himself had to kill her. No one else could lock her down."

"That explains why he trapped her," I said quietly. "Grudge match." I walked down the stairs as quickly as would still appear natural. "I just hope she was going to the lobby desk or else we lost her."

"I get the grudge match, but why trap her here, specifically?" Bria asked in confusion. "Why not transfer her to that warehouse and stick her in a body or two? With a strong enough Necromancer, she could be made to follow orders. Her power would be useful."

"But they don't have a strong enough Necromancer. He had to scramble brains or whatever to make the spirits easier to handle, remember?"

"Still, they could've tried. Or done something else. Trapping her in the government building doesn't make sense."

When we reached the bottom of the stairs, I scanned the lobby, immediately finding the teen beside the large information desk. There was no sign of a white-haired man or anyone who would meet her description of the caster.

Bria followed my lead across the spacious floor, ducking in and out of people moving about their day.

"The teen said she was in the lobby when she saw him," I murmured. "And that today is the second calendar day she took. If it's what I suspect, then this is the second time he's been here since I last saw her. It sounds like he comes about once every two weeks. We'll see if that's exact, and if so, we can come back here in two weeks and catch him in the act."

"Or we can just steal the security footage from earlier, get his face, and get Kieran to find him," she replied.

I wasn't going to ask how she planned to get the footage. I suspected I wouldn't like the answer.

As we neared, the blue-skinned woman at the high desk glanced up with unnaturally green eyes, a welcoming smile adorning her lovely face. I had no idea what kind of magical creature she was, but wondered if she knew Valens's penchant for killing lovely things and putting them in his trophy room…

"Hello," Bria said, grabbing the edge of the desk.

I looked at the teen before shifting my gaze to Bria. "Where is it?"

Hopefully the teen would realize I was talking to her.

"That's what we're going to find out." Bria smiled at the front-desk woman. "Can you tell me where the rock wall is? I have a hankering for climbing."

The teen bent down, out of sight.

"Oops." I clucked my tongue. "I dropped my pen."

Bria frowned at me. "Well, don't expect me to get it."

"Lazy," I admonished, scooting around her. "It was on your side."

"I'm a climber, not a crawler." Bria winked at the front-desk woman.

I bent and peeked around the side of the desk, gasping when my nose nearly touched the ghost's. I pulled back a little.

The teen didn't. She held out her two thick sheets of paper. A large black date graced the bottom of each page, leaving room in the middle for an inspirational quote.

I took them out of her hand with a quiet "thanks" before standing and checking the dates. Fifteen days apart… I squinted and shook my head, trying to remember the date I was here last.

"Oh!" The receptionist frowned at the calendar pages, rising up a little to see better. "Where did you find those?"

"Ummm..." I stared at her like I had been caught holding a stolen necklace.

"They were down there," Bria said, pointing to the side of the desk. "I noticed them when I first walked up. I meant to pick them up, but..." She laughed and hit the heel of her hand off her head.

I handed them across the desk sheepishly.

"That is so strange." A look of perplexed wariness crossed her features. "I was watching that spirit guy work"—she pointed at the far end of the large front wall of glass, way to the side of the double door—"and I heard this ripping sound. I *swear* I saw the page disappear..." She laughed, a forced sound matching her uncomfortable expression. "This was the second time it happened. I mean..." She swiveled to gaze vaguely at the side of the desk. "How did it get over there? And why haven't I seen it all this time?" She wiped the pad of her finger across her forehead nervously.

"Weird," Bria said, either exceptional at hiding the adrenaline raging through her body, or missing the *huge* clue the attendant had just dropped.

"Yeah," the woman went on, blinking in confusion. She shook her head and lifted her pencil-thin, light blue eyebrows, moving on. "Honestly, they shouldn't allow that spirit guy to work in such a busy area. Who knows *what* he's dragging out of the depths, know what I mean? Both times this happened, he was here."

"Yeah, that's not right," Bria commiserated, grimacing. "You have to watch him work?"

The woman waved the thought away. "He's over in the corner, so it's not that big of a deal. And actually, the weird dance he does is kind of neat. It reminds me of those dances the Native Americans do." She grinned sheepishly. "Or maybe that's just because his hair reminds me of this Native American guy I dated once. You know…" She made a flowing gestured down the side of her head. "That really pretty long black hair?" Her lips curled. "That air elemental with him gives me the creeps, though." She shivered. "He tried to hit on me once at the solstice party, and no-thank-you."

"Wait," I said, holding up my hand. My heart thudded in my chest. The teen had seen a man with long white hair, but if she'd only glimpsed the spirit trapper while he was using magic, she'd probably seen him in the spirit plane, where the colors were neon, like negative images. That hadn't even occurred to me!

"I think we just saw those guys." Bria turned to me with excited eyes but an inquisitive expression. "Didn't the arrogant guy we just saw have long dark hair?" She put her hand up to her chest. "He was with that gangly ginger."

"Yes! That's him. He's gangly, right? And such a jerk. I mean, please, I have fae blood. Do you really think I need to lower myself for an air elemental that can only get a job with a spirit person? No." The woman smiled at someone passing by, easily masking her haughty tone. Clearly my freak show training wasn't a catch-all, because I had not seen any of this coming. "They just finished up not that long ago. They have to go to the back of the building to get the other half done, whatever that means. All I know is, good riddance. I wish they'd just stay back there all the time. I mean, we have guests coming through here."

"How often do they come?" I asked.

Bria shoved me and stepped in my path. "I know, right? How often do you need to deal with that?" she asked the woman. Clearly, I was way too blunt in my approach. Subtly, that was the key.

"Every two weeks about." She plastered on a welcoming smile, perking up as a flustered older woman with a large knit purse approached the desk. She looked back at us. "Oh, right, you want the rock wall. Well, you just go—"

I stepped away, my mind racing. They were here. Right now. Two of them. We could go after them and…

And what? They were Valens's guys and employed by the magical government. We were rogue rebels who needed to stay under the radar. If anyone saw us, we would be the ones apprehended, not them. In a building full of professionals, a couple of oddly dressed girls attempting to hog-tie a couple of suave guys in suits would certainly get noticed.

"Let's make that appointment before we hit the rock wall," Bria said, grabbing my arm and jerking me away. Halfway through the lobby, she said, "Get a grip, would you?

"What's the plan?" I asked, ignoring her. My legs and arms trembled and anxiety squeezed my chest.

"We know what they look like," she said quietly, climbing the stairs we'd just come down. "All we have to do is find them."

"Yes. But *then what*?"

"What do you mean?" She pulled me into the alcove again, blasting a hard scowl at a woman looking our way. The woman ripped her notice to the ground and quickened her pace.

Oh yeah. We'd get noticed.

I said as much.

Bria slipped her backpack off of her shoulders and dropped into a crouch, ignoring me. She shoved her hand down into the bag. "A little stalking and then springing up unexpectedly will work perfectly for those clowns."

The teen appeared right next to Bria, her eyes staring solemnly at us.

"Why is Valens keeping you here?" I asked her, shifting from foot to foot as my adrenaline surged uncomfortably. "Did they ever try to move you?"

"We need a code word for when you start randomly talking to a ghost," Bria mumbled. "Did they ever try to shove you into a different skin?" she asked, pulling a small shoe box out of her pack.

The teen picked at her button, her gaze shifting down to Bria. "Twice. I hated it. It felt weird."

I relayed what she said.

"I can imagine," Bria said, setting the box down and digging into her bag again. "Then what happened?"

"It was like trying on gloves that didn't fit," the teen said. "They felt slimy. I tried to push away, but I kept getting forced back in, so I dropped a chair on them and left."

After I relayed the information, Bria paused with a candle in her hand. "She left? How?"

The teen shrugged. "Teleported to the other side of the building. When they came for me, I just teleported again. Finally, they stopped looking."

Bria braced her forearms on her knees after I'd relayed the girl's answer. "Huh. They clearly didn't have someone strong enough to control the soul." She tilted her head and pulled back the lid on the shoe box. "Stands to reason, I guess. They said she was a strong class five. Still, moving something as big as a chair in the afterlife?" She lifted her eyebrows and pulled out something furry. "That's intense. No wonder Valens wants her trapped here. He probably wants to keep her in the rafters in case he can scrounge up someone strong enough to use her." Bria glanced up at me. "Like you."

I recoiled. "Ew. I wouldn't want to force a soul to do something like that."

"How do you think you'll ever make money?" Bria gently pulled out another furry thing and set it next to the first.

"Not like that," I mumbled. I squinted through the low light of the small alcove, trying to make out the shapes she was lining up on the ground. Bria added a third before closing the box and putting it away. "What are those?"

She glanced at the people walking by in the hall. "Rats. And we have to do this somewhere more private."

"Rats?" I took a step away. The teen's eyes widened and she blinked out of sight.

Bria looked up in confusion. "What's the matter? They're dead."

"What are you doing with dead rats in your backpack?" I asked, trying to keep my voice down but having a hard time of it.

"To seek so that I can destroy. I just need to animate them, set them on the trail, and hopefully they'll find our guys before they leave the building. I have a couple standby souls who love scurrying around in these little bodies. I just let them have at it until the bodies decay out from under them. Least I can do, right?"

I took another step back as she collected the bodies and stood, looking down the hall. "Let's find a bathroom, and then let's find our guys. We'll get them today, I know it."

I had no doubt she was right. My problem was, what would we do when we did get them? And how would we keep from setting Valens on our trail?

Chapter 35

KIERAN

KIERAN LEANED HIS elbows against his desk, the middle of his chest throbbing. The strange ache he'd felt since leaving Alexis's house had intensified until about an hour ago, when it had slowly but steadily diminished into nothing but a soft hum. That was when the other feelings had begun. Inexplicable anxiety, random uncertainty, bouts of excitement, and now, intense worry.

He scratched at the center of his chest, knowing the feelings had to do with Alexis in some way. Knowing she'd formed a sort of connection between them, and now he was getting a smattering of her emotions. He had a vaguely similar situation with his Six, whose intense emotions he could occasionally feel, but while he could suppress his awareness of the Six, he couldn't seem to do so with Alexis. Every surge of emotion caught his attention. Every degree of rising or falling intensity jogged him out of his thoughts.

He looked out of his window of his office at the blue

of the bay, one of the better views in the building. The feeling of worry intensified before another emotion took over. Something like fright and disgust mixed together.

Alexis had left her house earlier with Bria. The guys had seen it on the camera and notified him. Judging by the GPS tracker, the BMW had been left behind. That meant Bria had driven, except Zorn had verified that Bria's car had also been left behind...in a random neighborhood.

Bria only stole cars when she didn't want to be tracked. When she was doing dangerous work that might have repercussions.

He blew out a breath. *Why* had he pulled the detail off of Alexis's house?

But he knew why. He trusted her with every fiber of his being. He couldn't help it. When she'd looked at him with those big brown eyes and agreed to give up the investigation, he'd bought it. He'd forced himself to tear her presence from his life, believing that she'd keep herself hidden. Keep herself safe.

And maybe she'd meant it in the moment. Maybe she hadn't lied. But clearly, Alexis Price could not be trusted to stay out of the action. And now he knew.

His phone vibrated against the desk. Zorn's name came up. *The girl knows where Alexis has gone but won't say. Should I force it out of her?*

The girl was Daisy.

He texted back. *Ask Mordecai. Tell him that Alexis might be in danger.*

Mordecai wouldn't play games.

A rush of shimmering air magic flew past the window. Like a big blanket, it shifted as it settled, attaching to the walls.

He looked away and returned to his computer. Valens did a fairly useless territory marking every couple of weeks or so, probably intending to prove that he had the staff and resources to "protect" the entire building. No easy feat, sure, but what was the point? It didn't stop anyone from entering, and it didn't harden into a forcefield of any kind. It was just *there,* only visible to a select few and hardly noticeable at that. Unless it was fresh, he couldn't even see or feel it.

When Kieran had first noticed it, he'd thought Valens was making a statement to him personally, but it had apparently been going on for six years or more. His father was eccentric. There was no two ways about it.

A strange buzz washed over his skin, making him pause. It only lasted a fraction of a second before sliding away, but it was strange enough that he glanced back out the window. Something disrupted the familiar currents of the air magic—strange colors and odd blotches, woven into it. The air drape stilled and, because of that, mostly disappeared.

A burst of feeling unfurled in his middle, the actual emotion unintelligible, but the strength of it undeniable. He paused, waiting for more, when his phone vibrated against his desk.

Zorn: *She's in the magical government building.*

Kieran stood in a rush, and like rusty hinges given grease, his thoughts started to collect. Slowly at first, laboriously, but then in a rush.

She'd talked to a spirit here. It was here she'd first learned about what Valens was doing.

She had returned to the source, seeking more information.

He turned his head slowly, directing his gaze out the window.

Alexis had alluded to there being a spirit trap over the building.

Over the whole building.

In a daze, he crossed to the window, and slowly put out his hand. The buzzing he'd felt a moment ago ran across his skin like ants. Air magic didn't usually elicit that effect, and then there were those strange colors and patches...

He'd never seen the patches before today, or felt the buzzing.

He'd never been able to see ghosts before today, either. But he'd seen three in the building on his way to his office. Two old people and a teenager picking at a sweater button.

Tingles spread through his body.

The answer had been drifting by his window every couple weeks.

The air drape wasn't Valens's way of marking his territory. Nor had it been put there as a warning. It somehow carried the magic of a Ghost Whisperer, or some other spirit magic, creating a prison for the spirits inside.

Like flicking on a light in the pitch dark, suddenly he could *see*.

Kieran remembered something that happened soon after he set up an office in this building. One of Valens's Elite had been murdered. A crime of passion, people had thought, pinpointing a scorned lover. The clues had overwhelmingly pointed to the lover's guilt. The case was closed in no time.

But a few days later, miraculously, the suspected murderer had been released. In his place, they arrested a mundane looking guy who had previously lived in a rental on the periphery of town, minding his own business, with a temp admin job in the magical government building. He'd already given his notice, and was ready to head out of town.

Unbeknownst to literally everyone, he was a spy.

Under the pressure of Kieran's father, the spy had cracked, spilling all of his secrets.

The guy had knocked off dozens of high-profile professionals in his day. He was responsible for toppling the magistrate of Scotland, for forcing the Demigod of Paris to renege on an agreement, and for exposing the illegal trade of magical beasts between the South Africans and Russians.

There had been virtually no clues. No evidence to lead Valens and his team to make that arrest. It wasn't the first time Valens had pulled off a seemingly impossible coup, sending the world a message: I'm immune to even the best. Nothing can take me down.

Kieran shook his head slowly, incredulous, as he fitted the pieces together.

Valens always got his mark because he never lost a spirit to the Line and the protections of whatever lay beyond it. The dead became their own eyewitnesses. Before the shock and memories from the traumatic event could evaporate, the brain's natural coping mechanism, his lackeys would move the spirit of the murdered person into another body so they could recount their own murder.

Genius.

Alexis had helped Kieran uncover another chink in his father's chainmail: his father didn't know the unknowable at all. He wasn't any more insightful than any other expertly trained and experienced Demigod…he just knew how to collect information from the dead. And soon, when Kieran found the originator of the spirit trap, he'd wipe out his father's neat little trick.

Reality seeped back in. The gravity of the situation blared through the quiet room.

The spirit trap had just been set. That meant the creator—or creators, since clearly an air elemental had laid the foundation—were on the premises. He'd felt it, which meant Alexis must've felt it, too.

Bria never ran from a fight. Never. Alexis had courage in spades, and wouldn't leave a comrade behind.

Those women would go after the magical workers responsible for the spirit trap. Maybe they *were* already going after them. He knew it as well as he knew his own name. The problem was, if that air elemental was in any way trained—and he had to assume that was the case since draping a building this size was no easy feat—the ladies would be outgunned. Alexis didn't know how to fight with her magic, and Bria could only take on an air elemental in close combat. Put any space between them, and that elemental would toss her like a tumbleweed.

He jogged toward the door. If he didn't find one of the parties before they found each other, the ladies might not come out of the altercation alive.

Chapter 36

ALEXIS

"WE GOT 'EM!" Bria shooed the large, wire-tailed rat in front of her, grinning from ear to ear. "I told you these guys were good."

My heart pounded and blood rhythmically *thrushed* in my ears. I hurried behind Bria across a well-appointed hall and through swinging doors with scrapes on the sides. The lavish furnishings fell away, replaced by off-white walls lined with metal racks. We darted to the right down a service hall, able to move faster now that well to-do people weren't paying attention.

Bria took another turn, following her rat. Squeaking rose up from a crack I hadn't noticed, and a different rat darted out.

I jumped to the side as it dashed between my feet and up to its friend. "Gross!"

"It's just a ghost-powered furry creature, Alexis, honestly." Bria slowed with the rats, reaching another swinging door, this one a little off-kilter and in need of repair. She stopped beside it and pushed the door a little, peeking out. "Looks like they're heading for the side exit, closest to the East parking lot. Good. They aren't checking in with Valens."

"If they've been doing this for a while, there would be no reason to." I pushed up against her to peer out, then flinched back when a furry body ran over my foot. "These things better not have diseases."

"Nah. The diseases die with the rodent." She stiffened. "Actually, I don't know if that's true. I should probably look into that. Sometimes they get ornery and bite."

"You could've just called them back and let them stay as spirits. Then we could've actually spoken to them."

"*You* could've spoken to them. I would've just stood around with my thumb up my butt, hoping you'd fill me in. Okay." She pushed through the door. "Come on."

My phone vibrated in my pocket, but Bria put on the jets just then, her legs churning as she weaved in and out of people meandering through the hall, so I couldn't do much more than brush my hand against the fabric containing it. The smell of food and clank of dishes became more pronounced as we reached a large opening. A cafeteria. People idled outside, chatting or holding their snacks or lunches, no one glancing at us as we passed. Vending machines with drinks and sugary sweets hugged the wall opposite us, and a large area covered in circular tables spanned out on the other side.

Bria took a right, away from the cafeteria, as someone screamed behind us. Another person yelled. The third rat joined us, catching up with the other two leading the way.

My phone vibrated again, shaking against my thigh. Bria slowed, approaching another corner, before resuming an unassuming stroll. I followed her lead, immediately recognizing the men from earlier, side-by-side with their nice suits, as we turned. If they had any friends in the building, they clearly hadn't stopped to talk.

"Okay. We're just going to chat like girlfriends and follow their lead," Bria murmured, smiling for show. A double door waited at the end of the corridor. "This entrance has a camera that covers the doorway, but nothing beyond that for about twenty feet. After that, a camera looks out at the first couple rows of cars, where the important people have their spaces reserved. Hopefully you're right and these guys aren't important. After that, no cameras."

"We can't very well hog-tie them in the middle of the parking lot," I said, looking at the ground because I didn't know where else to look.

"I have a roomy trunk. It'll be great."

The black-haired guy pushed the door open, the

metal bar clinking as it compressed. Light sliced through the doorway. The red-haired guy waited for his friend to exit, turning to glance back at us as he did. His gaze slid by Bria, touched me, and then stuck.

"Damn you and that face," Bria murmured before turning my way and chuckling a little. She raised her voice. "I actually hate roast duck. It's super greasy."

"I've never had it," I said honestly, directing my gaze at the wall.

But why would I look at the wall? Surely that would seem odd.

I shifted my gaze to my feet as the light at the end of the corridor dimmed. The door thunked closed.

"Hurry, hurry, hurry." Bria jogged to the end before stalling for a moment, glancing down at the rats waiting by her side. "Stall them, if you can," she said to them. Then she looked up at me and said, "Another reason for bodies. Other people can see them."

"Like the people in a cafeteria, yeah," I muttered.

She pushed the door wide and let me go first before following, shielding her hand against the light. Well-tended bushes, budding with yellow flowers, lined the paved sidewalk leading up a gentle slope to the corner of the parking lot. The guys angled to the side, passing the first row of expensive vehicles.

"Keep going, you rat bastards," she said, watching them. She wasn't talking about the ghost-powered furry creatures. "Go to the back. Be less important than you look."

I glanced back at the windows, climbing high and sparkling in the sun. Many of the blinds were open, anyone at all able to look down at us.

"This is a bad idea," I murmured. "Too many potential witnesses." The parking lot stretched out to the side and then wrapped around the building to the front. We'd parked on the way other side. That would be much too far to drag a couple of tied-up bodies, and hanging out between cars with them while waiting for the (probably stolen) SUV to be brought around was too risky.

"No." I took out my phone and glanced at the screen. Two missed calls from Kieran, and a text. I ignored it for the moment, my mind working. "Let's not do this here. Let's follow them. We can get more info. They only spent half a day here, and we've already discovered a few of Valens's spirit traps. Let's hope they head to another of those. Or hell, a place to get a bite to eat. Anywhere but here."

Bria huffed as the red-headed guy glanced back again, spying us for the second time—or the third, if he remembered us from upstairs. He slowed, narrowly missing the rat darting out from the car right behind him.

"You're right," she said, grabbing my arm and stopping me. She put up her hand to block the sun as she looked around in confusion. "This is the wrong spot," she said loudly, turning in a circle.

Another rat practically ran over the feet of the black-haired man. He jumped back with a start, drawing the attention of the red-headed guy.

"Go, go," Bria said, whipping me around and back toward the building. "Wait, *shit*." She stiffened as she stared at the black keypad next to the door. "They'd catch me breaking in. Bugger." She yanked me toward the wall and started walking. "Hurry up. *Don't look*."

I ripped my gaze away from the two guys dancing around, the rats running at their feet, but not before the guy with the black hair looked directly at us, his eyes narrowed suspiciously. I did a double-take as the rat at his feet slowed, then stopped, before convulsing. Another went into convulsions right behind it.

"Can a Necromancer rip the soul out of another Necromancer's cadaver?" I asked, my voice tight.

"Sure, if they're set up for it."

"Like with incense and stuff?"

"Yeah. Why?"

"What if they don't have that stuff?" I asked, desperately trying not to look back. I could see their shapes out of the corner of my eye. Whatever they suspected, they weren't following us. Not yet.

"If it's a human cadaver, and if they were class—"

"What if it's a fucking rat, Bria? Would that guy know those rats aren't really rats?"

Her head jerked left and I stupidly followed, my lips tight and my hand gripping her arm. I looked like anything but a carefree woman headed to lunch with her friend, and I knew it.

"Shit." She swung her head back to face front. "That's unfortunate."

"Why? What?"

She picked up the pace. "Something like a rat is much easier, yes. But you have to be accustomed to a critter to know where to find its soul. Most people only focus on humans and large animals. The caverns for their souls are bigger, thus easier to find and work with. Very few know how to use rats and the like."

"He knows about rats?"

"Yeah. It means he's savvy. Like me. Let's hope he's also not unpredictable like me."

I grimaced as we reached the corner of the building and cut through the landscaping back to the parking lot. The guys stood at a cross-over type SUV, the vehicle not matching their suits.

"They dress up for their job," I murmured, cutting right down the center of the row of cars. "Or maybe they just dress up to come here."

"Hurry. Jog."

My worn-in dress flats held me back, but my long

legs gave me an edge. I kept up with her easily, rushing around the large building and to our SUV way in the corner, which still had not been found by the cops. She quickly sat into the driver's seat and used the push-start ignition. That should've meant she had a key, but I still didn't ask about the nature of the situation.

"Let's hope those bastards aren't already—Got 'em." She pulled out of the space as the blue crossover pulled out of the parking lot.

She wasn't far behind, rolling through the lot way too fast and skidding her tires against the street.

"Don't worry, Lexi. I've tailed a couple bad guys in my day."

She did everything like I'd seen in the movies: stayed a few cars back, didn't change lanes hastily, and didn't follow their movements exactly. If they knew we were tailing them, they didn't show it.

I yanked the phone out of my pocket, reading Kieran's text. *Where are you?*

I debated not answering as I caught sight of the crossover turning three cars up. But soon he'd know what I was doing, anyway. Bria wasn't about to let this go. We'd catch these guys, and we'd subdue them until Kieran showed up. He'd eventually figure out I'd lied about dropping the case.

What could he do to me?

Scenes of torture rolled through my head.

What *would* he do to me, I amended.

The memory of his hands on my body and his lips between my legs boiled my blood.

I took a deep breath and unlocked my screen. I could handle that.

"I'll be damned," Bria whispered before I could type the first word.

The cars thinned out until it was just them and us driving down a lonely road, headed to a neighborhood forgotten by everyone except the ghost hunters and thrill seekers. We were headed to the ghost neighborhood and John.

"They use the air to carry the spirit magic," Bria said, turning off the road. "Air can drape over things. Somehow, it can hold the spirit magic in place."

"And a combination of them must be able to slice through the air, because it's cutting into the spirits in that house."

"Yes. It's genius, when you think about it. I've never heard of pairing an Air Elemental up with spirit magic. Someone was thinking outside the box. It's almost like they found a way to duplicate your magic."

"It's more effective than my magic," I said as the SUV crawled toward the neighborhood, entering it from the opposite direction this time. The two guys were likely to take the more direct route.

She pulled in and parked, out of sight from the

main house with the trapped spirits at the other end of the street. "No, it's not," she said. "Which you'd know if you knew anything."

"Totally," I said dryly, climbing from the car. I absently rubbed at my chest. The ache had returned, and it momentarily pulled my focus.

The brittle weeds crunched as Bria trekked across the forgotten yard of an empty house. She flattened against the buzzing wood.

"I can't feel any souls. Can you?" she asked as she peered around the side of the house.

I shook my head, my phone still clutched in my hand. "No."

"Their car is parked at the other end, right outside the house of horrors."

"Can you see them?"

She ducked and slipped around the side of the house, scooting along behind the pillars of the porch before jogging across the front of the yard and ducking behind the next house over. I followed her lead, now able to see for myself.

From this distance, I couldn't tell if anyone was in the car, but no one lingered outside. The door to the haunted house looked like it was open, but I couldn't be sure.

"They wouldn't need to go inside, would they?" I asked quietly.

"They went inside of the government building, so I don't know. Let's get as close as we can and see how they do it. We'll grab them on the way out."

My adrenaline started pumping again as I followed her from house to house. Each dash left us completely visible, but no movement caught my eye from the house at the end. Three-quarters of the way down we slowed. I could clearly see the door of the last house now, wide open. John, the man I'd spoken to before, waited in the doorway, looking out at the car parked in front.

"Wait," I said, grabbing Bria's arm. "Something isn't right."

John seemed like a guy who needed to be in the action. For him to be staring out at the car meant there was no one inside with him.

I squinted at the car's windows. Sun shimmered, the light waxy against the pane of glass. Still nothing moved within, and I couldn't make out any shapes.

My phone vibrated in my hand as a presence niggled at my awareness. Subtle but building, the soft strength of a soul moved somewhere on the other side of the street, one house down. A moment later, another joined it.

"They're there," I whispered, pointing.

Bria's brow furrowed and she shook her head. "I don't feel anything."

"Trust me. They're there. They must know we're

here—" I cut off at the *creakkkk* of the wooden gate in the fence of the house where I'd sensed the souls. It drifted open and two stiff shapes stepped out, their movements jerky.

I sucked in a breath, my eyes widening at what I was seeing.

The first was a lanky man with stained and hole-ridden clothes. A flap of scalp hung down the side of his head and only one patch of hair adorned the otherwise bare head. His stringy arms hung limp at his sides with one of his fingers missing, and his knees knocked whenever he moved, their ligaments or whatever held them straight clearly lacking.

The woman behind was just as messed up, with half her jaw depressed, an eye missing, and tattered and ripped clothes hanging from her skeletal body. If they were alive, they were on their death bed.

"Clearly they don't like being followed," Bria said, unslinging her backpack. "They're raising an army of the dead to take us out."

Chapter 37

ALEXIS

"WHAT THE HELL does that mean?" I asked, clutching my chest. My legs quivered from the primal instinct to run away from something so clearly unnatural as the creatures emerging from the backyard.

"What do you think it means?" Bria ripped out her necromancy materials, her movements rushed and her hands shaking. "He's got cadavers, he's got souls aplenty in that house, and he's clearly got a *lot* of Red Bull. I gotta tear those fuckers down before they get control of their new digs."

"You mean they're not going to stay like that?"

She organized her materials for ease of use. "Remember the rats?"

"Those were new bodies, though."

"Doesn't matter. As soon as the soul learns to pull the strings, things speed up. These souls can't be that strong, since I didn't feel them, but that doesn't mean worse aren't coming. Lord only knows what magic they have."

Their magic throbbed in their middles, much less potent than that of the guy who'd put them there.

"No, they aren't powerful," I said, opening and closing my hands, feeling the souls pulse in the bodies.

"The power level of the magic and the soul are sometimes two different things, especially if the Necromancer used non-magical cadavers."

"I know. Neither the souls nor their magic are very powerful. Way less than the guys we're tailing, who are less powerful than us."

She didn't stop in her harried preparation, but her head tilted. "How do you know that?"

"I did something to Kieran last night and now I just know." Two more souls popped up on my radar, farther down the road, creeping toward us. After another moment, another presence flared to life. "What can I do?"

"You can rip the souls out of those bodies. That'd be really helpful." Bria slid her thumb across the top of a lighter. It sparked before the flame flickered to life. "Barring that, just keep them off me, if you can."

Memories of the night before with Kieran rolled through my head. I remembered seeping into his chest and stroking his soul. He'd let me do it, I was pretty sure, but he was also a live Demigod with protections in place to keep his soul put. These suckers were just hosts for a bunch of poor sods who should've been well past the Line by now.

"Okay," I said, stalking into the street. Another soul flared to life down the way, stronger than the one before it. "Definitely Red Bull," I said, watching the animated dead people learn to walk. They were already much smoother, picking it up quickly. "I need to start grabbing these souls."

I closed my eyes and felt through the closest body, finding the squishy middle easily. I dug down, ready for the hard plate protecting the soul. Instead, I punched through into nothing, and found myself immersed in someone else's junk.

"Ah crap," I said as the soul latched on and started crawling up the link I'd just created. "Ew. Get off."

I yanked back, my version of flinching away. Without meaning to, I dragged the soul with me.

A man materialized on the edge of the lawn, his eyes rounded and a surprised look on his face. Behind him, the body crashed down to the ground, lifeless without its pilot.

"Wow. That happened," I said in a rush of breath, energy rippling through my body. "Do you...ah..." I looked at the man, feeling another soul flare into the world. The magical worker was a machine. That, or it was super easy to grab a soul waiting in the world of the living and stuff it into a ready body. It was certainly easy to pull one out. "Do you want me to put you across the Line...or..."

"Did you do it?" Bria asked, surprised. Smoke tendrils curled around her into the air.

The spirit man looked around, confused. The reanimated dead woman cracked her neck and stepped off of the curb. She was getting ready to charge me.

"Uh-oh." I punched my theoretical fist through her middle, hitting that cavernous area with next to no effort and snatching the trespasser. Just like the first soul, this one tried to crawl along the connection.

The heebie-jeebies washed over me. It was like I'd swatted a spider, only for it to come sailing toward me on spider silk. I yanked away, super grossed out and not wanting that thing touching me. Energy pumped into my body and the spirit went flying, smacking the ground and rolling like a real person might've.

I cracked a smile. I couldn't help it. That was kind of badass.

"Okay. That part's easy," I said to Bria, letting go of the woman. "What should I do with them now?"

"Are you serious?" Bria asked, crouched over her setup with her hands up and out. A strange, wide-brimmed yellow hat adorned her platinum blonde head. "Did you seriously just rip the souls out of those bodies? Just like that?"

More reanimated dead people staggered into a front

yard down the street, learning their new bodies, and learning them quickly.

"Yeah," I said, turning toward them. "When a person dies, clearly the vault holding the soul breaks open to let the soul free. I wonder if it can be put back in place..." My brain started to wander, thinking through how someone might Duct tape that sucker in there so it wasn't so easy to yank out.

"Focus," Bria said, not having risen. "Can you do it again? Should I put this stuff away?"

"Yes, yes." I waved at her to hurry up. "Like I was saying, without that vault, the soul is just hanging out in there, desperate for a way to escape."

Bria stared at me for a moment, hands still out to her sides. Like a dam bursting, she was suddenly all action, bending to her incense and snuffing them out.

"Great. Head off those others," she said, grabbing the candle. Hot green wax spilled across her hand and she sucked a breath through her teeth. "I'll be there in a minute."

"But what about—"

"I do not care what you do with the souls, Alexis," she said, throwing blunted incense into her pack. "Just do it fast. We have to get to that air elemental before he knows we're coming. He's the danger now."

I nodded and turned, just in time to hear, *"Watch out,"* from one of the newly released souls.

A rotting body, the sex hard to tell, took a running leap, flinging itself at me. Discolored teeth gnashed in a face screwed up in rage.

I threw up my hands to protect myself as the body slammed into me, driving me back. My butt hit the ground first, but I was already moving, grappling with the reaching hands. I pushed the body off me as I grabbed the soul, easily ripping it out and throwing it to the side.

Two more souls, moving fast, caught my attention as a jagged point from the bone in a finger from the falling body scraped across my skin.

"You better not have the plague," I said through gritted teeth, grabbing the souls from the other bodies as they reached me.

Once again, the spirits tried to crawl up my connection. My survival instinct kicked in, and I kept the souls put, knowing the enemy Necromancer was controlling them somehow. Could I take over? I probed around with my magic until I found a strange pulse of power, foreign to the souls and more alive than the bodies. Focusing hard, I tried to inject my own agenda into that spot while shoving my hand against a gnashing face. These things were acting like zombies. I didn't want to go down that road.

The souls crawled along my connection again, trying to escape the bodies, and that weird spot of magic stayed strong, ignoring my advances. I pushed harder, trying to get the upper hand. Trying to take over.

"What the hell are you doing?"

Suddenly the body above me flew to the side. The soul came away in my grasp and a startled man in his thirties looked down on me. Bria jumped over me, running for the body she'd just kicked away, but slowed when she saw it was no longer moving.

"Stop screwing around," she yelled.

"I was trying to control them." I pulled out the souls and let them go immediately before sending out a shock wave of banishment, throwing everybody at the Line.

"Thank youuuuu," someone yelled as they disappeared. Wind from the Line blew down over me, ruffling my soul.

"No, no, no, cut that out," Bria said, clutching her chest.

"Sorry!" I hopped up and energy surged through me. "I think I get energy from taking those souls out," I said as she slung her backpack over her shoulder.

"Probably. Who knows. You're a damn freak of nature. Hurry, let's go."

She took off at a fast jog, running toward the house of horrors. I tried to keep up, but my shoes kept trying to slip off, hindering my progress. She dodged to the side and kicked open the aging gate. Wood splintered and a hinge broke. She kicked it again before battering her way through.

Hobbling now, I stepped over the curb and ran onto the weeds and dirt of the front yard, angling for that fence.

"There's two of them," John yelled from the house, confirming what Bria had already sensed. "They went around back."

My shoe flipped off and my heel crashed down onto a rock. I cried out and staggered to the side, pain throbbing up through my ankle and into my calf.

"Mother trucker..." I slipped the shoe back on and hurried forward as a surge of debris flew through the air. I ducked down as I went through the fence, but the strange, shimmering debris flew high over the house, untroubled by gravity.

Another soul flared to life as I limped down the side yard, picking my footing a little more carefully.

"Alexis," I heard, Bria's call ending in a grunt.

More debris, transparent and sparkling, sailed up through the air at the end of the house. I followed the fence, which wrapped around the back, ending in some badly leaning tattered boards.

A vicious howl rent the air as I stepped around the side of the house. The man with the black hair sat cross-legged amid curling smoke and flickering candles, his face screwed up in intense focus and his hands resting on his knees. A body shook and trembled as it straightened up from the other two dead people, their faces slack and eyes staring at nothing. The animated dead body turned its head up to the sky and let out another howl.

On the other side of the yard Bria jabbed at the red-headed guy and clipped him on the chin. He lifted his hands and I could feel magic build before Bria struck flesh again, dragging a heavy boot across his thigh.

He staggered but didn't fall and shook his head. She was after him again, but I had already shifted my focus back to the black-haired Necromancer. His eyes flickered open and his face, flush with fatigue, turned toward me slowly. The animated body shook next to him before facing me.

"You've left your materials behind," the Necromancer said in a taunting voice. "Game over."

"You got me all wrong, bub," I said as the jacked up, reanimated body lurched toward me, a thick guy with a face that looked like it was melting off.

For effect, I held out my hand with my fingers open as I reached into the chest of the (currently) slowly moving body. I squeezed my fingers into a fist, grabbing the soul. The body shook and the soul skittered up my connection.

"Ew," I said, yanking my hand out and shaking it off. I hated that feeling.

The soul tumbled to the side, a look of shock replacing a disgruntled expression. The jacked-up body collapsed into a pile of gross.

"What—" The black-haired man's eyes widened and he jolted backward. He looked down at the body in utter disbelief.

"Yeah. Game *on*." I ran at him and planted one foot before pulling back the other. My shoe flew off, but I didn't let that stop me. I kicked forward, my foot hitting his face like it was a soccer ball.

He grunted. Spit flew to the side. Lights out.

He collapsed like his previously animated bodies.

A blast of air pulled my focus.

Bria staggered back in the sudden gale, her arms windmilling to keep her balance. The red-haired man kicked out with perfect form. The bottom of his shoe sole hit Bria mid-chest. She grunted and bent as he seamlessly transitioned into a round-house kick.

"No!" I said, too far away to help.

His foot hit her square in the face.

Crack.

She didn't even stagger backward. She just dropped, knocked unconscious.

I didn't have time to call out. The red-haired guy shoved his fists through the air and a gale burst forth, slamming into me and picking me up off my feet. I flew, rotating ass-over-end again and again, and crashed into the ground. The dead bodies caught my fall, lifeless and weirdly squishy.

Spikes of air sparkled in a ray of sunlight as they gathered above me, lengthening like daggers. The ends gleamed and I knew they'd be as sharp as any knife. Air wrapped around me. Clumsy but effective, the hold trapped my arms to my sides.

"Good trick," I said in grunts. "Very quick way to end a fight."

I tried to fall into a trance to call the power of the Line, but the air bands around me squeezed, cutting short my breath. Panic crept in and I attempted to reach into his chest, my mind hazy, my mental efforts clumsy. He grunted as more of the strange debris rose into the air.

No, not debris. Air particles. Because of Kieran, I could see air magic now.

The lack of oxygen hazed my brain and slowed my thoughts. The air particles hovered, lengthening, turning into spikes. My heart raged. My chest struggled for air. Black blotches clouded my vision.

A dark chuckle drifted from the red-haired man. The air daggers trembled, before raining down.

Chapter 38

ALEXIS

THE GROUND RUMBLED. The spikes of air above me stopped dead, one foot away, before dissipating entirely. The bands around my body loosened and peeled back.

Kieran stalked into the yard, his magic terrible and humbling. The ground quaked now, and his power electrified the surroundings. Swirls of light danced through the air—a stark contrast to the rage masking his expression. Clouds crawled into the sky above us and heavy fog drifted in, swirling around the yard in angry black-gray swirls.

He was ready to unleash the full power of a Demi-god.

He stopped by my side, his heavy boots trampling the ground. His stormy eyes dipped, his gaze meeting mine before drifting over my body.

"Are you okay?" he asked, and his rough voice sent a thrill through me, fear from a primal sense of his extreme danger, and intense relief because he was on my side.

"Yes," I gushed, even though my lungs still burned from the near miss, I was lying in a pile of death, and was sore from head to toe. But now that he was here, yes, I was okay. More than okay.

He looked up and squared those muscular shoulders, facing the cowering redhead at the other end of the yard. Air whipped around us. Pressure shoved down from the sky, almost solid it was so powerful. Confidence and authority radiated out from his robust frame.

"You dare attack a woman under my protection?" His voice was liquid steel.

The redhead's face paled, even his freckles losing color. He sank down to his knees and threw up his hands. "I'm sorry, sir," he bleated before clasping his fingers together. "I'm sorry! I didn't know. She attacked us. I was only—"

"Enough," Kieran barked. A surge of power sliced through my chest, rattling my rib cage and jiggling my soul deep in my body.

That was my power! How the hell could he use my power when *I* couldn't even properly use it?

The redhead clutched at his chest and gagged, sinking to the ground. "What..." He gulped, clearly drowning in fear. "What was..."

Without another word, Kieran turned and bent, scooping me up and hugging me close.

"Wait...Bria!" I twisted in his arms, trying to see her. My body screamed in protest, the lumps and bruises from being flung and rolled pounding pain.

"She's alive. I can feel the strength of her magic. She'll be taken care of," Kieran said softly, leaving the redhead cowering in our wake as he carried me down the side of the house to the street. His warmth coated me and his strong arms held me tight.

I melted in his arms. I couldn't help it. My head touched down on his shoulder and I breathed in his familiar smell, salty sea foam and chocolate. Power moved within me, and our magic twisted tighter together.

"Secure them," Kieran said, and I lifted my head to see who he was talking to. Thane, Zorn, and Donovan stepped forward. "The air elemental is conscious but subdued. He won't be a problem. Bria is down."

Zorn stalked forward, his face expressionless but his eyes tight. He held out a phone as he went by, not glancing my way.

"Oh." I reached for it gingerly, noticing a bad gash on my hand. I sure hoped that wasn't from the exposed bone of that dead person. "I must've dropped it."

Thane followed Zorn, and Donovan fell in behind them. The other three of the Six stood out near the cars, their feet planted and eyes hard.

"You must've," Kieran said, slowing halfway

through the yard but not turning, still facing the street. His body stiffened. "Do spirits normally look like that?"

I blinked stupidly for a moment. "You can see spirits now?"

"Yes. Do they normally look like the people in that house?" He turned a little, indicating what he was talking about.

I was still blinking stupidly, but he shifted me enough so I could see through the door. John still stood there, looking out. Probably wondering what was going on. His face was lanced and blackened, and new gashes marred his sides. He must've sensed the weakening of the walls and tried to break out of the house with everything he had. The air infused with spirit magic had kept him at bay.

Behind him, a woman wailed in agony. She sprinted away, before sprinting back, tearing at her hair. A man wandered past, walking awkwardly and missing half of his head.

"No, they don't. Those spirits are being physically and mentally tortured. None of the other traps I've seen do this, though I might not have seen them all."

He nodded and then turned to look at John in the doorway. "Valens is responsible for keeping you here. Alexis"—he hefted me a little—"will be responsible for your freedom. Should you be willing to stay, to help take Valens down, you're welcome to."

"One day of seeing spirits and already you're enlisting them to your agenda," I murmured, grinning and not sure why. "Except they can't do much besides close a door or two, and cause a fright."

"That's why we have Bria to put them in bodies. More the merrier." He shifted away from the door, but before he could take a step, John called out, "I'll fight."

Kieran paused.

"I'll fight," someone else screamed.

"Fight!" Someone yelled.

"But you won't want everyone who applies," John said in a dry voice. "I can weed them out for you."

I huffed out a laugh as Kieran turned back to nod in approval.

Zorn jogged from the side of the house with Bria's limp body in his arms. Her head lolled against his shoulder with blood dripping down her face.

"Broken nose," Zorn said as he passed. "Unconscious but vitals are stable."

Kieran nodded, watching Zorn hurry her to a car and delicately tuck her inside.

"Do you want me to strip the spirit trap away now, or wait..." I let my voice trail away as Zorn sat into the driver's seat.

Kieran looked down at me, his gaze focusing on my lips. "Do you have the energy?"

I laughed again. "I feel like shit, but energy is one

thing I have in abundance. Every time I yank a spirit out of a body, I get a rush. If I thought about it a little harder, it would probably be gross, but…"

He nodded, giving me the go-ahead, as he said, "You've been ripping spirits out of bodies?"

I dropped my head again, feeling the buzz from the house, weaker now than just a couple days ago. The Line pulsed around me, offering limitless power for me to borrow. And then something amazing happened.

"Put me down," I said, straining away from Kieran.

Now that I looked more closely, I could just barely make out the air magic draped over the house, running along the walls and collecting at the bottom. Within it, drifting through the air currents, was the power I recognized and could now easily see, swirling and throbbing through the air.

Kieran was using some of my magic, and he'd gifted me with some of his.

Or I'd gifted him and forced a trade. Either way…

"Wash away that air, Kieran," I said. "You can see the air drape, I take it?"

"Yes," he said, turning to it more firmly. "The one at the government building disappears the day after they bolster it, but they must've made this one ten times stronger. It's still visible."

With a flick of his hand, the magic covering the house peeled away in places. Parts disintegrated, but the spirit magic kept it mostly stuck together.

"Huh," I said, eating through that spirit. With a rush, the air magic continued to disintegrate until it was gone.

"He wouldn't have been able to make a spirit trap without the air elemental," I said, feeling the pulse of the Line around me, beckoning to the newly freed spirits. "He needed a way to string all the parts together."

John looked up at the frame of the door before directing his gaze to me again. He took a purposeful step, crossing the threshold. Then another, his face grim.

"Let's get out of here before they attach themselves to us..." I murmured.

John nodded at me, then directed his words to Kieran. "I need to check on some things. To look around. Where should I report back?"

I put my hand on Kieran's arm, leaning hard. My back throbbed. I'd clearly tweaked it in my unplanned series of somersaults.

"Report back here," Kieran said, his voice smooth and authoritative. He was born to lead. "As soon as the rest of the magic dissipates, there will be plenty of places for you to stay. I'll return with instructions."

John nodded before his body vanished. Spirits poured out of the house, looking around in wonder. Gazing at me in either hostility (because their minds were gone) or devotion.

"Let's go…" I tapped Kieran's arm. "Come on, donkey. Pick me up. Let's go."

"It's a sweeter gesture when it's my idea," Kieran said dryly, doing as I said. He turned, stalking toward the cluster of vehicles haphazardly parked in the street. Instead of choosing his, he nodded at Jack, who stood in front of the Range Rover Bria had been driving earlier.

Jack gave me a sour expression before opening the back door.

"Not cool, stealing a man's ride," he murmured as Kieran gently set me inside.

"I thought you drove a BMW like mine?" I said.

"That's the work car. This is my baby. I don't appreciate when it goes missing…"

"I didn't know," I said, putting up my hands. "I swear. I suspected it was stolen, but I didn't ask in case it got called in. Ignorance is bliss."

Kieran tossed his keys to Boman before crossing around the back and getting in next to me. Jack closed my door and sat in the driver's seat.

"Are you sure you're okay?" Kieran asked me as we got underway, his voice so soft, his eyes softer. He took my hand.

"I'm sore, but I'll heal." I dropped my phone on my lap and swallowed. Might as well just get this over with. "How'd you find me?"

Kieran held my gaze for a quiet moment, before tapping the center of his chest. "When you shared your magic with me, you planted a homing device. If I think about you hard enough...I simply need to follow the ache until it quiets. And there you are."

Butterflies tickled my belly. I sucked in a deep breath, trying to still the nervous tremors. "I didn't mean to do that. I mean...I might've, but it wasn't a conscious effort. It just...happened."

He nodded, not commenting.

"I'll find a way to undo it. I'm sure I can. I just have to..."

His head was already shaking.

Silence descended on the SUV as I met his inviting gaze and held it. I felt the electricity flowing through his limbs and supercharging mine. His power, so mighty, beyond any of the classes and in a league of its own. He had more power over air than an actual air elemental. He could play the tides like a guitar, and the seas like his personal playground.

He was a Demigod, descended from one of the Power Three, and he was sitting in the back of a Range Rover, holding my hand. Holding my focus in a way no other man ever had.

Slowly, I let myself feel the connection between us, thick and solid, attaching the middle of my person to the middle of his. Attaching my soul...to his. Our souls oozed toward each other and met in the middle, where our magic mingled and flowered. I didn't have the power he did, but I could use some of his magic, and he mine.

Except he used mine a lot better than I did.

"I choked back there," I admitted, a tiny flower of fear budding within me. "I was in the thick of it, and I couldn't save myself."

"Didn't you rip souls out of bodies?" he asked quietly.

"Yeah, but they were dead people's bodies. The souls weren't attached. That was easy."

He tapped the center of his chest, indicating what I'd done to his soul.

"Yes, okay, but you were open to that," I said, my face heating. "That's different. And I'll undo it, I promise. Somehow…"

"You have had less than a week of training, Lexi." He traced my jaw with his thumb. "You barely know your magic, you barely know the world of magic, and you don't at all know how magical people fight. And yet, you littered the streets with bodies and took down a class-four Necromancer who showed some exceptional insight and experience. You did more than anyone could possibly have hoped."

I let out a deep breath and grimaced. "Then you're not mad at me?"

A grin tickled his full, kissable lips. "I'm livid. You lied to me, ignored my calls, put yourself into danger, and nearly got yourself killed. If I hadn't figured out how to track you, you'd be dead."

My heart amped up and a cold sweat popped out on my forehead. With a speech like that, his gorgeous smirk confused matters.

"But you look too pathetic to punish," he said finally. "It'll have to wait."

Chapter 39

ALEXIS

"WHAT'S UP, INVALID?" Daisy closed the door and stopped in the entryway, her hands braced on her hips and dirt and grime marring her light blue shirt.

I sat up on the couch, only grimacing a little. Nearly a week had passed since that air elemental had made a plastic bag out of me and rolled me across the yard, and still I had aches and pains. I felt a lot older than my twenty-five years, and in desperate need of some physical fitness.

Thankfully for me, and not thankfully for her, Bria was also sore as hell, with a black-and-blue face and out-of-shape nose, and didn't want to think about training until she could control her rage over losing to an air elemental one class lower on the power scale than her.

Once we were both healed, I had a feeling she'd kick my ass to get into gear. I was not looking forward to it.

"Just living the dream," I said, not bothering to

comment on the state of her shirt. Zorn was still training her every day. He'd probably had her crawling through the sewers on her belly or something.

"You going to watch Mordie's first change?" She turned toward the kitchen.

A wash of nervousness stole my breath. I clenched my teeth. Jack had assured me that Mordecai would be fine. Mordecai's body was more than strong enough. His constitution was better still. He was primed, he was ready, and he had someone with experience to talk him through it. Sure, Jack couldn't actually change with him, being that he was an enormous sea creature, but his knowledge was enough.

Or so he said.

Still. So much could go wrong with a shifter's first change. So much. I was afraid to lose Mordecai all over again.

"Yes. Are they getting close?" I asked, lugging myself off of the couch.

"Yeah. Fifteen minutes." The faucet handle squeaked as she turned it. Clear water filled her glass. She leaned her butt against the counter and turned toward me. "Have you heard from that stalking Demigod?"

A blast of emotion stole through me: warmth from thinking about him, passion from the memory of his touch, longing because I hadn't seen him since he'd deposited me in my bed after saving my life, and nervousness that the kids somehow knew we'd spent every night chatting via back-and-forth texts.

I'd *thoroughly* finished my job this time. I'd found the spirit trappers, and, in a roundabout way, delivered them into the hands of my ex-boss. Kieran knew all the various places and items they'd been paid to maintain traps on, and now that they were no longer making their rounds, those traps would disintegrate and release the trapped souls.

My part in all of this was done. Well and truly done.

Except, Valens would soon realize what was going on—that his employees were not doing their job. He'd want to know why, and given his suspicious nature, he'd almost certainly expect foul play. This was the calm before the storm. A storm Kieran did not want me to be a part of. That my kids did not want me to be a part of. That I'd be *stupid* to be a part of…

"Nope," I lied, stretching my arms so as to hide my burning face. I hadn't gotten any better at lying to them.

"Hmm." Her eyes narrowed. "So he didn't tell you why he has one of his Six watching the house again?"

"He doesn't have to. He doesn't trust me to stay put."

She gulped her water, set the glass on the counter, and pushed forward. "Fair enough."

"No, no, no." I pointed at the glass. "Put that in the

dishwasher."

Tired of doing dishes, the guys had installed a dish-washer. They were still cooking every night. Well, on a rotating schedule—one was doing the cooking, and the rest showed up to eat. Daisy and Mordecai didn't complain, which made me wonder if they were still so determined to be rid of Kieran and all the perks that went with having him in our lives.

Daisy rolled her eyes before turning back.

A moment later, I hesitated at the front door, taking a deep breath before pulling it open. A collection of people stood on my green-brown grass and along the sidewalk in front of my house. One nutter hung out in the middle of the street, grinning manically at an oncoming car that wouldn't be slowing.

"They won't leave," Frank said, standing just off my porch, his back to the house. "Even if I strong-arm them off of your property, which I have done, they just come back. They keep coming back."

I lifted my eyebrows and sighed. "Yeah. Now you know how I feel."

Some of the spirits I'd released from the ghost house had somehow attached themselves to me after all. Not just the devoted ones, either. I had a couple surly bastards who hung around, scowling at everyone they saw. I was now their home base, but since they couldn't get in my house past the banishment magic I had up, they loitered outside. Most of them wanted to help me. Some were afraid to leave this plane. Still others didn't know what was going on—they were just going with the flow and playing chicken with cars.

Soon I'd crack and banish them. I knew I would. But for now, while I didn't know the score with Kieran, I tolerated it.

Mordecai stood in a cleared area at the side of the house, his shirt off and definition showing beneath his dark skin. The calories, his health, his shifter genes, and his hard work were paying off. And paying off quickly. His parents had passed down some great genetics...except for the little issue that had nearly killed him.

Lines etched around his light hazel eyes, his fear of what would come leaving its mark. His fingers curled into fists before straightening out again.

Jack stood before him, his own shirt off, revealing perfectly sculpted muscles and a brawn that would give any enemy pause. His face was calm, his bearing alert. Donovan blocked off the way to the street, his shirt off as well, and Zorn blocked off the path to the backyard.

I sucked in a breath when I saw Zorn's bare torso. Jagged white lines criss-crossed his well-built body, his torso a mess of scars—some straight and even, some long and bent—that carried across his shoulders and surely continued on to his back. It was clear someone had taken great pains to carve him up.

"He was tortured for information about Kieran," Daisy whispered. "You aren't the only one Kieran has saved."

I swallowed. "I got away easy, it looks like."

"Yeah. You totally would've broken. Zorn is the most stubborn dickhead I've ever met. I have mad respect for him."

"If my shoulder didn't hurt, I'd punch you in the face."

"Dickhead isn't a swear, it's an adjective."

"Stand back, ladies." Donovan waved us back as people crowded in behind us, Frank included. Just because they'd lost their bodies didn't mean they were any less nosy. "He'll be disorientated his first time. There's no telling what he'll do in shifter form."

Mordecai glanced over, and through his fear, I saw a spark of excitement. A smile bent his lips and his shoulders loosened.

"Deep breaths," Jack said in an easy voice. "Can you feel the need to change building?"

"It'll be a full moon tonight," Daisy whispered, as if I hadn't been living in the same house and hearing the same discussions non-stop. "The pull to shift is really strong. The guys thought it would be easiest—"

"For a first time. I know, I know," I said quietly.

Mordecai nodded nervously. His tongue darted out, wetting his bottom lip.

"Sink into it," Jack coached. "Sink into that feeling. Let it wash over you. Let it consume you."

Mordecai closed his eyes and his hands fisted.

"Let it consume you," Jack said again.

The throb of power from Mordecai intensified. The air turned hazy around him, shimmering.

"Here we go," Daisy said, grabbing my arm. "He's been having really bad dreams."

Again, it was like she'd forgotten we all lived together. Daisy and I had both needed to wake him up in the dead of night when he was screaming and wrestling with his sheets.

"Now rush into it," Jack barked, his body shimmering, too. The intense power within him was also building.

A burst of magic preceded Mordecai's jaw clenching. His skin, then his limbs, turned hazy, as though a cloud had drifted over him. His body bent. His face changed, elongating into a snout.

"Faster, Mordecai," Jack yelled. "The pain from the first handful of changes will last as long as it takes to change. Rush into it. Give in to it."

Mordecai grunted and his brow lowered. His legs bent and his skin erupted into fur. Teeth grew out of his mouth.

"Ew," Daisy said, her fingers digging into my arm.

I had to agree. This was one of the grossest things

I'd seen, and given that I'd been working with dead bodies, that was really saying something.

"If you don't hurry, the pain will make you pass out," Jack said, stepping forward. "The first time is always the most painful."

Mordecai didn't hurry. The change didn't go any faster. But not once did he cry out. Not once did he howl in pain. The only indication that the shape change had an effect on him was a few grunts and lots of silence.

"What the hell?" Donovan said, stepping to the side to further block us off.

"What's the matter?" Daisy asked, her nails cutting through my skin.

I took her hand away, certainty calming me. Tears filled my eyes. "He's going slow so he can learn control. He's used to dealing with intense pain in silence. He has for years. His whole life. Even now, he's trying to make it so we don't worry. This is his rite of passage, but he's putting us first."

Daisy looked at me, her eyes heavy and intense. She chewed her lip as she glanced back.

"He's better than me," she said softly. "He's a better person than me."

"He's a better person than all of us. We'll take credit for it. That'll make us good people by association."

She nodded. "Good idea."

The haze cleared and the throbbing magic settled. In place of the human stood a lean but enormous wolf, its muzzle dark gray with an odd spot near its left eye, and the rest of his body like a timber wolf, with grays and whites. Intelligent hazel eyes stared out from a wolf's face, and a long pink tongue lolled out over sharp white teeth.

"His teeth are even lovely and white in wolf form," I marveled. "See, Mordecai? See why I always harp on you about hygiene?"

"Wow. You need to let it go," Daisy muttered.

Mordecai shook like a dog before trotting forward. Jack braced himself, holding his hands up. Mordecai stopped, turned, and trotted in a circle, not nearing any one person. The guys all loosened, dropping their hands.

"Incredible," Jack said, bracing his hands on his hips.

Donovan stepped over to Jack. "I haven't seen many newbies shift, but he acclimated really quickly, didn't he?"

"Extremely quickly. I've seen a lot of newbies shift. A couple as old as him. This is…unexpected." Jack shook his head and blinked a few times in disbelief. "It just goes to show, men are way easier to deal with than women."

Daisy huffed and crossed her arms over her chest.

"I'll feed you those words on the end of a razor-tipped fork."

Jack chuckled, looking back at her. "Any time you're ready, little girl."

"You won't know I'm ready until you taste steel."

The guys all started to laugh. This was the new normal since Daisy had started training with Zorn—someone baiting Daisy to see what she'd come back with.

Little did they know, she was serious, didn't forget being taunted, and they wouldn't like it when she got even.

I smiled and turned away. I'd look forward to watching and laughing.

"Hey."

I turned back to Zorn, waiting for him to continue. He wasn't a big fan of using names, for some reason. Or details.

"He wants you to meet him," Zorn said.

I still waited for more. None came.

"Where?" I asked.

Zorn tapped his chest. "He said you'd figure it out."

I stared like an idiot, because yes, I was pretty sure I could. I'd focused on that ache in my chest all week, digging into the feeling and closing my eyes, following our connection with my mind's eye. Miraculously, I could practically envision where he was at any time.

And if I reduced down into a trance, I could feel what was going on. Like last night, when I'd felt him stroking himself while he texted with me… The pleasure had washed over my body until I was keeping pace, letting the desire build up and the ecstasy take me away. In the middle of it he'd figured out what was happening, and then our mutual sensations had spiraled until it felt like we were physically together, touching each other's bodies, kissing each other's lips.

That said, I didn't need the kids realizing any of this. Not until I figured out how to tell them what I'd decided.

Daisy's hard stare beat into my head as I nodded and turned. Soft padding crunched the brittle, mostly dead grass as Mordecai approached me.

"He saved my life. I have to at least say thank you," I said, hurrying away.

A small growl rumbled from Mordecai's throat.

"Yeah," Daisy said. "I agree. This is bad news, and not because I am now talking to an overgrown dog."

Mordecai growled again.

I grabbed my handbag and thought about changing into nicer clothes. But that would make it obvious that I had lost my mind where it concerned Kieran. Some-where along the way, it had become less about helping others by taking Valens down, and more about helping him. About speaking to him, and spending time with him.

"This is bad," I said, trying to ignore my excitement at seeing him again.

As expected, there was nothing to finding him. Nothing at all. I looked internally, felt his solid presence connecting to my middle, and followed the shimmering path to his soul. The handsy souls in the ghost neighborhood had given me the heebie-jeebies, but when Kieran's soul reached for me, I didn't want to shake him off. I wanted to pull him closer.

The train of terrible ideas was screaming down the tracks, and I didn't want to jump. I wanted to ride it all the way in.

Such bad news.

I smiled when I reached the little outlet, engulfed in swirling gray fog, and found his bright red Ferrari parked beside the road. It was the same place I'd met him to talk about the job. Sure enough, I followed the trail beside the magical zone barrier, through the windswept trees, and emerged in a clearing high on the cliff.

Kieran sat on the lonely bench overlooking the vast blue ocean. His T-shirt stretched across his large shoulders, and a muscular arm was thrown over the back of the bench.

Heart thumping and stomach flipping, I silently made my way to his side.

"You found me." His deep voice rumbled in his chest. He looked up, and those stormy blue eyes opened up all the way down to his soul. To the place I'd latched on to.

"Yes." I sat on the far end of the bench, leaving space between us.

His focus stayed on my face, absolute.

"You disobeyed me the other week," he started, though if he'd meant his tone to be severe, he wasn't doing a great job.

I clasped my hands. "I didn't want to leave the job half finished. I know I signed on to help your mom, but I promised myself I'd help those other souls, too. I know you said you'd find the guys responsible, but—"

"The solution had been staring me in the face the whole time," he interrupted. "Since before we met. I knew about that air draping spell. Knew about it, and discounted it to the point that when you spoke about a spirit trap on the building, I didn't even think of it. My mother as well. I'd been in my father's room. I'd seen that picture. I'd seen the fountain." He shook his head, his eyes sparkling. "I hadn't made the connection."

I shrugged. "You didn't have the benefit of seeing your mother in her younger form. It was a lot easier to compare her spirit to that fountain."

He stayed silent for a beat, his stare beating into me. "I don't agree. You have a knack for reading people.

You have a pure soul that lets your magic shine. I know for a fact—I can feel it. It's so light. So lovely. Like you."

My face heated and my heart lurched. I shrugged again, not knowing what to say. Scared of the strength of what I felt.

"My father will notice the absence of his employees soon," Kieran went on. "He'll know what it means, even if he doesn't know it was me. Yet." He paused. "He'll know some serious power was behind this. Power in the spirit realm."

I controlled my breathing, and tried to control my face. I knew what would come next. He didn't disappoint me.

"It's time for me to get you out of town, Alexis."

A weight settled on my chest and squeezed my heart. I refrained from commenting, not trusting my voice.

"It wasn't fair of me to try and cut you off before you finished the job," he went on. "I should've known you'd want to keep going until those spirits were released. I should've guessed you wouldn't leave it alone. But it's done now. I've visited every site. I've spoken to the spirits. Then I've let them go."

"I know. I got the pictures. And some of the buggers showed up at my house and milled on the grass." I'd had to just assume some of the lights and orbs in the pictures were a host of spirits and not just one. They didn't show up very well on camera, to the dismay of countless Ghost Whisperers who wanted proof they could do their job.

He nodded. "Your task is well and truly finished. I have a house ready for you and the kids in Sydney. They have an excellent dual-society zone there. I've already arranged for training for all of you. The shifter packs in the area are led by honorable alphas. The spies who would take on an apprentice are cunning. I have friends there. I will make sure you are all sorted." His eyes sparked. "Valens doesn't mess with Sydney. The ruler there, a class-five fire elemental, can't stand him. She'll cause a problem if he goes sticking his nose in her territory. And with his home turf…issues, he won't risk dividing his forces, even to face a lesser power."

"And Bria?" I asked, my words thick.

"She'll stay here with me. I need a Necromancer. I have a lot of spirits willing to fight."

I took a deep breath and made sure my voice was steady before I went on. "I take it you'd like to keep my magic so you can communicate with the spirits?"

He surveyed me silently. "No," he said, and I paused with my mouth open, because that wasn't the answer I'd expected. He continued surprising me. "You must know that you've had an effect on me. I haven't been with another woman since I met you. I haven't had the interest. I can't stop thinking about you, Lexi. You're on my mind constantly. I fear for your safety. I lose sleep, pained that harm might come to you. I find joy when you laugh, and get aroused when you tell me no. You're a peculiar woman, and it turns out, peculiar women are my type." Our connection throbbed in my chest, and I longed to reach out to him. To sit in his lap. "But I might not have a future, Alexis. My father is extremely powerful, cunning, and has been at this for years. He also watched me closely throughout my childhood. He knows what I'm good at, and he's documented my weaknesses. When he realizes I mean to oppose him, he'll cut me at the wick." The hand that was draped over the bench fisted. "I have no illusions. I know what I'm up against. But I have a duty to my mother. I have a duty to the people of this city. He needs to be held accountable for his choices. I'm the only one who can...who will."

He shook his head and directed his gaze out across the ocean. I let silence descend, listening to the crash of the waves below. Feeling the pull of the tides and enjoying the wind against my face.

Finally, he spoke again. "So no, I don't want to keep your magic so that I can communicate with spirits." He looked back at me. "I want to keep your magic—keep this connection—so I can find you if you get in trouble. So I can be near you even when we're oceans apart. So I have a piece of you, even in my last moments."

Chapter 40

KIERAN

KIERAN FELT EMOTION rise through him, hot and powerful. He couldn't tell if it was his or hers. Her eyes sparkled with unshed tears and a soft smile drifted across her beautiful face.

"And here I thought you'd be mad that I...did whatever I did," she said, and a tear wobbled free, cutting a trail down her cheek.

He held out his hand, inviting her closer. She scooted along the bench immediately, sliding against him. His cock hardened with the contact, and his desire for her burned through his veins.

But he kept it at bay. He was pushing her away. He didn't want to confuse matters by giving in to his desire.

"The tickets have been bought," he whispered, falling into those deep brown eyes. "I can ship whatever you want from your house. The house in Sydney is fully furnished, but I've set up accounts so you can change it however you want. The kids will have their own rooms. And new clothes, because Alexis, they look homeless."

She shuddered with a soggy laugh. "They were at one stage." She wiped her face with the back of her hand. "So...you're forcing me away?"

"Yes," he said, and this time, the burning ache in his heart was all his. The first woman he'd cared for, and he couldn't keep her. Life had a way of kicking a guy in the balls. "I'm sorry. It's for the best."

She nodded, and wiped away another tear. She took a deep breath, and a surge of feeling rose within her. He could feel it. It mirrored his own.

But it wasn't meant to be.

"Don't waste your heart on me, Alexis," he said softly, looking out at the ocean. He couldn't bear to see her tears. It was bad enough that he could feel her pain. "I'm not what you need. There's a full life waiting for you in Sydney. Live it."

"What about my father?" she asked, and he jerked his head toward her.

That had come out of left field.

"Uh..." he said stupidly, regrouping. The woman didn't think in a linear line. "We've had to go about determining who your father is under the radar. It's taking longer than usual."

"So you still don't know which one he is?"

"No." It dawned on him why she was asking. "Even if it is Magnus, he won't find you. How could he?"

She shrugged. "How did you?"

He opened his mouth, but closed it again before he said "fate." He didn't need to pour salt in the wound.

"Thank you for helping me, Alexis. Thank you for…everything."

She nodded, but didn't speak.

He wasn't sure what else to say. "I'm just going to sit here for a while…"

She nodded again, but didn't get up.

"What makes you think that I'm going to do anything you say?" she said finally.

"This isn't up for discussion—"

She surged up from the bench and spun toward him, her face flushed and eyes shooting fire.

"I love taking handouts, don't get me wrong," she started, and he couldn't help a smile. "But if you think I'm going to let you walk into danger all by yourself, after everything you've done for me and my family, you've got a screw loose. I'm in this now, Kieran. I might not know what the hell I'm doing, and I might not be an incredible asset like the others, but I'm really good at plucking souls out of dead bodies. And I'm excellent at banishing souls. And…communicating with them. And that's something."

She balled her fists and dug in her heels. "Don't waste my heart on you? Fine. I won't. But I also won't waste my life hiding from a fight because it might not go my way. I've lived in that dual-society hellhole all my life. If anyone should fight for the people in the magical government not to be such turds, it's me. I have a score to settle, too. Someone has to get Valens back for treating spirits badly. For killing fairies and illegal game. I mean, fuck that guy! So screw you. I'm joining this fight. I'm joining the ranks. There's nothing you can do to stop me. Besides kill me, and I'll haunt the shit out of you."

He surged up before he knew what he was doing. He'd wanted to do what his mother had said. To do the right thing. He'd tried. But if the woman wouldn't go…

He grabbed her neck and reeled her in, crashing his lips to hers and kissing her for all he was worth. She shoved him back, making him butt up against the bench and fall back onto it. Her hands yanked at his pants and his fingers ripped at her jeans buttons. He pushed down the fabric as she stroked his cock, her touch fanning the fire inside him.

She stepped out of her jeans and straddled him on the bench, no hesitation. Passionate and headstrong, like he liked 'em. She lowered and rubbed the tip of his cock down her wet slit, already ready for him. Eager, like he was for her.

He grabbed her shoulders, and when she'd lined them up, pulled down. He groaned as her tight warmth sank down on him, his world bursting into color. Her middle—her soul—throbbed and her touch stroked the very center of him, an incredibly intimate feeling that heightened the sensation of her physical body wrapped around his cock.

She bobbed with abandon and he reached between them, massaging her clit as he thrust, hard and deep. Pleasure tugged on his gut and the sensations wound, tight and hot. Electricity raced through his body and he lost all semblance of control.

He stood, wrapping his arms around her waist and taking her weight. He rocked his hips up, crashing into her. Loving this feeling of her hanging off of him. Of plunging into her wet depths over and over.

His balls tightened and the pleasure dragged him under to a place where only she existed. Only the feel of her body and the connection between their souls.

"Don't leave," he commanded. Or maybe he begged. "Stay."

"I was…always…going to," she said, then moaned, a low, feminine sound. "I'm not…going…anywhere."

His world exploded as he climaxed. A delicious, incredible climax. He groaned as he emptied into her depths, soaking up the exquisite sensation. She cried out, and then she was shaking, too, calling his name. He thrust again, riding the intense wave as bliss washed over him. One more time and the strength went out of his body.

He staggered back, trying not to drop her, feeling

her shiver again before she relaxed against him. He sat down, hard, onto the wooden seat. His breath came in heavy gasps, hers was ragged.

"Hmm," she moaned, before lightly trailing her lips against his neck. "I have one request, though."

"Let me guess…" He leaned back, holding her firm. He didn't want her getting off of him just yet. That would mean the moment was over, and he would have to face the hard truth of what lay ahead of him. "You don't want me to tell the kids about any of this."

She laughed against his skin. "Just until I can break it to them gently. I need to figure out the right angle."

"And you think that angle exists?"

She didn't say anything, just lay against him, her middle throbbing happily.

Fear wormed into his gut. Ten minutes ago, the worst thing the future could bring was death. With Alexis safe, and his mother freed, that was a fate he'd been willing to face.

Now, however, it wasn't just his death on the line. It was hers. And they both knew some things were worse than death. Specifically, what Valens would do to her if he found out what she was.

Success was now infinitely more dire.

Chapter 41

ALEXIS

I HELD MY head high as I stepped onto my front steps and stopped outside the door.

"Well you look...refreshed," Frank said with a smirk. A couple men behind him started laughing and an older woman scowled.

"Shut up," I whispered, one hand on the door knob. I smoothed my hair with the other, trying not to react.

We hadn't stopped with just the one lovemaking session. He'd gotten hard again before I could even climb off him, and we'd had another go, the second time slower and more emotional. I'd meant to leave quickly. To hurry home and act like nothing untoward had happened. But I couldn't bring myself to say the words. Before I knew it, we'd been sitting there for hours, half naked and not worried about it, overlooking the ocean and chatting about everything and nothing.

Don't waste your heart on me, Alexis.

Maybe he'd meant it in a different way, but he was right. I doubted we'd have a future together. We were from two different worlds, and I wasn't sure either of us wanted to cross over. Kieran would be a leader some-day. I knew that in my heart. He'd sort out the issue with his father and go on to rule a territory, probably a large one. Maybe he'd even take over magical San Francisco and fix it up a little. Kieran was destined for great things, and while I could joke about being a prince's wife, sans the duties, I knew where I belonged. I was an outcast. A misfit. The girl who took in strays and lived in the crack of societies. That was all I knew. Maybe it was all I ever wanted to know. I could put my head down and do whatever I wanted. I didn't have to listen to anyone, and was only responsible for a couple people, while he'd be a pillar of a community.

But man, being with him was a thrill. Sexy and ex-hilarating and heart-pumping.

Don't waste your heart on me, Alexis.

"Yeah, yeah, I heard ya," I muttered, rubbing at the ache in my chest. I might have to remind myself of that from time to time. Like every five minutes or so. Logic was having a hard time winning over how I felt when I was with him. A really hard time.

I took a deep breath. Time to face the kids.

The smell of BBQ wafted at me as I slowly opened the door. My stomach growled and I slipped inside, hearing voices from the kitchen.

The floor creaked under the weight of my foot. I

paused. So did the talking.

Two quick steps brought an expressionless Daisy to the edge of the kitchen. She took one look at me, rolled her eyes, and turned.

"You were right, Bria," she said. "We're staying."

"I knew it," Jack hollered.

The toilet flushed down the hall and Zorn stepped out of the bathroom. His gaze drifted over me. He walked past me without a word, heading into the kitchen with the others.

Mordecai sat on a chair at the dining table, his face excited but fatigued, and his shoulders slumped. Jack stood at the counter, laughing—at me, apparently—and chopping something. Daisy slid into a chair next to Bria and pulled over a cutting board and a pile of green beans.

"We need a bigger house to congregate at," Bria said, her voice nasally. There were still white bandages over her nose. She hadn't wanted the Healer to meddle in her affairs, so she said. I had a feeling it was to get the pain meds.

"This kitchen is tiny," Zorn said and reached over Jack to grab the salt and pepper shakers.

"Well excuse us, Mr. Money Bags," Daisy said. "I don't see you inviting us over to your house for dinner."

"You're not magical. You're not welcome on my side of the tracks," he said, deadpan.

Daisy narrowed her eyes at him.

"I got you," Bria told her. "It's in the works."

"What's in the works?" Jack asked.

"Don't you nevermind." Bria winked at Daisy before turning her attention to me. "You're not moving to Sydney, I take it?"

I shifted uncomfortably, wondering how much they knew. "No. This is my home. I'm staying here."

"I sure hope you didn't pass up a new house for sentimental reasons," Daisy said.

"She didn't," Mordecai said, drooping. "She wouldn't pass up a free house. She's obviously invested in Kieran's cause and wants to join the fight."

"Is it the fight, or the man?" Jack asked, turning around.

All eyes drifted my way, but no one spoke, everyone waiting for an answer.

"Toot, toot," Bria said, pulling the imaginary chain.

"Hey," someone called down the hall.

I leaned that way so I could see.

Donovan smiled and came forward, leaving the back door open behind him. "What's up, Lexi? You're back, I see. What's the verdict? We have a bet going."

"She's staying," Jack called. "Pay up!"

"No way!" Donovan laughed, putting his hand on his chest as he swaggered toward me. "Demigod Kieran was dead set on you leaving. *Dead set.*"

"We found someone who doesn't mind saying no to him," Zorn said. "That might be useful."

Jack turned toward Zorn with his eyes wide and mouth opened in an incredulous smile. "Oh how the tables have turned, Zorn. Suddenly you don't blindly follow our fearless leader?"

Zorn's brows lowered. "I've never blindly followed anyone."

"We all know he sometimes gets an idea in his head," Donovan said, stopping by me, "and gets stuck on it even though it's not the absolute best approach."

Zorn nodded and handed a tray of seasoned steaks to him. "Occasionally he can be unreasonable. Especially regarding the safety of a certain...pain in the ass."

"He means you." Daisy pointed at me.

"I think we all knew that, Daisy," Mordecai said.

"Well, he could have just as easily meant me, Fido," she retorted, and earned a scowl.

"There are times when it's wise to...back off," Zorn finished.

"And those are the times we'll send in Lexi." Jack nodded. "Good plan."

Bria shook her head. "You should run to Sydney, Alexis. Not walk, *run*. But don't worry, I won't let them use you."

"I feel like I've walked into a fun house," I mumbled. When had I seen the Six act so easy going and loose? Then again, they were usually only together like this when Kieran was present.

I was starting to realize everyone else saw a very different side of Kieran than I usually did. A harsher side, with more impenetrable walls and harder angles. A guy who didn't tolerate the word no, and reduced people to quivering messes on the battlefield.

I wasn't sure how to feel about that.

Don't waste your heart on me, Alexis.

Oh yeah. That was how.

"Oh, did you show her?" Donovan asked as Thane called from the back door, "What's the hold up?"

Jack snapped his fingers and turned toward the fridge.

"Oh hey, Alexis." Thane walked down to me, just another large, muscular man in a very tiny house.

"We do need another place to congregate," I said, flattening against the wall so Thane could join us.

"You staying or going?" Thane asked.

"Staying," Jack sang. He pulled a newspaper from the top of the fridge and handed it to me.

"Damn," Thane said with a smirk. "I mean, great, because that vitals-grabbing thing you do will sure be helpful, but damn, I thought Demigod Kieran was going to put his foot down this time. He was set on it. Demigods don't usually bend."

"I wouldn't talk about the boss's lady grabbing your

vitals," Donovan said with a smirk.

"She defies logic." Jack tapped a story on the right column on the front page. "They got their man, and all it took was Demigod Kieran vouching for your authenticity."

"Huh?" I asked, looking at the paper.

"That's that guy, Lexi," Daisy said, smiling at me. Mordecai perked up, his tired eyes shining. "That guy at the freak show, remember? The one you called the cops about? See? I told you they'd track you down. But you were right—"

"I can't believe you're admitting it," Mordecai said.

She scowled at him. "Shut up, Rover, I was right, too." She refocused on me. "Like you said, it led them to Kieran's office. He talked to the cop shop about you being legit."

"You don't seem so weird when a Demigod is vouching for you," Jack said, laughing.

"All aboard," Bria called.

I pushed away the banter and zeroed in on the newspaper article.

The criminal from the freak show that seemed like forever ago stared at the camera in his mug shot, his expression pissed off and his hair mussed. In the four-color picture above, a SWAT team surrounded an opened locker, the contents hidden.

"They got enough evidence to put him away," Mordecai said. "The cop you called took point."

I glanced over the story, chuckling. "Guess I can't use it for a new business, even if I wanted to, since the credit went to an anonymous caller."

"Demigod Kieran figured you'd want to keep your privacy," Zorn said.

Bria huffed out laughter, but didn't say anything.

"We could easily get around all that," Daisy said confidently. "We could definitely make a business work."

"Chump change," Donovan said, smiling over my shoulder. "You're working for Demigod Kieran now. You don't need no freaking freak show." He laughed and handed off the steaks to Thane before patting me on the back. "That's cool, though. You helped bring down a murderer."

"And soon, you'll help bring down another," Bria said with a violent gleam in her eye.

"Hear-hear!" Donovan said as he followed Thane out to the grill.

"Are we really signed on to help bring Valens down?" Mordecai asked quietly.

Jack glanced back, then Zorn did, as if they were equally as interested in the answer.

"Not we, Mordecai," I said. "Me. *I* signed on to—"

"No." Daisy held up her hand, stopping me. "We. We go where you go. We're a family. If you're getting involved, we're all getting involved. Maybe not on the front line, but we're in this with you. That's non-negotiable. I still maintain that Kieran is a possessive, stalking asshole and a bad idea, but these other yahoos are okay, so I'm good to join this team."

"You'd make too many bad decisions without us," Mordecai said seriously. Jack and Bria burst out laughing. They didn't know that it was mostly true.

I took a deep breath, fire burning through my veins. I'd never taken a stand like this before. I'd never aggressively stepped up to authority and put myself out there. But if I did it against anyone, it was always going to be Valens. It was always going to be the guy who thought he was above the law.

"Yes," I said, the fire overflowing and strengthening my words. "Yes, we're going to get involved. And come hell or high water, possibly literally, we're going to win."

"Atta girl," Jack said, clapping. "Let the games begin."

THE END

About the Author

K.F. Breene is a *USA Today* Bestselling and Top 10 Kindle All-Star author of paranormal romance, urban fantasy and fantasy novels. With two million books sold, when she's not penning stories about magic and what goes bump in the night, she's sipping wine and planning shenanigans. She lives in Northern California with her husband, two children and out of work treadmill.

Sign up for her newsletter to hear about the latest news and receive free bonus content.

www.kfbreene.com

CPSIA information can be obtained
at www.ICGtesting.com
Printed in the USA
BVHW071402150222
629077BV00007B/81

9 781732 798984